THE LAST ETERNITY

THE LAST ETERNITY

TONY PEAK

The Last Eternity

Author website: www.tonypeak.net
Facebook: https://www.facebook.com/tonypeak78
Twitter: @tonypeak78
Amazon Author Page: https://www.amazon.com/Tony-Peak/e/B00H70H7IE/ref=dp_byline_cont_all_1

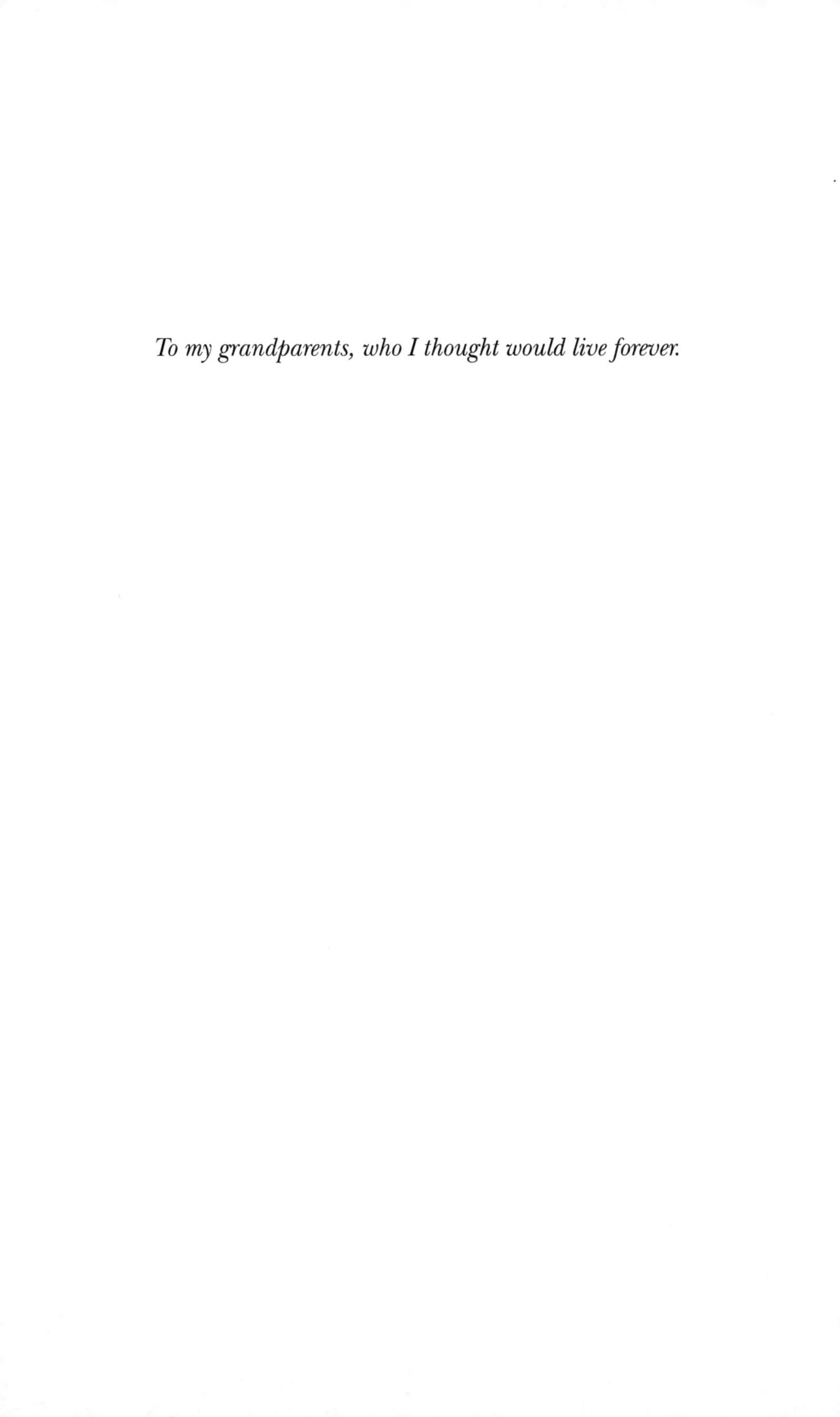

To my grandparents, who I thought would live forever.

ACKNOWLEDGMENT

First I'd like to thank my agent Ethan Ellenberg for publishing this novel. Thanks to my beta readers: Ian Welke, Meredith Morgenstern Lopez, Gregory Clifford, and Dusty Wallace; you all provided valuable input. A special thank you to everyone who has offered support and encouragement in my darkest moments—you know who you are. Extra gratitude to my family who reminded me to keep believing in myself and my work.

Chapter 1

The Rebirth Initiative guarantees that our brightest, most gifted individuals are given one more lifetime, one more existence, to strengthen our civilization. One more sacrifice, until we secure the future of our species.

Elder States Archives, Vol. XXIV

Jerr rolled off the bunk and slammed his head into something hard. He sucked his teeth against the pain and glared up at metal bars.

"Son of a bitch." Back in the brig again.

He sat up and rubbed his temples. Hangovers were worse in the Shroud since gravitational pressures increased the closer a ship came to its destination. It aggravated headaches, induced nausea, and reduced the ability to focus. Maybe it reduced judgement, too. He'd vowed not to get drunk again while onboard.

Some promises were meant to broken.

After getting to his feet, Jerr stood in place a few moments. One's equilibrium could be thrown off in the Shroud, even experienced 'nauts. He probably needed to puke. But not yet, without knowing how long he'd be in the cramped cell.

While he stretched, Jerr pieced together his scattered memories. Rebirth often left some psychological residue, like people's faces he'd seen, or a tune he'd never hear again. His former self could die on a world three hundred light years away, while the reborn version would recall those snippets.

These particular memories left him cold.

His previous rebirth was married, with a young son, maybe six years old. A pretty wife from a low-gravity world, judging from her delicate bone structure. Jerr remembered embracing them. Squeezing her hand, promising the boy a memento from the next campaign. Boarding a ship, then waving at them as the hatch shut.

Boarding a ship. Surrounded by soldiers. A cup slips from someone's hand. Jerr reaches for it, but misses. The cup strikes the floor.

That was new. He never recalled reaching for a cup before.

He swallowed and licked his lips. A drink would do wonders right now. He'd boozed it up after the last mission, ending a political disturbance in the Elium Rim. That was the official story: it'd been a revolt backed by Veja Qor, a terrorist organization. His company had eliminated the leaders and restored order. Sympathizers had hijacked factory robos, using them against the sector garrison. Jerr outthought and outfought them, too. Only a few real humans perished.

Those bodies at the garrison spaceport, though. Torn and burning. Some of the rebels brought their children, hoping to escape. None did. Jerr doubled over and braced his hands against the wall. Alcohol was the only way he could deal with it.

Sweat soaked his shirt as he grasped the bars—they didn't shock him. The current was turned off. If his superiors didn't regard him as a dangerous prisoner, then putting him in here was overkill.

"Hey," he called, glancing up and down the corridor. It was dimly lit, so as not to hurt his Urian eyesight, sensitive to high wavelengths. *Bhaellator*'s silence was typical of a vessel within the Shroud. No rumbling engines or thrumming reactors, gently vibrating the walls and floor. It was like standing still, except for the reality once one disembarked.

Standing still. Unmoving. That summed up Jerr's life. Every time he was reborn, his superiors assigned him the same duties. The same existence, but with other reborn like himself, in a different part of the galaxy. Until he died again.

Jerr frowned and shook the bars. "Hey!"

His voice echoed down the corridor, each reverberation more distant. Much like his rebirths; he was living his twenty-sixth. Jerr couldn't remember much about himself before the twenty-fourth—and then only faint sensations, like a distaste for Cuori spices, or green being his favorite color. Personality quirks but little else.

If he could just remember his wife and son's names. If they were well-cared for.

If they even knew he'd died.

Rattling the bars again, he scowled up and down the corridor. Another drink would wash such nonsense from his mind. "Damn, c'mon—!"

A slight whoosh sounded on his left as someone entered the corridor. Jerr released the bars and stood back, trying to look anything but hungover and pissed off.

The scent of spearmint mixed with vinyl made Jerr sigh. Not her again.

Xade halted before the bars, regarding him with cobalt eyes that looked more human than his own. Her sleek figure was an amalgamation of polished, navy-blue exoskeleton and perfect, pastel-blue flesh. A biomechanical Theux, Xade had chosen a feminine physique long ago, to better serve the Dominion. Or so he'd heard.

All Dominion ships kept one Theux among their crews. Unlike cold mainframes, a Theux's mind couldn't be hacked, electro-pulsed, or influenced in any way. They could simultaneously calculate the tasks of fifty intelligent people. Without her, piloting *Bhaellator* would require many more personnel or risky mainframes.

She was also caretaker of *Bhaellator*'s reborn. Watching his every move.

Jerr smiled. "You see I'm fit for duty now. Okay? Now let me out."

Xade studied him. Her short blue hair didn't move as she passed beneath a vent.

"Well?" he asked.

She didn't bat an eye.

Though out of uniform, Jerr straightened and stared. "As an officer, I demand to be released from this cell."

Xade opened her palm and a nodus flickered into existence over it. The transparent sphere displayed his face: Jerr Manivo, Captain of Company K, Consular Brigade. Next came his blood alcohol levels, metabolism—three times that of a normal human—heartrate, and blood pressure. Which was climbing.

The smile was getting harder to maintain. "Xade? The door?"

"Odious." She manipulated the nodus until it showed his blood alcohol before departing their last destination in the Elium Rim. It was amazing he still lived.

Jerr's smile fell. Xade only spoke in single word sentences, and always ones ending with 'ous'. It annoyed him less than her penchant for regulations.

"I know, I screwed up. It got out of hand, that's all. But as you can see, I'm fine now. So…open the door."

She regarded his climbing heartrate on the nodus, then arched an eyebrow. As a reborn he was expected to remain in peak condition and was constantly monitored. If he even farted too much, no doubt Xade would appear to find out why.

"These bars are insulting. I'm not an animal."

Images played across her nodus. Onboard camera feeds showed him staggering through an officer berth. Drunk, snickering, punching out wall panels. Shoving aside MPs. Overturning tables in the mess hall. Urinating on the Dominion insignia.

Xade's features softened. "Piteous."

Jerr sighed to hide his shame. "Open. The. Door. That's an order."

The nodus disappeared and Xade waved a hand over the control panel. The cell door slid aside, but before Jerr could exit, she touched his arm. Her soft blue dermaflesh, more resilient than steel, contrasted his own dark complexion. It reminded him of Aeoly Prime's rivers, a planet visited by a previous rebirth. Blue waters snaking through plains covered in fresh loam…

The Aeolyians flee as he reloads another gauss cartridge. Several trip over the dead ringleaders he's killed. Blue currents rush past his feet, mixing with their blood.

The memory came unbidden, causing him to hesitate. Xade cocked her head. Her fingers ran along his skin as her palm throbbed a few times.

"Can I go now?"

"Tremulous." She indicated her nodus. His heartrate was in flux, though he felt fine. It was probably the Shroud again, bringing the Aeoly mission back to his consciousness. Those not accustomed to traveling through it often confused their memories, thinking something transpired a day ago that had, in reality, happened last week. And they wondered why he needed a drink every now and then.

"Oh, come on—"

She swung at him.

Jerr weaved, sidestepped, and punched. Just as quick, she slipped to his outside.

Her nodus charted his honed reflexes.

"Satisfied?" He tried to sound confident, but damn she was fast.

"Dexterous." She smiled, dispelling her typical austerity. Though he could count the other times she'd displayed emotion on one hand, Jerr chuckled and smiled back.

"Listen, I'm fine. You try sleeping in that cell." He winked at her.

"Ludicrous." She hurried up the corridor.

"I know, Theux don't sleep." He ran to keep up. "Hey, it was just a joke!"

Chapter 2

Academics always question how a physically weak species such as humans could not only conquer a galaxy, but maintain hegemony over it. It is not flesh and blood that binds empires, but the merciless will to destroy anything that threatens said empire. Humanity surpasses all other species in this regard.

Narrative of the Armada, Chapter 8

The corridor led to a staging area for Company K, extending thousands of feet in all directions. Tier upon tier, inset into the ship's walls, housed a variable gravity training field, equipment racks, evolving firing ranges, and hundreds of soldier berths. The concave walls were engraved with famous battle scenes from Dominion history.

Men and women sparred in unarmed combat drills, battled simulations of various alien species, or flew in armored suits, adaptable to most environments.

More than a few of the men had his face.

After being a reborn for so many years, it no longer bothered Jerr to serve alongside others who shared his features, his voice. Normal citizens seemed to find it odd, even offensive, to share one's likeness. But Jerr trusted these soldiers more than any friend or relative—they had his skills, his morals. The empire was safer because of it.

No one paid him any heed, engrossed with their training. Most were new conscripts, replacing the losses suffered in the Rim. Only the elite, with the most experience and best records, were entitled to rebirth. It was the same across the Dominion: the most gifted scientists, engineers, and other vital personnel were all reborn. There was no special uniform or insignia denoting them. Jerr preferred it that way.

The next staging area housed a Repta brigade, their scaled bodies a genetic amalgamation of human characteristics mixed with reptilian features. Jerr had fought against, as well as alongside, them in previous campaigns. Previous rebirths. They numbered among the empire's deadliest auxiliary troops. A female warrior watched him with unusual interest, fingering her sheathed blades.

"Hey, when I was drunk…I didn't…you know, bring anyone back to my cabin?"

Xade noticed the Repta female, then gave him a reproachful look. "Ridiculous."

He sighed with relief. "Thank the stars."

Bhaellator housed many species-exclusive units in separate berths: Squidrans, Idreuns, Repta, and others. Thus a Leviathan could field any force, tailored to any world, anywhere in the galaxy. Like Jerr, many of their best officers were reborn.

"So where are we headed this time?" He tugged his sweaty shirt, eager to shower.

"Scandalous." Her tone was icy, scolding.

"Really?" He grinned at Xade's irritation. If she thought he was going to forget she had him tossed in the brig, she was mistaken. "Remind me."

As they entered another corridor terminating in a dark shaft, Xade held up her nodus. Its words and images made Jerr groan.

"The Idreun Periphery? Hasn't the Dominion fought enough wars out there?"

"Libelous," Xade said in a warning tone.

Jerr snorted as they sat on a long tram car inside the shaft. The other seats were filled with soldiers and technicians in full kit. It meant the ship was about to exit the Shroud—and that he was off schedule.

So the hell what? He'd needed that drink. Needed to drive that family from his mind. They weren't welcome in his current reality, since their existence suggested he'd had something before this. Something special, lasting.

Xade sat down first, her posture too perfect, her bearing too purposeful. The other soldiers had everything buckled and tucked in the right places, staring ahead with latent obedience. It grated on his nerves more than usual. He didn't know why.

Polarized and shielded, the tram sped through *Bhaellator*'s interior, utilizing the Shroud's space-time warping to send them anywhere onboard within seconds. Otherwise, conventional transport would take hours, since *Bhaellator* was a Leviathan class vessel. At one-hundred fifty miles long, the Leviathans were the only craft large enough to hold the gravity generators necessary to enter the Shroud. Large enough to bend space-time, and travel much faster than light. Even faster than pre-Armada starships.

Jerr closed his eyes. This wasn't going to help his hangover.

Though less than one-fifth of *Bhaellator* contained crew quarters, supplies, and other amenities, the rest housed the gravity engine. Like other Leviathans, it sported parks and arcologies. Housing a million permanent residents, each vessel was its own self-contained world. Onboard hydroponics and shield farming all but guaranteed self-sufficiency. Most people stationed on a Leviathan never saw their homeworld again, living out their lives on the massive starship.

Jerr wondered where home was for all these crewmen. Millions of worlds scattered across the galaxy. United as the Dominion, now in its 83rd Millennium.

The tram appeared in a transparent shaft high above Agri Deck 3. Jerr was numb for a few seconds, then he looked down.

Trees, moss yards, crop fields. An arcology stood over it all, with a continually updated knowledge vault accessible by mental nodes. He wondered how many families—

Jerr frowned. How many versions of himself had viewed the same scene? He'd never get to walk beneath those trees, or visit the vaults—as a soldier, he had one duty: kill the Dominion's enemies. The one constant he could never forget, regardless of how many times he was reborn. He recalled every battle, every tactic, every weapon he'd ever used. Lifetimes of combat experience, coupled with hair-trigger senses and the fortitude of a torture drone. The artificial world below wasn't for him.

It had never bothered him before. Or had it?

He caught Xade watching him intently. Did she have to study him all the time?

Turning from her, Jerr stared through *Bhaellator*'s viewports. The sight was as static as a still image: a field of stars and galaxies, dusted with the occasional nebula, punctuated by a few supernovae. It was an inert reality contradicting his presence aboard a moving starship. Like they didn't travel at all, but were caught in a moment of time.

The Shroud was a dimension that paralleled space-time. No one lived there. It did not contain planets, systems, or stars, though Jerr's universe could be seen and accessed from it. He'd heard stories of older ships exploding in the Shroud, with the survivors trapped in a stasis between life and death. Never to return.

At the edges of his sight, the universe blurred into ripples of light and dark. Gradually spreading until more stars, more galaxies were stretched and blurred.

The Shroud only appeared so when their destination was near.

Jerr started to reach out…

The cup falls away with terminal slowness. But he is slower.

"Anxious?" Xade asked.

The concern in her voice embarrassed him. Jerr exited the tram as soon as it stopped. He'd seen the cup about to spill again and he'd almost grabbed it. But he held no cup. Not then, not now. Maybe the Shroud had finally driven him mad. A 'blind 'naut', they called them, those driven insane by exposure to gravitational energies.

He needed a drink.

"Arriving at Stalis in five minutes," an intercom said.

Jerr hurried to his quarters on K deck. He waved his hand over the door panel, confirming his DNA, and entered. Still regarding him with unease, Xade followed. Ignoring her, he stripped, showered, and donned the gray Dominion uniform he'd worn for several lifetimes. Xade watched him without shame, but he didn't care. Having a walking, talking computer gawk at him was a trifling thing.

His quarters were sparse, with no realizers simulating favorite locales or loved ones in three-dimensional glory. But he knew where to hide an extra bottle of whiskey. As he shrugged into his jacket, Jerr felt under the counter.

The hidden bottle was missing.

As he turned, Xade held the bottle of Yuggan whiskey over the disposal chute.

"What the hell?" He glowered. "We talked about this."

"Contemptuous." Her pose dared him to argue.

"I have it under control now. Trust me."

"Vacuous." Her nodus showed an 87% probability that he didn't.

Fury rose within him. That bottle could provide short-term salvation, at least.

He jabbed a finger at her. "You're always judging me."

Xade swiped her nodus. His long-term aspartate transaminase and alanine transaminase levels were high. A carbohydrate deficiency was developing in his body.

He was an alcoholic.

"You only care because they want you to." He paced the room.

"Ruinous." The empathy in her eyes increased his anger.

"What does it matter? I'm a reborn. Here, let me have it, and I promise—"

Xade flung it down the chute. The sound of the bottle smashing took his breath.

"You had no right," he muttered.

"Superfluous."

"You had no goddamned right!" He stalked toward her.

Her nodus showed a 94% chance he'd lose. A 100% chance for court-martial.

"I don't care," he said. "You better respect my privacy. Us humans need—"

A voice buzzed over the room's intercom. "We've exited the Shroud, Manivo. The Idreun have agreed to speak with the Stalis enclave, but there might be a few dissenters looking to create an incident. Report to the dispersal deck in full kit."

Garrand's voice stilled Jerr's further protestations. "Acknowledged."

Without looking at Xade, Jerr stomped from his quarters and made for the egress chutes nearby. They allowed access to adjacent decks in the event of an attack disabling the tram. But that was a distant possibility. There were no known starships that could even hope to destroy a Leviathan. A boarding action would be suicide.

Inside the chute, a realizer version of Garrand appeared beside Jerr. He looked, felt, and even smelled like *Bhaellator*'s commander, the illusion was so complete. He wore a light grey uniform with black piping. "All you need to do is stand on that asteroid and look dangerous. The Idreun still view negotiation as surrender, so be wary."

"I'll do my part, sir," Jerr said.

Garrand's pale features reddened. "Damn right you will. You're my best solider, so I expect the best judgement. Another Inebriation Demerit and I'll court-martial you."

"Yes, sir." Everybody was in a court-martial mood.

Realizer Garrand vanished and Jerr sighed. Did he have any privacy on this ship?

By the time Jerr arrived on the dispersal deck, the dropship was prepped and the other soldiers were already suited up. Dominion troops wore Starjumper suits outfitted with heavy gauss cannon and diffusion blasters, enabling each individual to pacify large areas planetside. After the wars of the Armada Era, the Dominion sought to preserve worlds and infrastructure as much as possible. The age of massive fleets battling each other in the void, or grand armies clashing on asteroids, were mere tales now.

Jerr approached a skinny human repairing his reserve combat suit, which hung from a recharge rack. It was only then he realized

Xade had followed him down the chute. He'd tell Garrand to keep her off his back, Dominion asset or not.

"Is it ready?" Jerr asked.

Darei, the skinny guy, smiled. "It's always ready when I work on it. Though if you'd bother filing a damage report every other century, some of this crap would be easier to maintain." Darei was Jerr's technician, with tool pouches on his belt, legs, and arms. Blonde dreadlocks dangled over tattooed shoulders.

"I use it to shoot things, I don't keep track of where it's been," Jerr said.

"Kinda like that manmeat you keep in your trousers." Darei snickered. "Heard you had another booze-up. Did you pull that shit out on anyone this time?"

"And make you jealous?" Jerr snorted. "Not in a million light years."

Darei tsked as he tightened a capacitor. "I'm happily married, you slag. Hey, you're more pissed off than usual. What's grinding you?"

Jerr indicated Xade with his eyes. Darei snickered again.

"Let's get this one over with." Jerr stepped under the rack and the suit fitted around him. A Gahn Starjumper. He glanced at the HUD, then rolled his eyes upon spotting the current Build. "4.3? This is supposed to be a reserve, not a garbage hauler."

"You smashed up your primary back in the Rim," Darei said. "Remember?"

"This is the best they'll give us?"

"This far from the Settled Zone?" Darei laughed. "You're lucky to have a sharp knife out here, let alone an old piece of shit like this. What'd you expect, a Build 7?"

"At least a Build 5.5," Jerr said. "This is getting ridiculous. Don't they know what's out here in the Periphery? This heap doesn't even have auto-reload."

"You whine more than my last husband," Darei said. "Besides, you're a High and Mighty Reborn. If you die out there, so the fuck what? The Dominion will just grow another you. A brand new Jerr Manivo. Maybe one with a better personality next time."

"Gee, thanks," Jerr said.

"Anytime." Darei activated the suit's pressure regulator. Jerr grunted at the shock.

"You could've warned me," Jerr said between clenched teeth.

"Hey, at least it helped you forget about the hangover, right?" Darei smirked.

"You're an asshole, Darei." Jerr snapped the Starjumper fully into place and frowned at how little ammo the cannons had.

"And you always come back for more." Darei swatted the suit's rump.

"Careful, I'll tell one of your husbands." Jerr smiled.

Darei gave him the finger.

"Villainous." Xade nudged Darei aside and climbed up beside Jerr on the rack. She inspected the weapons and thrusters, then stared at Darei.

"The hell?" Darei cried. "I have to get approval from Miss Blue Theux, now?"

"Impecunious." She pulled a driver still attached to the suit and gave it to Darei.

"Sure, whatever." Darei slid the driver into a tool pouch.

Jerr bit back a reply as the Idreun and Stalis ambassadors were escorted into the dropship. The tall, mantis-like Idreun moved with grace, its gray flesh inset with various gadgets. The Stalis was simply a red, biomorphic vapor inside a transparent hoverdome. What they could possibly want to trade with one another, Jerr couldn't guess. Sometimes it was better being a grunt and not knowing.

The dispersal deck shook. Orange caution lights lit the walkways. Xade climbed down while Darei rushed to the next chamber. Soon, Jerr and his comrades would be out in the vacuum, and no one ... wait, why was Xade still standing there?

She stared at him a long moment. Jerr felt awkward under her azure-eyed perusal. As if she expected something, but had yet to see it. Or perhaps she was ensuring *Bhaellator*'s most expensive soldier had everything he needed—sobriety included—for the coming mission. People like Darei had it all wrong. It wasn't an honor, being a reborn. There were expectations no one else had to face, there were assumptions no one else were saddled with. Like those comments about Jerr's death.

Maybe Darei was right: so what if Jerr died again? There'd be no family to mourn him. His loss was an ephemeral one: unrecorded, unlamented.

He looked back down. Xade had gone.

Shit. He should've apologized. Yuggan whiskey always gave him the worst hangovers anyway. Xade was just looking out for him. At least someone cared.

The bay door opened and the soldiers looked at him.

"Okay, snowflakes, let's do this," Jerr said into his mic. "Company K, fall out!"

Company K hurried into the dropship. One hundred forty men and women, capable of laying waste to a city. Their names tallied on his HUD; none were familiar.

Normal troops had slower reflexes, less muscle mass, lower pain thresholds than he. Reborn commandos enjoyed the best genetically tailored physiques: blood congealed faster, and their immune system rescinded the worst cancers and bioterminators. Yet he was a transient demigod, while they enjoyed real, meaningful lives after a tour or two.

Maybe the Dominion would let him retire one day and he could have that life.

As men with his own face saluted him, though, Jerr smiled. The galaxy was indeed safer, with him and his reborn on duty. Protecting civilization.

Protecting his family, wherever they might be.

Chapter 3

Many an experienced 'naut went insane during the first century of Shroud exploration. Not for lack of shielding aboard Leviathans; gravitational radiation was an easy victim of scientific progress. Rather, it was the sensation of perpetual inertia, while the universe outside continued at a greater pace. One could leave her homeworld, then return after campaign, finding a terraformed sphere ruled by her great-grandchildren.

Elder States Archives, Vol. XVII

Bringing up the rear, Jerr glanced at the field of stars beyond the shielded hangar.

They were still blurred at the edges as if he remained in the Shroud. Jerr blinked and checked his scanners, but the view kept distorting, shifting.

"Worlds will melt, and stars will fade. Though more is built, all shall fall."

"Huh?" Jerr checked his radio, switched the bands back and forth. "Say again?"

"We warned them. We showed them, we implored, we even sacrificed, but they would not listen. Hear us, see us. Reveal us."

Jerr tapped his earbud and double-checked his sensors as the dropship started its engine. "Anybody reading that?"

"Negative, sir," came the other soldiers' replies. From the observation deck above, Xade and Darei looked on with confusion.

"Hear us. See us."

"Anybody at all?" Adjusting his mic, Jerr boarded the dropship. "Reveal us."

The field of stars blurred further. Jerr shrank back. Two Leviathans collide above a desert planet. Thousands of bodies float in the debris-filled vacuum.

Jerr watched it all, gripping the railing with his vise-like gloves until the dropship left *Bhaellator*. The field of stars leapt away as if torn from his consciousness.

"We warned them."

Blinking, Jerr stared all around. His troops regarded him with quizzical frowns.

The dropship neared Stalis, one of many worlds within the Periphery. Its teal brilliance appeared in half-shadow, a termination line bisecting it with nocturnal finality. Though Jerr had seen hundreds of worlds—and no doubt hundreds more, from previous rebirths—he was ever awed by their tranquil grandeur. It was typically his only opportunity to enjoy such a view, for upon landing, he'd be focused on tactics, enemies, how many rounds he had left. His training superseded any appreciation of beauty.

Their destination was an asteroid merchant station riddled with craters. A few starports clung to it, but their typical traffic was grounded due to the Idreun blockade. It numbered over sixty warships—insects compared to *Bhaellator*'s might.

"Everything proceeding well, Manivo?" Garrand asked over the open channel. "It's just another trade rights issue. Don't get trigger-happy."

"Sir, you getting any radio interference?" Jerr asked.

"None," Garrand said. "What's wrong?"

Jerr waited before answering. No visions, no voices. "Just a … faulty earbud, sir."

"Obvious." Xade's feed lit up on his HUD, displaying her face.

So she could look even more emotionless. "Thanks, Xade."

"I checked all systems beforehand," Darei said over the radio. "Quit screwing with the bud's frequency. It's interfering with your mapping feed."

"Glad the gang's all here." Jerr loaded the HUD map. "Mapping online. Happy?"

"Just keep that shitcan in one piece, you hear me?" Darei asked.

"If I rough it up a little, think of it as job security," Jerr said.

"The only thing secure around you is a glass of water," Darei said.

"Asshole," they said simultaneously. Jerr chuckled.

The merchant station relayed a message explaining its neutrality, a typical snoozefest of legalese meant to please Dominion bureaucrats. Jerr muted it and tuned a private channel to Xade's feed—then didn't know what to say.

"Nervous?" she finally asked.

Jerr stared out the window at *Bhaellator*'s cylindrical presence, casting its silhouette on the planet below. "You know better than that."

Neither of them spoke for a few moments.

"I don't know why you care, and I'm still pissed, but…"

Xade waited, brows lowered.

"Thanks for throwing it away. I need to quit."

"Duteous." Her jaw relaxed.

Jerr nodded to her and cut the channel.

It wasn't necessary, apologizing. If that could be called an apology. But Jerr had enough enemies out here, with a Dominion target on his back. No sense in making more.

"Sir?" a private beside him asked. "Think the Idreuns will try something stupid?"

"They're known for it," Jerr said. "Keep your eyes open, we'll be fine."

"I hope they do." The private patted her diffusion blaster. "I'll mow 'em down!"

"Tear them up like we did the Veja Qor in the Rim!" another cried.

"Fuck yeah!" a corporal shouted. A few soldiers laughed and cheered.

He should tell them to can it, reign in their juvenile enthusiasm. He'd been like them, once. Maybe worse, since he carried out the mission, then tried drowning the guilt afterwards with drink after drink.

Thinking of its burning taste made his mouth water.

The dropship is aflame, filled with dead soldiers. Blood stains the bulkheads.

"Captain? You all right?" The private shook his arm.

Blinking, Jerr righted himself. The vision felt real. "As you were."

Several soldiers stole glances his way. Since he'd rampaged through the officer's mess, he doubted any of these grunts knew about his inebriated episode. He found no comfort in their ignorance. To Xade, Garrand, and the rest who knew, he was a pariah.

"Two minutes to drop zone," the pilot said.

The announcement made Jerr focus. "Everyone power up your weapon systems. Secure those excess magazines, I want everything tight. Make sure your Starjumper is adjusted to any gravity fluctuation. And get that gauss cannon online, soldier!"

His voice erased all grins, straightened backs. K Company stood in rigid lines inside the dropship bay, each soldier an extension of Dominion will. Giving orders, feeling the weight of his Starjumper, nearing the drop zone—it thrilled him, serving as an expectorant for action. He roused the soldiers with the imperial rallying cry.

"Eighty-four!" he shouted. The soldiers yelled it back as one unit. Eighty-four. Implying all their struggles were to ensure the Dominion saw an 84th Millennium. In previous eras, soldiers had cried the number of the coming millennium. An oath of fealty that their life—and death—would continue humanity's eternal hegemony.

"One minute to drop zone," the pilot said.

Taking a deep breath, Jerr's reality felt right again. In his element, performing his duty, exercising the talents trained and bred into him. The emotional rush was contagious. His troops beamed with pride, shook with elation. All because he anchored their purpose.

Maybe he wouldn't want a drink afterwards.

"We warned them."

Jerr started to adjust his mic again, but the voice sounded so close, the speaker could have been inside the suit with him.

"We warned them."

"What?" His voice shook.

Flames erupt from the asteroid's craters.

"Stop," he said.

Another explosion shakes the dropship as Jerr clambers through the exit hatch. Their landing has been contested, with two soldiers dead and three wounded. Arming all weapons, he bursts from the dropship. Sensors relate how many combatants occupy the asteroid: where to shoot, and exactly when the enemy missile will shred the dropship to wreckage. Jerr raises his right arm, the diffusion blaster charged and ready.

"Stop!"

The dropship rocketed to their target as Jerr yelled in wordless frustration.

Chapter 4

Humanity prided itself on possessing superior mental capabilities, despite weak physiques. Such was the reasoning on our now lost homeworld. Yet nearly every intelligent species we encountered exhibited cognitive maturity. Humanity required more than primitive tenacity and brutish firepower to win. Thus Rezal training, perfected after centuries of eugenic controls, provided a much-needed advantage. Vestal House assisted.

Psychopomp Errata, Sector 94, Confessor
Balyra Peran, Vestal House

A voice in Jerr's earbud startled him.

"Manivo, what the hell are you doing? You're spooking the rookies."

It was Garrand speaking on a private channel from *Bhaellator.* Jerr paused and realized he wasn't in a combat situation at all. No dead soldiers, no explosions. His scanners remained clear. The dropship was still flying toward the merchant station on the asteroid, where an Idreun delegation waited.

His right arm was extended, the blaster humming. Trembling, Jerr lowered it.

"Manivo? Sound off!"

Jerr ignored the other soldiers' puzzled looks. "Manivo here. Everything's fine."

"Bullshit," Garrand said. "You were shouting like a maniac. What's come over—"

"Everything's fine." Jerr muted the feed and stared at his feet. He had to play it off as nothing. If he but hinted he was seeing or hearing things, Garrand would toss him into a psycho ward, or think he was deviating from his genetic template. It couldn't be his drinking. He always dreamt weird stuff during a hangover, but this felt too real.

"Sir, the detachment is waiting for us below," the dropship pilot said.

Seconds ticked by. Everyone awaited his command.

"Drink your float juice," Jerr said. The other soldiers supped liquid from cups passed around by a steward drone. The juice's nanite mix cushioned veins and organs in adverse gravities. It went down like milk but left a metallic aftertaste.

Jerr studied the merchant station's layout, still a few thousand feet away. Had the voice in his head warned of an ambush? The craters around the station looked empty. All sensors revealed nothing unusual. Besides, the Idreun would have to be crazy to push this dispute with a Leviathan present.

"Inbound, eight seconds," the pilot said.

"Wait," Jerr said. "Hold position."

The asteroid wasn't large—just a few hundred miles across—but it was pocked with even more craters, blanketed in shadow. If anything was hidden there, it would be small. Not artillery or soldiers.

Explosives.

"Hover over the station, but don't touchdown," Jerr said.

"The Stalis ambassador wants to know why we delay," the pilot said.

"Tell him we're doing our job." Jerr kept scanning, his thoughts tainted by the fever dream he'd just experienced. He had to lay off the Yuggan stuff. Maybe switch to some of that swill Darei liked to drink.

Drink…

The dropship shuddered. One of the crewman stumbled. Jerr's hand shot out, grabbing the juice cup the man had just dropped. The soldiers beamed with appreciation.

"Fucker's got reflexes," one muttered.

"Shit, sir, you're fast," another soldier said.

Jerr shrugged to hide his own dismay. "Once you've been out here long enough, you can catch a meteorite." Though the troops laughed, he shook inside his suit.

He'd seen that cup falling in his mind earlier. Like he knew it would happen.

Knew it would happen!

"Manivo, Garrand here. What's the hold-up? The Idreun and Stalis ambassadors are crawling up my ass."

Jerr gazed at the asteroid, as if viewing it for the first time. He'd seen what would happen once the dropship touched down. He'd seen all these soldiers die afterward. And though the deaths were bad enough, such an incident would guarantee war between the Idreuns and Stalis, something the Dominion wished to avoid.

That stupid cup. Knew it would happen.

"Sir…" Jerr mulled over what he'd say. "Sir, sensors won't penetrate the shadows in the craters. Unless we do a close topical scan, we might be flying into anything."

The soldiers regarded Jerr with apprehension. They looked up to him, but spooking a unit before battle was never good. Still, he couldn't abandon his intuition.

"The Idreuns might view that as threatening," Garrand said. "Unless you have a damn good reason, order the pilot to land that dropship and take your positions."

"Reveal us."

The voice set Jerr further on edge. The suit's HUD displayed his rising heartrate.

"We warned them."

"I…" Jerr stared at the cup, sweat coursing down his cheeks.

The starfield outside appeared normal. No blurs, no stretching. He could look away, pretend he'd not seen, not heard. He was just a drunken grunt anyway, reborn dozens of times, who knew where those voices came from, he should follow orders…

"Sir?" the pilot asked. The dropship hovered above the station.

"Take us in, but prepare for evasive on my command," Jerr said. "There might be explosives planted in those darker craters. Seal your helmets, everyone."

Garrand started arguing on the radio, but Jerr cut the channel. If he was wrong, he'd rather hear about it later, than right now.

The dropship maneuvered closer to the asteroid. Company K became restless. Jerr kept scanning the craters, eyes darting back and forth over a landscape that had never seen life, never known comfort. Much like his own recycled existence.

"We warned them."

Jerr shook as he gaped, wide-eyed, at the asteroid. There was nothing there, that cup didn't mean a damn thing, he was going mad—

Knew it would happen.

"Evasive!" he cried as the dropship came within three hundred feet of the station.

The pilot shouted over his shoulder. "Sir, there's nothing—!"

"Do it!" Jerr yelled.

The dropship swerved away as the craters around the station exploded, flinging shrapnel and stone out into space. Part of the asteroid crumbled. The station's outer towers burst with flame, then blew apart in terrifying silence, the vacuum extinguishing the brief fires. Warning alarms blared aboard the dropship as pebbles and wreckage enfiladed its hull. The main cabin depressurized, but with every soldier in a Starjumper, and the crew in full gear, no one would suffocate. The loss of pressure made the vessel wobble, however, and more wreckage struck it. Jerr's bones shook from the impact.

The dropship spun away from the asteroid.

Jerr's boots kept him in place with magna-grips, but his stomach churned from the spin's velocity. His HUD lit up with g-force warnings. Several soldiers puked in their suits; a few blacked out. Some, their bodies not enhanced like Jerr's, screamed as the forces inflicted pain. He tried reaching the cockpit but too many troops blocked his path.

They were spinning toward *Bhaellator*. It would be like a fly impacting a solar shield array on Uria, his homeworld.

"We warned them."

Jerr let his mind slip into Rezal state. Only the most elite Dominion troops mastered it and scant few among those could maintain it longer than a few seconds.

A few seconds was all he needed.

Rezal was a trance-like state of mind, during which the brain received even more of the body's energy, calculating faster. One could make snap decisions, normally requiring too many precious seconds, in the most stressful situations. Rezal state had saved Jerr's life, and the lives of his comrades, on a hundred different worlds.

Blast open hull fire thrusters then cannonade while braced against the bulkhead.

The plan, complete with estimated chronology, trajectories, and success ratios, zipped through his mind. He had to catch his breath after devoting so much energy to the brain. If not for his suit, he'd probably be lying in a heap on the deck.

The dropship continued spinning. More soldiers blacked out. The pilot sat limp in his restraints. The HUD warned of mounting g-force pressures. *Bhaellator* loomed closer.

Firing his diffusion blasters, Jerr turned the portside hatch into slag. One final shot flung it off its liquefied hinges. Atmosphere blew out the opening, along with a few cups and tools. The ship's spin slowed but the rotation's direction remained the problem. If he was wrong, they'd all become scrap within twenty seconds.

Jerr braced himself against the starboard hull. Timed his shot with the interval of spotting *Bhaellator* above and the interval of observing nothing but space. Without Rezal he'd never make such a mark. He fired.

The gauss cannon's recoil pressed him against the hull and the rounds flew out the hatch like fireflies of death. The salvo acted as propulsion, thrusting the dropship into a different trajectory and slowing its spin further.

Bhaellator passed above them as the dropship slowly spun off into space.

Only then did Jerr relax. He greedily sucked in air, not caring if he drained his supply. The radio band indicator lit up his HUD, but he waited a few moments before turning it back on. The voices, the visions in his head—both had been right. These soldiers, the crew, all would be dead now if not for his willingness to … to what, listen?

To believe?

But he'd caught that damned cup. Avoided those explosions.

Jerr stared out the ruined hatch at the stars. Wondering which his family called home. Wondering if they remembered him. If he'd been a good father, a good husband.

Hell, he doubted it. All he knew was how to be a good soldier.

He took deep breaths. Jerr had disobeyed orders, all because of visions, a dream—whatever it was. Now the Idreun and Stalis would wage war.

Jerr stiffened. The ambassadors were still onboard, in the stern. He needed to verify their survival. As he clanked over the deck, he spotted shapes outside the windows. Many shapes, with two larger than the rest.

Whoever set those explosives was coming to finish the job—and the ambassadors, their target. Unless Jerr made himself that target.

While the rest of Company K lay stunned or wounded, Jerr jetted his boot thrusters. He shot out the damaged hatch. Soon the vessel receded into blackness behind him. He tried the radio, but it was a static-filled uproar. Probably some jamming or cross traffic. He powered up the gauss cannon and checked the diffusion blaster's dampener.

Something streaked past his right shoulder. His suit beeped about slight heat damage. Using his HUD overlay, Jerr tracked the source. Twenty Idreun rebels in suits and two skiffs. The shuttle, his troops, the ambassadors—they had no chance. *Bhaellator* couldn't fire its weapons without hitting the dropship, and by the time they got a track for missile lock, the craft would be battered with deadly fire.

It was just him.

Jerr locked on to targets while thinking about his wife and son. Recalled hugging them on the dock, somewhere out there in the vastness. The last time he saw them.

The next instant he fired a gauss cannon barrage. It was instinctual, ingrained even, to go from passive musing to turning enemies into space dust. The rounds zipped past the rebels and clipped one of the skiffs. The vehicle spiraled off, pieces exploding away into the void. It lowered on the HUD's threat level and Jerr paid it no mind.

Scattershot rained at him. Two pellets melted through the outer casing on his left calf. He deactivated the alarm and swept a diffusion shot along the rebels' main line. The superheated light beam dissipated, but not before clipping off one Idreun's hand and cracking another's helmet. His intent was to make them scatter, which they did. The skiff homed in on him, which he'd also planned.

Jerr fired his wrist and boot thrusters, jetting toward *Bhaellator*. He had to insure no missed shots would pass him and strike the dropship. It was risky, because now the dropship lay defenseless. The rebels took the bait.

Using Rezal state again, Jerr aligned all his weapons with the HUD's tracking and fired his boot thrusters while turning in a spiral. Like a corkscrew, he barreled into the attackers just as they came in range of the dropship. To preserve momentum, he couldn't fire any weapons. The slightest push in the opposite direction would derail his flightpath.

As he passed the rebels, he dropped mine drones in their vicinity. They fired at the mines, while he pulled up, righted himself, and blasted three rebels apart. The concentrated light seared through armor, shredding bodies in brief explosions of red dust. A bad way to die, but at least it was quick. The mines still managed to take out a fourth rebel before the skiff destroyed the rest with a pulse shot.

The shockwave threw Jerr back, but he kept his eyes focused on the HUD. If he blacked out for one second, he and his friends on the dropship were dead.

"You cannot save them. The threads are frayed. They will all die."

The voice broke his Rezal concentration for a fraction of a second, but he corrected in time to fly behind the rebels. His diffusion dampener was still cooling the weapon, so he selected the gauss cannon. Though each shot's recoil would toss him away from the action, it was his only chance. The glowing hot rounds plowed through two rebels at once, leaving less than dust. Jerr hurried to reload.

One rebel spun about and returned fire. Scatter pellets sheared armor off his right shoulder, melting the dampener. The blaster went white hot.

"Shit, shit…" Jerr ripped the bindings off his right forearm. The diffusion blaster drifted away. He discharged his boot thruster at it. The overheated weapon flew right into the other rebels and exploded. Limp forms floated past in the void.

Distorted colors flared across his sight as Jerr slowly spun, cast adrift by the impetus of his weaponry and actions. The fate of humanity, exerting itself to ruination, only to drift forever in an oblivion of its own making—

Jerr blinked. He tried to reenter Rezal state, but the colors in his eyesight kept flaring. Blurring. Lensing at the edges, as if he looked at a black hole through a telescope, its gravitational pull distorting the wavelengths in his sight.

Floating, spinning…

Jerr coughed. Had he fallen asleep? Maybe that last explosion had given him a concussion. The dropship was a tiny dot now. The planet below rejected him, since he was too far away from its gravity well. He continued drifting.

"They murdered us."

"Huh?" he asked with a dry throat.

"They betrayed the Weavers. They murdered us."

Jerr blinked again as stars in his vison lensed into blurred, amorphous images like an oil slick in a rainstorm. He reached out with a burnt glove. The hubris of his species, thinking one could simply extend a hand, a fleet, or space-time, and there the object of their desire would be.

Faces appear in the oil slick, which morph back and forth to stars in his vision. Jerr coughed, then gasped as his air supply depleted. Maybe he was hallucinating.

His wife's face. She is crying. His son has survived a lava farm explosion, but Jerr has been absent, out on campaign. Out saving the Dominion, but not his family.

"I tried … not my fault …" Each word hurt his throat. His hungry lungs shriveled. But he couldn't let that accusation go. He'd deny it with his last breath.

The images blur until he sees himself, flying in a shuttle above a Hub World. Fighters dart after him, their thrusters ablaze, their cockpits gleaming from the starshine of a ringed world …

It must be his drinking. That, combined with whatever he'd suffered in the battle.

"You must run. The strands will not bind, but they can strangle. You must run."

Jerr tapped the buttons for his backup oxygen, but he couldn't keep his eyes open.

Emergency warnings flashed on the HUD. Shielding his eyes, Jerr thumbed the radio on. Static squealed in his ears. He mashed the volume button down.

"Manivo? Is there anyone out there?" Garrand asked.

Jerr activated his mic. "*Bhaellator* …" He coughed. "*Bhaellator,* this is Manivo. Dropship is crippled, but no apparent casualties. Request evac ASAP."

A flurry of replies filled the channels: dismayed Stalis voices and angry, accusing Idreun ones. But nothing else from Garrand. He probably wanted to chew Jerr's ass in private. So be it. Jerr had saved lives. Nothing else a good soldier was supposed to do.

A pale blue face lit up on his HUD. "Glorious."

Jerr snorted. "I bet. Does everyone feel that way about my decision?"

Anxiety tightened Xade's face. "Nonunanimous."

"Huh?"

She stared at him for several moments, then her image faded from the HUD.

"Well, shit." Jerr continued floating like forgotten wreckage. Though he'd taken little combat damage, two servos had locked up from the intense g-forces he'd put the Starjumper through. His thrusters could do little more than fart sparks.

Within half an hour, two gunboats deployed from *Bhaellator*, watching over the battered asteroid as well as the Idreun blockade. The dropship was finally brought onboard, with Company K and crew taken to sickbay. Both ambassadors were unhurt.

It wasn't lost on Jerr, being the last one recovered. And by a tug-ship at that, with all the comforts of cramped shithouse. Garrand probably had a court-martial and an empty prison cell ready. No one spoke to him on the way back to *Bhaellator*, even via radio. He thought about messaging Xade but didn't. She'd pester him soon enough.

Back on the dispersal deck, Darei watched as a crane lifted Jerr from the tugship and planted him on the suit rack. "Looks like you didn't die after all. Now I owe the boys in Munitions some money."

"Hello, prick." Jerr groaned as a service drone started removing his suit. The emergency seals had been activated, making it tighter than a clam against his body.

"My third husband used to call me names." Darei flicked on a hand torch and sheared through a bent shoulder plate right beside Jerr's head. "That's why I left him back on Cuori. Then I remarried."

"That the guy who dumped you for a Squidran?" Jerr winced as another plate fell.

"Yeah, sorry bastard." Darei chuckled. "Can't win 'em all, you know? But you, Mister Fucking Reborn, you always seem to win."

Jerr tensed as the torch neared his chest. "So you wanted us to lose out there?"

Darei shrugged. "Job security."

"You asshole."

Darei smiled and cut into the armor's crotch plate. "You know, a smart man would shut up about right now."

"C'mon. I'm betting you're all cuddly inside." Jerr bit the inside of his jaw as the fiery beam passed over his groin. "Now wait—"

The torch sputtered out. Darei shook it and frowned.

"See? You even cut off the torch."

"It ran out of fuel." Darei pulled a replacement canister from his belt pouch. "Now, where were we?"

Xade walked up to them. "Precarious."

Darei sighed. "Great. Miss Blue Theux to the rescue." He put away the torch as the drone easily removed the rest of Jerr's armor with a few well-placed cuts. The suit fell with a clatter.

Jerr glared. "You mean, that's all it…you asshole!"

"I'll bill you later." Darei walked away, laughing.

"That little shit." Jerr couldn't help but laugh too.

Xade's eyes scolded Jerr while worrying about him at the same time. "Nauseous."

"It's good to see you, too." Jerr limped off the rack and injected himself with a normalizer. He needed to get rid of his post-adrenaline shock before seeing Garrand.

Xade shook her head and touched her stomach. "Nauseous."

He started to laugh again, but the emotion in her eyes was real. "Don't worry, we're out of danger. I'm fine."

"Nauseous."

"I didn't think your kind…well, you know, got sick," Jerr said.

She stamped her foot. "Nauseous!"

Jerr frowned, then vomited on her boots. The normalizer had relaxed his nerves too much, producing a typical physical reaction. "Sorry."

The service drone dowsed her feet and legs with disinfectant. The stink of bleach and soap stung Jerr's nose.

"Torturous!" She stalked to the nearest chute. After walking twenty feet, she turned. Her frigid stare demanded he follow.

"Sure, I'm coming." Jerr caught up to her and she pressed him into a chute. When he exited it several decks above, she was right behind him, pushing him down the corridor, her demeanor chillier than a locker full of ice. Well, he had puked on her.

A squad of MPs waited, carrying piercer rifles.

"What's going on?" Jerr asked. In the second it would take for them to aim, he could take out at least one. Maybe two. Not all four.

He hated that about his training. He could never turn it off.

Xade gripped his arm. "Anxious."

"About me? I've done nothing wrong."

A sergeant saluted. "Sir, we will escort you to Commander Garrand's conference chamber. This is but a precaution."

Jerr forced himself to calm down. Precaution against what?

The MPs—with Xade in tow—led Jerr to an officer's tram, which was restricted to all but a few high-ranking personnel. Jerr burned with questions but Xade could only communicate so much. He knew the military police wouldn't tell anything. In all his rebirths, Jerr had never been court-martialed or found in dereliction of duty. He was a model soldier. Like Darei often joked, Mister Fucking Reborn.

As the tram whisked through *Bhaellator,* Jerr reflected on the battle. He'd obeyed voices in his head. Like a crazy person. Once, he'd captured escapees from an asylum on Phona IX, just outside the Affiliate Worlds. Now, he might be joining them.

Yet…those voices helped him save everyone on the dropship. Including himself. For whatever reason, he'd known about the falling cup. The sabotaged asteroid.

Beside him, Xade pulled up her palm nodus and examined a few lists. He didn't let on he was watching but sensed she wanted him to.

The nodus showed the official statements of the Idreun and Stalis factions—both denying any wrongdoing, of course—and the Dominion's stance, which claimed it was still investigating. *Bhaellator* had quarantined the entire sector, which meant it would be staying here for a time. Leviathans gave the Dominion its true power, governing an empire spanning the Elder States, the Elium Rim, the

Affiliate Worlds, the Idreun Periphery, and all in between. They rarely remained in one location, keeping order across the galaxy. Even though the Dominion possessed thousands of such vessels, it wasn't enough to control so many million worlds, with trillions upon trillions of citizens.

That was why they rebirthed people like him. More than being mere clones, the reborn possessed all of their original person's skills and instincts, and were always grown to the age when the original had signed the contract. Conditioned through exacting standards to be proficient and trustworthy. Not imagining voices and strange visions.

Knew it would happen.

If Jerr's superiors found his behavior questionable, the Dominion might execute him. Then rebirth and station him elsewhere. Glancing at Xade, he wondered who she'd fuss over then. Whether she'd miss him, or even remember him after few generations. Theux lived for millennia; they'd even fought and surrendered to humans during the Armada Era. He'd always wanted to ask Xade her age. What she remembered.

The tram came to an abrupt stop, yanking Jerr from his thoughts.

The MPs disembarked first, then watched with calm stares as he and Xade exited the vehicle. They entered a wide chamber spaced with viewports, potted plants, and four realizers, their lifelike illusions deactivated for the moment.

Two squads of reborn marines awaited them. Jerr's reborn.

Garrand walked among the trees, sporting a casual smile. His eyes were emotionless glass. "Captain Jerr Manivo. I'm glad to see you escaped in one piece."

The marines took up positions along the walls. Calm, dismissive stances. Jerr knew they watched his every move.

"Me too, sir."

Garrand looked at Xade, who nodded once. "In fact, it's amazing any of you survived that terrorist attack. I'm told you received an early warning about it? A warning you communicated to the dropship pilot?"

If Jerr lied, slight changes in his blood pressure and cortisol levels would give him away to the room's sensors. Then he'd end up back in the brig—and not for drinking. "I received no warning, sir. It was an intuition."

Garrand stopped pacing. "An intuition? You sound like a drugged mystic."

"Call it a soldier's intuition … sir."

"I would almost believe that—save for your Starjumper minutes," Garrand said. "They indicate you did not enter Rezal state until after the explosion. And Rezal is the only 'intuition' the Dominion teaches its elite commandos."

"It's the only way I can describe it, sir." Jerr stared forward to mask his frustration. Garrand demanded more from a rebirth, since he was one himself. Their interactions had always been neutral, but Garrand's undertone made Jerr anxious.

"Perhaps." Garrand initiated the realizers. "Here is footage recorded from the dropship. Watch."

The realizers cast three dimensional images into the air, with full-size representations of Jerr, the pilot, and Company K. They appeared as real as he was. He could even smell the burnt metal and rubber stink of the dropship bay. See the sweat sliding down his face in the Starjumper suit.

The recording played back those moments when Jerr warned the pilot of explosives within the asteroid's craters. Jerr was embarrassed at the crazed look on his realizer face. Hell, he looked like a madman. The realizer played the rest of the event, down to the moment when the dropship spun out of control. By then, the vessel's systems had been damaged, and the recording ended. His virtual doppelganger winked out of existence. Jerr flinched. It was that easy to die, to disappear from history.

"An intuition." Garrand's statement mocked Jerr.

"If not for me, the ambassadors would be—"

"I don't require validation of your abilities." Garrand raised his brows. "I need to know how you knew there would be an ambush. And why you didn't warn us."

"I did," Jerr said. "Right before it happened, sir."

"And how did you know to warn us?" Garrand asked.

"It was a hunch," Jerr said. "An educated guess, sir."

"Xade, if you please?" Garrand glanced at her.

Though her expression remained impartial, Jerr caught the anxiety in her eyes as she conjured up her nodus. It showed his rising blood pressure. His nervous inhalations.

"I want the truth." Garrand's eyes locked on Jerr. "Only the truth."

Jerr looked from Garrand to Xade, then squared his jaw. "I saw it. I saw the explosion in my mind. Before it happened."

Garrand's mouth hung open, then he straightened. "What do you mean, you saw it? You are Urian, you can't see wavelengths in shadows any more than I can."

"I saw the event take place in my mind." Jerr fought to keep frustration from his tone. "What would happen, if the dropship had landed. I saw my soldiers dying—"

"Where did this information come from?" Garrand's question echoed in the room.

"I…I don't—"

"Where?" Garrand yelled.

"Instinct, sir!" Jerr shouted back. Not a lie, for even he was ignorant of the truth.

The marines' postures straightened. Gazes narrowed. Fingers neared triggers.

Xade scrolled through her nodus. "Penurious."

"Yes, a poor assumption." Garrand faced Jerr. "Would you not agree, Captain?"

"I can't explain how it happened," Jerr said. "I saved my company. Why is my integrity being questioned?"

Garrand motioned and the marines surrounded Jerr. Xade's eyes widened, but she stepped back. "I'm confining you to quarters until we reach Ghela Beta in the Affiliate Worlds. Once there, you will face an inquest."

"You're placing me under arrest?" Jerr realized the violent timbre in his voice. His fists were balled, ready to strike. They'd made him like this, one rebirth after another.

Garrand's thin smile was as genuine as fool's gold. "You are not under arrest. The Dominion cares about its personnel, especially one of its most elite soldiers. I cannot send you into action, risking your life, if there is a disparity in your mental faculties. But I'm sure everything will be cleared up. Officer Xade, see that he receives constant care."

That meant Xade would monitor him until they reached Ghela Beta. Which was at least four days away via the Shroud. Hundreds of light years passed in milliseconds.

"Thank you … sir." Jerr saluted.

Xade led him out by the arm. Her grip was much tighter than usual.

Chapter 5

Cast your nets across darkest seas,
Under a million-fold horizon
But the starry depths, forever burning,
Under a billion-fold horizon
And your prideful snares, so unforgiving,
Strangling that which you sought to catch.

Epiphanies of the Shroud

After staring at the wall for an hour, Jerr found he preferred the brig to his own quarters. At least in there he could look out the bars into the corridor. Here, he had nothing but four walls, a cot, a screen, and a small pantry. He showered and lay on the cot in his underwear for a nap. Staying awake only reminded him of his situation.

Garrand probably thought Jerr was deviating from his rebirth template. There was no other explanation. They couldn't question him further onboard *Bhaellator,* for Rezal state allowed resistance to all known mental interrogation methods. But there would be Vestal Confessors on Ghela Prime. They could force an innocent man to confess murdering an entire world.

Maybe he should've told Garrand the entire story. The voices, the other visions. But Jerr would be in a padded cell now, rather than his quarters. There was no way out.

Unless…

Jerr got up. There was no silverware in the pantry. No cot sheets in the closet. Nothing he could use to hang himself, slit his wrists, or slice his jugular.

For a reborn, suicide was the unspoken option. End this life, wake up in the next. Religious fanatics in the Faqar Belt hated his kind, saying the reborn broke natural laws, scorning their gods. Rumors claimed the Avae, one of the sapien species defeated by the Armada, kidnapped any reborn they found, trying to discover how the Dominion not only regrew the deceased's body, but regenerated their mind and personality as well. The strangest reaction came from the Cultists of Mur, who worshipped the reborn as deities. He'd heard of renegade reborn dwelling among them in luxury.

Jerr sat back down. Reborn or not, he wouldn't kill himself. Though the Dominion would regrow him, he might not remember them: his wife and son.

It was the only thing he feared to lose. And it was only a memory.

A chime rang and the door opened. Xade stood there, but he spotted a marine over her shoulder in full Gahn armor. Garrand wasn't screwing around.

Xade walked to the center of the room, eyes fixed on him. He leaned back, hands behind his head, propping his bare feet on the cot's frame.

She finally spoke. "Contentious."

"That pretty much sums up my situation," Jerr said. "You here to interrogate me?" Having a lengthy conversation with her could already be torture.

She exhaled slowly and gave him an aggravated look.

He snorted. "You copy human emotions so well. How long have you lived among us? A few centuries? Or even before the 83rd Millennium? You know, the big 8-3?" His condescending tone was intentional. No doubt Garrand sent her here, a familiar face to glean whatever they could from him. If he even wiped his nose a certain way, they'd read something into it. The Dominion had mastered combative psychology.

Xade summoned her palm nodus. It read, '42nd Millennium'.

"Huh?" Jerr sat up and stared at her anew. Her exoskeleton, her blue dermaflesh, her curves. Mimicking a young human woman in every way. She could have stepped off a morga assembly line, save for her sorrowful eyes. Forty thousand years and more, she'd lived among his kind. Questions erupted in his brain.

"How many rebirths of me have you seen?" He leapt off the cot and stood before her, taller by only a few inches. The marine brandished his rifle.

"Fallacious." She tapped his chest once.

"So this is the only … one … they assigned you to." Jerr slumped back onto the cot. "Is this all you've ever done? Taken care of reborn?"

She nodded.

"Then what do you want?" Jerr expected some Theux weapon to slide from her hand and stab his heart. Theux could take different shapes, though he didn't understand their rational culture, one that surrendered to the Armada, and served the Dominion faithfully, for so very long. They didn't need to be anyone's servants.

"Meticulous." She beckoned him toward her.

He could fight her. Jerr was in his prime; the Dominion ensured that every single time it regrew him on a Hub World. The marine at the door wouldn't have time to shoot.

Something altered in Xade's expression: a slight narrowing of the eyes, a tightness of the jaw. She expected him to attack, fight his way out. Or at least try. Which suggested more about him than it did her.

"Fine," he muttered. "Do what you have to do."

Xade swiped a hand above his chest, her dermal sensors tingling his own flesh. They'd already scanned him fifty different ways with as many devices, but she sought something else. He hated his sudden nervousness. She'd never affected him this way.

Forty thousand years. Damn.

The nodus indicated tension in his shoulders, pinching his back. Xade dug her fingers into the thick muscle, kneading the trapezius, deltoids. His heart rate leveled off. He slowly exhaled. It wasn't the first massage she'd given him. Equal parts nutritionist, trainer, and physician, Xade always ensured his well-being personally. Not even the science division reborn in Research Berth received such treatment from her.

If only that treatment extended to helping him escape.

"How's it feel to be an old woman?" Maybe he could unbalance her, irritate her. It might be his only chance.

"Precarious."

He couldn't help but smile. "Really? I bet you drive all the Theux boys crazy."

Xade withered him with a look. "Vacuous." Her nodus displayed a small set of facts: Theux homeworlds destroyed by the Armada. Less than a half a million Theux left in the galaxy. No two Theux physically allowed to be in the same system, by law.

Jerr stared at the floor while she completed her scan.

As she made for the door, Jerr sat up straight. "Hey."

She paused, a grim will in her eyes.

"Is that why you made yourself look like that? To fit in?"

Xade gently touched her cheek, then examined the flesh on her hands. Her shoulders drooped. Without looking back, she left. The door whooshed shut and locked.

Bhaellator shook slightly.

Jerr stiffened. Xade had left less than an hour ago and he'd been unable to nap. What he'd seen on her nodus about her people, her age—the pain in her face—he couldn't think about anything else.

Forty thousand years old. He must come across as a stupid infant.

Now he awaited the ship's transition. When a Leviathan shook like that, it meant they were about to enter the Shroud. The journey to Ghela Beta would take a few agonizing days. Jerr wondered if he'd be able to sleep. If the voices would come again.

An invisible force tugged at Jerr, like fingers trying to pry the bones from his body. His stomach roiled. He couldn't breathe. As quickly as it came, the sensations disappeared. He felt slight fatigue but little else. He'd seen people get Shroud sickness and vomit, their muscles clenched tighter than a vise, their lungs refusing to fully inflate. Once in the Shroud, though, the only sensation was a passive inertia.

Jerr lay on the cot and supped from a water bottle. It tasted fresh, but he suspected it contained tracking enzymes. Just in case he was carrying any terrorist bactroids. Garrand was probably analyzing Jerr's piss for suspicious contaminates, too.

Bored, Jerr activated the wall screen and paged through the available programs. Wait, they'd be monitoring that, too. He selected one displaying a tropical seashore on Kavo with the surf audio maxed out. Let Garrand wonder about the significance of that.

In reality, he wanted to view current news from his homeworld, Uria. Located just inside the Affiliate, it was a high-gravity planet, the fourth from its yellow, middle-aged star. Though the atmosphere was breathable, the surface was mostly grey-blue cliffs and ravines. Native, furry athalbors could rip a person in two. After the Armada's victories, it'd been settled with an outdated, controversial terraforming method. Urian water still contained elements meant to strengthen those reared drinking it—but it left their eyes teal, almost turquoise, in color. Though Jerr's eyesight was excellent, the taint of that era stared at him whenever he looked in a mirror. A reminder that, even before his birth, the Dominion had tried fabricating better people.

For the first time in a long while, Jerr tried remembering his parents. It was easy recalling old squad mates, former commanding officers, or some of the ships he'd served on—but anyone he'd formed a real emotional connection with were absent in his memories. Since he was reborn at the same age every time, that meant he might not have any lovers, friends, or kinsmen still alive.

Save for the memory of his wife and son. Her tan skin. The colorful tunics she wore, in greens and blues, Uria's traditional colors. His son's braided black hair. Those slightly darker teal eyes, gotten from Jerr himself.

Those people had existed. He'd known them. Loved them. Why couldn't he return to them?

"We warned them."

Jerr snapped his head around.

"They took it from us with blue fire and death."

He started to examine the room, then realized the wall sensors would let Garrand see and hear everything. If he searched for something, they'd ask why.

"Do you hear, murderer?"

Jerr dared not answer.

"Your kind trapped us in the Shroud. The Weavers were unable to return."

He lay on the cot and covered his eyes. All he heard was his furious heartbeat. The screen continued playing the tropical scene, but his ears attuned to the voice.

"They took it from us."

Gritting his teeth, Jerr tried thinking of anything else. Xade's age, his wife and son, Darei's shit personality, how he'd explain things to a Confessor—

"With blue fire and death."

Jerr leapt off the cot and did pushups. One hundred. Two hundred. His pectorals, deltoids, and triceps burned, pumping out rep after rep.

"The Weavers are gone. Because of those like you."

He did crunches and squats. Sweat ran down his body.

"Weavers, gone."

He pushed harder and harder.

"Because of you."

Jerr stopped. Closed his eyes. He wanted to curse, shout, pound the wall. Instead, he entered Rezal state. Rather than calm him, though, new images gripped his mind.

Starships traverse the Shroud as their engines hemorrhage, their hulls splitting with awful slowness. Right as the vessel leaves the Shroud, the hull collapses, flinging passengers and wreckage across the cosmos.

"No," he murmured.

"The Weavers were murdered after the theft. Our strings cannot be linked again."

Jerr wiped his face with trembling hands.

Planets tremble as their surfaces are bombarded in grand shockwaves of cosmic fury. Fleets drift through space, filled with the long dead. Worlds once alight with the golden veins of cities become dark spheres hurtling around their dying stars.

"Why?" he mumbled, then mentally cursed for having spoken at all.

"We, the Weavers, warned you. Now we will all suffer."

If only he had a drink, some whiskey, some …

A Hub World in the Lagoon Cluster, its millions of vats filled with reborn. Meat sacs growing on an electric vine. They all have his face.

Jerr stood and paced the room.

"Do you understand, murderer?"

"Get out," he whispered.

"We will be silent no longer. Reveal us."

"I said, get out," Jerr said in a loud voice.

"Reveal us!"

"Get out!"

The door opened. Xade hurried in. Two medics followed, along with two MPs.

Jerr sprung. "Get out, get the fuck out!"

He shoved both medics from his path. One crashed into the wall screen. Shards and sparks flew. One MP raised a prod, but Jerr back-handed her into the corridor, then crammed the other MP's head through the wall. He ran for the door.

"Murderer."

"Get out of my mind!"

Xade flattened him with an open-palmed blow to the chest.

He lay on his back. More medics and marines ran in. They restrained his wrists and ankles with flesh magnets, which bit into his skin. His only concern was escape. He managed to pry one magnet free, but a marine slammed his rifle butt into Jerr's head.

The room swayed. Bright colors fizzled and popped in Jerr's vision.

"Monstrous!" Xade put herself between Jerr and the marine as the rifle butt came down again. It struck her in the back. She didn't flinch.

"Officer Xade, you tried to calm him, now let others do their job!" Garrand shouted over the intercom. "I want him restrained until we reach our destination. I want a nonstop watch on him, starting right now!"

"Reveal us, murderer."

"You're wrong!" Jerr yelled. "I don't know what you are, but you're wrong!"

Xade gaped at Jerr as another MP escorted her from the room. The medics tightened the magnets and produced a full-face muzzle.

"Reveal…"

"You're wrong, you're—!" The muzzle snapped into place over Jerr's mouth.

While marines carried him to the brig, Jerr's thoughts were filled with more voices, more panoramas of destruction. There was no hope, no redemption, no life in anything shown to him. Nothing but a never-ending epic of entropy spanning the cosmos.

Though he struggled and grunted, it wasn't against those restraining him. He wanted to escape who—or what—was inside his head. By the time they tossed him into the brig, Jerr was exhausted from the mental drain of trying to resist the voices.

But Xade had stopped him, then took a hit for him. Why? A being as long-lived as she would have other concerns than the fate of a grunt who was going insane.

A grunt. A body in a suit, another faceless murderer bent on killing. Is that what he really was? That's what the voices called him. Accusing him of killing the 'Weavers'.

Except… they'd also warned him about the sabotaged asteroid.

Chapter 6

Class II Repta proved resistant to torture due to higher pain thresholds; a side effect from their breeding for cheap, biological slaves. Yet when Class III Repta were introduced to test worlds in the Faqar Belt, we discovered this threshold had lessened, even though their physiology remained unchanged. We finally ascertained it was their enhanced emotional sensitivity, comparable to human experience, which made them more susceptible to such stimulus. We then proceeded accordingly.

Psychopomp Errata, Sector 191, Sister Kerase Dhaej, Vestal House

Ghela Beta was a miniscule tropical moon orbiting an ugly, orange-yellow gas giant in the Ghela system. Balyra disliked it instantly. Its star was an unremarkable red giant, it lacked planets with adequate magnetic fields, and the asteroid belt was more methane ice than minerals. In all respects it was a backwater within the Affiliate, but Revor had sent her here, after reports of a deviated reborn aboard *Bhaellator*.

Revor, head of the Dominion itself. He'd never personally gotten involved in something as routine as an interrogation. Such concerns were beneath him.

Balyra wondered if he'd finally uncovered her disloyalty at last. Perhaps she was going to her own interrogation.

As her ship *Lux Aeterna* neared the moon, Balyra paced the bridge. A new transmission played from Vestal House.

"You have arrived, Confessor Balyra?" The voice belonged to the Matriarch, her superior within the order.

"A clone no longer up to standards, frustrating it's superiors aboard a Leviathan?" Balyra glared out the viewport. "Sending me on such a mission is pointless. Just terminate the offender and grow another one. Vestal House has greater concerns."

There was little harm one person could inflict on such a massive vessel. Leviathans were the predators of the cosmos, and the Shroud, their lair.

"Curator Revor thinks otherwise," the Matriarch said in a testy tone.

"I haven't interrogated anyone in a decade," Balyra said. "The Dominion faces no real enemies now. No imminent dangers."

"Perhaps this reborn is an exception." The Matriarch sighed. "You know how paranoid they can be about any personnel aboard a Leviathan. Yet I trust that you will carry out the order?"

Balyra glowered at the speaker. Her superior was such a tool. "Of course."

The connection ended, but her frustration grew.

Even a Vestal such as herself was seldom allowed aboard a Leviathan unless the need was dire. The secrecy surrounding those starships bordered on fanaticism. She didn't need a behemoth filled with millions of would-be colonists, soldiers, and scientists. She had a stripped-down cruiser all to herself, *Lux Aeterna*. The one conceit allowed her after millennia of service.

Vestal House might not be the power it was before the Armada, but it still commanded respect. Rooted in religious and medical traditions, the organization was made up entirely of human women. Or it had been, before most became cyborgs to spread their knowledge for eternity rather than one measly lifetime. A Vestal endured disease, war, and worse in order to study it and thus eliminate it with the Eternal Flame.

Lux Aeterna entered the moon's orbit. Balyra spotted *Bhaellator* on the bridge's nodus display. She'd lost track of how much she had sacrificed so that Revor could have those ships protecting his empire. No doubt the clone already waited on the moon below.

Maybe this was about her after all. It was she that paid Idreun revolutionaries to plant explosives on the asteroid. *Bhaellator* had been responsible for safeguarding that trade deal. It was simply another plot she'd orchestrated to undermine Revor's control. Only someone with her lifespan and patience could expect such small calamities to build into a galactic emergency. Even Veja Qor was unaware of her patronage.

Just more grains sinking in the hourglass. A proverb from her homeworld.

Vestal House shaped her, taught her. Provided a life after fellow Sisters discovered her in a garbage trough on that desert planet. She knew about injustice, she had survived men's anger, repression, and violence. She'd risen in rank until she became the High Confessor, for none resisted her long. Whether she defeated their will through logic, deception, pain, seduction, or harming that person's loved ones, Balyra never failed. Other Sisters said she could crack diamonds if given the time.

Once, those methods provided gratification, but more and more, her mind and body's acceptance of pleasure was eroding. The Flame consumed all. Even her identity.

Perhaps she should have agreed to be reborn like so many others serving the Dominion. Forever young, forever escaping death. But Balyra preferred a level of control. Vestal or not, she had vowed, after getting rescued from that garbage trough, to never again be another's victim. And from her viewpoint, the reborn were the greatest victims in human history. Never dying, never changing—never progressing.

Except for the Dominion's leaders. The Ageless, some dubbed them, with Revor being the oldest. The one she hated most. The Reborn Initiative was his brainchild: millions of clones trained and conditioned to maintain the Dominion, since he trusted few to run his empire. It had made humanity stagnant.

One day, the Flame within her would cleanse it. A victim of Revor no longer.

The nodus morphed into a fuller image of Ghela Beta. Balyra swiped the access codes into the console and waited for the morga pilots to land *Lux Aeterna*. Manufactured to ancient Elium standards, morga resembled humans save for their segmented joints. Balyra's were attired in red jumpsuits with white armor, like the Vestal legions of old. She preferred them to human guards, since she knew all too well how far loyalty went.

She cinched her unisuit and adjusted her endoskeleton to the moon's slightly higher gravity. Though she preferred the weightlessness of zero gravity whenever possible. That was another thing she'd learned.

Never let anything drag her down.

Jerr's stomach growled as MPs led him from the shuttle onto a landing pad. Out of habit, he glanced at the light violet sky and spotted *Bhaellator* in orbit, its angular light configuration unmistakable. As the ship passed overhead it blotted out nearby stars. A sudden thought occurred to Jerr: he couldn't remember when a Leviathan wasn't orbiting the current planet he was on.

"C'mon, stop dragging your ass," one MP said.

Jerr shadowed their brisk pace, shackled with larger magnets and spring clamps, which even a lifter drone would have trouble snapping. Dressed in a yellow jumpsuit, Jerr sweltered in the moon's tropic humidity. Trees surrounded the pad, moist with fresh rain. Fog rose from the forest canopy below, a vast wilderness far from any urban area. There were probably two companies hidden in the trees, armed and ready. Jerr knew: he'd escorted alleged spies to such locations.

Xade and a squad of Repta auxiliaries followed in escort. Neutral as usual, she avoided eye contact. She was probably ashamed of him. If a Theux felt shame.

The Repta female he'd spotted earlier commanded the auxiliary unit. Again, she studied him with unabashed attention. Her warrior culture held traitors in great disdain.

A platoon of marines met them, accompanied by a tall, pale woman. She had the typical red eyes of a Vestal and sported long, lustrous blonde hair. Her dark red unisuit hugged her, a symbiont more than a garment, providing nutrients and protection. There was a smoothness to her movements that belied sophisticated training.

"Prisoner transfer 659," a soldier said. "He's all yours now, Confessor Balyra."

Jerr studied her face, noting the lack of empathy—hell, anything—in her crimson gaze. He was as good as dead.

"Take him to Detainment." Balyra's voice was perfunctory and crisp. She flicked a glance at Xade and the Repta. "Your presence isn't necessary."

Xade raised her hand, which displayed Garrand's face on her palm nodus. "Officer Xade must oversee the interrogation for *Bhaellator*'s records. Captain Manivo's sentence remains my responsibility."

A flicker of annoyance travelled over Balyra's features. "Then come."

She led them to a large elevator which lowered them below the tree canopy. Though glass surrounded the elevator tube, Jerr was allowed a grander view of Ghela Beta's surface. Winnow-like, green-leaved trees sprouted from the earth like oversized stalks. A few warble birds flew about, but they spotted no other wildlife. Jerr assumed the gas giant's proximity hampered the development and survival of most known animal species. So much green, so much possibility.

Once, he'd have given anything to live in such a place. He'd qualified for the Reborn Initiative after his commando training and signed the contract. All so he could travel the galaxy, serve with honor, and eventually retire. But now, after countless tours and battles, he knew the truth: a reborn never retired.

"You admire the arboreal surroundings," Balyra said. "You saw so very few trees on Uria, your homeworld."

Jerr stiffened. "I guess you know all about me."

Balyra smiled. "I am confident you will fill in the parts that I don't."

Her threat made him smirk. "Good, then you can tell me about my previous rebirths. Since you know so much."

One marine raised his sidearm, but Balyra waved him off. "It's refreshing that you talk so willingly, Captain Manivo. This doesn't have to be unpleasant."

"But it will be, won't it?" he asked.

She smiled again and exited the elevator when the door opened.

Xade walked closer to Jerr, though he wondered why Garrand really sent her. Any information Balyra claimed she'd gotten out of Jerr could easily be relayed via transmission. But it didn't matter. His end would be the same, regardless.

Detainment was an austere, octagonal room lacking windows. The platoon waited outside, while Jerr, Balyra, Xade, and two MPs entered. The room had but one chair: a metal affair fitted with magnet cuffs. It looked too simple, meant to lure a prisoner into a false sense of security. He had no illusions about what was coming.

The door shut. Balyra motioned for the soldiers to place Jerr into the chair. They need not have bothered. As soon as he neared it, his magnetic cuffs linked with the chair, and he was yanked into it with a clang. Again, he knew this was meant to intimidate him. He hoped he died with some dignity. Xade would record it all for posterity.

"We warned them."

The voice made him break out in a sweat, to which Balyra nodded.

"You are very nervous for such a high-ranked reborn soldier. You have died many times. Surely this situation does not bother you that much?"

"We even begged them."

Jerr tried to ignore the voice and stared back at Balyra.

"Your previous rebirths all shared a spotless service record." Balyra slowly paced around the chair. "You have one of the best genetic makeups in the empire, with more combat hours and training than an entire veteran brigade combined. And yet you gained information regarding an attack. Afterward, you assaulted your comrades when they tried to restrain you. To most, that alone would prove your guilt."

Xade watched with interest. Balyra kept pacing, not looking at him.

"Nothing to add?" Balyra faced him. "Then tell me about your 'intuition', as the dropship approached the asteroid. You told Garrand that you 'saw' what would happen."

"That's all it was," Jerr said. "An intuition."

"Soldiers make the worst liars," Balyra said.

"The craters were dark," Jerr said. "They were a perfect place to hide the explosives. Since my scanners couldn't detect anything—"

Balyra waved a hand and the magnetic cuffs burned his flesh. Jerr cried out in surprise as well as pain. Across the room, Xade showed no emotional response. Such was loyalty to a biomechanical. She might as well be carrying out the interrogation herself.

"Your intuition, Captain?" Balyra asked. "You have displayed no such 'intuition' before. Not on any prior missions. Nor did any of your rebirths."

That answered something for him: no previous version of himself had acted on the voices and visions—if they'd experienced them at all.

"Who were you speaking to in your quarters aboard *Bhaellator*?" Balyra waved again. The magnetic cuffs squeezed around his wrists and ankles. He gasped.

"Who did you tell to 'get out'?" Balyra leaned over him. "There was no one in the room with you. You were awake, so it couldn't have been a reaction to a bad dream. You were not interacting with a program on your wall screen. So who—or what—did you demand to 'get out'?"

"You'll kill me no matter what I say," Jerr muttered.

Xade's eyes narrowed.

"Lost forever in the Shroud, where you left us. Murdering us wasn't enough."

Balyra leaned on his shoulder and lowered her voice. "It isn't human nature to keep secrets. You yearn to tell me, to release the guilt from your heart. This secret is worthless to you. It has gained you nothing. Tell me and I will stop this."

"I…" He entered Rezal, obfuscating his thoughts behind walls of calculations. It was stubborn, but he didn't want to tell her. Didn't want it on his perfect record.

That he might be insane.

The magnets zapped him. He sucked in a breath.

"Rezal will not help you," Balyra said. "Vestal House helped the empire develop that branch of neurological training."

Multiple syringes darted from the chair's armrests, pricking his flesh.

"First, I inhibit you from metabolizing glucose and ketones." Balyra caressed his face. "Starving your brain so you cannot use Rezal."

Jerr clenched his teeth and tried maintaining the mental barrier.

"You can't feel the bactroids that were also injected into your bloodstream." Balyra's breath was hot on his neck. "They are one of Vestal House's greatest secrets."

Fatigue weakening him, Jerr hyperventilated. His Rezal defense was all but gone.

"Now you know why," Balyra said. "They disrupt the rate of neurons firing in your brain. The Dominion has outlawed them in all systems, fearing they might spread and replicate. See? I did not have to torture you to break you. Now tell me."

"But what will you gain?" He grunted as the magnets pulled tighter.

"Do you really care?" Balyra asked. "You are a reborn. What should one care about, when one has lived a hundred times, and will live a hundred times again, once this is done? In a thousand years, this will not even be a memory for that incarnation of Jerr Manivo. So why bother yourself with it? Let it go. Nothing is easier."

Xade watched with extreme interest. No doubt Garrand wanted to know whatever secret they thought Jerr possessed. They would be disappointed.

"I hear…" Jerr swallowed, every word sapping more energy. Sweat darkened his yellow jumpsuit. Muscles twitched as his glycogen stores evaporated.

"Yes?" Balyra straddled his lap and cupped his chin.

"I hear … them."

"Who?" Her fingers tightened on his chin.

"Voices," Jerr breathed. "In my head."

Balyra stood, all sultriness gone like a flame in a windstorm. "Voices?"

Xade scowled. "Incredulous."

"Quiet, Officer Xade." Balyra walked around Jerr. "What voices, Captain?"

He closed his eyes, seeing the images. The destruction. "From the Shroud."

She struck his face. "That is impossible. What voices?"

Jerr struggled at his bonds. "The Shroud, I said!"

Balyra gripped his throat and slammed his head back against the chair. "Everyone knows that nothing lives there. Now, what voices?"

"The ones in the fucking Shroud!" he yelled. Balyra slapped him, drawing blood.

Her eyes glowed red as humanity left her demeanor. All machine, all demands, like something out of a drone crafter's nightmare. "The Dominion has never found anything within that realm. It is not a place. It is a function of space-time. But tell me, Captain: what did these voices say?"

Jerr glowered up at her. "They said that the Weavers were murdered. That they were trapped in the Shroud after they were killed. That something was stolen from them."

Xade's lower lip quivered. That frightened him more than the torture.

"They?" Balyra bared her teeth. "Who are they? Tell me, you vat-grown oaf!"

"I don't…fuck you, I don't know—"

Balyra squeezed his neck until he couldn't breathe. "The Weavers plot revenge on us after all these eons? Why would they speak through reborn filth like you?"

"Probably…" Jerr spat blood on her perfect cheek. "Because people like you…will never listen…"

Balyra didn't bother wiping her face. "You genetic vermin. The Vestals have listened for millennia. We know everything, see everything. If the Weavers were still alive, still plotting against us, do you think we wouldn't know about it?"

"Contentious."

Xade's voice startled Balyra from her maddened reverie. She yanked away from Jerr and glared. "One more interruption and I guarantee you will not speak any words."

"World after world was ravaged, leaving nothing but charred mantle."

Eyes fluttering, Jerr shuddered in the chair. Weariness consumed him.

"Some tried escaping via the Shroud, but all succumbed."

His head lolled to one side. Drool slid from his mouth.

"But you had help, murderer. Our ancient enemies helped you."

Jerr chuckled, no longer sure of who spoke, of where he was.

"They helped you!"

As Balyra whirled on him, he guffawed with mad laughter.

"Did the voices tell a joke?" Balyra swiped a hand over the chair.

Jerr thrashed at the sensation of his wrists and ankles breaking.

Xade turned away, her jaw firm.

He laughed harder, louder. Balyra increased the pain level. The room's realizer made it look like she'd ripped out his intestines. Both hands hung at odd angles.

"The Shroud must be full of comedians. Please, share their humor with me."

Jerr smirked as she started to swipe again. "You're just pissed."

Balyra's eyes flared bright red. "What?"

"Pissed that they spoke to me…and not you."

Balyra grabbed his head with both hands. "If you truly received information from the Shroud, then tell me! Is that how you knew the explosives would be on that asteroid?"

Saliva bubbled from his lips as he quivered. She'd increased the pain.

"I saw the dropship full of bodies," Jerr whispered. "I saw it burning. I saw the fire in the craters as the bombs blew."

"Impossible. There is no such thing as predestination, regardless of experiments on Weaver brains." She raised her fist, then hesitated. Her eyes roved over Jerr's person without really seeing him. The chair's pain augmenter lessened and the realizer shut off. No broken wrists, no eviscerated bowels. He still trembled from shock.

"Now, explain," Balyra said.

"You Vestals are supposed to make those connections, see all this shit," Jerr said. "I'm telling you, the last few times I was in the Shroud…they spoke to me. Showed me."

Balyra finally wiped her cheek. The blood smeared her jaw crimson. "Then what will happen next, my little vat prophet? If you know the future, why did you allow yourself to be captured?"

"Stop asking stupid questions," Jerr said. "Ask the good ones."

Xade regarded him with pride, which surprised him. What did she care?

Grudging respect entered Balyra eyes. "Very well. Why did they choose you to deliver this information?"

"I don't know," Jerr said.

"Is it a threat? Do these visions hint at their plans?"

"Damn it, there were other things," Jerr said. "Smaller things, like a falling cup. Well, I caught that same cup. It's stuff like that, all coming to pass. Like the Idreun asteroid. I acted on what they showed me would happen. They were right."

The words spilled from him. Whether from the bactroids' influence, exhaustion, or the desire to end his pain, Jerr cared not. His execution was nigh.

Balyra motioned and the door opened. "Take him and clean him up. Officer Xade, notify Commander Garrand that we will use

Bhaellator to assess the veracity of Captain Manivo's testimony. The test will require his cooperation."

While Xade sent the message via her nodus, marines entered and pulled Jerr from the chair. The shock was wearing off; his body ached where Balyra hit him.

"What test?" Jerr asked.

"I am going to examine you while we are in the Shroud," Balyra said. "I need confirmation that you really are hearing and seeing these things."

Xade and the Repta captain shared a look.

As the marines dragged him outside, he scowled at Balyra. "And what happens when I'm right? What happens when something else I've seen comes true?"

"Unfortunately for you … that is not up to me." Balyra walked ahead, as if conversing with him tainted her somehow.

Chapter 7

The accusations of war crimes only come from those who haven't endured invasion and desolation. They are the rumblings of academics who will never see their comrades die horrible deaths, nor witness the destructive capability of such a single-minded, coldly efficient machine as a modern military. Thus, it is only genocide when enemies survive who can name it so.

Narrative of the Armada, Chapter 23

The trip back to *Bhaellator* was a grander affair than the initial descent to Ghela Beta. Two strike cruisers and fifteen gunboats acted as escort. Inside the shuttle, a platoon of marines watched Jerr—still shackled—while Balyra argued with Garrand on the radio. She finally cut the channel and glared out the viewport.

"When a Vestal is denied, blood rains from the sky," Jerr muttered.

"Every star system has such trite little proverbs about my Sisters," Balyra said. "They are created by the guilty and under-confident."

"Or the ravaged," Jerr said.

"You are the very ravager, being a Dominion soldier," Balyra said. "Do you even remember how many you have killed in service to the empire?"

Jerr shrugged. "I've never killed a Vestal."

She glowered at him and entered the cockpit.

Xade shook her head at him. "Facetious."

"Somebody has to be," Jerr said.

"Both of you, shut the hell up," a marine said.

From what Jerr could ascertain, Garrand disagreed with Balyra over her proposed 'test', and demanded Jerr be returned immediately. It was a pissing contest, one he sensed Garrand would lose. A Vestal Confessor was denied nothing.

Minutes later, the shuttle boarded. The marines led Jerr to a detainment area on *Bhaellator*'s lower decks. An entire platoon came along, plus three dozen Repta, led by the same female. The blue-green scales on their heads and hands gleamed under the corridor lights, contrasting their black unisuits. Jerr wondered what their original species looked like, before the empire bioengineered them to appear more humanoid. Such had been the fate of most defeated races during the Armada Era: assimilate or face extinction.

Two morga accompanied Balyra, dressed in white armor over red uniforms. Their mechanical joints gleamed chrome. Having them was an old-fashioned touch, hearkening back to Vestal slave armies predating the Dominion. Before they made soldiers like him.

Balyra stood before Jerr as the morga affixed his magnet cuffs to the far wall. The chamber was plain and rectangular, with a few observation windows. He spotted Xade and Garrand staring at him from one. Through another, several Dominion scientists readied their equipment.

The morga fitted a neuroscanner to Jerr's head, along with diodes all over his body. A med drone floated nearby, bearing an assortment of syringes ready to put him asleep, summon his adrenaline—even kill him.

"How does this confirm whether or not he is a deviation?" Garrand's voice sounded tinny over the room's speaker. "Your first interrogation revealed nothing."

"As I have told you," Balyra said with an edge to her voice, "be patient."

The Repta female kept looking at Jerr, serpent-like eyes cool and nonchalant.

"Journey to the coordinates I gave you, Commander," Balyra said.

Bhaellator shook for a moment, then all went still.

Jerr swallowed and waited. With everyone watching him, he feared more than ever what he might hear or see. He was but a conduit for whatever warned him about the Idreun asteroid. Maybe the Dominion wanted to keep using him as a conduit.

"We are in the Shroud," Garrand said.

Balyra nodded, her attention focused on Jerr. Though she was, or at least had been, a human, the Vestal bore the idiosyncrasies of a machine more so than Xade, who was biomechanical. He imagined a metronome in Balyra's brain, counting off the moments until she expected a result from him. Patient and calculating.

A few minutes passed. Garrand kept checking the time. Xade consulted her nodus. The Repta grew restless, the female leader in particular. Balyra acted as if nothing existed in the universe save for Jerr.

"What were you expecting?" Jerr finally asked.

No one reacted to him.

"Hey," he called. "I said, what were you ..."

A blurred, lensing effect surrounded everyone else in the chamber. The same effect Jerr noticed on stars and galaxies outside the viewports while traveling in the Shroud. Time hadn't stopped: people blinked, their chests rose with regular breaths, Balyra asked questions—but there was no sound. The lensing effect expanded to the entire chamber, until it seemed Jerr viewed reality through a telescope getting stretched from horizon to horizon.

"They helped kill the Weavers."

Jerr froze as the familiar voice entered his thoughts.

"Ones like her. They helped destroy us."

He started to sweat. Now, as the voice echoed through his mind, he discerned images in the lensing around the people in the chamber.

"They hunted us and tortured us and studied us and murdered us and—"

He struggled as an invisible force pressed down on his chest. It felt like submersion in a pool, with the pressure mounting the deeper he went. The lensing increased until a flurry of images surrounded each person around him.

The marines were encircled by images of their corpses. *Burnt armor, busted weapons.* None of them would live.

"—and hunted us and studied us and murdered us…"

Jerr flinched as his gaze passed over Balyra. She lays on the floor, smoke rising from her chest. Her glowing red eyes go dark. Tiny machine parts are visible through tears in her flesh.

Balyra continued speaking, but he heard none of her words. Heard nothing except the crackling of flames, the distant alarms going off as the marines lay in crimson pools.

As he stared about the room, he spotted the Repta—a few of them dead, but most carrying weapons and supplies to a different chamber, possibly inside another starship.

"Their threads can be cut, like the Kieta cut down the Weavers."

"I don't want… I don't want to cut them. Who were the Weavers? The Kieta?" Jerr's words came out too fast. Balyra was still asking a question as if he hadn't spoken.

"See how the Shroud unravels. See what will happen."

Jerr gasped as a series of images crashed into his thoughts. Human soldiers gunning down alien troops, of a species he can't identify. They resemble floating, inverted triangles, with tentacles grasping weapons. The humans are aided by creatures that are little more than swirling tendrils of silver, atomizing anything they touch.

"Why are you doing this to me?" he breathed.

"How do you know about the Kieta?" Balyra asked.

Garrand was bounded by images of himself: burnt, twitching, but furious as he leads Jerr through Bhaellator to Bridge Deck.

"Who were they?" he asked the voices, but their answers melded into a noise akin to wind scraping metal across metal. Not words anymore, but a chorus of information hammering at his mind.

Last, his gaze passed over Xade. She is cool as ever, cerulean perfection. Shooting a Dominion marine in the back with a diffusion pistol.

The next moment Balyra's hand was on his chin. The lensing effect was gone. Sound returned to normal as the Vestal's voice slammed questions at him.

"What did you see?" Balyra asked. "Your brain activity multiplied by a factor of forty during that interval in the Shroud. Yet your cortisol and stress levels are the same, as if your mind and body were in two separate places. What did you see, Captain?"

There was desperation in her voice. Balyra cupped his chin with a motherly touch, while her other hand balled into a fist. It was as if she sought conversation, but the only language she understood was violence. A vernacular encoded into her, like the skills every version of himself recalled upon leaving the rebirth vat on a Hub World.

"I saw…" Jerr's voice was a dry rasp, like he hadn't had water for a week. "I saw those marines, all dead. The others… dead, wounded."

"And me?" The want in Balyra's voice was so palpable Jerr had to lick his lips. He realized this comprised her one joy: not emotional needs, not physical pleasures, but the acquirement of knowledge—especially if gained through her talents.

"Broken… ripped open, and your body… a smoking pile of junk."

Balyra gnashed her teeth and raised her fist, but Garrand's voice stopped her.

"Confessor, his physical readings are anything but normal. We were in the Shroud for a few minutes, before returning to Ghela Beta—"

"He has seen lifetimes." Her voice was tight with tension. "What was that you mentioned? The Kieta, the Weavers. None in this room should even know about them."

Some of the Repta stirred. Xade's eyes widened.

"I don't know," Jerr said.

"Think." Balyra mopped his brow with her sleeve. "Tell me everything."

"After you tortured me?" He snorted. "Go to hell."

She stood upright. "Everything could fall apart. Don't you understand?"

Jerr caught movement from the corner of his eye, but he already knew what was happening. The Repta female shot a marine in the back and drew her sword. Her warriors did the same. Each body that fell, each scream reaching his ears, was something akin to déjà vu. It was cinematic, watching it all with the detachment of the dead.

Balyra wheeled around and smashed a Repta's head with her fist. The warrior fell, his skull crushed. Though the morga defended Balyra with deft strikes, both were soon overwhelmed. The other marines managed to turn and fire once or twice, but the Repta were quick. It was all over in seconds, with the bodies arranged like Jerr had seen.

Amidst the carnage stood Xade, her diffusion pistol smoking over a dead marine.

Jerr gasped for breath, his muscles numb, his arms limp.

He'd seen this happen. He could have warned them. They might still be alive.

But he'd been unable to change that future, unlike the asteroid incident. He'd not called out. He'd not told Balyra enough. He might as well have killed them himself.

Balyra slew two more Repta before the rest shot her down. The Vestal hit the floor and twitched, circuitry showing through her exposed, burned flesh. The red eyes glowed once then dimmed.

Garrand shouted for security and ran to an exit, but the female Repta shot him. He went down screaming, patting out diffusion fires on his shoulder.

"Get Jerr Manivo and deliver what Xade promised," the Repta told Xade.

"What?" Jerr coughed at the stink of burnt armor and boiled blood. "What the hell did you promise them? This is mutiny!"

Xade rushed in and ripped off his magnetic restraints. "Obvious."

"Why?" he cried. "I'm a reborn, remember? I might have come back after this. You're not like me. They will destroy you. Forever."

She hauled him up into her arms with ease. "Repetitious."

"I'm not worth this, damn it! I'm just a grunt they'll regrow!"

While sparks popped off the dead marines' combat armor, and Balyra continued twitching, Xade carried him from the chamber. The female Repta and three others waited outside, holding Garrand hostage. Just like in Jerr's vision, his face and hands were burnt from the diffusion shots.

Bhaellator's general alarm sounded.

"They'll fucking scatter you all across the galaxy." Garrand started to say more until the Repta female lay a blade at his throat.

"Tunva does not scatter so well. Tunva needs to take command of *Bhaellator*."

"What?" Jerr asked. "There's no way. It can't be done."

"Audacious." Xade, still carrying him, led the way through a hatch to a tram. Tunva followed, with her warriors forcing Garrand along. Shortly afterward, the tram whisked them to *Bhaellator*'s upper decks.

The intercom buzzed. "Companies E, J, and K report in full kit to Auxiliary Deck 2. Repeat, Companies E, J, and K…"

Jerr's heart thumped. Company K was his unit. His reborn.

"There is no escape," Garrand said. "No matter where you go, we will find you. Every Leviathan leaves gravitational information in its wake, in the Shroud."

"Tunva is not interested in conversation." She covered Garrand's mouth.

"You planned this?" Jerr nudged Xade. "For how long?"

She didn't reply, focused on the tram controls while tracking *Bhaellator*'s security patrols on her nodus.

"Planned ever since the Armada massacred the Repta," Tunva said.

Jerr faced Tunva. "I won't be used. I'm not fronting some revolution."

"Revolution?" Tunva laughed with a slight hissing sound. "Tunva doesn't want revolution or revenge. Tunva wants release."

Fatigued from his ordeal, Jerr slumped against Xade's shoulder as she piloted through *Bhaellator*'s tram system. Alarms blared everywhere they went, and she avoided any stops where soldiers took positions at the docking platforms. Which was every one.

"This is crazy," Jerr said.

"Meticulous," Xade said.

"It doesn't matter how well you've planned this," Jerr said. "Besides, where will we go if we steal *Bhaellator*? How will we keep it? There's over a million people onboard who will want our assess for this!"

"The Leviathan will give birth," Tunva said.

He stared at her for a moment, then laughed.

Tunva grabbed him by the collar. "Tunva is not a comedian. We will only use the parts of the Leviathan that the Weavers once did."

Xade nodded. "Treacherous."

The tram stopped on the dispersal deck, where Starjumper suits hung in racks. Darei stared at them wide-eyed while the other technicians fled. Xade beckoned him.

"I … I changed my mind," Darei said.

"Fatuous." Xade's frown left no room for negotiation.

The intercom popped with static, then a voice spoke. "Auxiliaries are now regarded as Hostiles. Shoot to kill. Repeat, shoot to kill."

Xade checked her nodus. It showed a series of security feeds from Auxiliary Deck. Imperial soldiers—Company K among them—engaged in brutal firefights with Repta, Squidrans, Idreuns, and other conscripted humanoids.

"What the hell have you done?" Jerr asked.

The fighting spread to neighboring decks. Noncombatants caught in the crossfire were mowed down. Some feeds showed silent corridors piled with bodies.

"Thousands will die!" Jerr yelled.

"They die for Jerr Manivo," Tunva said. "Their blood pays for Jerr's escape."

"You're insane." Jerr kept shaking his head, refusing to believe it.

Xade gestured for Darei to hurry.

"It's not worth it." Darei backed away.

"You asshole," Jerr said. "How long have you been in on this?"

Tunva aimed at Darei. "Jerr Manivo will need an armor tech on this voyage."

"Do I look like I want to be executed for treason?" Darei asked.

"Halt!" a sergeant yelled, aiming a rifle at them. The other soldiers did likewise.

Conflicting emotions weighed Jerr's heart. These were supposed to be his comrades. He couldn't simply go from saving them, to gunning them down. The instinct to surrender, or assault those in the tram beside him, frightened him with its power.

"Get your asses out here and lie on your stomachs!" the sergeant cried. "Now!"

Repta charged from an opposite entrance. Both sides battled with unchained ferocity, diffusion blasts and scatter shot turning bodies and walls into slag. Stray shots blasted several suits off the racks. Sparks jetted in deathly geysers.

A soldier sneaks near the tram, aiming at Darei…

"Watch your left!" Jerr nudged Tunva.

Tunva shot the trooper creeping up behind Darei. "Tunva says now!"

"If you insist!" Darei leapt onto the tram. Xade piloted them to the bridge deck.

Jerr knew Xade and Tunva's rescue wasn't altruistic. They would expect things of him if they managed to escape. Unless he turned on them. He was a soldier of the Dominion, he owed the empire his very existence. Maybe Garrand would regale him as a hero and restore his command.

But Darei would be dead, if not for that vision. They all would be.

The room popped with a few still-burning bodies as Balyra stirred. Her internal systems had taken a shock, but it wasn't irreparable. She slowly stood, wondering how far Jerr and his traitorous fellows had gotten. There was nowhere to hide on a Leviathan. Every move would be tracked and they'd eventually need to eat and rest. She staggered to the control nodus outside the detainment chamber and accessed *Bhaellator*'s mainframe. She locked down all hangars and med wards while alerting the entire ship.

Balyra would take no chances. She had the interrogation data, the recordings of what Jerr said. Now she had something to evaluate and weigh his abilities against.

But such abilities were unknown. In all eighty-three millenniums of the empire, there was no record of a human showing any telepathic or psychic abilities. The very idea was ludicrous; a peasant's superstition. Yet she couldn't deny he had described the very scene around her now: dead marines, her damaged and smoking body.

It still wasn't enough to verify the truth of her hunch. What had he seen while in the Shroud? His brain readings were phenomenal. As if he were in forty places at once, rather than utilizing forty times his normal mental output. Far beyond Rezal state.

And the Weavers… none had so much as whispered their name for generations. Jerr had mentioned them twice. Common people thought nothing lived in the Shroud. A lie Vestal House had long perpetuated. But the Weavers had almost succeeded.

During the Armada Era, Revor trailed down and destroyed them. Vestal House had supported it with religious zealotry, aided by the Kieta, the true natives of the Shroud. She remembered what that battle had cost her. Was still costing her.

Even now, she couldn't forgive Revor for it. Or herself.

Afterward, Vestal House had decreed that the ability to cheat time and defy space was sacred. The privilege of the few. Tacit support of Revor's imperialist policies.

Uncounted epochs and lifetimes had erased those convictions in her. Jerr's predictions had spawned a new one: the conviction that this was a real chance to usurp Revor. Through her, Vestal House could once again become humanity's savior.

Smiling at the control nodus, Balyra left Bridge Deck open.

Chapter 8

With humanity strewn about the cosmos, it was impossible maintaining contact with every colony. A thousand different governments rose and fell; and in their ashes, feudalism, tyrannies, and theocracies inhibited human progress for centuries. Not even the Molexi engines, used by our ancestors to travel the firmament, or Theux minds, the most flawless computer, provided a solution. Humanity became a virus, a chaotic engine devouring all before it until the Shroud's discovery. Therein lay our salvation. In that moment, we transcended from mere sapiens, to the rulers of the universe.

Elder States Archives, Vol. XXXIX

The tram stopped on the dock leading to Bridge Deck. Though Xade helped Jerr from the transport, he could walk on his own now. He scanned every corner, every shadow. Tactics and escape plans passed through his mind, but nothing would make up for it: they were outnumbered, outgunned, and trapped on a hostile ship.

Bridge Deck was a massive chamber with no viewports. Hundreds of realizers displayed planets, fleets, galaxies, even *Bhaellator*'s officers, in a holographic gallery. Nodus screens monitored every aspect of the ship, from engine power to the minutiae of restroom wipes. Each system was independent, ensuring network stability.

The entire vessel was on alert but there was no security personnel. No alarms.

"Something's wrong," Jerr whispered as they all remained on the dock.

"Damn, you're a bright one." Darei quieted when Tunva elbowed him.

"Spurious." Xade looked at Garrand.

"Yes, but every system will be locked down," Jerr said. "We'll have to use him."

Tunva held up Garrand, whose burn wounds needed treatment.

"I'll not do it," Garrand said. "You will all be taken soon enough."

"Cumbrous," Xade said.

"Then let Tunva get rid of him." She raised a blade to Garrand's throat, but Jerr pushed it down. They stared at each other for long moments.

"You can't even work together." Garrand leered. "You're not going to survive."

Xade glared hard at Tunva, who finally released Garrand.

"A bunch of barbarians and traitors." Garrand laughed. "That's all—"

Jerr grabbed Garrand's collar. "You think the Dominion will want you after this, since you've screwed up here? You're as good as dead yourself."

"What chance do I have with you assholes?" Garrand asked.

"A tiny one," Jerr said. "With the Dominion? None."

"I don't know what the hell you've become," Garrand said. "But I swear I'll see you pay for this. You are supposed to be our best, the hero that kids on a hundred thousand worlds cheer about. Now you're going to be their monster."

"Maybe I always was a monster," Jerr said. "Now get us in the bridge."

Xade checked her nodus, narrowed her eyes, then left the dock.

"Wait—" Jerr said. Once the bridge crew spotted her, they were done for.

Nothing contested Xade's entrance. The ray barriers were down, which normally incinerated intruders. She passed a few realizers and swiped their controls. Full access.

Garrand stiffened.

"Looks like we have some friends onboard." Jerr led the others into the bridge.

Darei snorted. "Not for long. You going to let me go now?"

Jerr faced him. "We shot a Confessor and a bunch of marines. That means everyone associated with me on this ship will be under investigation. Including you."

Darei blanched. "I never should've listened to Miss Blue Theux. Why'd you have to ruin this post for me? Shit, I'm not a reborn, I don't get to come back!"

"Help us out," Jerr said, "and I'll get you two of whatever Xade promised you."

It was insanity, making offers when he didn't even know why Xade and Tunva saved him. Why they wanted to commandeer a Leviathan. They could be terrorists for all he knew. But at this point, he had to trust someone.

"There is only one." Darei gave him a dark look. Jerr frowned in puzzlement.

"First, Elium Rim," Tunva said.

"Yes," Jerr said as he hurried between realizer planetary globes. "In the Lagoon Cluster. I … I saw it while we were in the Shroud."

"You're going to listen to him, a deviated clone?" Garrand asked.

They fell silent, didn't look at him. Jerr felt hot and more than a little foolish.

"Like I told that Vestal, I can't explain—"

The bridge crew noticed Jerr and the others.

"Surrender and you can go in peace—"

Ignoring Jerr, the crew swiped at their nodi, trying to raise alarms or summon security robos. At Tunva's command, the Repta surged through the deck, killing any in their path. Xade shielded Garand and Darei, her expression scrunched in horror.

Furious, Jerr snapped a Repta's neck, took its pistol, and blasted a warrior about to gut a crewman. The others trained their weapons on him. Tunva hissed.

"You're not butchering them." Jerr was so angry his voice shook. "Is that what you wanted, Xade? Is this why you rescued me?"

"Scandalous," she murmured, glowering at Tunva.

"Traitors!" Tunva cried. "Only blood clears the way!"

A dying crewwoman swiped her nodus and activated the bridge alarm.

The entire Bridge Deck locked down. Twenty armed robos hovered down from ceiling enclosures. Each spheroid figure carried a diffusion repeater. Garrand beamed.

"Shut it all down." Jerr told Garrand. "Say the passphrase."

The robos covered the surviving bridge crew as they fled out another exit. When they swiveled their attention to Jerr, he pressed the pistol into Garrand's chest. The robos halted, programmed not to endanger the commander's life.

"This standoff won't last," Garrand said.

"Say it, goddammit." Jerr aimed at Garrand's head.

"You can't kill me." Garrand gave a short laugh. "Go on and try it, you vat-grown son of a bitch. We made you just the way we wanted, Manivo."

The gun shook in Jerr's grasp while the alarm continued. Try as he might, he couldn't pull the trigger. He wondered if it was his own morality, or the Dominion's conditioning, preventing him from murdering a superior officer.

"Those little voices not tell you about that?" Garrand grinned. "What a shame."

"Speak the words!" Tunva aimed at Garrand. "Tunva won't hesitate."

Garrand shrugged. "Xade knows it, being my First Officer ... but we all know how much she's able to talk."

Jerr rammed a fist into Garrand's gut. The commander spat blood and crumbled to his knees. Xade frowned at Jerr, but he yanked Garrand up. "Say it and we'll leave you here with Balyra. That'll give you a chance to come after me."

"I don't believe you," Garrand managed between heaves.

Tunva lay her sword on Garrand's neck. The robos targeted her, ready to fire.

"Better find some faith real fast," Jerr said.

Garrand finally said the passphrase. The alarm ceased and the robos returned to their enclosures. Yet, several realizers on the bridge displayed security and military officers, gathering squads to assault the bridge. They'd arrive within a minute.

"They think we can't pilot this thing ourselves." Jerr gave Xade a hopeful glance. "Um, we can pilot it, right?"

"Are you shitting me?" Darei asked. "You said you planned this ahead of time!"

"Pompous." Xade shoved Garrand out the door and secured it. She swiped the helm nodus, bringing up an entire realizer wall of *Bhaellator*'s statistics and settings.

The realizers showed the security forces docking their tram with Bridge Deck.

"We need to enter the Shroud," Jerr said. "How long will it take? Can you do it?"

"Efficacious." Xade accessed multiple systems until the gravity engine was activated. Jerr blinked and had to look away. There were so many integers, diagrams, and equations on the realizer. All he'd been trained—and rebirthed for—was to shoot at whoever the Dominion deemed an enemy. How limited his world really was.

The miniature world aboard *Bhaellator* was falling apart as Jerr stared at several nodi feeds. The Auxiliaries had taken two decks, while three others had become charnel houses. Using trams, both sides slaughtered one group of enemies, then hurried to the next. It was all a diversion to aid his escape. Jerr wondered if they knew that.

"*Bhaellator* must give birth," Tunva said.

"Huh?" Darei said. "I thought we decided that was nuts."

Xade accessed multiple nodi, doing the work of the entire staff. "Dangerous."

The realizers mimicked Garrand ordering the troops to attack the bridge.

"What does she mean?" Jerr wiped his brow, keeping an eye on Tunva's warriors.

"She wants to dump *Bhaellator*'s citizen compartments and the military bays," Darei said. "That'd leave the main crew area. More than enough, if it's just us."

The ray barrier went back up. Several robos deployed against the security forces outside. The soldiers, wearing Starjumpers, blasted the robos with gauss rounds.

Jerr shook his head. "Whatever. Get us going!"

Repta took up positions near the entrance. The ray barrier crackled as soldiers tried barging through it. Tunva murmured words over her blade and waited.

"Xade?" Jerr took cover behind a console. "They're going to break through!"

The racket of battle fired Jerr's blood. In moments the soldiers would rip past the very bulkheads and be at their throats.

What he wouldn't give for a drink.

Xade swiped a plethora of commands on the transparent nodi. Moments later, *Bhaellator* shook slightly. The realizers winked out, then displayed real-time data and video feeds of the transition. Xade effortlessly maneuvered through a barrage of overrides and security protocols to complete the order. Darei watched her, open-mouthed.

The chamber outside the bridge locked off and disconnected. The realizers showed Garrand and the remaining soldiers scrambling for the tram. Jerr loosed a deep breath and patted Xade's shoulder. Darei rubbed his face with both hands. Tunva smiled.

The immediate decks around *Bhaellator*'s bridge sealed themselves off and separated from the hull. Garrand was on one of them, no doubt cursing Jerr's name. Single-use thrusters flung the disengaged berths from the mother vessel. On the realizers, the scene resembled a jigsaw puzzle coming apart. Much like his reality.

Jerr closed a dead crewman's eyes. He stared at Tunva. "You murdered him."

"Jerr has never done this?" Tunva gave him a derisive glance. "Jerr Manivo, reborn again and again, has not committed murder? Tunva hears Jerr's lie."

"I promised to let them go if they surrendered," Jerr said.

Tunva cleaned and sheathed her blade, never taking her eyes off him.

"What the hell do you people want from me?" Jerr asked. "Should I worry about getting my neck cut, too?"

Xade collapsed a few nodi as *Bhaellator* ejected the rest of its main living and military areas—roughly half its mass. Entire sections came free, though still shielded with minimal power. They drifted into Ghela Beta's orbit. Regardless, fighting raged on several decks. Radio and video feeds exploded with queries until Xade muted them all.

"Jerr mentioned the Weavers," Tunva said. "Tunva would see the Weavers avenged. The Dominion needs reminding."

"You think I can find them for you." Jerr shook his head. "I don't know whose voices I hear in the Shroud. But attacking the Dominion isn't—"

"You hear voices?" Darei snorted. "Man, lay off the bottle."

Tunva studied Darei, hand on her sword. "Jerr Manivo hears the will of the Shroud. Does the skinny technician contest this?"

Darei raised his hands. "Okay, great, he hears stuff."

They continued arguing as Jerr examined a realizer image of Ghela Beta. Now it had several new satellites in orbit. They'd just deposited over a million people into a system they'd never visited before, with no hope of rescue until another Leviathan came. The castaways' energy and food stores would last months, maybe years, but without central engine power, they were doomed. Those who'd survived the mutiny.

"Leprous." Xade touched his shoulder.

"Then why'd you do it?"

She regarded him with the same resigned sadness as before. There was much she wasn't telling. Like how she'd worked out an escape plan, convincing thousands of Auxiliaries to mutiny. Or what she knew about the Weavers that Tunva kept mentioning.

No one spoke as *Bhaellator* drifted farther away from Ghela Beta and its gas giant. To enter the Shroud, a Leviathan had to distance itself from other celestial bodies, else the gravitational forces—harnessed by the engine core—could affect objects in the immediate vicinity. Jerr had seen a departing Leviathan tear an entire fleet apart by mistake as their flight paths grew too close.

Bhaellator shook for a moment, then all went still.

"Now what do we do?" Jerr leaned on a console and stared at Xade. "You saved me for a reason. Where are we going and why?"

"Hazardous," Xade said.

Darei rolled his eyes. "No shit."

"The Weavers were the masters of the Shroud," Tunva said. "We find out more about the Weavers, we might know why Jerr Manivo sees and hears them."

"So where do we start?" Jerr asked.

Xade held up her nodus. It showed a Hub World in the Lagoon Cluster: Stavia X. The same one from his premonitions. His skin prickled. He wasn't a star navigator, had no idea how to chart a course—yet she was taking them all to the place he'd envisioned.

"Why there?" Darei asked.

A rebirth vat appeared on Xade's nodus.

A chill washed over Jerr. "Because that's one of the places my reborn are grown."

Tunva nodded. "We must know if they all hear and see what Jerr Manivo does."

"What will that prove?" Jerr asked.

"Whether or not you are the only one the Weavers have chosen," Tunva said.

On *Lux Aeterna*, a med drone attached a new hand to Balyra's left arm. The ambush had damaged it, her diaphragm, and several discs in her spine. She preferred treatment back at Vestal House itself, but these facilities would suffice. Biotics to resuscitate or repair most known lifeforms were aboard, even substrate for a Theux. Balyra stocked them to mend tortured prisoners, rather than honor Vestal medic tradition.

Soldiers had taken her to *Lux Aeterna* inside *Bhaellator*'s lower hangar deck, right before it separated from the Leviathan. Affixed to the operating stand, she gleaned data from a multi-tiered nodus visible only in infrared.

Bhaellator had departed for the Elium Rim, in the vicinity of the Lagoon Cluster. They might take one route after another, hoping to confuse pursuers—but she doubted it. It was a major feat stealing *Bhaellator* in the first place. It would require a great deal of effort to operate it. She assumed Garrand's traitorous Theux facilitated that.

And yet, she'd aided them too. It was the greatest gamble she'd ever dared.

"Priority message from Curator Revor," one of her morga said.

As the drone snapped a new disc into her spine, Balyra scowled, though not from any pain. She had hoped to avoid his direct involvement. "I will view it shortly."

As head of the Curators, Revor ruled the Dominion from his own personal Leviathan, *Liberator*. Such individuals oversaw thousands of solar systems, commanded millions of soldiers, and lived in constantly upgraded bodies. Revor was their senior. A god traveling the cosmos in his own little world.

She remembered, many centuries ago, how she'd prayed to the goddesses of Vestal House, when the priestesses still taught that garbage. How she'd remained chaste, keeping her body free of toxins and addictions. But when she learned of the Curators and their manufactured immortality, of their power and influence, Balyra lost her faith. In the first year afterward, she'd not consumed enough drink, vapors, or sexual partners to fill the void within her. The other Sisters finally beat it out of her. That struggle had provided its own pleasures.

The wooden rod struck Balyra again, this time in the back. She maintained her posture, staring straight ahead, naked. Bruises and gashes gnawed at her nerves like leeches draining her sanity. Her dignity. She would not let them.

The Confessor glared at Balyra as the Martial Bride raised the rod. "You think you are strong enough to be a Vestal. Look at you. You are bleeding all over. A scab on the rump of the universe. It is not strength I see, holding you up. It is pride."

The Martial Bride swung. Balyra bit her lip as the rod wacked her right thigh.

"Pride is the downfall of humanity," the Confessor said. "It once made men think they were superior to women. Then it made humans think they are superior to gods. The Dominion abolished that pride under the watchful eye of Vestal House. As I will abolish yours." She grabbed the rod and smacked Balyra across the face with it.

Balyra, trembling with pain, returned her gaze forward, bloodied lips held shut.

The Confessor leaned in close. "You came from wealth and education; I can see it in your demeanor. You came here thinking those things would continue the privilege you have known all your life. It only buys you the privilege of the rod!"

The rod struck Balyra's stomach. Her knees. Her neck. Each strike made her shake more, bleed more. But she did not lower her eyes or slump.

"How many men have you fucked?" the Confessor asked. "One? Twenty?"

The rod swatted Balyra's rump a dozen times.

"How many would have wed a rich girl like you?"

The rod bashed Balyra's temple. Blood ran down her ear, along her jaw.

"How many?" the Confessor yelled in her face.

The rod busted the skin on Balyra's right arm. Blood slicked down her fingers.

"Confessor?" the Martial Bride asked in a concerned tone.

The Confessor relented, glowering at Balyra as if she were responsible for the ritual hazing. She grudgingly handed the rod back to the Bride and walked to the door.

Balyra stood straighter and took a deep breath. "Is that all, Confessor?"

The Confessor wheeled around and grabbed the rod again.

Balyra was the Head Confessor now. Vestal House would be her rod.

Another drone inserted a new diaphragm into her torso, into a cavity that did not bleed, serving a body that breathed only as a pumping action for the internal motor. There were no pleasures left her, no vices to feed her desires. And, human or machine, those desires never abated. That was the folly of the Theux, and of the morga, who were little more than sentient drones.

The folly was that flesh and metal were both weak. Both had their advantages, their limitations. Yet possessing a metalloid body and a synthetic brain did not remove the needs all intelligent beings have. The old stories of emotionless robos were children's tales. And a Vestal was nothing but a daughter of raw emotion, seeking solace in the burning fires of stars, or the ashes beneath a blackened stake in a town square.

That was how she felt regarding Jerr Manivo and what he knew. To ask Revor for aid would surrender that feeling to him. But she needed more resources.

"Confessor, Curator Revor demands your attention," the morga said.

Before she could answer, the realizer on the wall activated. It reproduced a three dimensional figure so realistic, she could smell Revor's trademark Laijan musk.

"Confessor Balyra. Your lack of a prompt response concerns me."

Revor was still tall and athletic, like the Revor who originally commanded the Armada. He even wore the same black and white uniform, complete with a bloodstained, burnt cape that had witnessed the scouring of worlds, the murder of countless dreams. An androgynous silver mask covered his face. Tinted lenses shielded his eyes.

A legend claimed that only the Weavers had seen him unmasked. And even then, only in the penultimate moment before their obliteration.

"As you can see, Curator, I am rather indisposed," Balyra said.

The realizer even added the sound of Revor's footsteps as he paced around the med table. "Indisposed, but not inoperable. Considering that a Leviathan was stolen right from under you, I would expect you to be mere dust. The Balyra I know would have fought harder. Yet here you are. Beautiful and whole, while a single renegade grunt challenges the Dominion. Perhaps Vestal House has deteriorated more than I thought."

"The Flame burns brighter than ever." She hated how he stared down at her, naked, her torso still open. Revealing how hollow her existence really was. "You sent me to interrogate him, so you must know something about this 'grunt'."

"The Kieta informed me of an anomaly in the Shroud. One centered on him."

Balyra wasn't as surprised as she might have been. "Truly."

"This soldier—Jerr Manivo—had help?" Revor eyed a spare heart on the counter and a realizer copy appeared in his hand. "The auxiliaries battled on his behalf?"

"More importantly, *Bhaellator*'s Theux facilitated his escape," Balyra said.

"Xade?"

None but a Confessor could have detected the surprise in his tone. "Yes."

Revor moved right beside the table, his waist level with her head. "Why?"

"The void knows." Balyra stared into those tinted eye slits. "Yet your 'grunt' knows things he shouldn't."

"Oh?" Revor looked from the heart in his hand, to the one thrumming in Balyra's chest cavity. "What could a mere deviant reborn know that would make Xade turn?"

"I'm certain Garrand mentioned all this in his report—"

The heart popped and hissed as he crushed it in one hand. "I want your report."

Revor's threat made his ignorance transparent, but she hid her smile. "Jerr has developed some sort of precognition. He sees things before they happen." She described the asteroid incident and Jerr's forewarning about her wounding in Xade's uprising.

"Interesting," Revor said. "But why did you require he be tested in the Shroud?"

After she told him of Jerr's increased brain activity in the Shroud, Revor waited.

"He also claimed to hear voices," Balyra said. "Telling him of the Weavers."

The only sound was the squish of a drone reapplying her inner dermal lining.

"Curator?" She had never seen him at a loss for words.

"That ... cannot be possible." Revor straightened.

"He also spoke of the Kieta," she said. "He knows we allied with them to—"

"How could he know that?" Revor asked. "We trapped the Weavers and their wrecked fleets in the Shroud, after exterminating their host bodies."

Balyra tensed. Did he suspect her after all?

"Time and space have different properties there," she said. "It could be possible that Jerr is able to sense the echoes of their existence, through space-time."

"Echoes." He paced again, his anger a palpable force in the room.

"Xade knew. It is obvious she planned well in advance for such an opportunity."

He stood still. "She never forgot, it would seem. Or forgave."

Balyra chose her words carefully. "Forgot what, Curator?"

Revor took a deep breath. "Jerr must be found and destroyed. Xade as well, should she resist. Spare no expense."

"Then I may call on Vestal House to aid me?"

"Yes. Officially, Jerr Manivo is simply a rogue reborn. His other ... abilities ... are not to be entered into the imperial record. Take Commander Garrand along, so that it appears he will assume control of *Bhaellator* once you are successful."

"Appears?" Balyra asked.

"Other than Jerr and his traitorous allies, Garrand is the only one who knows what was said during your interrogation." Revor flexed his gloved fingers. "Use Garrand as a bloodhound, then kill him. We cannot have anyone else knowing the truth."

"Of course."

He ran a finger along her exposed heart. "Exceed my expectations, Confessor. Manivo threatens our stability. We have given up too much, you and I, to allow that."

The realizer shut off before she could reply.

The drones completed their work and Balyra slowly sealed her unisuit. That bastard had promised her glory for her role in eliminating the Weavers. Glory that was just as artificial as her body. Believing him was her one regret.

Balyra entered *Lux Aeterna*'s bridge and accessed a transmitter capable of messaging via the Shroud. A whisper across the stars, summoning wrath.

Revor had given her a mandate. Vestal House would answer.

Chapter 9

The Kieta were little more than spiders,
Spinning webs around our worlds,
While fitting irons around our hearts.
Boundless were their voyages,
Glorious was their endeavors,
Yet stunted was their empathy; rotten was their worth.

Epiphanies of the Shroud

With the battle far behind them, and adrenaline gone, exhaustion forced Jerr to plop down on the floor between the realizers. "I want to know if it was worth it. Worth all those people dying."

"Inglorious." Xade crossed her arms and looked elsewhere.

"How long did you wait?" Jerr asked. "How long have you prepared for this?"

Darei leaned against a console. "This should be good."

Xade said nothing, but Jerr cornered her.

"Why risk the wrath of ten thousand Leviathans to save my ass?"

"Because Tunva knew you," Tunva said in a quiet voice.

"What?" Jerr looked from her to Xade.

"Tunva was a blade sister with Jerr Manivo's earlier reborn," Tunva said. "Tunva watched him die on Boschalan. Tunva held his bleeding body until the soldiers took him. Saw him again on a mission in the Faqar Belt. That Jerr Manivo did not know Tunva."

"I've never been to Boschalan," Jerr said.

"Tunva never lies." She stood straight.

Jerr sighed. "There are thousands of my reborn out there. Just soldiers trying to do their jobs. Not his fault he didn't know you."

Tunva scowled. "My Jerr was killed by troops with his face. There is much fault with your 'just soldiers', Jerr Manivo."

"What do you mean?" Jerr glared at them.

"Exiguous." Xade walked around a realizer console. As if she were placing it between them. Seeking fortification, protection.

"Bullshit," Darei said. "Tell us."

Jerr hopped over the console and blocked Xade's path. "No more secrets."

Xade stared into his eyes, then activated a row of realizers.

Each showed his face. Some were younger or older. One had a scarred cheek. Another wore an eyepatch. The realizers underscored each portrait with a different name. Some had families; most did not. A few were of higher rank. Every one of them had his teal eyes, his jawline, the same swarthy complexion and close-cropped, black hair.

"Shit, doesn't that freak you out?" Darei asked.

"It's what I signed up for," Jerr muttered.

He was a template they'd used again and again. Always a soldier, always placed in the toughest, most war-torn regions. He wondered how current the data was. How many still lived. Could he and these others even be called men? The very fundamentals of human existence were denied them: childhood, parents, domestic life. Even death, the one guarantee every living thing could never be forbidden.

Though he could think, feel, hate, even love—he'd never truly lived.

"Why show me this?" Jerr asked. "I know what I am. What I, and all my reborn, serve and protect. Because of us the Dominion has peace."

"Criminous," Xade murmured.

"What?" Jerr gave her a harsh glance.

"They are the Dominion's best killers," Tunva said.

"No," Jerr said. "We are its best soldiers."

"They are the same," Tunva said with force.

Jerr scowled. "You don't know a damn—"

"Tunva knows what her blade brother was like, fighting for Repta homes. He saved Tunva's life. Tunva remembers the next one did not know her." Tunva's tough façade dropped to one of shy hurt.

Anger gave way to curiosity as Jerr lowered his voice. "What was he like?"

"Strong," Tunva said. "Stubborn. But he taught Tunva the best Dominion tactics. He taught Tunva how to be patient. When to strike. How to defeat the empire."

Jerr turned away, but Tunva continued. "He wanted a home, but the Dominion put him in a Leviathan. He almost lived with Tunva … but he died in Tunva's arms instead."

"So you were friends with a traitor," Jerr said. "Where's the honor in that?"

Tunva glared at him.

"Oh shit," Darei murmured.

Tunva gestured for her surviving warriors to clean up the dead, then walked over to Jerr. "Xade, show Jerr Manivo the Massacre of 12 Ewoui A."

After swiping a nodus, Xade summoned an antiquated video on the nearest realizer. Soldiers in Build 2.0 Starjumpers attacked an octagonal fortress, reminiscent of old colony outposts. The soldiers blasted through the walls. Incinerated escaping forms.

Each soldier looked like Jerr. He regarded their efficiency with appreciation.

The hostiles were Class III Repta. Men, women. Children.

Jerr waited for the Repta to fight back, to ambush the imperial troops, but the only visible resistance was upraised hands against withering piercer fire.

A cold ball formed in his gut. A deepening frown hurt his face.

"What was their crime?" Jerr asked, avoiding eye contact.

"Electing native governors," Tunva said. "Not Dominion ones."

"Bullshit. I've fought Repta pirates who'd peel your face off for a few—"

Tunva gripped Jerr's arm. "A few what, Jerr Manivo? Seconds of freedom?"

"Hey, you saw that video," Darei said. "They killed kids."

"I've never been ordered to do any such thing." Jerr's voice shook with fury.

Xade loaded more feeds. More massacres. Repta, Idreuns, others. All perpetrated by men and women in Dominion armor. Many of them were Jerr's reborn.

Jerr stood on shaky legs. "I told you. I'm not supporting any revolution or Veja Qor, whatever they call themselves."

"Me either, but you can't pretend you didn't see that," Darei said.

"Hell, am I on trial here?" Jerr asked. "What's your stake in this?"

"I've got my reasons, Mister Mighty Reborn."

"I'm waiting." Jerr's face grew hot.

Darei looked at his feet. "It's personal. Just lay off it."

Jerr threw his hands up. "Oh, come the fuck on—"

"You don't see me doing that crazy shit," Darei said.

"They're not me," Jerr said.

"They steal Jerr Manivo's face, steal Jerr Manivo's honor, and all Jerr can say is that they are not him?" Tunva's scaly face scrunched with disgust. "They could be."

"I didn't kill those people!" he yelled. "What do you want me to do about it?"

"Listen to the Weavers so that we can end it," Tunva said.

"We warned them."

Jerr stumbled into a realizer. One where his reborn butchered protesting miners.

"We begged them."

"I didn't kill them," Jerr whispered. "I … I couldn't …"

"They took it from us, with blue fire and death."

The realizers continued playing. Quashed revolts. Forced conscriptions.

Population control.

His reborn weren't protecting anything but Dominion power.

"Shut them off," Jerr said.

Xade swiped. Looked at him with a sympathetic defiance.

There was no denying the evidence. How the Dominion used him. The countless victims out there, fearing his face. Did those other reborn feel any remorse? Did they tell their families what they'd done? He himself couldn't recall much past his twenty-fourth rebirth. Any number of his previous selves might have existed as pure murderers.

"Murderer…"

A soft hand lay on his shoulder. The simple empathy of physical contact made him close his eyes, sigh deeply.

"Reveal us. Avenge us."

Everything Jerr thought he stood for, all he believed he had died again and again to safeguard—was a lie. He'd been right, telling Garrand he was the monster.

He opened his eyes to Xade standing beside him.

"Gracious." She squeezed his shoulder.

They shared a brief smile, then Jerr spoke.

"I swore an oath to protect the Dominion and all its citizens. I intend to keep it. If that means stopping these atrocities—stopping my other rebirths—then let's do it."

The sound of running water woke Jerr. He yawned and sat up on the bunk. He was naked. Brows lowered in confusion, he looked around the room. Everything was blurry, colors bleeding into one another. He tried to stand as the visions returned.

"Tunva enjoyed that. Very much." She grins, eyes full of emotion. Jerr embraces her as Dominion troops flee Boschalan. Even as he bleeds to death.

Jerr started to speak, but the edges of Tunva's body blurred into something else.

Two Leviathans appear in the sky above, blotting out the planet's moons. A metropolis surrounds the causeway Jerr stands on, where inverted pyramids dominate the cityscape. Explosions and debris pepper the sky. Across the causeway, hundreds of dead or dying soldiers lay in his wake.

He's killed them.

"No," he breathed. As a soldier of the Dominion, he was trained not to—

"You cannot be a Weaver. You will try, but the lines are tangled. You are only good for cutting them, like the rest of your kind."

"No!" His skin blazed like a furnace.

The water is still running. Xade stares down at him.

"How long…?"

She holds up two fingers.

"Two hours?" he asks.

She shakes her head.

"What the hell?" He rolled off the bunk and hit the floor. Xade stood over the sink, shutting off the water. Dirty towelettes filled the bin where she'd washed him.

Xade wheeled around and rushed to his side. She touched his neck, then his forehead. Her palm nodus appeared, showing he'd been running a fever. Balyra's torture had taken a toll, but he'd not needed so much rest since the last time he was shot.

Fully awake, Jerr's trained eyes absorbed his surroundings. The small quarters belonged to one of the bridge crew, complete with variable gravity exerciser, realizer, kitchenette, and toilet. Pictures of a crewwoman with a morga husband annoyed him. They looked too happy, too perfect. He was supposed to be above such petty jealousies.

"How long…" He pinched the bridge of his nose and breathed deep. Knowing, even fearing, how she would answer. "How long have I been asleep?"

She held up two fingers.

"Two hours?" he asked.

She shook her head.

The vision had ended there. Jerr hesitated. Xade indicated her nodus, displaying irregular brain activity, an increased pulse.

"Two…two days?" His mouth was parched. A drink would be great.

Her nodus confirmed it, charting his nocturnal timetable. Highly active REM periods. Fevers. Insulin spikes that had to be countered with intravenous feeding.

He groaned and closed his eyes. "Shit."

Xade returned to the sink and brought a small basin and sponge. It was so old fashioned, he gawked at her. Sitting on the bunk's edge, she sponged his forehead and neck. Though the cool water assuaged Jerr's burning skin, he gently took her wrist.

"It's okay, I can do it."

She shook her head and continued sponging.

"Xade, this is what servants did for despots, in our—in humanity's past."

Xade dabbed his cheeks. Rivulets coursed through his stubble.

The way she touched him, her serene expression, the slight upward curve of her lips…she liked it. Helping him. Feeling him.

The nodus revealed his rising heartbeat, the glorious endorphin release each moist, soothing swipe on his flesh brought. Being naked around her now was unsettling.

"Listen, I…"

She gently mashed the sponge against his collarbone. Water slid down his chest.

Jerr stopped her. "You're not my slave, just because you're a—"

Xade stopped and stared. Ready for, perhaps daring, him to finish the sentence.

"I…never mind."

"Ridiculous," she murmured.

"You don't understand. It's a human thing." He tried taking the sponge from her, but Xade squeezed all water from it with vengeful fingers.

"Hey—"

"Ridiculous!" She flung sponge and basin at him. Water doused him and soaked the bunk as she stormed to the door.

"Damn it, will you listen!" Jerr leapt off the bunk, but, still weak, he hit the floor.

Xade knelt and pulled him to his knees. Her eyes were furious sapphires.

"You don't have to keep doing things for me," he said. "In fact, you shouldn't."

She arched an eyebrow.

Jerr sighed. "You've been the Dominion's willing slave for so long. Like me. I don't want you serving me like that. I don't want you lowering yourself, caring for a man who's only worth is measured in the enemies he can kill before his next rebirth."

She shook her head vehemently.

"Please," he said.

"Odious," she muttered.

"The only thing I can give back is—"

She touched his mouth and shook her head.

Again, he wanted to know how long she'd been his caretaker. How long she'd known him. He'd never heard of a Theux showing affection.

But he couldn't return it. He still yearned to know the wife and son he'd had, still wanted to know why they'd been taken from him. If they yet lived. Besides, she was forty millenniums old. He wasn't even thirty in his current body.

Xade finally pulled him up, then changed his bunk sheets and helped him dress. When he lay back down, she sat beside him. He realized she waited for him to speak.

"I had strange visions this time," Jerr said. "But the voices still come and go."

She cocked her head, intent on his every word. He described all he'd envisioned.

"Invidious," she said.

"What? I guess. The voices tell me I can't be a Weaver. What are they, anyway?"

Xade's nodus materialized, showing their destination: the Lagoon Cluster. Seventy-eight thousand stars in a formation nineteen light years across. Among the dying red giants was Stavia X. The epicenter of Dominion authority in that sector.

"That's the place I saw. But where are the Weavers?"

She hesitated, uncertainty in her eyes, then she finally shrugged.

"What if we go somewhere else? What if that isn't the future?"

"Calamitous?"

Jerr frowned. "Can these Weavers really help us? Help me?"

Xade looked away.

He sensed there was more she wanted to tell, but Theux had never perfected speech. For minds accustomed to imparting information at the speed of thought, then to stumble over enunciating every word, it must be irritating. That she didn't simply write it down, or display it on her nodus, hinted she wished to overcome her handicap. It might explain why her emotional expressions and reactions were so genuine—it was all she had to communicate, other than simple one word sentences. He respected that now.

"Why are you trying to help me?" he whispered.

Her fingers brushed his cheek. The cabin blurred around them.

"Xade?" He cradles her close as a piercer round melts the decking near his right boot. "Xade, we're going to make it. They're here. I saw them ..."

She touches his face.

They both blinked and stared at one another. Her nodus flared with activity.

"What's wrong?"

Trembling, Xade withdrew her hand and stood.

"Wait, I'm not trying—"

The door slid shut behind her.

After pacing a while, Jerr found a bottle of nutrient water in the kitchenette. Staring into space, he broke the seal. Tried pretending it was Ghaskan gin, or cloud beer.

Tried pretending it didn't matter if Xade cared about him.

He raised the water to his lips, then flung it against the wall.

❧ ❧ ❧

Balyra waited as *Lux Aeterna* entered the bowels of *Prophetess*, Vestal House's only Leviathan-class starship. Though the craft had a different berth configuration, the gravity engine remained the same, adding at least a hundred miles to the vessel's overall length. A massive, empty cylinder where invisible gods dwelled and moved reality.

That was the tale the Matriarch told all new Sisters. It was no different than the lie that chastity could be maintained after their bodies were broken by the thralls. That purity could be achieved only after they had been violated in ways no human should endure.

She wasn't human now, having suffered more than the gods in their banal myths.

That was the way of Vestal House: break it down and build it stronger.

Prophetess lacked armies, gunships, or bombs … but it carried the will of Vestal House across the galaxy. That alone made it a weapon more powerful than any other. Some people still believed in the Eternal Flame, despite the unraveling of miracles and the deconstruction of mythology. Vestals were the mythology now … and Balyra, their metalloid angel, her sword of fire ready to smite any who challenged her.

"We cannot stand on ceremony for long, Confessor." Garrand paced the deck. "*Bhaellator*'s gravitational residue is decaying as we speak."

The stolen Leviathan's commander bore himself as if he gave the orders now. *Prophetess* had rescued his detached berth, but left the rest under the care of trusted Sisters. Vestal House always maintained the appearance of helping imperial citizens.

"You doubt Vestal House's ability to bring Manivo to justice?" she asked.

Garrand's smile was anything but polite. "Of course not. But I remind you—"

Balyra blocked his path. "A Vestal never needs reminding. You are here only because you will assume command of *Bhaellator* once we find them."

"Careful, Confessor." Garrand's smile widened. "We have yet to discover who lowered *Bhaellator*'s bridge defense system during the mutiny. It would be unfortunate if all system access during that time were verified."

She allowed no emotions to show. "Unfortunate for some."

"Then you will surrender Captain Manivo into my custody once we have him."

"It was once a sin, blackmailing a Sister." She circled around him, a bird of prey.

"Sin?" Garrand touched the edges of her ritual winged cuirass. "How can I blackmail one who is already blackened with corruption?" His hand neared her thigh.

Balyra grabbed his hand and snapped the wrist bones.

Garrand cried out. "You bitch—!"

She wrenched his arm out of socket, forcing Garrand to his knees. "Unless you wish to sit in the magnet chair, I suggest you show respect. You were his superior officer. The Dominion rarely differentiates between the guilty and those guilty by association."

Cradling his arm, Garrand left the bridge.

Balyra wasn't shocked by Garrand's ambition, his own corruption, or misogyny. It surprised her that he actually believed he could threaten her with such things.

After *Lux Aeterna* docked within *Prophetess*, Balyra waited at the exit hatch. Vestals hadn't donned spacesuits in millennia; they must appear immune to the constraints of the human body. Wearing a suit admitted that the universe could destroy her, extinguish her Flame. Some myths needn't be dispelled.

Prophetess shook but a moment. Balyra adopted her best smile.

The hatch opened. Acolytes in white chemises waited in a corridor on the other side. Balyra, hair pinned up into a golden coil coiffure, strode past them into the Sanctum, *Prophetess*'s main audience chamber. It measured several miles in diameter.

Capable of accommodating entire starships, the Sanctum was replete with marble colossi sculpted like winged Vestals. These towered hundreds of feet over the deck. Columned causeways were lit by millions of lamps. The distant hull, wreathed in shadow, was covered in backlit Flame iconography the size of skyscrapers.

Since a Leviathan was constructed in space, never landing or breaking atmosphere, and Shroud travel required no thrust, such extravagances were possible.

Garrand and a platoon of reborn marines followed, but female morga in white armor barred their entrance with crossed pikes.

"Your quarters are ready below, commander. Only fellow Sisters may enter the Sanctum." She didn't bother waiting for his reply.

Balyra walked up the steps of a floating dais. Other Vestals waited around the dais's edge, holding incense canisters. They gave off the pleasant aromas of coriander and red bitter weed, two flora from opposite ends of the galaxy. Without the Shroud, it would be impossible to ever unite both plants in such a manner.

As Balyra gazed at the Matriarch atop the dais, she wondered what had been united within her over the centuries. When younger, she would have answered with immortality. Now she knew what a challenge such a gift was. She might answer with security. A fleeting illusion, no matter what the Dominion told its trillions of citizens.

Those two things had united within Balyra: eternal insecurity. It was on the Matriarch's metalloid face, it was in the red gazes of her fellow Sisters.

Balyra bowed her head to the Matriarch. Several Vestals frowned. Bowing to the knee was customary, but three years had passed since Balyra stood in the holy presence. Protocol was no longer necessary. The leader of the Vestals was little more than a statue seated on a column, sheer robes clinging to perfect features. Like other religious, philosophical, and scientific orders originating from the Elder States, Vestal House only existed now because it served Revor. He allowed them to maintain their traditions and structure. The current Matriarch had long been his puppet.

"High Confessor Balyra Peran," the Matriarch said in a deep feminine voice. "Your flame burns ever bright. It has served as inspiration for Vestal House."

Balyra didn't have time for the typical empty pleasantries. "It has also inspired Curator Revor to send me your aid in a delicate matter best not left to mere soldiers."

"We would review the evidence to justify an intervention from Vestal House."

She'd been expecting this. "The missing Leviathan, *Bhaellator*, should be the first case for evidence, since its absence demonstrates a threat to the Dominion."

"And a threat to Vestal House?" the Matriarch asked.

"Whatever harms one, will certainly harm the other," Balyra said.

"Explain."

"Captain Jerr Manivo is an elite soldier, a reborn," Balyra said. "He hears voices and experiences visions when he travels through the Shroud."

The Vestals glanced at one another. The Matriarch grunted with disbelief.

"He foresaw a terrorist attack on an asteroid in the Idreun Periphery," Balyra said. "I interrogated him to discover how he knew it would happen. He never changed his narrative: that he received this information from some entity within the Shroud."

"That is contemptuous," a Sister said. "Prescience is a human legend. It is not possible to predict the future in such a way."

"It is biologically impossible," another Sister said.

Balyra held her frustration in check. This was why she loathed contacting her Sisters: their thought processes were stagnant, incapable of adapting to new threats.

"He has learned other things," Balyra said. "Things no simple grunt could know."

"Yes?" The Matriarch's voice dripped scorn.

"Captain Jerr Manivo has heard from the Weavers."

The Sisters and Matriarch all spoke at once, denying such a thing could happen. Finally, Balyra drew her blade—a razor-sharp ritual sword, forged in the original Vestal House—and struck the dais. Its mini-reactor caused the edge to flame. The strike burned a long mark into the platform. Smoke rose from the indentation.

"You dare damage the Sanctum?" the Matriarch cried. "It has been flawless for—"

"That is how Manivo will grab your attention," Balyra said. "You will ignore him until he is burning Vestal House down around us. No one has ever stolen a Leviathan before. No one has ever traversed the Shroud and claimed to have heard voices from it—and then act upon such information. If he really is communicating with the Weavers, then Manivo threatens everything. Will you wait until Veja Qor finds and uses him?"

"That cannot be allowed to happen," a Sister said.

"Your report details your assumption he has departed for the Elium Rim," the Matriarch said. "The hotbed of anti-Dominion sentiment. Perhaps that isn't coincidence."

Balyra hid her smile. Of course it wasn't a coincidence. While these galactic nursemaids played caretaker behind the safety of Leviathan bulkheads, Balyra still traveled the galaxy. The Flame wasn't meant to remain static; neither would she.

"Jerr Manivo must be captured and studied," Balyra said. "Vestal House could learn much if the source of his precognition can be discerned."

"What does Revor suggest?" one Sister asked.

"It is with his permission that I answered your summons," the Matriarch said.

"Revor wants Manivo eliminated," Balyra said. "I see no reason we cannot examine him, before his execution?"

A Sister grunted. "We risk overstepping our bounds."

Balyra hardened her gaze. "Since when did Vestal House possess boundaries?"

The others murmured and shared glances. Balyra knew she'd struck a nerve.

"We will act on your suggestion, Confessor," the Matriarch said. "Set course for the coordinates provided in the report. Now, I would speak with the Confessor alone."

While the other Sisters departed the Sanctum, Balyra waited on the platform.

"Put away your fire, Sister," the Matriarch said. Her voice was lighter, silkier. Familiar. It made Balyra's anxiety rise. She glanced around, hand still on her sword.

"There is no betrayal in Vestal House," the Matriarch said. "There are so few of us left. The old infighting is gone. Unless you finally intend to take the dais from me?"

Balyra put her blade away. "It belongs to you only in name. Revor controls all."

"Unless we take Jerr Manivo first and use him against the Curator?" The Matriarch studied Balyra for a moment. "This is a dangerous game you play."

"Would you have us be his perpetual slaves? The Flame smolders in the ashes that were Vestal House. Jerr Manivo could end our servitude. Then I will kill him."

"Without Revor and the other Curators, the galaxy would fall into chaos," the Matriarch said. "You think to control the one who would bring that about?"

Balyra didn't hide her cold smile. "Let Jerr and his voices destroy it all. Vestal House will be the one to offer leadership afterward. We will be the galaxy's saviors."

"I forbid it," the Matriarch said.

"We may never get another chance," Balyra said.

"Let Revor have the galaxy. I have you." The Matriarch nodded and smiled. She wasn't supposed to move in the presence of others, since true enlightenment came from an immobile body. A body incapable of indulging temptation.

Balyra had long been her superior's only temptation.

The Matriarch came free of the column and eased down against her.

"Even if they cannot see, they will know," Balyra murmured as the Matriarch undid Balyra's unisuit. Metalloid fingers caressed her breasts. Amazing it could still excite her, even though she knew the flesh was grown, and the nerves, adjustable. It wasn't real blood beneath the skin, warming at another's touch. So much was mere simulation now, but the tragedy was that many still required such stimulus.

Despite all that, Balyra kissed the Matriarch. The secondary reason for summoning *Prophetess* became known, though centuries of training wouldn't allow them to admit it. Not even to themselves.

"Our Sisters only know what we wish them to," the Matriarch said.

"I have only one wish." Balyra tugged the Matriarch's robes off.

They held each other in the near dark, a false eternity shared within the bowels of *Prophetess.* It was a darkness Balyra didn't wish to penetrate or dispel. Even while the Matriarch clasped Balyra's thighs and hungrily tasted what engineers had tried to perfect. She let herself go in those blissful moments, as much to influence her superior, as to enjoy the pleasure itself.

Afterward, Balyra lie still while the Matriarch traced fingers over Balyra's nipples. When they were both mere Sisters, they had shared men and women until it was obvious who they really wanted. The passage of centuries had dimmed their passion, but not the desire for it. Something still existed between them. Something she hoped to use.

Balyra sat up. "Do you ever regret joining Vestal House?"

"Of course not."

"Not even when you consider how much it has changed us?" Balyra asked.

"Stop talking blasphemy." The Matriarch kissed her stomach.

"Blasphemy is the one vice we have left," Balyra said.

"A vice of last resort. You never asked this before. What has happened to you out there? Each interval between us changes you. I am not sure I approve."

Balyra stared at the colossi. Only one had ever seemed like a goddess to her.

"Have you been visiting that statue-filled chamber again? You torture yourself."

"It is only a question." Balyra started to rise.

"The answer to such queries would condemn us." The Matriarch cupped Balyra's face in both hands. "Vestals provide answers for others. We aren't entitled to our own."

"Then what am I entitled to?" Balyra kissed her lips, her neck. "You?"

"Not when you are like this." The Matriarch studied her face. "I need to know: what are you planning? It consumes you, Balyra. I worry."

Balyra drew back. "Enough to give me what I want?"

"You want everything." She sniffed Balyra's hair. "You always have."

Balyra pushed her away—but not too much. Just enough to bait her again.

The Matriarch gaped with hurt. "Is that your answer? Tell me!"

Unleashing her needs, Balyra gave her reply. Straddling her. An hour later, they still lay together beneath the countless lamps. Forgotten goddesses beneath false starlight.

It wasn't love between them. Their coitus was a denial of everything they served, since it had denied them so much for so very long. Now it was mere exploitation: the Matriarch's lust for flesh; Balyra's lust for power. Balyra wished it were different.

She wondered who Jerr loved. If a reborn could even understand the concept.

"Manivo could end all of this if the Weavers tell him everything."

The Matriarch withdrew as if Balyra had suddenly caught fire. "Then you will ensure that he doesn't. Whatever the cost. You will do it."

The intimate moment was destroyed. Balyra stood and slowly dressed.

"You will kill him?" The Matriarch's voice bordered on desperation. "For me?"

"Yes, your holiness." This time, Balyra bowed fully as the Matriarch stood over her. Only in the festering dark could she acknowledge her true mistress. And it wasn't the Matriarch, or any of the colossi watching over them.

It was the fear of losing what the darkness hid from everything outside.

After leaving his quarters, Jerr strolled around the empty bridge deck. *Bhaellator*'s stillness was beyond eerie. A sterile universe unto itself. Even with the bulk of the ship jettisoned, one could still get lost in the remaining labyrinthine corridors. It made him wonder if he was having another dream. He hoped not. The Shroud aggravated his condition, his curse, his gift—whatever it was.

Xade, Darei, and Jerr himself had taken quarters formerly used by the bridge crew, but Tunva and her warriors occupied the security berth, where robos, Starjumper racks, and the ship's few remaining armaments were stored. Tactical, if not subtle. A few dozen Repta had managed to escape with them. They regarded Jerr with cautious respect.

For over an hour he rummaged through kitchenettes and the deck's two mess halls, finding no alcohol. Desperate, he'd even checked the garbage chutes. Nothing.

Making his way around the deck, he spotted sparks flying from an alcove. He reached for a weapon, then realized he was unarmed. Had a few Dominion troops stowed onboard? Maybe they were trying to cut their way into the bridge.

He crept toward the alcove and sprung.

"What the hell are you doing?" Darei held up his torch and raised his goggles.

Jerr straightened. "Looking for stowaways."

"Liar," Darei said. "You won't find anything to drink. Xade's thorough."

"What are you doing?" Jerr was eager to change the subject.

"Fixing your armor. Gahn Industries should pay me to make them a new Starjumper series. This piece of shit might fly after I'm done." Darei gestured at a combat suit on a rack in the alcove, where the technician had set up shop.

"Thanks… for helping back there," Jerr said.

Darei rolled his eyes. "I'm not a hero. What choice did I have? Like you said, the Dominion are probably interrogating everybody that was onboard *Bhaellator*, right?"

"You could've shot me," Jerr said. "That would've earned points with the brass."

"Well, I didn't, so lay off that shit, okay?" Darei lowered his goggles. "I got work to do, so you can have work to do, once we reach the Lagoon Cluster."

Jerr frowned. "I'm hoping we won't have to fight."

"You crawl out of the rebirth vat yesterday?" Darei welded a thigh plate back in place. "The Dominion considers you its property. Mister Mighty Fucking Reborn. You're a walking, gun-toting, hymen-busting investment. They're not letting you go."

"What's your problem?" Jerr pushed the torch down and made Darei face him.

"Scram, let me do my job." Darei didn't make eye contact.

"What did Xade promise you?" Jerr asked.

"That's between me and Miss Blue Theux." Darei reattached a thruster coupling.

"Because you sure as hell didn't do it for me. You hate the reborn. Don't you?" He didn't know how much it would hurt, asking Darei that.

Darei shoved an uplink power source into the armor.

"Are you jealous?" Jerr asked. "Do you think my life is great?"

"Just fuck off."

"I need to know who has my back," Jerr said. "Tell me."

Darei slumped against the wall and rubbed soot off his face. "Listen to your noise. You already get to live forever, now you think you're entitled to my personal shit?"

Jerr kicked the wall and started to walk off.

"My brother…he was the best engineer on our homeworld, in the Con-Union."

Jerr stopped.

"I learned every damn thing from him," Darei said. "Repairing these Gahn suits, hotwiring one of those old Molexi drives to a yacht for a rich Union magistrate—he showed me all kinds of shit. Until they took him."

Jerr didn't like where the conversation was going, but he had to know. "They?"

"The Dominion." Darei snapped a few armor fragments into place on the suit's torso. "They 'recruited' him, just like they did anyone with the best skills on my planet. Made him sign the rebirth contract. I never thought I'd see him again."

Jerr held a servo in place while Darei attached its routers. "But you did."

Darei stared off into space while absently putting parts into the armor, perfect each time. "Three years later, I was on my first merchant run, in the Settled Zone. A Con-Union shit like me, seeing those world metropolises for the first time. I saw him, all right. I saw my brother, commanding a maintenance crew. They were repairing a Leviathan's lower deck reactor. Now that's high-level genius, right there. I went right up to him."

Handing him a tool, Jerr said nothing.

Darei glared into nothingness. "I talked to him, tried hugging him…but my brother didn't know me. He had a new name. Fuck, he was even a little younger than me by then. That's when I knew. That's when I started hating you reborn assholes."

"Xade told you she'd take you to him. Didn't she?"

"You make it sound like a bad idea." Darei flung the tool away.

"Trust me," Jerr said. "He's not your brother anymore. I know."

"Don't act like you're the same," Darei said. "He builds shit. You destroy it."

"You think I like coming back from the dead, leaving people behind—"

"I don't give a shit," Darei said.

"You think I asked for this?" Jerr shouted.

"Fuck you, don't even try to understand it!" Darei yelled.

Jerr slammed Darei against the suit and held him by the throat. "I had a wife, a son! I still feel things for them, things I shouldn't because I don't fucking know who they are. At least you knew your brother once. At least you have memories of that. I don't have a goddamn thing. Nothing. It's not you, seeing your face replicated on a thousand grunts. It's not you, trained to be a killer, a killer that's so good, they bring me back again and again. You want to try to understand that? Can you?" Jerr released him. Darei hit the floor, his tools rolling across the deck.

"Looks like you are a killer, then." Darei slowly stood. "Good for you."

Jerr looked at his hands, at what he was about to do to Darei, then stormed off.

CHAPTER 10

Few of us remained after the Armada destroyed our home-worlds. We, who could adapt to any biosphere, any disaster, were the conquered. All the primitive intuitions had been bred out of our species, so that we lacked the will to fight such a young, aggressive race. The human propensity to destroy, consolidate—then bemoan that destruction, chafe against that consolidation—confused us. So we adapted once again, assuming their genders, their faces. Their emotions. Only then were we accorded respect. Only then, did the Theux generate awe. We were as bound to our conquerors as they to us.

Theux Codex, 78 Vaaqa D (reconstructed), unabridged excerpt

Jerr was busy raiding Garrand's quarters. Again.

The last day of the journey—if days still existed out there—he'd avoided everyone onboard. First he'd angered Xade, then Darei. If he angered Tunva, one of them would probably end up dead. So in the best interest of all, he became a recluse.

And he was terrible at it.

He searched the unused cabins a fourth time for the smallest drop of alcohol. Ran laps round the tram dock, did pullups on its precipice. Good motivation for not letting go. Used Rezal to calculate how much energy *Bhaellator* had saved since ejecting its berths. Tried a game of realizer chess, but he was always checkmated within ten moves.

Nothing could make him forget those video feeds. Those screaming faces.

Though trained to survive alone, or operate without superiors, Jerr was still miserable. He'd never wanted to talk to others more in his life. Well, this life at least.

He thought about calling for Xade, then went back to rifling through Garrand's last cabinet. The commander was a collector of sorts, with eighteen pistols engraved with his name and rank, and a motley assortment of blades bearing evidence of use. Jerr sheathed two of these into his belt and girded two pistols. One was a typical diffusion Devastator model, but with no energy dampener. Each shot would likely disintegrate an opponent. The other sidearm was an old but deadly Stinger from the mining uprisings in the Faqar Belt. The Matrisse diamond-tipped rounds could penetrate any armor, leaving a cleaner wound than the sharpest scalpel.

There were a few wrist blasters, but he didn't want to overdo it. The Shroud had shown that he would go to the Lagoon Cluster. Not what he would encounter there.

"Egregious."

He didn't turn as Xade entered. "Well, I've no idea what we're getting into."

Xade stood beside him, saying nothing.

"Do you?" He tried sounding gentle, but his grip tightened on the cabinet door.

She shut the cabinet. "Crankous."

"Wouldn't you be, knowing your face was the last thing those people saw?"

Xade touched his arm. He started to shrug her off until he spied her expression. There was no judgement, no anger. Only the deepest concern for him.

"You believe in my visions enough to risk everything. What is it you and Tunva hope these Weavers will do?"

A reverent look came over her face. "Miraculous."

"Right. But the only thing I'm good for is fighting."

Her stare took scolding to new levels.

"I'm serious. Do you have any idea what this shit's doing to me?"

"Nutritious." Xade's mocking tone could've cut granite. Her nodus showed his caloric intake over the last two days. He hadn't been eating much. Cortisol levels had spiked. Pulse was up. Cold sweats drenched his sleep.

"Proud of your little detox plan?" He spread his arms and gave a callous laugh. "Now I'm a prick instead of an alcoholic."

"Onerous." Her face scrunched in hurt.

"Hey, I didn't mean … c'mon, don't look at me that way."

She left the room before he'd even finished the sentence.

"Goddamn all this shit." He flung open the cabinet, then kicked it shut.

He felt more at home with these instruments of death, while Xade showed more affection than a member of his own species. But she was just a biomechanical creature.

Not a real woman.

He started to kick the cabinet again, then looked down at himself.

And he was supposed to be a man? Bracing his hands against the wall, he took deep breaths. He felt smaller than before, despite his newly acquired weapons.

"Shit." He left the room in a huff.

Outside Garrand's quarters, Jerr paused. Distant music reverberated down the corridor. With nothing else to do, and no one else to piss off, he strolled around Bridge Deck until he discovered the music's source in an unused crew cabin.

While tranquil Eulko wind melodies played, Tunva, stripped to halter top and loin cloth, performed combat katas in flowing, ceaseless movements. Her lithe, scaly body dodged, struck, and leapt across the room. Though she seemed oblivious to his presence, her voice betrayed that notion.

"Tunva's Jerr would knock."

Jerr rapped the doorframe with sarcastic slowness. "Happy now?"

She stopped in mid-kata. "Happiness eludes Jerr Manivo."

"Don't remind me." He looked her up and down. "Never figured you for music like that. Repta tunes are usually all percussion. The others train to it all the time."

"Tunva likes the 'tunes' of others. Tunva's collection was large before her assignment to *Bhaellator*." She twirled on one leg and lashed out with her other.

"Those are some pretty fancy moves. Onashi blade school?"

"The Onashi learned it from Tunva's people." She picked up a water bottle and misted herself. "Tunva taught them."

Jerr leered. "Right. Repta don't live that long…" His smirk vanished.

Tunva walked right up to him. "Does Jerr think differently of Tunva now?"

"No. Hell, of course not. I didn't know you're a reborn, too, that's all."

She offered him a water bottle. "Tunva served the Dominion for many lifetimes—until Veja Qor showed Tunva what she was used for. Ever since, Tunva has searched for a way to defeat the Dominion."

"What if these Weavers can't help us?" He sipped the water, wishing it were beer.

"They are speaking to you, Jerr Manivo." Tunva sat cross-legged on the floor. "If anyone knows how to defeat the Dominion, it is those who fought against them."

"Knowing and doing are two different things."

"Jerr must sit." She gestured at the floor before her.

He humored her, though he wasn't sure if it was because he needed reprieve from angst-ridden boredom, or because Tunva had never spoken so much to him.

"Xade knows more of the Weavers than Tunva," she said. "But even she does not know how the Weavers were defeated. That is why Jerr must speak for the Shroud."

"I'll try, but not for Veja Qor. I'm doing this for those who can't defend themselves. Not a bunch of terrorists."

Tunva's eyes went to slits. "Jerr thinks Veja Qor are bandits, or criminals? Veja Qor have always helped the defenseless. Xade trusts them. Jerr trusts Xade?"

Jerr had to look away. "It's not about trust."

The music continued. Soft voices swelling with the winds of a planet now long gone. Jerr had never paid it much mind before. What else had he ignored all this time?

"Is it because Xade is not a human, like Jerr?" Tunva asked softly.

He faced her. "I still have a family. Somewhere."

Tunva shook her head. "No, Jerr Manivo. Tunva is sorry, but no."

"Didn't you ever lose someone after a rebirth?" He started to rise.

"Tunva has lost much. So very much, Jerr Manivo. Friends, mates. Children."

"Then you know how much this still hurts."

"Xade knows, too. Xade has lost more than either of us."

"How? Why?" Jerr leaned forward, interested.

"That is not Tunva's story to tell." She straightened. "Now, will Jerr meditate with Tunva? The Eulko sang beautiful songs. They calm Tunva's mind, Tunva's anger."

Jerr studied the water bottle in his hand, then sat straight. "I'd be honored."

Hours later, *Bhaellator* gave a slight shudder. They'd left the Shroud.

Jerr rolled off his bunk and took his time walking the corridors. No one would be thrilled to see him. Considering the way he's been acting, he couldn't blame them. He didn't need Rezal to calculate the probability he'd treated his family the same way.

Maybe they were glad to be rid of him.

En route to the bridge, Darei passed him, wearing a cleaner jumpsuit and a new tool belt. "How's the fan club coming along?"

Jerr sighed and moved on.

The Repta had finally left the armory. Jerr did a quick count. Thirty-nine of them, armed and eager to follow Tunva into bloody glory. They hissed and tracked Jerr with their slit iris gazes. Tunva, her long black braids tied back, nodded with approval.

On the bridge proper, Xade ignored him, swiping commands into several nodi. The realizers detailed dozens of systems a few light years away, then displayed the one they were in: Stavia, an orange star slowly burning its way to a red giant.

Jerr approached Xade, but she conveniently walked to another nodus. He waited, neared her again. Xade flitted past him and activated *Bhaellator*'s orbital autopilot.

"Hey." He wondered if he sounded just as pathetic to her.

More nodi opened and Xade entered passcodes so the Stavian authorities would think everything was normal aboard the ship.

Jerr finally blocked her. "Will you listen?"

Xade's gaze scolded him harsher than usual. "Pertinacious?"

"What?"

She tried shoving him aside, but he caught her hand.

"Xade, c'mon."

She started to withdraw her hand, but he gently held on. "I can't go on like this. You've saved my life, and all I've done is resent you for it."

They stood there, him holding her wrist, her not making eye contact.

"You are such a strong person. You're good to me. Better than I deserve. I've never met a woman who—"

He hesitated, realizing how he'd phrased it. Xade looked up at him, mouth parted in surprise. "I mean … I'm sorry."

Her stuttering intake of breath, though she didn't require air, was so real, so natural, that he felt guilty for having the same sense, but in flesh and blood. It wasn't pretending, or repeating something programmed into her. She was all the more real because of it. Her eyes exploded with the need to express it.

The realizers glowed around them, displaying *Bhaellator*'s position, temperature, engine usage … but he had eyes only for the subtle changes in her face. The crinkles at the corners of her eyes, the slight tremor in her lower lip. The widening of her iris, like a camera lens eager to see everything he had to show her.

Jerr touched her face. Glided his thumb lightly over her cheekbone. Felt her tremble. Brushed her earlobe with his fingertips.

She closed her eyes and shivered.

"I…" He drew closer to her when Darei walked in.

"Hey… yeah. Anyway. I've got our suits ready. Tunva's waiting at the airlock on the dispersal deck." Darei glanced from him to Xade and walked out.

She withdrew and returned to swiping nodi. Keeping her back to him.

Lips tight, he wanted to say something, but silence was a barrier between them again, rather than the private realm it'd been moments before. Jerr left and caught up with Darei, who walked stiffer at his approach. Jerr said nothing.

As they neared the lift to the lower deck, Darei paused. "That was real dumb back there, but you lucked out. Miss Blue Theux was putty in your hands."

Jerr held back a vicious retort. "What do you mean?"

Darei entered the lift. "Your moves are shittastic, but… you pay attention to her. You seem to care what she thinks, how she feels. You touch her. That's more than most humans ever do for a Theux. Usually we just ask them to compute this, operate that."

Jerr entered the lift beside him. It took them down. Before the door opened, he cleared his throat. "I just want to be nicer to her."

"Whatever. I've had thirty-four husbands, I know what I'm talking about. But you'd better not be an asshole to her." Darei exited the lift and made for the airlock.

"Or what?" Jerr asked.

"Remember who fixes your pretty 4.3 Starjumper, that's what."

They shared a quick smile.

"You really are—"

"Watch it," Darei said.

"—a nice guy," Jerr said.

"Sure." Darei entered the bridge's smaller dispersal deck and readied the Starjumper he'd been working on. Tunva waited nearby, staring at Jerr.

"So what are we heading into out there?" Jerr tapped the Starjumper's torso.

"Jerr Manivo did not see it in his visions?" Tunva's tone bordered on playfulness.

"Apparently not."

"Tunva will be your prisoner so the Dominion will let us land. Then we find your reborn and see if they have heard from the Weavers as well."

"Huh?" Jerr shook his head. "That first part is fine, but the second?"

"You look more surprised than a naked Squidran in an aquarium," Darei said. "You worried? Or you think we'll have to fight one of your twins down there?"

A chill crept up Jerr's back. He rushed arming the suit. A Hub World. Dominion troops and ships would be everywhere. He'd heard no voices or saw any visions for the past twenty hours. He hoped they'd return, offering a clue as to what he was supposed to do now. Then again, he was ascribing purpose to a phenomena he didn't understand. Superstition wasn't in his profile.

Xade arrived and checked Jerr's suit. She glanced at him several times, but he could only nod. Damn, he wanted her to smile. Wanted to see that look on her face again.

She gave a short, shy nod back.

Darei chuckled. "You have a way with people, Mister Mighty Reborn."

"If you only knew." Jerr tested his leg thrusters and debugged the suit's uplink with *Bhaellator*'s network. Double-checked his ammo. Adjusted the HUD configuration.

"Jerr is afraid," Tunva said.

Darei and Xade stopped, watching him for a reaction.

She was right. Jerr had never felt more anxiety before a mission, nor ever fidgeted so much in his Starjumper. It wasn't combat, or even death he feared. He'd no idea how he would react, seeing the actual vats where his reborn were grown.

Instead of replying with machismo, Jerr met her eyes. "Wouldn't you be?"

Tunva's lips parted in a slight grin. "No."

Jerr snorted, started to speak, then laughed.

Tunva grinned wider and patted his armored hand. "Sometimes, you really are like the Jerr Manivo that Tunva once knew. He never lied to Tunva, either."

"That's the only promise I can make," Jerr said.

"I feel better already." Darei disengaged the suit's energy cable from the rack.

"We ready to do this?" Jerr asked.

Xade summoned her palm nodus, then expanded it to a large transparent globe above them. It showed Dominion gunships already approaching *Bhaellator*, the landing platform their shuttle would be escorted to, and the prisoner processing center beneath it.

Right beside a rebirthing facility.

"So that's the place." He couldn't look at the rest of them.

Xade nodded, her nodus showing a 100% probability.

"Now we will see if all Jerr Manivos are the same," Tunva said.

"And if we aren't?" He straightened.

"Serendipitous," Xade said.

"Huh?" Jerr asked.

"Xade means Jerr would be extra special," Tunva said.

"Great, I can already feel his ego growing," Darei said.

"Vacuous." Xade gave Darei a sharp look.

"Have you met this guy?" Darei jerked a thumb at Jerr.

Jerr's glower made Darei and Tunva both snicker.

"Seriously, won't we be suspected?" Darei asked. "A Leviathan arrives, missing its main berths, with one armored grunt bringing in a half-naked Repta for detainment?"

"Auspicious." The confidence in Xade's voice was unshakable.

"Let's hope so." Jerr led the way aboard the shuttle, clanking every step.

As they departed *Bhaellator*, he took in the view. Stavia X was a green and tan world, with jagged blue shapes denoting lakes, rivers, and seas. Even from this distance he spotted solid blocks of light on the surface, connected by uncountable lines of brilliant luminance. Like other Hub Worlds, Stavia X was over-industrialized, overpopulated, and overdeveloped until ruins and old streets formed part of the crust. Hundreds of stations orbited it. Two entire fleets massed neared Stavia IX, a small blue world with bright yellow rings. Even from here, he saw mining barrows traveling the rings, harvesting minerals and ice. Solar sails powered the freighters traveling from planet to planet.

Once, he'd smiled upon witnessing the Dominion's power: a human civilization taking advantage of every resource. It had made his battles worth it, every death maintaining the empire's gargantuan apparatus that was but one of millions in the galaxy.

But he'd grown among the generations for whom interstellar travel was a mere inconvenience. Gone was the drama, the romance, the primal purity of the endeavor. Wonder was viewed as a naïve reaction to what the Dominion considered humanity's entitlement. In other words, all that could be seen, and would ever be seen, with human eyes. Those who disagreed were extinct, or resembled Xade's race, sacrificing their own identity in exchange for the right to exist.

"It unravels. Before you, behind you. It unravels and you cannot stop it."

Jerr turned off his radio in case he actually answered the voice this time.

Four small fighters darted from Stavia's atmosphere to intercept them, but Xade swiped a default preset of protocols on the shuttle's console. Seconds later, the fighters escorted them to Stavia's surface—like Xade had planned.

Reentry shook their small vessel. No one spoke as the autopilot flew them to a military platform. The fighters hovered in place until the shuttle touched down.

A squad of MPs in full armor walked across the platform.

"What did you tell them?" Jerr asked.

"Bounteous," Xade said.

"Shit," Jerr muttered.

Darei placed magnet cuffs on Tunva. Jerr waited behind her, diffusion blaster charged. Xade adopted an even stiffer posture, nodus already hovering above her palm.

The shuttle's hatch slid open and they walked out onto the platform. They all coughed at the atmosphere's terrible taste, but it was breathable. Jerr's HUD displayed Stavia's pleasant temperature, its low surface gravity, atmospheric pressure, and other things he really didn't care about. He focused on the MPs instead. Searching for a familiar visage through their faceplates.

"Which of you is Commander Garrand?" a loud MP asked over the radio.

"Commander Garrand remained in orbit on *Bhaellator*," Jerr said. "First Officer Xade will oversee this transfer, and … and …"

The MPs shared confused looks.

Tunva glanced at him. Darei shifted on his feet. Xade kept her eyes on the MPs.

"And?" the first MP asked. "The message said this Repta was inciting a revolt in the neighboring sector. Was it so bad you had to jettison your Leviathan's berths?"

Jerr forgot the lie they'd prepared and realized he'd seen this before. *Four fighters. A ringed planet. Inverted pyramid-styled buildings.*

"Hey, the Shroud suck your brains out?" The lead MP stepped forward. "You going to answer me, Captain?"

"I …" Jerr could only stare at the MPs. If those voices in the Shroud told him the future, was he creating that very future by his actions?

"Well?" the MP asked.

The man's voice trails off into Jerr's consciousness as he floats in the void. Adrift, his thoughts lensing across the cosmos. Fleets explode in his wake. Worlds are emptied of life, replaced by the empire's domineering architecture. Silvery, swirling creatures appear from nothingness. They touch Jerr. The next instant, he appears elsewhere: a dark well where stars are born, enlarge, then explode. Where worlds go from molten spheres to inhabited cityscapes to cratered desolation. Over and over again, as if Jerr sees history begin and end, but unable to experience it. An exile from physical reality.

"Damn it, you'll speak when spoken to!"

Jerr shook his head and shoved his armored finger into the MP's face. "You'll address me by the proper rank … soldier. Fetch us some masks and stow the attitude."

The MP blinked, then gave a crisp salute. "Yes, sir."

While the MPs obeyed, Jerr tried to reassure his friends of his sanity with a smile. None of them returned it. And no wonder. He'd almost blown the mission.

Damn, he really wanted a drink.

CHAPTER 11

The Dominion, despite its fleet of Leviathans, cannot be everywhere at once. Their propaganda has inculcated this belief in citizens' minds, but even a million Leviathans cannot attend every galactic dispute. This is where fear and faith come in: the tried and true combination that has kept humanity in line for eons. For no matter how advanced our science, how utopian our society, there must be an invisible constant keeping order. That is Vestal House's prime task—one we pursue with utmost vigilance.

Psychopomp Errata, Sector 33, Confessor
Balyra Peran, Vestal House

Stavia's air was a combination of terraphylled crud with a low hydrogen content, making it breathable, but the taste was so awful, everybody wore masks. Of course, the MPs gave them cheap ones, which fit nobody's face. It squeezed their noses and made the air taste like burnt plastic that'd been urinated on.

It was better than using his suit's oxygen. With his instincts on edge, in a situation that could turn hostile at any moment, Jerr didn't want to waste any resources.

These discomforts didn't ruin Stavia's unique architecture and landforms. Artificial hills and valleys, landscaped over centuries into perfect terraces. Old starships lay sunken off the shores, acting as reefs housing marine life. Buildings rose thousands of feet into the atmosphere, then spread out like a wide-brimmed mushroom or a tree with a massive canopy of leaves. Trams and zip paths crossed in countless intersections of gold-tinted light, as vehicles were propelled along by electromagnetic power. The effect was a silent metropolis full of activity, with citizens walking promenades above the clouds, or dining in cafés held up entirely by drones. Arcologies towered over all else, their reverse-pyramid shapes defying gravity.

"Voluminous," Xade said, the only one not needing a mask.

"Nothing like a Hub World." Darei smiled. "I once had two husbands and three other lovers on one."

"Why so many?" Jerr asked, the mask pinching his nose.

"It's lonely as hell out there in case you haven't noticed," Darei said. "Besides, they come to me." He smirked and shrugged.

Tunva looked like she wanted to speak, but Jerr gave her a warning glance. As a prisoner, the MPs would beat her if she spoke.

They rode a tram down from the landing platform, flanked by MPs. The protocols Xade had activated on *Bhaellator* confirmed their identities. Upon learning he was a reborn, the MPs regarded Jerr with grudging respect.

During transit, the city became a magnificent blur around them. A halo of life, industry, and expression humanity sought to crown each colonized planet with. A stamp of ownership. Since light traveled forever through the cosmos, Stavia's artificial glow communicated that humanity had not only mastered that planet, but it was their property, forever. Jerr imagined another species studying these lights through a telescope a million years later, wondering who created that faraway, diffuse gleam imitating a star.

"They ordered all reborn to be taken into custody, didn't they?" Jerr asks.

"How did—?"

"Including you."

The vision was but a blip on his thoughts, but Jerr steadied himself on the tram.

The vehicle stopped at a magistrate's office on a lower level, where the MPs hurried them into the large, castle-like structure. Its formidable stonework looked like it dated from the Elder States era. The Dominion insignia, a sunburst over a raised hand, hung backlit above them. Beneath it, 'eighty-three' stood in large, carved letters.

"Avenge us."

Jerr tried ignoring the voice, since he needed to stay alert, but it continued.

"They unraveled space-time, killing us, trapping us. Stealing our ships, our knowledge, our history. Our voice remains the last surviving thread of the Weavers."

The air was much fresher inside and they removed their masks. The walls were hung with archaic banners from worlds long conquered and forgotten. The MPs started to take positions around Tunva, but Jerr waved them off.

"I've got this. Dismissed."

The MPs saluted and left.

An officer walked in, attired in a dark gray uniform. One of Jerr's reborn.

The man was older, with a mechanical right hand. He wore a permanent frown, with crows' feet around the eyes, and a mouth so tight it hadn't laughed in years.

"I am Lieutenant Wanrys." Though the accent was different, Wanrys had Jerr's voice: the same timbre and enunciation. "Stavia Reserves, 32nd Battalion."

"Captain Jerr Manivo," Jerr said. There wasn't any point in lying. "Company K, Consular Brigade. Stationed on *Bhaellator*."

They studied each other with the same stubborn resolve. The same thought process, trying to outmaneuver an opponent.

"She give you any trouble, sir?" Wanrys flicked disdainful eyes to Tunva.

"Not as much as she's going to receive," Jerr said.

"Those damned Veja Qor have been active in the surrounding systems," Wanrys said. "I hope you apprehended one of the ringleaders, sir."

"That's what we're going to find out." Jerr nudged Darei. "I brought our best interrogator and a Theux to analyze the data."

Wanrys's lip curled as he studied Darei and his tool pouches. "Detainment is just two levels below us, sir. I will show you—"

"We'll find it, lieutenant. Thanks." Jerr was thankful he outranked the man, or else their plan could be threatened. Wanrys saluted and walked into a nearby office. After a few moments, they took the lift down to Detainment.

"That guy has a bigger stick up his ass than you do." Darei chuckled.

"Stick, hell. More like the whole damn tree." Jerr smiled.

Tunva studied Jerr's rump and frowned. "Tunva has never understood human humor regarding the back of the pelvic area."

"Frivolous." Xade also reviewed Jerr's posterior.

Jerr winked at her. Xade hesitated, then winked back.

The lift stopped on the Detainment level, which ended all their jokes. Jerr nodded to Darei, who sneezed through his hands. The nasal eruption blew circoid dust off his gloves. Jerr waited until his HUD showed the circoids' dispersal.

A panel slid aside on Xade's shoulder exoskeleton. A tiny drone flew out. It whirred, then a full-sized realizer double appeared, one for each of them.

Darei poked at his illusory twin and frowned. "They won't buy this for long."

"Tunva does not need very long." She flexed after Darei removed her cuffs.

"The dust will disrupt any cams or sensors in this area for a few minutes. These realizers might buy us some extra time." Jerr looked at Xade. "Ready?"

Xade nodded, her nodus detailing their next destination: the rebirthing facility. She'd hacked the planetary mainframe, granting them access to every locale in the immediate vicinity. Though he realized her mind worked at blazing speeds, it still hinted at a premeditated scheme she'd planned for him. Years beforehand, even.

They took a different lift down to the facility a few hundred feet below. Jerr kept his uplink open. Coupled with their shuttle, he could summon it to their current location—which, if HUD mapping was correct, would be another platform nearby.

After the elevator stopped, Jerr led them through a transparent corridor to a maintenance access hatch. They couldn't risk running into the scientists inside. According to his mapping, the hatch would take them beneath the growth vats.

His hesitated, knowing the slightest delay might cost their lives. Beyond the door would be his artificial, surrogate womb. Eugenic gods who always resurrected him.

"Come on, let's get that blood sample and rocket the hell out of here," Darei said.

Jerr opened the hatch and entered. It was a wide area, with an open ceiling going up dozens of feet. Pipes and cords created a maze backlit by a few service terminals. The humid air stunk of decay and disinfectant. Sludge covered the floor. Heavy pumping sounds came from above.

"Up there." Darei pointed.

Above them hung tier after tier of growth vats. Each was a transparent yellow, shaped like a crude uterus. The moist containers bulged with interior movement.

"They are grown and almost ready for assignment," Tunva said.

"Think so?" Darei's voice shook. "Smells like their diapers need changing."

Jerr stared at the vats. "Just get what we need."

Xade accessed one of the terminals. Soon, snake-like probes lowered into each vat. Something writhed within. Seeking escape.

"Is Jerr still afraid?" Tunva asked.

"Only of how they'll be used." He'd seen men and women blasted apart, watched people suffocate in the void, incinerated enemies into atoms—but nothing had ever summoned such loathing in him. "Where they'll be deployed. Who they'll kill."

"This is fucking sick," Darei muttered.

"Tunva agrees. The Veja Qor once helped Tunva destroy many Repta reborn. Years afterward, Tunva still had nightmares of dying in those vats."

Darei turned away and wiped his eyes. Jerr pretended not to notice.

A minute passed. Then another.

"How much longer?" Jerr asked.

Xade's nodus displayed each reborn's brain activity. Normal. Jerr recalled what Balyra said of his own mental capabilities. Forty locations at once…

The three-dimensional sphere switched to DNA comparisons. All of the reborn matched Jerr's template—save for one genetic mutation. One only he possessed.

"Nonhomogeneous," Xade murmured.

"How is that possible?" Jerr scowled in confusion. "I have a mutation, but they don't? I was birthed before them. They're all based on me!"

Xade nodded. "Incredulous."

"Reveal us, before the threads are severed forever."

The terminals lit up and beeped. Jerr and the rest tensed, weapons held ready.

"Jerr's reborn are waking." Tunva stared at the vats, spiraling ever upward. Green lights blinked on each. Tubes shook and bulged as fluid was pumped from the containers.

"Then we need to go," Jerr said. "We have what we came for."

"Thank the fucking stars." Darei headed for the lift.

"The job is not complete, Jerr Manivo." Tunva fingered her blade.

He glanced at the vats, then glowered at her. "What do you mean?"

Tunva simply stared back, the answer in her eyes.

"Hell no," Jerr said. "They deserve a chance to live."

"They will kill and destroy," Tunva said.

"I didn't come here to do the same," Jerr said. "We're not terminating them."

"Outrageous." Xade stood at Jerr's side.

As Tunva reached for a terminal, a sidearm clicked behind them.

"Stop right there." The voice sounded familiar. Ice formed in Jerr's gut.

Wanrys entered the chamber, aiming a pistol at them. "Commander Garrand didn't send you. But he is here now. The order for your arrest was just announced."

Sure enough, the planetary warrant appeared on Xade's nodus. Now, not only would they be hunted on the planet's surface, but *Bhaellator* was at risk of being retaken.

Sweat dappled Wanrys's brow. The man had come after them alone.

"They ordered all reborn to be taken into custody, didn't they?" Jerr asked.

"How did—?"

"Including you." Jerr shook as the precognition became real.

The news feed on Xade's nodus confirmed it. All of Jerr's reborn were suspects.

"You bastard," Wanrys said. "Now my family is in danger."

A family. The man had a goddamn family.

Jerr thought fast. "Look at me. They lied to us. They use us to kill innocent people, to commit genocide. Access *Bhaellator*'s mainframe. The data is all there."

"Shut up." Wanrys grimaced as if he gazed upon a monster.

"He's right," Darei said. "Check it out."

"Tunva will vouch for—"

"Shut the hell up!" The pistol shook in Wanrys's grasp.

"Why'd you follow us down here alone?" Jerr asked.

"You're supposed to be a deviant clone," Wanrys said. "That means they will examine all of us. The empire might shitcan us and grow replacements. My family…"

"Vulturous." Xade frowned.

Tunva glanced at the hatch. "How many more will Tunva have to fight?"

"I shut off those stupid realizers you left behind," Wanrys said. "But no one else knows you're down here. Yet."

"They will soon enough," Jerr said. "Why are you doing this?"

Wanrys licked his lips, probably wanting a drink as much as Jerr did.

"Why?" Jerr asked, louder.

"You remember people from before?" Wanrys finally asked, staring at the vats. "I had a doglet once, if you can believe that. One with the whole fur coat and the original ears, like those breeds inside the Settled Zone. I loved the hell out of that thing. But I can't remember his name. I don't remember what happened to him."

"It's the same," Jerr said. "My wife and son…"

Wanrys shot him a look. "I've got a wife. Two little girls, seven and nine. They live in the high-rise beside Arcology IV. Both want to work there when they grow up."

"Come with us," Jerr said. "Show everyone what the Dominion makes us do."

Tunva gave signs she could attack Wanrys, but Jerr shook his head.

"I won't recall much about my family, will I?" Wanrys asked. "After rebirth."

Jerr swallowed. "No. You won't."

Wanrys stared at the vats.

"Help us," Jerr said.

Xade nodded. "Valorous."

Wanrys aimed at Jerr's head.

"Wait!" Jerr yelled.

"Dangerous!" Xade shouted.

Wanrys regarded Xade with a bewildered look. "You are one weird Theux. And that's saying something. Mine never gives a damn about me. Just runs tests."

"Transpicuous." Xade looked away.

"She's right," Jerr said. "Think of the others out there, like us. Those in these vats. We fight and die for the empire—killing the families of others."

"Too late," Wanrys said. "A Vestal representative is already on her way. Marines will be coming for you in minutes."

"It is never too late to be brave," Tunva said.

Darei grunted. "Never too late to haul ass, either."

"Listen to me," Jerr said. "You still have jurisdiction. Escort us out of here, place us in the military brig. Vestals can't say dick about that. You'd have time—"

"You act like we're working together," Wanrys said. "It's not happening."

"The Weavers tried to show them the way, but they wanted more."

Jerr ignored the voice. "Help us and we'll get you and your family out of here on *Bhaellator*. We'll take you anywhere in the galaxy. You'll never have to see us again."

"Meritorious." Xade sounded pleased with him.

"Huh?" Darei asked. "No shit?"

Wanrys narrowed his eyes. "A reclamation team is already trying to enter *Bhaellator*. I'd have to convince them to stand down."

"Get us up there and we'll do the rest," Jerr said.

"Tunva's warriors will defend the Leviathan."

Wanrys shook his head. "You're not killing those people. They're good soldiers."

"No one has to die," Jerr said. "I wasn't trained in Rezal for nothing."

Wanrys's eyebrows rose. "They trained you in Rezal? Damn."

"This can work," Jerr said.

Wanrys regarded the vats again, then faced Jerr. "It better."

"What is the delay?" Balyra willed the attendant to allow her entrance into the magistrate building, but the young woman maintained her pleasant nonsmile.

"Lieutenant Wanrys is escorting the prisoners to a secure cell block, Confessor," the attendant said. "Protocols forbid any entry or exit until transfer is complete."

Protocols. Balyra had learned—and broken—many over the centuries. To maintain appearances, she could wait a little longer.

The journey aboard *Prophetess* had provided much-needed relaxation, among other things. But now, here on Stavia X, impatience nibbled at her sanity. Jerr thought he could flee Vestal House, and on a stolen Leviathan, no less. It would be the stuff of legend, like the exploits of all criminals.

But no one would celebrate him. She would tinker and pry with him until she discovered how he gleaned information from the Shroud. Then she would kill him. He would have too much confidence after this endeavor. Let one man steal a Leviathan and he'd dream of stealing the galaxy. It would not be the first time.

That had been Revor. A decision he'd allowed her to live to regret. Even should she succeed here, he would never consider her an equal. Only a tool.

But a sharp tool was always a danger to its wielder.

It was Vestal House who'd helped him gain mastery of the Shroud. She'd enslaved the Kieta for him, who'd known the best way to defeat the Weavers. Those formless cretins could barely be called lifeforms. Killing them had been easy.

Gazing over the cityscape, her jaw hardened. It all existed because of that one choice. The Shroud remained humanity's domain because of her. In the years after that tragedy, she'd wept whenever she considered what she had lost. What they had lost.

Balyra pulled up the familar image on her nodus. That face. Those eyes.

So much time had passed that she feared forgetting those physical details.

She wondered if Revor could feel grief. How much of him was still natural. Though she was no more human than he, Balyra still used the same face and name. She'd never relinquish them, being the last vestiges of humanity she'd yet to surrender.

"I asked you to perform a simple task and they shot you. Why?"

"Vestal House is not as popular as it once was." Balyra lay on a cot in Med Deck 8 while the Matriarch fumed nearby.

"It never was." The Matriarch peered inside the cavity of Balyra's body and grimaced. "Ovaries? Whatever are you still carrying those around for?"

Balyra sighed. "They are circoid implants. Anyone who scans me will think they are ovaries. It is the same with my appendix. They contain the newer data dumps."

There were more advanced ways to store and retrieve information now. Balyra could recall all her experiences. Remembering them never soothed her real wounds.

"Yes," the Matriarch said absently. "Yes, of course. Now, why were you shot?"

Balyra watched as a drone cut out her ruined stomach and replaced it, complete with a newer waste reclamation tank. The last model had made her piss too much. "Protestors at the orphanage did not want me to recruit new Sisters from the girls."

"What fools," the Matriarch said. "We are saving their lives. But enough of that. I need you to raze that place to the ground. No one assaults a Vestal. We are here under Dominion authority, and we shall not be challenged in such a manner."

All those children…all those young girls. They had wailed when Balyra got shot, but cheered when she managed to stand and let the morga walk her to the shuttle. A Vestal always maintained appearances.

Balyra didn't flinch. "Yes, Matriarch."

As she gazed heavenward, she hated Revor even more. Not until after that loss had Balyra become callous and cold. Inhuman before the cyborg implants made her so.

Garrand's annoying voice came over her aural implant. "Confessor, all landing platforms in your vicinity have been cleared. Captain Manivo must be elsewhere."

"Rebirth Facility 1947 was tampered with within the last hour," she said. "He is here, commander."

"I know my soldiers better than you," Garrand said. "He would already have left."

"You speak out of order, commander. Shall I—?"

A shuttle rocketed from the platform atop the magistrate building.

She withered the attendant with a glare. "You claimed no one was allowed entrance or exit."

The attendant stared in utter confusion as the shuttle darted into the atmosphere. "Confessor, I have no idea what has happened."

"My prisoners are escaping. That is what has happened." Balyra regarded her as a snail. "Get me a transport immediately, or I shall have you working the whore pits on Gavellon. And sound the alarm. Now!"

Chapter 12

Though the Armada shattered the previous era's religious institutions, people still wanted their gods. The Curators, with their Rebirth Initiative, filled that role. A pantheon of nameless individuals, with prayer nodes set up across the galaxy for the faithful to impart their desires, their hatreds. But like the gods of early humanity, the Curators never showed themselves; never leaving the dark confines of their Leviathans, never interceding in the genocides that guaranteed human supremacy.

Elder States Archives, Volume LII

"**C**hivalrous," Xade whispered.

"I don't feel chivalrous," Jerr said.

They all waited in the patrol boat cockpit, currently docked in a hangar across from Arcology IV. Wanrys had allowed them to hide *Bhaellator*'s shuttle in the magistrate hangar, which Xade now piloted via remote. They watched the feed on her nodus as imperial fighters scrambled to intercept it.

"Think they'll shoot it down?" Darei asked.

"If they wanted us dead, they'd have already launched missiles at it," Jerr said. "They plan to disable it, take us alive."

It was a gamble: use the shuttle as a decoy while they escaped in the boat. Plus Wanrys could still change his mind and report them to the authorities. Or they might be spotted and arrested before Wanrys returned. The only advantage was that their presence hadn't been announced on public feeds—nor would it be. Nothing could dispel the illusion of peace and stability.

125

"The longer Tunva waits, the more Tunva wants to take off without your twin."

"I gave him my word," Jerr said.

"Hell, do his kids have to bring every fucking toy in the house?" Darei studied the ship's sensors, keeping an eye out for pursuers. "I bet they're spoiled little shits."

No longer posing as a prisoner, Tunva clipped her sword and pistol back on. "Jerr trusts his twin too much. The twin risks nothing. We risk everything."

"He's bringing his family—so he's risking every damn thing." Jerr was more afraid of what Wanrys's wife and kids would think, because Jerr would seem an imposter of the man they cherished and loved. Reborn became accustomed to others sharing the same facial features. It usually unnerved others.

Making his anxiety worse, his eyesight lensed into a waking vision every few minutes—and not because of his Urian sensitivity. The moon orbits between the parent planet's massive red ring and the smaller but brighter orange ring. Xade clasps his hand tight, but he's unable to smile. He tried focusing his attention elsewhere.

Darei played with a socket wrench. "This is crazy, waiting on him to rat on us."

"Give the guy a chance," Jerr said. "He did let Xade take his blood sample."

Xade nodded. "Gregarious."

"So?" Darei rolled his eyes.

"She said it turned up negative." Jerr looked to Xade to back him up.

Her nodus displayed the gene sequence absent in Jerr's reborn. During the flight to the Arcology hangar, she'd cross-referenced it with all of his known DNA templates. His was the only anomaly, though hundreds more reborn had been grown after him.

"So Jerr is the only one who hears the Weavers," Tunva said. "That will make it easier for Veja Qor to battle Jerr's reborn, if Jerr Manivo has the secrets."

Jerr shot her a look. "We won't have to fight them if we expose the atrocities."

Darei smacked the sensor terminal with the wrench. "Stop jerking us off."

Jerr turned in the chair, facing Darei. "What?"

"Admit it," Darei said. "You want all these rebirths of yourself to be noble, to do the right thing, all that stupid shit. That'd validate your precious hopes, right?"

Jerr stared. "They're not evil, just misled."

"The hope that you were chosen to be a reborn, not only because of your skills, but how 'good' you are? How far above us you are on that fucking moral ladder?"

"Oh, bullshit!" Jerr cried.

"It's not!" Darei spread his arms. "You want him to be like you, not his own damn person. Next, you'll be jealous that he's got kids and you don't."

Jerr reached for Darei but Xade blocked him. "Obnoxious!"

The shuttle hatch opened. Wanrys led a young woman and two girls, all dressed in blue naval fatigues, into the boat. Wanrys raised his brows at them.

"Everything all right in here?"

Jerr burned with embarrassment, all too aware of the stares fixed on him.

"My friends were getting impatient." Jerr tried not to meet the wife's eyes. She gawked at him in disbelief and revulsion. The two girls gaped up at Jerr in shock, their young faces registering their mother's fear. Jerr's heart chilled.

"Krana, this is my cousin. Jerr Manivo." Wanrys's voice held all the conviction of an addict swearing off drugs. "Isue, Lisua…say hello to your cousin."

Neither girl spoke.

"We'd better get underway." Jerr sat back down, turning his back on them. There was nothing rude about it. Rather, he spared them from having to look at him.

The others, even Darei, said nothing. Xade smiled at the children, but they crowded around their mother. Wanrys and his wife shared desperate, fierce whispers, until she led the children into the gunnery bay. Jerr didn't blame them. As soon as *Bhaellator* left the system, he'd deposit them on a decent planet.

Xade flew the shuttle through the lower stratosphere. Numerous feeds played on her nodus, showing sector activity. Tunva asked Wanrys something about the reclamation team sent to *Bhaellator*, and Darei cursed the sensors again, but it was all dull noise as Jerr mentally wrestled with more visions, more words.

"You hear me, goddammit?" Darei shouts over the radio. "Get out of there!"

Jerr cradled his head, ignoring Xade's worried glances.

He darts into the exposed berth slot and through an egress hatch before it shuts.

His thrusters give out.

"Migrainous?" Xade asked softly.

"I'm good," he muttered.

"Libelous."

"Does that mean no more chocolate rations?" Jerr asked.

She kicked his shin.

As Stavia's atmosphere evaporated before the darkness of space, Wanrys spoke. "We'll join the flotilla sent to investigate *Bhaellator*, use them for cover. Then, when we are close enough, we fly into your hangar and seal it. There's nothing in this system that can penetrate a Leviathan's hull."

"Do you have contact with the boarding party?" Jerr asked.

"Which one?" Wanrys gave him a flat look.

"Shit." Jerr wiped his face. "Tunva, are all your warriors on the dispersal deck?"

"Yes," she said. "It has the weakest armor."

"They suspect we don't have enough defenders to hold off simultaneous assaults." Jerr did a Rezal calculation. Even with the security robos defending the bridge proper, Bridge Deck remained a weak spot to exploit. And if it was taken—they were all dead.

"If we are fast, we can do it," Wanrys said. "I've brought 'lectro-pulsers and riot guns. Make it clean and non-fatal. I see a kill, our deal is off."

Jerr didn't mention Wanrys would be outnumbered should he nullify their bargain. If the man was anything like Jerr himself, Wanrys had a chance of beating them all. But Jerr didn't want a fight. Especially with the family onboard.

"How many in each group?" Tunva asked.

"A dozen or so marines," Wanrys said. "In Starjumpers."

"Wanrys expects Tunva to fight that with riot guns?" She flicked her tongue.

"Build?" Jerr asked.

"At least 7.0," Wanrys said. "Tough bastards."

Jerr frowned at Darei, who shrugged.

By the time they left Stavia's orbit, the cockpit HUD blinked with alarms and messages. Jerr glanced at the moving dots on Xade's nodus. They had a minute, if that.

Bhaellator waited ahead, its massive size tempting them with safety. Xade joined the flotilla's formation, flying alongside gunships and other patrol boats. It was a pathetic showing against a Leviathan—but the Dominion knew *Bhaellator* was poorly manned.

"The reclamation crew will've been told that our shuttle left the planet," Darei said. "Shit, they're expecting us to sneak back in. Anybody listening to me?"

"The best we can hope for is to make them think we're somebody else," Jerr said. "Xade, think you can make us scan as a marine squad sent to secure the ship?"

"Nebulous." She worked the controls with frantic gestures. On the display, the fighters fired at the shuttle. It was crippled within seconds. Two gunships neared it, preparing to board. Another feed showed new ships in the system. A hodgepodge of assorted vessels, from freighters to outdated Con-Union cruisers.

"What the hell?" Wanrys accused Jerr with a look. "Those aren't friendlies."

Jerr squinted at the image. "Friends of yours, Tunva?"

"Looks like we came here to do more than fill a syringe," Darei said.

Tunva's smile was sharp ivory. "Veja Qor received the signal. They will fight."

"They can't win." Though angry they were throwing their lives away, Jerr was still impressed with the rebels' courage.

"Not every battle is about winning," Tunva said.

"Right." Jerr rose and activated all his suit's weapon systems.

"Don't be stupid," Wanrys said. "That hunk of junk you're wearing can't engage those marines with any success. It's suicide."

Xade broke off from the flotilla and rocketed to *Bhaellator*'s bridge. As they neared the hangar below Bridge Deck, the flotilla changed course. Following them.

"Stay here with your family," Jerr said. "When all's clear, hurry aboard."

They stared at each other. Mirror reflections of a destiny betrayed.

"I understand," Wanrys said.

On Xade's command, the boat entered the hangar as it opened. The crevice was just wide enough to allow them entrance. No sooner than they were through, it shut. Jerr, Tunva, and Darei waited at the boat's airlock, weapons ready.

"Manivo," Wanrys called from the cockpit. "The flotilla has pulled back."

"Suspicious." Xade stood, clasping a prod in each hand.

"I know," he murmured, then called back to Wanrys. "We're going in!"

"Think he'll wait in this bucket?" Darei asked.

"Have we done anything with certainty so far?" Jerr asked.

Outside the viewport, Veja Qor ships attacked the flotilla. Explosions popped across the darkness. Each a tiny supernova of desperate, foolish hope.

"Jerr has led us with his visions," Tunva said. "That is certainty."

The airlock opened and they reentered *Bhaellator*.

Chapter 13

After rebirth became a common procedure, its beneficiaries developed personality traits once considered anathema to social development: conceit, megalomania, and belligerence. Knowing one will simply be regrown after death transforms the mindset. It gradually erodes the civilized maxims these individuals were selected to uphold and perpetuate. The imperial military exhibited the worst cases.

Psychopomp Errata, Sector 72, Sister Nhla Edrov, Vestal House

Jerr led them from the hangar into the adjoining corridor. *Bhaellator* was bereft of any sound, a ghost ship for all its activity. Which meant the boarding party hadn't gotten this far. After glancing at the others, he neared the first turn leading to Bridge Deck's access chute. Thanks to Xade, the chute remained locked down.

Smoke drifted through the next corridor. Glowing pellets cooled on the deck. Slag had formed corpulent metallic sculptures. Jerr readied his diffusion blaster.

"You cannot stop them. Not this way."

Though his HUD detected nothing out of the ordinary, the hole cut through the bulkhead confirmed his worst fears. It led to the dispersal deck. The path was littered with dead Repta warriors. Judging from the corpses' receding heat signatures, they were killed right before Jerr and his friends arrived in the patrol boat.

The marines were already onboard, then. Waiting.

Tunva quivered with raw fury. Xade consulted her nodus, growing more frustrated with each swipe.

"So much for surprising them," Darei said.

The marines knew Jerr would see this. They were baiting him into doing something stupid. He'd not oblige them. Entering Rezal state, he did a few calculations.

The first impulse was to hurry for the bridge, for one would assume it'd be the marines' primary target. Control it, and one controlled *Bhaellator*. Which meant they had an ambush planned for him there. He would trap them within *Bhaellator* instead.

Rezal allowed him to consider all the possible points of ambush and crossfire within a second. He left the short trance and caught his breath.

"What now?" Darei asked in a whisper. "They've got us by the balls."

"Tunva needs to avenge the fallen." She closed the eyes on a warrior's corpse.

"Horrendous." Xade stared at the bodies with pity.

Jerr checked his HUD. "We need to—"

Two marines darted from around the corner, their Starjumpers clanking over the deck. Both fired 'lectropulsers at Jerr, but he lunged into the next corridor. The shots struck the wall. Blue arcs sizzled through the air.

Two more marines charged from the dispersal deck, but Tunva shot both through their faceplates with the riot gun. Jaws and cheeks broken, the marines wobbled backward, then aimed at her. Xade clubbed both in the head with her pulse rods. The marines toppled to the deck.

Jerr crawled toward an alcove as the other pair continued firing. Their shots blasted the armor off his right leg. His HUD blinded him with all its flashing alarms, but he managed to roll and fire. The diffusion beam melted their gun barrels. While they hurriedly switched to another weapon, Jerr fired again. Both marines fell, their leg servos burned through. They tried to crawl away until Xade whacked their helmets with the pulse rods. Blue arcs crackled along their faceplates. Both soldiers went limp.

"That went well," Darei said.

"They're not trying to kill us—yet." Jerr examined the prone marines. Both still breathed. Tunva stood over the pair she'd shot and unsheathed her blade.

"Tunva's warriors should be avenged," Tunva said.

Jerr stood. "I'm sorry you lost your friends. But if we act like that, then we're no better than the Dominion. Is that how Veja Qor treats a fallen enemy?"

Tunva put her sword away, leaving the unconscious marines alone.

"Thank you," Jerr said. "C'mon, there's still enemies onboard."

The berth beneath the bridge consisted of a large circle containing the former crew's quarters, mess hall, and other such cabins now empty of personnel. Jerr led and Tunva brought up the rear. With the Repta slain, they were the vessel's sole defenders.

In the next corridor, sparks flew as a torch cut a gradual line down the bulkhead.

"Must be one of the other boarding parties." Jerr checked his HUD mapping. "They've got a dropship on the other side of this hull. Shit."

"Audacious." Xade showed the hull's blueprints on her nodus. Several small points were highlighted along the structural framing. Single-use thrusters.

"You can't be serious." Jerr studied the three dimensional plan again.

Darei looked it over. "It's either this, or we wait until they finish this new door."

"Tunva doesn't like waiting." She raised her weapons.

Though *Bhaellator*'s main berths had already been disconnected, each and every section could be discarded, until nothing but the gravity core remained. In this case, if Xade disengaged the bridge crew berth, it would rob them of comfortable quarters—yet it would send the boarding party off into the void. But they'd need a proper push.

"You're the only one in a suit," Darei said. "We'll wait on the dispersal deck."

"Courageous." Xade patted Jerr's arm, eyes full of concern.

Jerr motioned them to go as the fiery line grew longer. Curving over into a doorway. He powered up the gauss cannon, but with his right leg unarmored, he'd have to time everything perfect. Sparks blurred in his vision as he entered Rezal.

Damage dropship stabilizers then throttle to egress hatch and rendezvous.

A simple statement, but computing the variables—how many marines might've exited the dropship, how skilled its pilot was, the velocity of the berth once the frame thrusters activated, how much fuel his boot thrusters possessed—made him gasp.

Third Echelon glows beneath him, a gem held captive by two greedy, dying stars.

Jerr shook, unable to force the images from his mind. The sparks glowed brighter.

"I don't give a damn if you can't talk." Jerr embraces Xade. "All I care about…"

The erstwhile portal flew away. An armored figure appeared.

Jerr liquefied the marine's helmet with a diffusion shot. The headless man wobbled in place, his magna-boots still gripping the outer hull. Jerr leapt forward, his momentum knocking the corpse out into the void.

Outside, a dozen marines trained their weapons on him. Two dropships, not one, were attached to the outer hull. Instinct took over. Combined with Rezal and snippets of precognition, Jerr emptied his gauss cannon at the dropships as the berth detached from *Bhaellator* with a quick flash. Scatter shot and piercer rounds zipped his way.

"Cannot stop them…"

His HUD glowed red with danger warnings. It bled into his reality, tinting it vermilion, blurring as if he were in the Shroud. Pain erupted in his legs, his back. Reacting a split second before the marines, he coaxed his Starjumper to thrust right, left, blast a marine, thrust left, blast again. He became the apotheosis of all the Dominion had created him for. Blackened armor shards and frozen plasma drifted away from him.

"Jerr, you hear me, goddammit?" Darei shouted over the radio. "Get out of there!"

Deathly cold numbed his right leg. Jerr fired boot and wrist thrusters, flying over the edge of the berth as it shot away from *Bhaellator*. One dropship snapped free and spun into darkness. The other was mobbed by surviving marines, desperate to escape.

"Jerr, blow all fuel reserves!" Darei's shout made the line crackle. "Now!"

But he already knew. The reserves energized the thrusters to full power. Mind still blurred with imagery and numbers, Jerr barely controlled his trajectory. He darted into the exposed berth slot and through an egress hatch before it shut. His thrusters gave out.

Lying near the dock outside the bridge, Jerr lifted his head. Xade and Darei hurried to his side. Tunva examined two dead marines that had drifted in with him.

"Job security?" Jerr smiled at Darei as the technician unfastened the suit's still-glowing thrusters with insulated gloves.

"You're one crazy son of a bitch." Darei removed Jerr's helmet with a pop.

Jerr laughed until Xade jabbed a normalizer syringe into his shoulder. "Hey!"

"Necessitous." It was the first time he'd seen Xade smirk.

"Ow, damn it!" Jerr grimaced as the syringe's stopper slowly came down.

"Remember what I said about being an asshole?" Darei cut the right leg off Jerr's emergency liner, then through the jumpsuit underneath. If not for it, the limb would be frozen beyond restoration. Scattershot had bruised his back, but otherwise he was fine.

"Did that solve our problems?" Jerr sucked his teeth as Xade squirted warming solution over his exposed leg. A burning, writhing sensation dashed away his numbness.

"Tenuous." Xade checked his pulse, examined his eyes.

"There's the flotilla still fighting Veja Qor," Darei said. "And there might be—"

"We'll make it." With their help, Jerr removed the rest of the Starjumper. It was scratched and burnt all over. He eyed the dead marines' suits, then beckoned Darei.

"Upgrade?" Darei sighed and helped him take the newer suit from the corpse.

Tunva crossed her scaly arms, serpentine eyes wide with frustration. "Jerr broke his promise to Wanrys. Tunva kept hers."

"It couldn't be helped." Jerr buckled on the dead marine's greaves and boots.

"Jerr Manivo lies," Tunva said.

"Heinous." Xade scolded her with a look.

"Look, there was no time." Jerr stood as Darei helped him snap the breastplate on.

Tunva crammed the helmet onto Jerr's head. "Jerr Manivo better remember."

"Fine, but no one tell Wanrys," Jerr said as they piled the dead marines on the dispersal deck. But Wanrys and his family were already watching them, having just left the patrol boat. The mother clung to her daughters, who trembled visibly.

"You bastard," Wanrys said. "I told you I didn't want—"

Tunva started to speak, but Jerr shoved her behind him. "You're past that point, and you know it. The Dominion is your enemy now, like it or not. We'll leave you at the next system, as promised. Then you'll never see us again."

"Daddy, why does he sound like you?" one girl asked. The mother shushed her.

"He might sound like me, look like me." Wanrys didn't break eye contact with Jerr. "But he isn't me."

There was nothing Jerr could say. The pain in Wanrys's face said it all. A soldier never wanted his loved ones to see enemy bodies. Never wanted them to know how much the killing might have been enjoyable, justified by nonsensical ethics. Never wanted their kin to know that, if ordered, he was just as capable of killing someone else's family.

Xade led the others to Bridge Deck's chute, but Jerr grabbed Tunva's wrist.

"What did you mean, I'd better remember?"

"That Jerr Manivo is not a peacemaker." Tunva flicked her tongue. "Jerr will get us all killed, thinking the Dominion shares Jerr's honor."

He pointed outside the nearest viewport where ships exploded in battle above Stavia X. "Is that honorable? Using your friends as a diversion so we can escape?"

"Veja Qor understands the costs," she said. "Jerr doesn't. Not yet."

Jerr grabbed her by the shoulders, ignoring the rippling muscles that could break his neck. "Cost? You're a reborn, you dare lecture me about cost?"

"Costs are not always about Jerr Manivo," she whispered.

He slowly let her go. "The Jerr who died in your arms—did he ever understand?"

She tapped a clawed finger on his cheek, eyes roving up his body until they reached his face. "No. That is why that Jerr Manivo failed."

Though he didn't know why, the words wounded him. As if sensing it, she touched his chest, her gaze filled with sorrow.

"Tunva is … sorry."

"Yeah. Me too." They shared a brief smile and hurried after the others.

Chapter 14

Humans resented us for copying them in those early centuries of supremacy. They failed to understand that we assumed their appearance not in mockery, but as a way to learn, to share. Yet they found our emotional responses lacking, inappropriate. Theux were subjected to bigotry and murder, while human authorities disregarded the plight of their biomechanical citizens. In punishing us for our emotions, they sacrificed their own.

Theux Codex, 78 Vaaqa D (reconstructed), uncensored excerpt

"Xade, how long until we leave?" Jerr knew she'd only answer in her limited fashion, but talking eased his anxiety. Dominion fighters couldn't even dent *Bhaellator*'s hull, but with its major berths missing, so was the ship's armor. Their vessel was literally a skeleton of its former self. Stavia's flotilla might inflict enough damage to prevent them from entering the Shroud. If they were captured again, there wouldn't be a second escape.

Knew it, because he'd foreseen it.

"Dubious." Xade swiped several nodi, preparing *Bhaellator*'s engine. After dislodging the bridge crew berth, they suffered no other boarding attempts. Fighter squadrons and gunboat task-forces tried to make regular sweeps around their ship, but the Veja Qor fleet kept them occupied. Even that wouldn't last much longer.

"Huh?" Jerr asked.

Darei scowled at the bridge realizers that displayed their situation. "Not enough time, that's what she means. No way the

Dominion will let us go. They'll plant charges on the hull. I've seen that shit before."

"This ship is too valuable to them for that." Jerr let out a breath. "Xade, one of those taskforces keeps nearing our stern. See if you can work the thrusters, make them think twice about it."

Xade shook her head but swiped the commands anyway.

Wanrys glared at the realizer displays, then at Jerr. "It's impossible to break that blockade without causing serious damage to Stavia's fleet and orbiting docks."

His erstwhile twin's family watched from the bridge entrance. As if coming near Jerr would taint them. He made himself not look at them.

"*Bhaellator*'s weapons can clear a path," Tunva said.

"No. We can still make it." Jerr wriggled the toes of his right foot as the numbness finally receded from its brush with cold vacuum.

Xade shared a look with Tunva. "Disputatious."

Jerr leaned close to her. "I know Tunva wants a rebellion. What do you want?"

Depthless resolve filled her eyes as she squeezed his arm.

"Tell me …?"

"They hid the secret amidst circles of orange and red. The secret of our defeat."

Xade studied him with a puzzled expression as he left the question hanging.

The moon orbits between the parent planet's massive red ring and the smaller but brighter orange ring. Xade clasps his hand tight, but he's unable to smile …

"Gnebus," Jerr whispered. "It's on Gnebus."

Xade's brow rose. She gripped his shoulders, waiting for him to say more.

"They hid the secret so that—"

An alarm went off. The various realizers and nodi glowed red.

"I told you the Vestals would come." Wanrys wiped his brow. "Their own Leviathan is in the system: *Prophetess*."

Jerr paused. Even he'd heard that name, supposedly one of the first Leviathans built. But sending a religious cult after him, rather than a full military convoy to retake a valuable prize like *Bhaellator*... it meant one thing.

They wanted him alive for further questioning. They believed his story.

"They hid the secret so that the threads could never be repaired. What the Weavers wove was hidden, forgotten. Forbidden."

Jerr tried to understand what the words meant while everyone gave him bewildered looks. Wanrys's teeth gritted. Tunva paced before the weapon systems nodus. Xade nearly had the core online, an impossible feat for the rest of them in so short a time.

"Weave a new thread. Reveal us."

As the voice left Jerr's thoughts, Wanrys punched a control panel. "Damn, are you even listening? *Prophetess* is drawing up alongside us! We have to surrender."

"Fuck that," Darei said. "I want my payment. Now."

"We need to go to Gnebus first," Jerr said. "In the Settled Zone."

"I need my family safe." Wanrys lowered a hand to his holster.

Tunva kept glancing at Wanrys, her neck scales bristling. The family huddled together, the mother whispering in her daughters' ears.

"Everybody calm the hell down," Jerr said. "We can—"

Xade's eyes widened as she studied a nodus. "Alacritous!"

Darei stared at the translucent sphere. "Motherfucker."

"*Prophetess* is docking with *Bhaellator*," Tunva said.

"Insidious." Xade indicated a display of the upper hull.

The dispersal deck was breached. White-armored morga marched into *Bhaellator.*

"Damn it," Jerr said. "We shouldn't have detached that last berth. This section's armor went with it. Now they're walking right in."

Wanrys drew his pistol and aimed at Jerr. "That's it. I'm taking control of this vessel. Hands up, all of you."

"Tunva doesn't take orders from—"

"Hands up!" Wanrys shouted. His wife and daughters jumped at his voice.

"This is just wonderful." Darei raised his hands.

"Don't be stupid." Jerr tried keeping his voice neutral. "There's no reward if you turn us over to them. The Vestals will want you, too."

"I don't give a damn about rewards," Wanrys said. "This is about my family."

"Tunva's family was taken by the Dominion," Tunva said. "This will not help Wanrys keep his."

"You don't know a damn thing about it," Wanrys said. "The empire will listen. After all I've done for them, after all the times I've died and been reborn—"

"Just like me," Jerr said.

"We're not the same person!" Wanrys bellowed.

One of the realizers assumed Balyra's face. "In the name of Vestal House, surrender now. You will all be—"

Xade swiped the realizer off.

"Stop." Wanrys aimed at Xade.

Xade glanced back and forth between Jerr and Wanrys. Jerr should tell her to continue readying *Bhaellator,* because this man was just like him and wouldn't shoot. But Wanrys was right. They weren't the same. No way to predict each other's actions.

"Do you know why they want me?" Jerr was desperate. The shapes on the realizer were coming closer. "I see things before they happen. I saved my company—"

Wanrys shook his head. "Shut up."

"That's why they won't let you go." Jerr eased around a counter, putting himself between Wanrys and Xade. "They'll torture you despite what that blood test showed."

"Shut the hell up!" Wanrys yelled. "I'm not a traitor!"

More alarms beeped. *Bhaellator* trembled slightly.

Jerr saw it in his mind. Rushing Wanrys as he pulls the trigger. The shot strikes Jerr, not Xade. While Wanrys's family prevent him from firing again, Bhaellator escapes.

"You have to trust me." Jerr raised both hands. "They took my wife and son. Don't let them take your wife and daughters."

The gun wavered in Wanrys's grip. His shoulders slumped.

Jerr reached for the gun when Balyra stormed the bridge entrance. She wore red and chrome armor. Her robotic morga troops grabbed Wanrys's family. In the split second they'd focused on each other, Jerr and Wanrys had lowered their defenses.

Xade narrowed her eyes at Balyra. "Cancerous."

"The only disease I see here is sedition." Balyra raised a hand. The morga snapped magnetic cuffs on Wanrys's wife and daughters.

"Don't," Jerr whispered to Wanrys, who looked even more frantic.

"It is over, Manivo," Balyra said. "*Bhaellator* is surrounded. *Prophetess* is prepared to disable her, if necessary. Surrender and no one will be harmed."

"The Vestal lies." Tunva bristled with restrained violence. "Our fleet still fights."

Balyra smirked. "Perhaps in whatever miserable afterlife you savages imagine, but not in this one." Outside the viewports, the space battle was over.

"We will surrender," Jerr said. "If you let Wanrys and his family go."

"That is not possible," Balyra said. "Treason has been committed against the Dominion. He knows the punishment."

Wanrys's expression crumbled into a visage of rage. All inhibitions against his primal torrent of anger were broken. His family tried holding on to each other, but the morga kept them apart. Jerr wasn't sure who they feared more: Wanrys, or the Vestals.

"If you want my cooperation," Jerr said through clenched teeth, "they go free."

Tunva slowly shook her head at Jerr, while Darei stared from one group to the next, sweat dappling his brow. Xade remained cool and aloof, focused on Balyra.

Jerr did a quick Rezal analysis: there was scant chance of escape, but he wouldn't have innocent blood on his hands. He'd made

Wanrys a promise. To prove he was capable of trust, he needed to keep it. Prove he could choose his own way, rather than the voices, or the Dominion's training. That he was more than the sum of his parts.

"I accept," Balyra finally said.

Balyra's eyes widen. "No. That would mean—"

Jerr nods. "I know what it means."

Jerr looked at his friends, who slowly lowered their weapons—except Wanrys, who once again aimed at Jerr.

"You're going to get us all killed," Jerr said.

"It's him you want," Wanrys said. "I'm still loyal. See? I'm turning him in."

Balyra regarded Wanrys as a nuisance. "Stand down, or you will be put down." Additional morga troops entered the bridge and aimed at the crazed lieutenant.

"Daddy!" one of the girls cried as she tried to wrench away from a morga.

Wanrys quivered with anger. "You said we would go free."

"And you shall," Balyra said. "As soon as we have your accomplices in custody."

"That wasn't part of our plan." Garrand walked through the entrance, flanked by a squad of marines in Starjumpers. "My, it is nice to reclaim my former vessel. Like I reclaim my best commando, Jerr Manivo. Or, the next best thing." He smiled at Wanrys.

Balyra regarded Garrand coolly. "You are not helping, commander."

"On the contrary," Garrand said, "that is exactly what I'm doing. You have orders to shoot on sight, Confessor. Why is Manivo still alive?"

"He will be dealt with." Balyra's words were steel.

Garrand leered. "Lieutenant, the empire is willing to waive your participation in these unfortunate events. You can even replace Manivo here on *Bhaellator*."

"My family as well?" Wanrys asked.

"Of course." Garrand smiled wide. "All you need to do is shoot Manivo."

"I have jurisdiction here!" Balyra cried.

"We can't let Vestal House take all of our toys, can we?" Garrand smirked. "Do it, Lieutenant Wanrys. That's an order."

Face slicked with sweat, Wanrys looked from Garrand to Jerr.

Jerr saw it in his mind a second before it happened. One of the marines shoots Wanrys in the neck. His children wail, watching him die. Gunfire zips through the bridge realizers. Darei falls, bleeding. The two little girls scream—

"He's lying!" Jerr cried. "Duck!"

Wanrys, like Jerr, possessed hair-trigger reflexes. He ducked right before the piercer round hit. It soared over his head and smacked into the far wall.

Tunva lunged, knocking Jerr from the marines' line of fire. Their rounds still singed his left side. His flesh bubbled inside his jumpsuit and he cried out. He managed to roll behind a console as Tunva fired, covering them. The bridge's security robos, now controlled by Xade, hovered down from the ceiling.

"No prisoners!" Garrand shouted. The marines rushed forward.

The morga aimed at Tunva, but Wanrys blasted them, sending several to the deck. He yelled his rage. Jerr felt a kinship with it, so much he vaulted up and plowed through the marines. Two fell on their backs, but the others sprayed piercers at him. He ducked and weaved among the realizer displays as the marines kept firing. The light but deadly rounds only inflicted superficial damage; Garrand wouldn't dare risk heavier weapons on *Bhaellator*'s bridge. It gave Jerr his only chance.

The morga focus on the marines a millisecond too long as Tunva and Wanrys shoot them down, with the robos joining in. Xade fires Bhaellator's thrusters, breaking away from Prophetess and the flotilla. The marines aim and prepare to fire ...

The visions allowed Jerr to remain one step ahead of his enemies. A marine fired his piercer, but Jerr had already dodged. Two tried cornering him between the consoles—but he outflanked them and drew them into a crossfire. Tunva and Wanrys decimated Balyra's guards, who focused on the robos. Xade set *Bhaellator* adrift from *Prophetess* while ducking gunfire. All took place like a waking reverie. One he'd already dreamt.

He knew every action, reaction, and played upon them. The odds shifted.

"Keep shooting!" Garrand yelled, even as he tried exiting the bridge. Balyra and the surviving morga barred his path.

Xade swiped several nodi. The spheres showed *Prophetess* banking toward the Stavian flotilla. Balyra regarded the Theux with tight-lipped condemnation.

Jerr leapt from between two realizers and slammed Garrand to the deck. His old commander wheezed, the air knocked from him. Angry instincts took over. Jerr snapped Garrand's wrist, crushed his ribs with a knee. Garrand cried out until a marine punched Jerr across several consoles. Jerr hit the floor, tasting blood.

Darei tossed two scatter grenades at the entrance. Balyra shouted for her morga to retreat. A piercer ripped through Darei's shoulder. He screamed, still returning fire as the round ate through clothes, flesh, and bone.

As the morga retreated into the corridor, Wanrys continued shooting. A piercer shot had melted through his left knee, while another had taken off his right cheek. He was a grinning skull of death, stalking toward the dead morga, reloading his weapon.

"Goddamn you." Garrand scowled at Jerr. "You've sent us all to hell."

Darei scooted back beside Jerr as *Bhaellator*'s displays showed all systems prepared for entering the Shroud. A morga shot the last robo in a shower of sparks.

"Xade, the Shroud!" Jerr clutched his chest where the marine punched him.

"Not without my family!" Wanrys said, his voice disgorged, ragged.

Balyra pointed at Xade. "You will kill thousands in the fleet, and on Stavia below. You have tampered with Vestal networks. A Theux knows only pacifism!"

"Spurious." Xade activated the gravitational engine. *Bhaellator* entered the Shroud. Balyra's body faded from existence. Everyone fell still.

Trembling with pain and shock, Jerr simply stared. Tunva shot the last marine and aimed at Garrand, still prone and bleeding. Xade cocked her head at their reactions, then summoned her palm nodus. Its information made Jerr relax.

Darei coughed. "She was a realizer illusion? Bitch wasn't even onboard."

Garrand squirmed and tried crawling away, but Tunva yanked his good arm around, pinioning him in place. "There is only once place Garrand is going."

"Kill me and you'll never know why they want you," Garrand said.

"We're listening." Jerr forced himself up. Xade rushed over and steadied him.

"Get me a med drone first." Despite his situation, Garrand still managed a smirk.

"Tunva can be persuasive." She dug her claws into Garrand's arm.

Jerr started to reply when the sound of weeping gave them all pause.

Wanrys knelt by the bridge entrance, cradling the torn corpses of his daughters. There was even less left of his wife. Quivering morga bodies lay around them. Piercer rounds had shredded them. Holes still smoldered in small, lifeless limbs.

"Malicious." Xade's smooth voice choked with emotion. Jerr squeezed her arm.

"Get me a drone!" Garrand cried.

Shaking with anguish, Jerr stared at Garrand. "I should kill you right now. They gunned down his—"

"I shot them." Wanrys carefully lay down his daughters. His calm voice chilled Jerr's blood. "By accident. I couldn't stop pulling the trigger, with those morga ..."

Jerr pushed Xade behind him as Wanrys rose, still holding the pistol. Madness filled his eyes. There was nowhere to run. No future visions to guide his actions.

"I tried to save them," Wanrys said. "But now I will be reborn again. I will be a new killer, a new weapon. And I will do this every single time, until it finally ends."

"Help us stop it," Jerr said.

"Yes … I will." Wanrys aimed at his own head.

"Don't!" Jerr yelled.

Wanrys pulled the trigger. Brains flew across the bridge. Wanrys fell like a heavy tree in a logging camp. Jerr gaped as blood flowed from the jagged cavity. It could be him lying there. It's what might've happened, had he remained with his wife and son.

In the premonition, Jerr had seen Wanrys get shot, but by the marines. He'd either been wrong, or he'd changed the course of events by warning Wanrys. Either way the result was the same. Jerr had watched himself die. Watched a family and a future die.

"You see what happened, Manivo?" Garrand asked. "That is why this escape is useless. You and all your cursed reborn will always be killers."

"You're wrong." Jerr stalked over to him.

"Look around you," Garrand said.

"You're wrong!" Jerr loomed over Garrand. It would be easy, snapping his neck, crushing his spine. Make him suffer. The more Jerr thought about it, the heavier his breathing became. Liquid drops splattered his hands. Jerr realized he was crying.

"Jerr Manivo should weep," Tunva said. "Tunva has wept for her people. Tunva has bled to bring Jerr Manivo here, so the voice of the Shroud will lead us."

"What?" Jerr asked with a raw throat.

"They're using you, you stupid grunt," Garrand said.

"Why?" Darei asked, leaning against a console. Though a med drone had sealed the piercer wound, he remained terribly pale.

Garrand smiled. "Whoever can see the future controls it. Veja Qor probably thinks you can help them against Revor. Balyra must have similar plans."

"What were your plans for me?" Jerr nudged Garrand.

"To see you dead," Garrand said. "That had to be ordered by Curator Revor himself. No one else would have the authority to send all of Vestal House against you."

"Just because I see things?" Jerr grunted. "Bullshit."

The thought twisted Jerr's guts. A Curator, showing interest in him?

"You might have seen…but you didn't understand," Garrand said. "I captained for Revor back in the Armada days. I know what he can do. You can't win."

Jerr glanced at Xade. "Really? Is that why the Shroud told me to go to Gnebus?"

Arrogance drained from Garrand's face. "You're lying. Only Leviathan commanders and the Curators know those coordinates."

"Gnebus," Tunva muttered. "What is there, more soldiers like Jerr Manivo? More warriors for the Dominion? What did the Shroud tell Jerr?"

"That's where Xade found my brother…" Darei wheezed. "In her database."

"But not how to get there," Jerr said.

Xade's eyes lowered in embarrassment.

"It's okay, Miss Blue Theux. You had the right idea." Darei's smile was weak.

Garrand laughed, then winced at his wounds. "Reborn, Repta, Theux—none of you have the right idea. None of you could beat Revor then, and you won't now. You're just offshoots of humanity. Prepackaged, bastardized slaves. You're not even people—"

Darei fired. Garrand fell still.

"He could've told us more." Jerr glared at Darei. "Damn it, why'd you do it?"

"Because he's full of it." Darei dropped the pistol and groaned. "Fuck. You'll need someone else to fix your Starjumper now."

Jerr limped over to Darei. "You're giving up that easily?"

Darei chuckled. "Never had much stake in this. I was caught at the wrong place, wrong time. With the wrong friends."

"Contemptuous." Xade knelt and propped Darei up. Her palm nodus showed his vital stats: terminal. Jerr swallowed, tried to think of something to say.

"Darei made the right choice," Tunva said. "Garrand will not be mourned."

"We're about to find out." Darei fixated on Jerr. "Now tell me what you've seen in your little visions. About me."

Jerr looked at him in bewilderment. "What?"

"You know the future," Darei said. "Tell me mine."

"I don't—"

"You owe me that." Darei's voice became an agonized cough. Anguish spread over Xade's features as she clutched Darei close.

Jerr slowly nodded. "You find work on an Affiliate world. You have two husbands. You look happy."

"Two?" Darei grinned. "Yeah, I suppose I would be. So that's what you saw?"

"Yes, but why ask me? It could change."

"Because I want to know what I'll be missing out on."

"Darei?" Jerr leaned forward, but Darei was already dead. The med drone had merely sealed the shoulder wound, but the piercer had went straight down into his abdomen. How the skinny tech had managed to even talk was beyond Jerr.

Tunva sheathed one of her blades in Darei's belt while Xade closed his eyes.

Jerr squeezed Darei's shoulder and hung his head.

"Yeah. You looked happy."

Chapter 15

The first signs of 'possession' came during the Xaju Blood Riots. When questioning the perpetrators, Sisters discovered many acted upon 'voices' they heard. No amount of coercion, even by Vestal standards, brought us closer to the truth. The old psychopomp scanners were used on the populace, but it would be years before Vestal House discovered the truth. These heretics were not possessed by invasive bactroids or spirts from a peasant's tale, but something else: mania driven by desperation.

Psychopomp Errata, Sector 350, Martial
Bride Oja Jun, Vestal House

Balyra studied the soldiers arrayed before her on *Prophetess*'s interrogation deck: all of them manacled to the floor, all of them glowering with the same face. Jerr's face.

"These are the last from Stavia's rebirth vats?"

"All that could be found before our departure, Confessor," the morga said.

Like Jerr, the soldiers were high-gravity grunts with a physical age of two human decades. Their range of expressions was a gallery of human angst.

"Activate the psychopomp scanner," Balyra said.

The psychopomp had been used by Vestal House for nearly seventy thousand years. Some ancient Vestals claimed it could detect emotion, lies, even subconscious anxieties. Commoners thought it magical, revealing the presence of 'demons'. In truth, it perceived mental activity, brainwaves. With *Prophetess* back in the Shroud, she needed to know if their reactions matched Jerr's, when she'd examined him on *Bhaellator.*

The soldiers squirmed and groaned as the scanner mapped neural pathways, axon resilience, and synapse reaction time. The process was painful, especially for those with lower or failing mental faculties. The more scattered a mind, the more work the scanner must do, and thus the more stress it placed on a biological brain. Once, Balyra had used it on a Theux, but the creature simply stared at her for hours until she'd given up.

Seconds passed. Then minutes. The soldiers screamed, frothed at the mouth. Still Balyra waited. She had to find out more before Revor got involved further. There remained a stolen Leviathan on the loose, a Hub World and its fleet had suffered significant damage, and Jerr still wasn't in custody—the man who could see the future.

She knew, somehow, that he'd seen those events unfold on *Bhaellator.* Perhaps right before they happened. His Rezal-trained mind exploited such data on the fly.

Balyra shut off the scanner since the soldiers weren't emitting the same readings. "Take these away and bring in the next group."

While another morga squad escorted in the next group of reborn—females from the Settled Zone, professional concubines—Balyra considered what she'd seen on *Bhaellator.* Jerr's rebirthed twin, Lieutenant Wanrys, had shot his own wife and children in a maddened attempt to save them. She wondered if it had disturbed Jerr. If witnessing his clone destroy something Jerr himself could never have gave him nightmares.

Vestal House had inured Balyra to such nocturnal, mental incubi. Most Sisters had to kill at least a dozen heretics or criminals before their apathy reached the proper set point. Balyra only had to kill six.

But Jerr's brain wasn't as old and trained as hers. She needed his mind to remain strong if he was to help her against Revor.

The concubines knelt in their manacles, calmer in their demeanor than the soldiers. These women were accustomed to pleasing others, not resisting and killing. Balyra activated the scanner. Though the women reacted with gasps and moans instead of the veins-bulging, strained glares the men had displayed, the test results were the same.

Balyra tapped a finger against her lip. Jerr's Theux had hacked into the reborn database, accessing the DNA templates. It could have been an attempt at theft, stealing the data for sale to Dominion enemies—but she doubted it. In fact, she doubted any subterfuge from Jerr. He was a soldier, not a spy. Everything about him would be direct.

As she studied the young, nubile bodies kneeling before her, Balyra beckoned the morga guards. "Vestal House will not punish you. You will join *Prophetess*'s crew until your service is deemed at an end. Take them to their new quarters."

The concubines were led out by the morga but she didn't watch them go. She paced the interrogation chamber a long while, the psychopomp scanner a silent companion. There were two more reborn groups to question, though she was skeptical they could provide an answer. Balyra swiped the wall nodus for more data.

What had caused Jerr's genetic anomaly? It had appeared in no other strata of humanity. Not a single reported case in the entire galaxy. There was something about the process, regrowing the same person, again and again, that enabled the mutation.

She still didn't understand how it gave Jerr a view of the future.

Using the nodus, Balyra cycled through Vestal House's network. Her Sisters had amassed one of the greatest libraries in the galaxy. One could spend ten thousand years perusing it and still not complete it. She summoned entries on the Kieta and Weavers. The only two species to access the Shroud before humanity stole Weaver technology.

A rope-like creature native to the Shroud, the Kieta could naturally traverse space-time due to its cellular structure. This structure was copied by the Weavers, a hive mind artificial intelligence gifted with engineering genius, to create the predecessors to the Leviathans. The Weavers' true name and origin was never discovered. When they learned to move ships and planetoids through the Shroud, they became the Kieta's rivals.

Both considered the Shroud theirs—for whoever controlled it, controlled all else.

Balyra scanned through old Armada documents, many of them forbidden even for her eyes. Vestal House never discriminated when it came to acquiring information.

Entries on Weaver extermination, Kieta surrenders to Armada fleets, and captured gravity generators netted her nothing. Not a single clue as to how a human could foresee the future after exposure to the Shroud. Jerr's DNA contained no hybrid Kieta or Weaver strands, which would have been a genetic impossibility, even for imperial eugenics.

"Rebirthing him. Again and again." After sifting data for an hour, Balyra found Jerr's earliest genetic template. Its age surprised even her.

A notification alarm glowed on the wall. Balyra shut off the nodus and exited the chamber. The Matriarch wished to speak with her again, but Balyra took her time. She needed a stroll to sort her thoughts.

Like other Leviathans, *Prophetess* housed entire cities in its berths. In this case, it was the totality of Vestal House and its ancient legacy. Wide windows gave a view of the gardens far below, where titanic cathedrals and stone rings had been painstakingly removed from their worlds of origin and relocated aboard. Some of those worlds were gone now, through warfare, environmental disasters, and, in two cases, supernovas. A million or so faithful resided as caretakers, willfully ignorant of events in galactic society. Monks and nuns of the stars, they tended vineyards and recited Vestal scripture like their counterparts in the pre-industrial past.

Balyra found herself in her art chamber, where she kept statues from a thousand worlds and cultures. She walked among the collected grandeur, smiling sadly.

Humanity had been but a dream then, and the Vestals mere virgins with oil lamps, claiming to carry the very stars therein. Now their greatest and last vessel carried the whole of the order; a lamp that would not be extinguished.

A lamp Balyra found guttering in the solar winds of her heart.

She passed an idealized statue of herself, attired in the ancient Vestal robes. Another sculpture stood beside it. Beautiful. Hopeful. The source of her inspiration.

"I miss you." Balyra cupped the cold face, then squeezed her eyes shut.

If Jerr learned more from the Weavers, all of it might end. What little remained to her would come to an end. The fire within her would finally be extinguished. Unlike Jerr, she would not be reborn again and again.

She blinked, activated her wrist nodus. Swiped through the DNA data.

There it was. Right in front of her the whole time.

Balyra slid down the rail, slumped to her knees, and shook her head.

"By the Flame. His Theux must have known all along."

The bunk was cold against Jerr's body as the med drone finished pasting the dermaflesh to his left side. With the crewmember berth detached over Stavia, they now had to use Bridge Deck's med bays as cabins. The chill air aggravated his new skin.

The pseudo-organic material 'breathed' like human flesh, sporting tissue walls and blood vessels, but he wasn't accustomed to its sensory mapping. Right now, the slightest touch could make him grunt in pain.

Xade's cool gaze held him in place more than the restraints. She was finishing his routine blood lab, ensuring Garrand hadn't infected the ship with poisonous bactroids.

"I know, you wanted me to use anesthetic," Jerr said. "I've already heard the voices again, so I'm not interested in having them invade my mind while I'm out of it."

"Ridiculous." Xade squirted salve on his dermaflesh while he studied her own perfect blue skin. He assumed a Theux felt much more than a human via dermaflesh, but it remained alien to him.

But no more alien than watching another version of himself gun down a wife and two daughters. Or lying to an old friend about his future, only to watch him die afterward. The chill in his heart was far colder than the bunk.

Even if he had some alcohol, he doubted he'd even want it.

"You set coordinates for Gnebus, right? The ones I told you?"

She gently spread the salve on his new skin. "Obvious."

He caught himself staring at the way she swayed now. The subtle roll of her hips.

"I told you, you don't have to do these things for me." He tried to smile.

"Medicamentous." Her nodus displayed her wide range of medical skills.

"Any excuse," he muttered, then realized she was glaring at him. "Joking."

Xade put away the salve and sat beside him. Her body language was even more feminine than usual: the way she held her legs together, resting both hands in her lap.

Jerr chuckled despite himself. "Where did you learn that?"

Xade raised her palm nodus. It showed an image of Wanrys's wife.

"Turn it off." Jerr looked away.

"Contemptuous?" Her tone was apprehensive.

"Turn the damn thing off."

Xade deactivated the nodus and walked to the door.

"Wait." Jerr groaned as he rubbed the dermaflesh the wrong way on the bunk.

Xade turned, her expression sullen and hurt.

"She was…" He closed his eyes, then faced her. "She was Wanrys's wife. His mate. Not mine. She wasn't… it's not like we had the same taste in women. Yes, she was pretty. But I want you to be… just be you, okay?"

Her face softened.

"Please, try to understand. It makes me uneasy, for you to act like someone who is gone. Someone who was never my partner, my companion. Know what I mean?"

Xade nodded, then assumed a slightly different stance. Hand on outthrust hip, shoulders pushed back, head cocked. She'd made herself look like a starport prostitute.

"Not quite that, no." Jerr did look her over, though. She was showing more dermaflesh than usual.

Her eyes crinkled with thought, then Xade went stiff and domineering, her face sterner than a block of solid wood.

"Not Tunva. Please."

Xade grinned. "Grievous."

"She can be." Jerr grinned back.

The lab interface beeped, signaling the test's completion. A knotted double helix rotated on the nodus: his DNA. Xade assumed a tentative stance.

"What is it?"

Wanrys's DNA booted up on the nodus beside Jerr's.

"Why?" He shook his head. "Let the man have some peace. I owe him that."

Xade finished a computation on the nodus, then faced him.

There was a discrepancy between the blood samples. Which was impossible, since a reborn was supposed to be a perfect copy of the previous person.

"So Wanrys didn't have my mutation, either."

Shaking her head, Xade loaded more data. Jerr leaned forward, heart beating faster. New charts showed his DNA helix, altering. New genes. New genetic code.

"How?" Jerr was shaking.

Xade presented statistical impressions of what the new genetic coding would most likely produce in the next generation. Ten generations. And then, in a hundred generations. The system extrapolated it to a thousand generations.

"That's enough." He was numb all over.

Xade hurried to him, but the room blurred. Bright colors stung his eyes. The bunk, the lab table, the walls, all morphed into a different chamber. A different ship.

A woman with metalloid flesh stands on a causeway tens of miles long. Towering marble statues of Vestals line its edges. Millions of lamps illuminate the distant hull.

Balyra kneels before her. "Matriarch."

"It is true?" the woman asks. "His DNA has altered with each rebirth?"

Jerr rocked back and forth on the bunk, trying to catch his breath.

Balyra nods. "Jerr Manivo's DNA mutated over time. His genes have evolved to take advantage of—"

"Of what?" the Matriarch asks. "What you are inferring is impossible."

"Are Jerr's voices impossible?" Balyra stands, all pretense to subservience gone.

"Xade?" He reached for her, though all he saw was a conversation yet to happen.

"Why hasn't this befallen others who have journeyed in the Shroud?" The Matriarch regards Balyra with snide arrogance. "We have traveled it for millennia."

Balyra glares. "Such a mutation might come along in a million generations. But Jerr's DNA has been accelerated through the rebirth process. He is sensitive to gravitational variations in space-time. He is seeing the future through space-time itself."

Jerr shivered with the eager fear of one who has learned the day of their death.

"This is why Jerr Manivo has been reborn so many times as a soldier, on so many different worlds," Balyra says. "He senses what his opponent will do, right before they do. Over time, this advantage has grown. Deepened. Now, when he is exposed to the Shroud, he sees a future that has already happened."

"Already happened?" The Matriarch shrinks back.

"Then why can't I see my own fate?" Jerr shouted.

Colors and shapes normalized as his eyelids fluttered. The vision ended.

"Disastrous," Xade whispered.

"Do I even have free will anymore?" He touched her face. "Do I have anything?"

Xade lay on the bunk beside him. There was a longing in her eyes, and something else. He was human, he could identify it. She'd been around his species long enough to know how to signal such an inclination. Damn him for even wanting it.

"I'm still married. I have a son."

"Tenuous." She clasped his hands.

"Their names are..." Emotions warred in his heart, even as he leaned toward her.

She rubbed his chest, soft fingers gliding over his dark skin like waves over an ebony ocean. There was nothing coy in her eyes. Only genuine affection.

He wondered if his previous rebirths had loved her.

"Xade?" He cradles her close as a piercer round melts the decking near his right boot. "Xade, we're going to make it. They're here. I saw them..."

She touches his face. "Cheval—"

Jerr sat up and winced. Xade sat up with him, massaging his tingling dermaflesh.

"We can't," he said. "I'm something they created. I'm not even—"

"Blusterous," she said.

"Can't you see? I'm the most wanted man in the galaxy. All I see is death. I won't put you through that."

Xade shook her head. He sighed and started to speak, but she shook her head even more forcefully. She held his face in her hands and moved her lips to his.

Jerr pulled back. "No. I have a wife."

Brows lowered, she shook her head. "Spurious."

"Damn it, it's true!" He was shaking. "No matter how I feel about you."

They stared at one another. He stopped shaking. Anger left her face.

Jerr pulled Xade into his arms and kissed her.

Together they lowered to the bunk, speaking a silent language understood by all.

All of her exoskeleton retreated within her body. Revealing herself, right there for him to touch, trusting him. Other than his wife, Jerr had no memory of previous lovers. How many times he'd fallen in love across the light years, or how many had suffered as he'd died in battle, only to be reborn somewhere else. It was a terrible existence.

Xade in his arms, willingly offering herself, was the closest to living he'd felt in many lifetimes. To feel life, loosing overflowing emotions in his heart, confirmed that hope remained for them all. The pent-up feelings she unleashed left Jerr breathless. Like she'd repressed her love for centuries. The gamut of primal, pleasurable noises she uttered belied her limited speech. They more than excited Jerr's passions; they confirmed his capacity to feel. He wasn't a soldier drone. He was a complete human being.

In those hot, eager moments she was no longer a biomechanical, mimicking his species. No longer a walking think tank. No more a scapegoat for his own shortcomings.

She became joy in his arms. In his heart.

"When he is exposed to the Shroud, he sees a future that has already happened."

She lay beside him afterward, an azure virago refusing to let him travel the darkness alone. Smiling, caressing his chin as he relaxed, physiologically and psychologically satisfied by the simplest yet most intimate act.

"Weave a new thread. Avenge us."

The voice woke Jerr from his pleasant rest. He was alone on the bunk, still naked. Still smelling of sex and Xade's odd spearmint scent. He almost called for her, but she couldn't be far. Since Theux didn't sleep, he didn't blame her for not staying with him.

"Avenge us, or you will join us."

Jerr gripped the bunk's edge until his knuckles popped.

"Why?" he whispered. No answer came.

He started to rise as she came back in. Still nude.

"Dangerous." She eased him back down, which didn't take much effort. Smiling, he pulled her on top of him. They kissed for a time. He could almost forget the voice's warning, wrapped in Xade's embrace. Almost.

"If we run into more trouble, I won't be able to fight like this," Jerr said.

Grinning, she squeezed her bicep into a nice, hard muscle shape.

"You're pretty damn strong. But it won't be enough."

Her grin faded.

"I need one of those marines' Starjumpers. The armor will compensate for my wounds for a little while. Besides, if we're going to such a secret location, it'll be well-defended. Balyra will certainly be trailing us."

Xade finally nodded, but her hands gripped his.

"I wish this could last, too." Jerr touched her cheek. "But I can't stand by and let them use me. All of those like me. Not anymore."

Chapter 16

Our Armada became such a fixation in the minds of collective humanity that it defined an entire era. It formed a demarcation line, between a time when we ruled a few solar systems, to the empire's millions of systems. No other military force ever achieved that, for by name alone, it won victories, kept the peace, and struck fear into enemies.

Narrative of the Armada, Chapter 30

Jerr felt numb while Xade helped him into the Starjumper. He missed Darei already, who knew how to snug the joints and set the equilibrium just right for Jerr's body mass and control presets. He had to show Xade these things, though she needed to be told just once. She attached everything with care as if it were a sacred ritual. In a way, it was. They were honoring Darei with something he'd taken pride in, something that had saved Jerr's life—at least this life—countless times.

After she snapped a shoulder plate into place, Xade lay a hand on Jerr's chest.

"Odious."

"I know," Jerr said. "I would've liked to seen him reunited with his brother. But we did all we could do. Darei would understand."

"They hid the secret amidst circles of orange and red. The secret of our defeat."

Xade clasped his hand tight, but Jerr didn't smile. Tunva was right about the cost.

Bhaellator had just exited the Shroud in the Gnebus system, where Darei's brother resided. Beforehand, Jerr, Xade, and Tunva had laid their friend in a funerary capsule and loaded it into the shuttle. Now, they were all tense.

"Avenge us."

Jerr wondered what the man would think upon opening the capsule. Finding not only a body, but Darei's personal data. Containing images and video of the brothers, together throughout their lives, before going their separate ways. Plus Darei's DNA, an unmistakable declaration of who, and what, the dead tech was to his reborn sibling.

"Darei might get Jerr inside the research compound, but not back out." Tunva wore another Starjumper salvaged from Garrand's dead marines. Being unaccustomed to the suit's human ergonomics setup, her movements were a little clumsy.

Xade showed their route on her nodus. "Precarious."

The plan was to escort Darei's body to his brother, using it to get inside the compound on the planet below. Jerr hoped they could find the secrets the voices told him about, but Tunva was right. They had no escape plan should they fall under suspicion.

"If you have any better ideas, I'm listening." Jerr stood with Tunva behind the cockpit as Xade slid into the pilot station. The shuttle departed the hangar.

"Jerr should have cleaned these suits earlier." Tunva's nose twitched.

He smirked. "Thought you might enjoy their marine-like ambiance."

"They stink," Tunva said. "Xade, you have not trained Jerr to be better than this?"

"Scandalous." Xade grinned.

"Watch it." Smiling, Jerr touched Xade's shoulder.

Blues and reds reflected in Tunva's vertical irises as her faceplate HUD came online. "Jerr Manivo and Xade make a good match. Tunva approves."

A brief moment of silence followed. Jerr shared a look with Xade.

"Delicious." Xade's tone was nonchalant, innocent.

Tunva gave Jerr a knowing look.

"Yeah, well…thanks." Jerr cleared his throat. Tunva chuckled.

True to Jerr's visions, Gnebus was a small, rust-colored moon orbiting a dull green gas giant. It circled between the planet's inner red ring and a wider, brighter, orange ring. The effect flooded the cockpit in vermilion and tangerine hues. For a moment, Jerr stared in wonder. His Urian eyesight detected the planet's formless radiation glow, which bolstered the rings' reddish effulgence.

"Jerr looks peaceful," Tunva said. "What does Jerr see?"

He paused before answering. "I've viewed images of what others with your eyes—humans, Repta, Idreun—can see. To you, space is mostly darkness. Cold. But to me, it's so alive. Reds, purples, and blues, surrounding every planet, nebula, supernova, or star cluster. It's why I became a reborn, so I could see it all. For me, space is warm."

"Jerr has a poet's heart," Tunva said.

"Nope. Just the eyes." He smiled.

The arrival of a Leviathan startled Gnebus's flight control operators, but Xade knew the correct passcodes and protocols. Their shuttle was cleared to land. Jerr was surprised that only a small gunboat fleet protected the moon. But then, anything traveling the Shroud would leave a space-time ripple in its wake, making it traceable—thus giving away the moon's location. Meaning they didn't have much time.

Volcanoes and geysers covered Gnebus's young, geologically active surface. The low gravity and even lighter atmosphere, however, meant that all expulsions were jetted out into space. Magma ejecta glittered as it cooled right above the thermosphere.

Xade flew the shuttle past several such obstructions toward a collection of tower-like structures. Each was thousands of feet in height. Getting closer, Jerr realized they were starships. He surmised that if the eruptions became too much, the facility could simply launch into orbit. Regardless, it had to be expensive, maintaining even a one-pad starport here—let alone a secret research base. Which only worried him more.

"It is hidden here. Take it. Reveal us. Avenge us. We cannot abide it any longer."

After they landed on a pad at least two hundred stories from the surface, Jerr led the others outside with the funerary capsule. It hovered between them. He and Tunva activated their suit life-support systems, but Xade merely remorphed her exoskeleton to cover everything but her head. No one came out to greet them. The airlock opened.

"Friendly," Jerr said. "What if this is a trap?"

"Jerr has not seen what will happen?" Tunva scanned the area.

"It doesn't work like that."

Past the airlock was an elevator. It took them up a few more levels then opened to a quiet lobby with wide windows overlooking the hellish landscape. A few security robos floated by a counter where a morga sat at a desk, watching with unblinking eyes.

A skinny young man leaned on the lobby counter in evergreen R&D fatigues. His blond hair was short and his stance oozed less attitude, but the semblance to Darei was uncanny. He turned and gave them a bored look. "You the reason I was pulled off duty?"

"We brought your brother," Jerr said. "Darei Inao, technical specialist, Company K, Consular Brigade, *Bhaellator.*"

"I'm Vyrio Jan," the young man said. "Don't have any brothers."

"You do now." Jerr brought the capsule about and activated its data screen.

Vyrio read it and glared at them. "This some kind of prank?"

"No." Jerr turned on the capsule's realizer. While normally used to display videos and images of the deceased during a funeral, Xade had loaded all of Darei's personal data into the feed. His Con-Union homeworld, the status of his reborn sibling.

Vyrio turned away and stared at the lobby elevator.

"Take it and weave a new thread…"

"What rebirth are you on?" Jerr asked while Tunva kept an eye on the robos.

Seconds passed before Vyrio answered. "Fourth. My work is pretty dangerous."

"I'm on my twenty-fourth…I think." Jerr stood beside him. "Not easy, is it?"

"What the hell are you talking about?" Vyrio didn't look at him.

"Not remembering your parents," Jerr said. "Who your friends were, before."

Vyrio's jaw quivered. "Comes with the job. Why do you care? Just leave."

"Darei was my friend," Jerr said. "Seeing you again was his dying wish."

"You didn't make it come true, though, did you?" Vyrio neared the elevator.

"Don't you even want to know what he died for?" Jerr scowled.

Vyrio kept walking.

Though Xade and Tunva gave him uneasy looks, Jerr clanked after the young tech. "Darei hated the Reborn Initiative. Hated people like me, because I reminded him of how the Dominion took you away from him all those years ago. He says he even met one of your previous rebirths once—but you didn't recognize him."

Vyrio wheeled about. "How could I have? It wasn't my fault!"

"It wasn't his, either," Jerr said.

The capsule's realizer, still playing, showed an old home video of Darei and Vyrio in their teenage years, building a Molexi engine coil from scrap. The illusion was so complete that Jerr smelled burnt metal as Darei welded parts together. Both brothers laughed at some joke, working in a rapport only years together could produce.

The realizer shut off. Vyrio's sorrow felt like another presence in the room.

"Help us," Jerr whispered.

"What do you want from me?" Vyrio asked.

"Give us access to your work. The Weaver and Kieta research."

Vyrio gaped at them, shaking his head. "The Dominion would kill us all."

Tunva stepped forward. "That is what Darei died for. Darei knew this."

"But why?" Vyrio grimaced. "This is the way it's always been."

Jerr pointed at the capsule. "If you're researching the Weavers, then you know what happened to them. To everyone else who's ever resisted the Dominion. Reborn like you and I, we're enabling that. We're perpetuating it. Darei wanted to change that."

"I'm not my brother," Vyrio said.

"If Vyrio admits that kinship," Tunva said, "then Vyrio admits this is wrong."

"There's nothing I can do," Vyrio said. "I'm not going to end up like Darei."

"Give us access to your work," Jerr said. "The rest is up to us."

Vyrio ran a hand over the funeral capsule, then made a fist. "I can get you in, but that's it. I'm staying up here to see that my brother receives some dignity. What you do down there, how you get out—none of that's my problem."

"Gracious," Xade said.

Vyrio sent data from his wrist nodus to Xade's. "I never want to see you again."

"You have my word." Jerr started following the others to the elevator, then turned. "For what it's worth…I'm sorry. Darei was the best friend I ever had."

Vyrio turned on the realizer, watching videos of his dead brother again. "Judging from all this…looks like we had that in common."

Jerr hurried into the elevator and didn't look back.

Their descent seemed to take forever. The elevator lacked windows but was large enough to hold a platoon of soldiers. It gave no indication of movement. Only the declining numbers on the terminal showed they weren't at a standstill. The effect reminded Jerr of the Shroud's eternal lethargy.

"Tunva is proud of Jerr."

"Fabulous." Xade patted his armored shoulder.

"I just hope Vyrio finds some peace," Jerr said.

An octahedron rests on a pedestal within a laboratory. It is chipped, blackened.

He staggered against the elevator wall. The mental image burned into his consciousness, refusing to be dispelled by Rezal or random thoughts.

"Tell us who you are. Will you create new threads?"

"I…"

"Or will you destroy them?"

Tunva and Xade held him up, worry in their eyes.

"Tell us who you are."

"I'm here to help," Jerr said. "I want to—"

Human soldiers gun down alien troops that resemble floating, inverted triangles, with tentacles grasping weapons. The humans are aided by swirling tendrils of silver.

"See us. Reveal us."

The same vision he saw during Balyra's interrogation now became clearer, more complete. This time, Jerr felt the anguish of death. Their fear as the silvery Kieta killed them by ripping them from the continuum of space-time. The fall of the Weavers.

Vestal soldiers, their metalloid wings the color of blood, stab at the Weavers with gleaming blue shards, causing the victims to vanish. Their screams echo across epochs. Echo in the Shroud until they combine with the shrieks of other species wiped out by the Dominion: the original Repta, before they were enslaved and altered. The Squidrans, the Eulko. Others whose names are now gone, erased by Revor and his confidants.

The elevator doors opened, intruding on Jerr's vision.

"Is Jerr Manivo ready?" Tunva asked.

Xade's nodus showed his pulse, blood pressure, cortisol levels—all elevated.

"More than ever." He nodded to them, then exited the lift on his own.

Vyrio's passcode had sent them to Research Level 58, as indicated by a large screen just outside the elevator. It displayed who was present for duty, which was a small number of people. Sentry robos patrolled the area, floating above a series of connected, circular platforms. These overlooked the structure's colossal berths where reactors eked geothermal power from Gnebus's volcanoes.

"What could demand this massive output of energy?" Tunva asked.

"Let's find out." Jerr led them across a few railed walkways, which separated them from a drop thousands of feet deep. He and Tunva kept their helmets on since the air was of poor quality. Other scientists wore masks, paying them little heed.

Unlike the sentry robo who stopped them.

The reactors' afterglow cast a red gleam over the robo's spherical form. Its voice was sexless, emotionless. "Present credentials."

Jerr glanced at Xade, recalling their practiced spiel. "We're escorting *Bhaellator*'s resident Theux, Officer Xade, to gather data on combating Veja Qor rebels who might have access to Kieta technology."

"Appointment not in database," the robo said.

"It's in Commander Garrand's." Jerr waited as Xade showed the falsified information on her palm nodus. It was risky, but he hoped, like on Stavia, that word of *Bhaellator*'s capture hadn't reached Gnebus yet. The Dominion still wanted to keep him and the hijacking a secret. Now he might finally discover why.

"Credentials verified." The robo floated away.

"Tenuous," Xade said.

"I know, they might revoke access at any time." Jerr looked around. "This way."

They passed numerous circular laboratories where scientists examined pieces of ancient Weaver hulls, dissected Avae, outlawed bioterminators, and other things long thought destroyed or lost. There was even a group studying Theux substrate, the source Xade's race was birthed from. But the sample appeared dead, now a dried cube that had been amorphous once. Xade said nothing, but her gaze could have melted titanium.

"Reveal us."

Jerr sighted a lab isolated from the rest. More reactors were linked to it than any other circle. Inside, an azure-hued octahedron, five inches across, rested all by itself on a pedestal bordered by transparent walls. It was chipped, blackened.

"Heinous," Xade said.

"You've seen this before?" He entered the lab with caution.

Xade nodded, her stare haunted with grief.

"The Kieta refused to share. They untangled the strands and left us here."

Jerr leaned over the pedestal for a closer look, then realized a morga waited nearby. Its thin, androgynous form looked more like a lab instrument than a body.

"That is the only etherspace box that survived the Armada Era," it said.

Xade covered her throat, as if someone had just threatened to cut it.

The morga paced around them, its chrome face beaming. "I have not seen a Theux visitor to our moon since the 71st Millennium. A pleasure. I am Jhe 97."

"Larcenous." Xade edged away from Jhe 97.

"The Dominion would never steal from the Kieta, the makers of this artifact." Jhe 97 whirred over to Tunva, its smile never waning. "Now, this is a lovely specimen."

"Tunva is—"

"Grateful," Jerr said as he pushed Tunva's armored fist down. "Why do you say nothing would be stolen from the Kieta?"

"You know nothing of Kieta history?" Jhe 97's tone bore no mockery.

"No." Jerr took a deep breath. "Please, tell me."

"The Kieta are the only species known to be native to the Shroud," Jhe 97 said. "They occupy space-time here, as well as within that invisible domain. Their term for our universe is 'etherspace'."

"Tunva is confused." She pointed at the object on the pedestal. "That is no box."

"Their species regards the universe as a box," Jhe 97 said. "Thus, all of their technology is given the same term. A narrative box, for example, records and stores a Kieta's experiences."

"Which can only be accessed while in the Shroud?" Jerr asked.

Jhe 97 viewed him with fresh esteem. "Yes. How did you know?"

"Lucky guess," Jerr said.

"It is because the Shroud is limitless to them," Jhe 97 said, "while everything else, even our universe, has boundaries. Like a box. You are quite clever for a reborn soldier."

Jerr forced a smile. "And the etherspace box? What's it do?"

Rubbing metalloid hands together, Jhe 97 paced faster. "Kieta once used the shards that make up an etherspace box to punish the criminals among their species. It rips them apart at the subatomic level before they can reshape themselves in space-time."

"Murderous," Xade murmured.

Vestal soldiers stab at the Weavers with gleaming blue shards…

"What if someone from our universe were to use one?" Jerr asked.

Jhe 97 stopped pacing. "Why, that is preposterous."

"You mean you don't know?" Jerr asked.

The morga studied Jerr for an uncomfortable moment. Its tone became less jovial. "It could sever one's connection to their current relationship with space-time."

"So that person would be dead?" Jerr asked.

"That, and removed from this dimension," Jhe 97 said.

"What if I struck a Kieta with it?" Jerr backed Jhe 97 against the pedestal.

"Not only would it destroy the Kieta—which is impossible with all other known armaments—but if used against non-Shroud natives, such as you or I, it also traps that being into the Shroud. Exiled from our universe and unable to return."

"What if the box were destroyed?" Jerr asked.

"Detonation, as in a bomb?" Jhe 97 asked. "Why, it would most likely produce the same effect, but over a much larger area."

"Like trapping a Leviathan in the Shroud?" Jerr asked in a low voice.

Jhe 97 flinched. "Yes. Whatever would you want to do something like that?"

Staring at the box, Jerr suppressed a shiver. Revor had used such weapons not only to kill the Weavers, but to hide evidence of their defeat. As if they'd never existed.

But why? Wasn't death enough for the Weavers?

"Well, you know," Jerr said. "Reborn soldiers think that way."

"How does it work?" Tunva asked.

"As I said, each 'box' is a collection of shards," Jhe 97 said. "I suppose one could stab an enemy with it, but it could also be fitted on a high energy weapon, like a diffusion gun. The beam is fired through the shards, which achieves the desired result."

"Why would Kieta give humans something that could destroy them?" Jerr asked.

"The Kieta are Dominion allies," Jhe 97 said. "They need never worry about this weapon being used on them, after helping the Armada eliminate the treacherous Weavers. Their alliance is infallible." Jhe 97 nodded in self-satisfaction.

Turning her back to the morga, Xade showed Jerr her nodus. It calculated the chances of such an alliance being that strong: 8%.

"The Kieta were greedy, refusing to share the Shroud with the Weavers. They betrayed us, and now are the slaves of our murderers. Such is the reward of traitors."

If he could break that alliance, he and his friends might have a chance.

Jerr reached for the etherspace box. "May I?"

The octahedron blurred and melted in his sight. While he still moved, the others were frozen in the moment. The box's eight surfaces slid aside one by one until only a glowing blue core remained. Jerr tensed.

No voices. No visions. Just the vague idea of colors and shapes. Jerr morphs through them, from darkness to even greater darkness. Shifting sideways down. Sliding.

It took Jerr a few moments to realize he was seeing a Kieta's experiences.

The Shroud is his world. His true home. Invaders keep sliding through it, keep trying to shape it, control it. One race abuses it. Traversing the galaxy in one voyage.

The Weavers.

"To destroy us, the Kieta aided the murderers. They did not want to share. We did not come to take. But they gave the murderers the means to untangle our threads. The Kieta were fooled, for the murderers took our ships and enslaved the Kieta. Sensing them whenever they traveled the Shroud, killing them until the Kieta surrendered."

Third Echelon glows beneath him, a gem held captive by two greedy, dying stars.

"Careful, you might damage it!" Jhe 97 cried.

The morga's voice made Jerr open his eyes. He lay against the pedestal's base, out of breath. The etherspace box remained in place.

Xade knelt beside him, scanning his vitals on her nodus. "Overzealous."

"They are Revor's slaves," Jerr breathed. "Not his allies."

"I am checking your credentials," Jhe 97 said in a frigid tone. "This is a research laboratory, not a—"

Tunva grabbed Jhe 97 by the neck. "Tunva and her friends are leaving."

With Xade's help, Jerr stood. He scanned the immediate area for robos. "You're our credentials now, Jhe. We'd like it if you could escort us back to our shuttle."

"This is absurd!" Jhe 97's chrome smile didn't wane. "I will summon security!"

"Not unless you want a one-way trip to those reactors below," Jerr said. "No? Then let's go. Tunva, don't let him go. Xade…bring the etherspace box."

She took the box and shot him a look. Though he'd merely reached for it, Jerr had felt as if he were in the Shroud. Which made him afraid to touch or carry it, at least with so many hostiles around.

"I am not a 'him'," Jhe 97 said as Tunva led it by the arm. "I am sexless. Which is the kind of soldier the Dominion should grow, not you breeders. Your passions make you emotional to the point of stupidity."

As they entered the lift, Jerr clasped Xade's hand. "Nothing stupid about this."

She smiled.

"A Theux, displaying affection?" Jhe 97 shuddered despite Tunva's grip. "What will plague the Dominion next? Perhaps when you are caught, they will place you down here, to be studied with all the other oddities."

While the elevator sped them back up to their shuttle, Xade's expression became neutral again. Jhe 97's comment bothered Jerr, too. He knew he cared about her, had no doubts about her own feelings … but was there a future for them, together? She was a Theux. She would outlive him by epochs. They'd never have children.

Once the lift stopped, Jerr hurried into the same lobby from before. Vyrio and the funeral capsule were gone. Regardless, Jerr kept his weapons ready. Their shuttle was still waiting for them on the pad outside.

"You cannot escape," Jhe 97 said. "One word from me, and you will have—"

Tunva jerked the morga through the airlock and dangled it over the pad's edge.

"—a pleasant journey," Jhe 97 said. Tunva dumped it back onto the pad.

As Jerr and Xade hurried onboard, Tunva paused. "Should Tunva shoot Jhe 98?"

"Jhe 97," Jerr said. "And no."

The shuttle engine thrummed to life. Xade set a return flight-path to *Bhaellator*.

"You will destroy yourselves with that etherspace box," Jhe 97 said. "I regret I will not be there to see it."

"C'mon, let's go," Jerr called out the hatch.

Tunva fired a piercer round, liquefying Jhe 97's head. The morga wobbled, then plummeted off the landing pad.

"What the hell?" Jerr cried.

"Now it will be Jhe 98." Tunva brushed past him and boarded the shuttle.

During the trip back, Jerr shook his head. "You shot him."

"Jhe 97 declared that Jhe 97 was an 'it'." Tunva removed her helmet and flicked her tongue. "Maybe Jhe 98 will be different?"

"Dubious," Xade said.

Jerr looked from one to the other. "You two are something else."

Xade smirked. Tunva grinned.

"Well…it did have that stupid smile, even at the end," Jerr said.

Chapter 17

Revor's best officers and soldiers were the first beneficiaries of the Reborn Initiative. It wasn't merely their tactical and martial prowess he wanted recreated. Their propensity to follow orders, regardless of outcome—self-destruction, loss of friends, genocide—was absolute. Eugenicists finally learned that humans possessed a greater submission to authority than other sapien species. This was exploited in all future reborn.

Narrative of the Armada, Chapter 14

"Priority message from Curator Revor," the morga said.

Balyra turned from the nodus, which displayed a galactic map. While tracking *Bhaellator*'s movements, she'd mulled whether or not the Matriarch should know about Jerr's mutation. Her Vestal superior wouldn't see the threat—but Revor obviously did.

After the other Sisters left the conference room, Balyra nodded. "Play it."

The wall realizer came on. The next instant, Revor stood beside her. He wasn't wearing his cape. His thick chest rose and fell with frustrated breaths.

"Jerr Manivo visited Gnebus." Revor's voice was ice-calm.

Balyra flicked her eyes to the map. "*Prophetess* is already inbound to intercept—"

"The etherspace box was taken," Revor said.

She gazed back at him, not letting her joy show. "That is unfortunate."

"Unfortunate?" Revor paced around her. "That is all you can say?"

"He only has the one—"

"He only needs one!" he shouted in her face.

She said nothing, allowing Revor to collect himself.

"Veja Qor has become brave," he said in a quieter tone. "Word has gotten out that a Leviathan was stolen by the rebels. There are uprisings all across the Elium Rim. Uprisings that must be contained by reborn soldiers. Can I trust those soldiers now?"

"Jerr alone has the mutation that has gifted him precognition," Balyra said. "Your soldiers are still ignorant, still loyal. Still eager to be used."

"I cannot risk that now." Revor stared at the galactic map. "If there is even the slimmest chance that another like him could be grown, then there is only one choice."

Balyra's surprise was not feigned. "You cannot be serious."

"If he is somehow in contact with the Weavers, if he can see what happens before we do—then what else will he learn? What else will they tell him?"

"Do you fear the dead, then?" She didn't flinch as he whirled on her.

"You know better than most what had to be done to defeat the Weavers. If they are seeking revenge through Jerr, then he will be merciless. So must we."

"Very well," Balyra said. "How may Vestal House be of service?"

"Tell your Matriarch to rendezvous with me at Third Echelon," Revor said. "It will begin there."

"Destroying a facility of that size will generate sympathy for Veja Qor," she said.

"Good," he said. "Let us hope they make an appearance."

"And if Jerr shows up?"

"Destroy him." Revor vanished as the message ended.

A humorless smile spread over Balyra's face. Yes, she knew better than most what he had made her do that day. When the moment came, she would remind him.

❧ ❧ ❧

Jerr nibbled Xade's ear lobe as she quivered from an intense orgasm. Stimulating her like this was beyond addictive. Spooned together, he ceased thrusting, his own passion spent. She gently slid him out of her and rolled over on her side to face him.

He took her hand. Kissed every finger. "So this what you meant by 'amorous'."

Legs rubbing together, she watched with delightful wonder. "Luscious."

"You haven't seen anything yet—"

The bunk collapsed, spilling them onto the med room floor. Xade landed atop him. The side table turned over, scattering tools. The shock on her face made him laugh.

"Guess it really was meant for one patient."

She grinned, then kissed him.

Third Echelon glows beneath him, a gem held captive by two greedy, dying stars.

"Mmm?" Jerr drew her close, not wanting to see.

A Leviathan orbits the planet. Bombarding a rebirth facility.

"No," he muttered. Xade frowned, then kissed him harder.

Running down causeways as buildings topple over. A Leviathan blots out the twin suns overhead.

"No, wait—"

Bright rounds slip through armor and flesh like magical light beams. The dead are slumped over in heaps. Jerr keeps running. He sees in his mind the man about to shoot him. Ducking, Jerr shoots him first.

Jerr cried out and struggled, but Xade held him until he calmed down.

"Portentous?" The fear in her voice stung him.

"I'm sorry." He sat up, pressed her against him. "I'm so sorry."

Moments passed as they sat naked on the floor, holding each other.

Xade slowly pried herself free, eyes searching his face. "Portentous?"

After taking a deep breath, he nodded. "Yeah, it was another vision. They feel more and more real. This time I saw a Leviathan. It was firing on a Hub World."

She opened her palm, displaying her nodus. "Treasonous."

"I know what I saw." As she scowled at him, Jerr blinked. "Oh. You meant them, whoever it will be. I've been catching glimpses of some place called Third Echelon..."

The nodus sphere showed their galaxy, then zoomed in to a binary system between the Settled Zone and the Affiliate Worlds.

"Why would the Dominion do that?"

Xade studied him for a long moment, then swiped her nodus.

The sphere showed what was produced on Third Echelon. Or rather, who.

"Goddamn them," Jerr said. "Are they that desperate? Killing my reborn?"

"Egregious."

"To hell with that, then." Jerr rose, lifted her up, and kissed her cheek.

"Duteous?" Her exoskeleton morphed back out of her flesh.

"Yes." Jerr reached for his fatigues. "But not for the empire. For Veja Qor."

"Jerr Manivo wants to save his twins?" Tunva completed her blade kata, spinning herself in a tight arc, sword outstretched. "What finally changed Jerr's mind?"

Jerr paced back and forth in the storeroom where Tunva had made her quarters. "I don't want to just save them. I want to recruit them."

The scales on the back of Tunva's neck bristled. "Does Jerr remember Wanrys?"

"He cracked," Jerr said. "That doesn't mean the others will."

"Credulous." Xade handed over a water bottle and Tunva misted herself.

"If only a fraction joined us it would be worth it," Jerr said. "Besides, a Leviathan killing Dominion citizens—"

"They are reborn, Jerr Manivo." Tunva began another kata.

"They're still citizens." Jerr caught her arm and weathered her glare. "This will give Veja Qor some support. People will see the Dominion for the lying murderer it is."

Tunva sheathed her blade. "Veja Qor does not have Leviathans. They will have few ships in that system and no way to bring in more."

"Then we'll hit them quick and get out," Jerr said.

Balyra's eyes widened. "No. That would mean—"

Jerr nodded. "I know what it means."

He was gambling on what he was seeing—even though he'd not always gotten the predictions right. Darei's death, for instance. Or Wanrys's. But the vision had felt all too real. And now, a future conversation with Balyra, of all people.

"Avenge us… or join us."

It wasn't an ultimatum or threat. Jerr knew there was no turning back.

"Tunva has believed in Jerr Manivo this far." She looked at her hand, then at Jerr's. "We fight for the future of others, for we surrendered ours long ago. Tunva will send Veja Qor a message: that Jerr Manivo is ready to lead."

"Hey, I never said I wanted that," Jerr said.

"Would Jerr rather take orders from Tunva?"

It took him a second to recognize her teasing. "Hell no."

She flicked her tongue at him and smiled. "First, Tunva must meditate. Will Jerr and Xade join Tunva?"

Xade clasped his hand and gently pulled him down beside her.

"One condition," Jerr said. "Xade, do you have any Urian mantras in your—"

Her nodus played one of his native songs, featuring two female vocalists and one male. Their breathy ululations sent nostalgia washing over him, despite barely recalling what his homeworld looked like. Nevertheless, the connection was there, easing his anxiety. Jerr closed his eyes, holding Xade's hand as Tunva mumbled Repta proverbs.

"Weave a new thread, before they untangle yours."

"This is why Jerr Manivo has been reborn so many times as a soldier, on so many different worlds," Balyra said. "He senses what his opponent will do, right before they do. Over time, this advantage has grown. Deepened. Now, when he is exposed to the Shroud, he sees a future that has already happened."

"Already happened?" The Matriarch shrunk back.

"Revor wants him and his reborn destroyed at all costs." Balyra waited on one knee as the Matriarch mulled that over. She'd run the tests many times, all with the same result: Jerr was unique. Another chance might never come.

"*Prophetess* is one day away from her destination," the Matriarch said. "Yet Revor presents these demands to me now? Why did you not alert me to his message?"

"He didn't display his typical patience," Balyra said. "Perhaps this has tired him."

"Perhaps this quest has tired you, Balyra. Even a Sister must rest and take communion with her betters."

She had slighted the Matriarch, but her superior dared not punish her for it—since Revor sent the message to Balyra personally. "This threat demands much from us all."

The Matriarch glared. "No threat demands anything of a Sister. Especially a reborn soldier that is little more than a trained thug. He will be easily defeated."

Balyra stared down the narrow causeway where kings and emperors had once bowed. The structure and most of the chamber around it had called many worlds home over the epochs. It all found permanent residence on *Prophetess* in the 68th Millennium. For fifteen thousand years, Vestals had bowed here before the Matriarch. Balyra remembered the awe, the pageantry. Now the great unlit gulf extending from the causeway represented the darkness of her existence, lit only by distant stars and the brief points of joy she'd once found in being a Vestal. She'd had lovers, riches. Being a slave to Vestal House, she'd seen both destroyed. And still this miserable structure remained.

Jerr Manivo had seen the future, though. A future she could mold and shape.

"You disagree?" Centuries ago, the Matriarch's tone would have lashed Balyra's conscience with scorn. "Once *Prophetess* finds him, his rebellion shan't survive."

"That conclusion is at odds with the tests I conducted."

"Oh?"

Balyra rose, feeding on the Matriarch's curiosity. "If Vestal House is to survive what Manivo has set in motion, perhaps it should be free of Revor's influence."

The Matriarch glowered. The morga guards all stared at Balyra, hands on their weapons. Balyra had no intention of testing their mettle. That was the disease all long-lived rulers developed: chronic fear of losing their power

"You imply that my decision to consolidate Vestal House was in error?" the Matriarch asked. "That my cautious submission to Revor has weakened us?"

"Caution is a dead variable in this new game we play," Balyra said. "If Revor falls, we will fall with him. I propose an alternative."

The Matriarch's eyes blazed red. "There is no alternative. If we split our power, Revor will dismantle us as he pleases. The Shroud guarantees our survival, it allows us the illusion of omnipresence. Our enemies would destroy us otherwise."

"One cannot destroy what died long ago," Balyra said. "We are simply caretakers of this massive tomb that travels the Shroud. That doesn't mean we have to rot in it."

"That is blasphemy." There was no conviction in the Matriarch's voice.

"No," Balyra said. "It is the future."

"Bring Jerr's head to me," the Matriarch said. "Or I know what yours will be."

Not breaking eye contact, Balyra bowed to her. It would be the last time.

CHAPTER 18

Humans had no idea what to do with us after our surrender. So they gave us menial data tasks. Computating banal calculations, solving equations any lifeless mainframe could do, or piloting their grandiose Leviathans. That was how they saw us, regardless of our form: a mere device whose sole purpose was to further their progress.
Theux Codex, 78 Vaaqa D (reconstructed), unabridged excerpt

As *Bhaellator* left the Shroud, Jerr flinched. Reality lensed and rippled about him. Brief flashes of numerous futures lighted his mind like explosions over a battlefield.

"Look at me, asshole." The reborn lifts his visor. It is a younger version of himself. "Look at the future."

"Veja Qor has messaged Tunva. They are ready."

Jerr could only nod as more scenes hammered his thoughts.

Balyra braces herself as tendril-like forms appear from out of nowhere.

The viewport opened. The brightness of Third Echelon's sun made him squint.

"You wanted this to happen," Jerr says in her ear. "That mass murder down there isn't all I've seen."

The visions finally cleared from his mind as Xade touched his hand.

"Titanous," she said.

"Yeah," he mumbled.

Her description didn't do the vista justice. At five hundred thousand miles distant, Third Echelon dominated the blackness. Orbiting shipyards twined about the deep red planet in thin metallic spirals. Wide bands of light beckoned from the surface, denoting industrialized regions housing billions. Third Echelon's binary star system was safe from the influence of gas giants and contained fewer comets and asteroids overall. It seemed peaceful, like the Hub Worlds Jerr heard about as a child.

What had he heard in childhood? Jerr barely remembered his parents. He wasn't even sure if he'd had siblings. The sparse memories he possessed were faint but pleasant: climbing Uria's steep cliffs, the planet's high gravity gifting him great physical strength. The powdery, sweet cuisine, cooked in sodium geodes. His mother smiling through her tears after his father survived the mine collapse.

"Fugacious," Xade said as she joined him at the viewport.

"Yes, it is," he said. "But I'm the one in transition."

Images of Third Echelon kept replaying in his thoughts. Running down causeways as buildings topple over. A Leviathan blots out the twin suns overhead.

"There has to be a way I can reverse what I see," Jerr said. "The future can be changed. I saw Darei get wounded, yet he died in my arms. I saw that asteroid exploding, killing hundreds, but I prevented that from happening. I have to stop whatever's going to happen here. There's nothing else I can use this for."

"Hazardous." Xade gestured at the bulkheads around them.

"There is much Jerr Manivo's gift can do." Tunva swept a hand across the view outside the window. "It can bring hope. It can bring light to the dark worlds of Tunva's people. But combined with Jerr's new plan, it will certainly bring blood."

"Yes." Jerr sighed. "You keep reminding me."

"Tunva knows Jerr wants it to end. Death, pain. Tunva wants it to end, too."

He gazed at *Bhaellator*'s interior. For at least twenty-four lifetimes, it'd been his home. Knowing he'd never set foot inside it again made Jerr's chest tighten.

Balyra's eyes widen. "No. That would mean—"

Jerr nods. "I know what it means."

"Xade, send out a general announcement," Jerr said. "*Bhaellator* is under orders to acquire a new contingent of reborn soldiers to fight Veja Qor. Hurry."

"Jerr has the Kieta box?" Tunva asked.

"It's in my suit's spare magazine, but it cost me some ammo." Jerr led them into the shuttle. "You activated all of *Bhaellator*'s presets?"

"Fastidious." Xade gave him a weary look. He'd already asked her three times.

"We'll have to be." Jerr set his suit's sensor network to act in tandem with *Bhaellator*'s scanners. He wanted to know as soon as another Leviathan arrived.

The shuttle darted from the hangar. Jerr's heart rate increased. Stupid anxiety.

Third Echelon's name originated from being the third successful colony outside the Affiliate Worlds. It hearkened back to humanity's ancient past, when colonies were sparse and spread far apart. Now it was a burgeoning world of thirty billion citizens.

The shuttle landed on a wide platform outside a hovering spherical structure. The system's twin suns, one red and one blue, pierced the thin atmosphere in mauve glory. Wind scoured the maroon surface, a labyrinth of causeways, power stations, and barracks. Tens of thousands of windmills harvested the constant breeze.

Though his Starjumper compensated, the planet's low gravity made him queasy. The planet's wavelengths irritated his ultraviolet sensitivity, making him squint.

"Nauseous?" Xade asked.

"I'll make it," he said.

"Conspicuous." Her eyes lingered on him.

He chuckled. "Stop worrying about me and land this thing."

Two fighter wings escorted them through the lower atmosphere. Wind propulsion plants drifted among the lightning-streaked clouds, ensuring constant high pressure systems. It was like descending into an underworld from a Faqar death story.

"Miraculous." Xade pointed at symmetrical, artificial canyons where thousands of buildings were constructed into the bedrock, safe from the roughest winds.

"Yes, but I wouldn't want to live here," Jerr said. "Too much red."

Xade nodded. "Nonglamorous."

A sudden heartache overcame him, a reminder of the choice he'd made: letting go of the family he'd never see again, in exchange for Xade's irresistible tenderness. He wasn't sure if he loved her, but he needed her. Maybe that's what love really was.

It'd taken him two dozen lifetimes to figure it out.

After touching down, a squad of MPs and a eugenicist greeted them. Xade showed her palm nodus: using Garrand's name and rank cleared them for entrance, but for anything more than that, Jerr wasn't sure.

The platform lowered into the sphere. A thick door sealed shut behind them. The sounds of wind died away. Jerr tried to look like a bored officer while security robos completed their inspection of the shuttle.

The eugenicist removed his helmet, revealing a young, smiling visage topped with short brown hair. "Welcome to Rebirth Facility Alpha 12. I am Chief Eugenicist Holte. I hope your journey through the Shroud was pleasant?"

"Always. What new acquisitions do you have available for immediate shipping?" He knew the terminology from studying Garrand's log files, but still loathed using it. One in-depth discussion and even a fool would realize he knew nothing about the process.

"Your Theux informed us that you need two brigades of Class A warrior elite." Holte led them around a wide balcony while the MPs followed, rifles held at rest. "That is a tall request, Captain Manivo. Has another uprising began in the Idreun Periphery to justify such a deployment?"

"I have my orders." Jerr frowned over the balcony as if he'd seen cleaner, better rebirth chambers. "Their deployment is classified."

Holte glanced at Tunva and grimaced. "Are we reduced to once again rebirthing Class III Repta? With that many reborn humans, you should be able to conquer a planet, without bringing this one with you."

Tunva glared at Holte, and Jerr interjected before either said anything else.

"This one is my personal guard," Jerr said. "If she offends, I can send her away."

"Please do." Holte continued walking without waiting for them.

Jerr gave Tunva a subtle nod, who walked back to the platform exit. He knew, even as he and Xade trailed after their quarry, that Tunva wouldn't find her way back to the shuttle. He'd expected Dominion bigotry, and now played off it. He just hoped Tunva could restrain herself until the moment came. One false move and they'd all die.

Holte gestured over the balcony as he swiped his arm nodus. "We have more than enough ready, Captain. Any preference? Male, female, or a mixed roster?"

"Male." Jerr paused at the next balcony. In a circular chamber extending far below, thousands of vats hung from holding rings. He made out faces and limbs through the yellow muck. Each occupant possessed a pre-generated name.

Jerr's mouth went dry as he thought about waking up on a bunk, his earliest memory of his service on *Bhaellator*. It was likelier he'd woken up here first.

"I don't blame you," Holte said. "Males are still the stronger, more dependable strata when it comes to human troops. Any hint of the mission? I can configure your request to give you the very best choices. I have assassins, infiltrators, gunners, and marine grunts willing to ignore a severed arm and keep on shooting—"

"My Theux has already filed a detailed request." Jerr tried to appear disinterested.

Holte sighed with disappointment, like a salesman unable to convince a customer. "Very well. Elite trooper, male, full skill set. I have the perfect specimen."

He led them to another balcony. Jerr's blood ran cold. The next vat ring was filled with slightly younger versions of himself.

All floated unconscious in the yellow liquid. Incubated here after being grown to full adulthood from a mere speck of blood.

"Weave the thread. Reveal us."

Jerr shook his head to get the voice out of his mind.

"No, Captain?" Holte asked.

"I meant that for my Theux," Jerr said. "Yes, I want these suited up and ready to go immediately. We're already overdue."

Xade swept her nodus without comment, her face neutral. But she stood closer.

"No one with a Leviathan is overdue—they will be ready within the half hour." Holte entered the data into his arm nodus.

Jerr pretended to study Xade's nodus as he recalled the vision in his mind. Third Echelon would be attacked. There would be more than one Leviathan present. The people of this world were in danger, but they could be saved—if he convinced his reborn that the Dominion was wrong.

The first vat ring lowered over the balcony. Comatose versions of himself were roused with adrenaline shots. Like him, their genetically tailored organs allowed for the quickest waking, the fastest nutrient intake. An engine that could ignite from a cold start five times faster than normal. As the figures opened their eyes and drones fitted them in new Starjumpers, Jerr wondered what the hell he would do with such men.

What he would do with himself.

CHAPTER 19

After stealing the Weavers' gravitational technology, humans underwent a renaissance in colonization and technical progress. With worlds separated by a journey of days, rather than centuries, a new culture developed. But another fundamental change arose: humans felt the weight of mortality less. The Shroud allowed them to travel from one end of the galaxy to the other. The Reborn Initiative gave immortality to a select few. Humanity could now cheat time and space. Their only rival was an uncertain future.

Theux Codex, 78 Vaaqa D (reconstructed), uncensored excerpt

As soon as *Prophetess* exited the Shroud near Third Echelon, its scanners detected *Bhaellator*. Balyra faced the bridge realizer, a recreation of her superior.

"It is as I told you, Matriarch. This is where the Shroud told Jerr Manivo to go."

Standing on the ship's bridge, Balyra was surrounded by Sisters who operated the nodi and piloting controls. It was an anachronism; morga did the actual work, but Vestal House was all about appearances, even among its own. Sisters had to look useful and engaged in the current situation. For Balyra, no acting was required.

"You are certain of Jerr Manivo's intentions?" the Matriarch asked. More formalities, for the older Sister had already given Balyra command of the mission. The façade was another thing she would eliminate if everything went according to her plan. Jerr

Manivo's plan, really: he was seeing it, the future. She was simply guaranteeing it.

"Yes, Matriarch." Balyra wore her full uniform: a red unisuit with metalloid cuirass, plus an armored skirt around her thighs. A red and white scarf was tied into her hair, drawn into an elaborate ponytail. Her metallic wings offered basic particle shielding in lieu of flight. It'd been four thousand years since she'd wore the complete panoply.

In the past, the appearance of an armed Sister usually quelled conflicts. Vestal House had long perfected war before it perfected peace. Yet she felt emasculated.

"May the Eternal Flame burn our enemies and light the path," the Matriarch said.

The old adage meant nothing now. The only light lay in the possibilities Jerr offered. Balyra shivered, wishing she could remain loyal. Wishing she could ignore it.

A private message reached her nodus from the Matriarch. It read, 'Please tell me what you want. I do not know what you intend, but think of us. Think of what we'll lose.'

She swiped the message off. Started to reply, then didn't. It had been decades since the Matriarch voiced such affection. Yet all Balyra could feel was the heartache of millennia past, when Revor had forced her to destroy what she cherished most.

It was too late to change. Too soon to forgive.

"Ready the landing party," Balyra said. "Ensure that the local governor receives the Vestal Disclosure and Devotion Agreement before we reach the surface."

The Matriarch expected her to retake *Bhaellator.* Balyra had a different goal.

As she strode to the shuttle dock, an alarm sounded. She turned as a Sister swept a nodus displaying another large vessel in the system.

"Balyra, what is this?" the Matriarch's realizer avatar asked.

"Report!" Balyra cried as she hurried back into the bridge.

"It is another Leviathan, Confessor," the Sister said.

"No … it is larger." Balyra gaped as a massive shadow crept over Third Echelon. It was three times the size of *Prophetess*. The dark gray hull lacked insignia or design.

"*Liberator*," she whispered. Revor's personal ship. So he'd meant what he said.

She was still following through with her plan, Flame be damned.

"For the third time, Captain, what will you name this unit?" Holte's tone grew more impatient by the minute. Now, over two hundred reborn soldiers waited on the causeway outside, outfitted in Starjumpers. Though awake, the soldiers remained in a chemically controlled stupor. All Jerr needed to do was activate their neural locks and they'd be ready to fight. Each was a killing machine unto himself, capable of terminating enemy battalions. A mere name wouldn't do them justice.

"Immortals," Jerr finally said.

Holte gave him a sardonic look. "How appropriate, sir. I'm uploading the manifest to your Theux. It will have all the information you require."

"She." Jerr stared at him.

"Pardon?" Holte frowned.

"She's not an 'it'," Jerr said. "Xade is a 'she'. Look at her."

Though she didn't look at him, Xade smiled.

"Of course, sir." Holte scowled as if he'd tasted something bad. "To finalize, I need your DNA signature and what ship they will be serving on."

Jerr started to sweep Holte's nodus when it flashed red.

Holte gave Jerr a cold look. "Captain Manivo … orbital patrol states that *Bhaellator* has been taken into custody as a stolen vessel."

The squad of MPs snapped their weapons up and aimed at Jerr.

A wicked grin split Holte's face. "You are under arrest, Captain. Perhaps I should allow your 'recruits' to take you in? It would be a fascinating display."

"I don't have the time. Neither do you." Jerr targeted them all in his HUD.

Holte glowered. "You insolent—!"

The MPs screamed and gurgled as Tunva attacked them from behind. Her blade sliced through necks, their suit's power supplies, ammo bandoleers—anything to disrupt and damage. As Holte turned, Jerr kicked him against a vat. Holte groaned and lay on the floor as Tunva killed the last MP.

"Duplicitous," Xade said.

"No choice." Jerr hurried out to the causeway. Grouped in ranks, the reborn stirred as alarms blared through the facility. A dark shape loomed into orbit. Jerr looked up in resignation. Just like his vision, it was larger than a Leviathan.

"Dangerous." Xade showed the news broadcast on her nodus.

"They betrayed us, rent us apart, scattered us to the Shroud."

"Holte said they already have *Bhaellator*," Jerr said. "That means they'll be coming down here."

"Will Jerr light the very sky itself?" Tunva asked. "Veja Qor is ready to attack."

"Reveal us. Avenge us. Weave a new thread, for ours are gone."

Xade gave him a questioning look. He nodded. She swiped her nodus.

Jerr stared skyward. So far, his visons regarding Third Echelon had come true. He'd already heard these alarms, seen the blood on Tunva's swords. Knew someone other than Vestal House had come to stop him.

Knew he'd have to detonate *Bhaellator* so they could escape.

"Think about what drives these ships," Jerr says.

Balyra watches as Xade draws up a Leviathan schematic on her nodus.

"A gravity engine," Jerr says. "It creates an artificial neutron star every time a Leviathan travels. That gravity is pushed outward, creating a rift in space-time."

"Go on." Balyra stands very still.

"What if we could reverse that gravity? What if the Leviathan draws things to it, instead of pushing them away?"

Balyra's eyes widen. "No. That would mean—"

Jerr nods. "I know what it means."

The future conversation finally made sense.

"Rebellious." Xade's nodus showed that she'd hacked access to every reborn facility on the planet. Tens of thousands of individuals, primed to serve their purpose again and again. Men, women, scientists, soldiers, engineers. One swipe away from waking up to the lie of their existence, like the soldiers waiting outside.

"Reveal us!"

"This is what we came here for." Jerr closed his eyes and sighed. "Do it."

Xade's light blue fingers swept the nodus. More alarms sounded. Feeds from various facilities lit up Jerr's HUD in a rainbow of pain, epiphany, and anger. A collective consciousness stirred in that moment, demanding its freedom. Jerr trembled, unsure whether he was a savior or the harbinger of apocalypse.

In addition to the normal waking procedures, Xade had imprinted a short memory sequence into the reborns' minds. It was little more than a burst of information. Few of them would remember it for long. Jerr would remember it for all eternity.

All at once, thousands of psyches were introduced to Dominion atrocities. The same footage and imagery Jerr had been shown. Carried out by people with their face.

The action brought the 'Immortals' out of their stupor. Jerr led Xade and Tunva onto the causeway. Overhead, Dominion fighters and gunships filled the skies.

"What's going on?" one reborn soldier asked.

"I don't recall that mission!" one yelled.

"Bastards," one muttered.

"At ease," Jerr called. His HUD blinked with all weapon systems ready.

The soldiers kept their weapons raised, some of them subtly aiming at Jerr. He didn't blame them. They were under duress.

Training took precedence over any other thinking. Like animals, they had those killer instincts, ones he felt as well.

"I'm Captain Jerr Manivo, a reborn like you. Nothing you've been trained for will prepare you for what's coming, so I need your full attention."

A distant rebirth facility exploded. Black smoke columned into the sky. The soldiers muttered and brought their Starjumper weapons online.

"Xade, upload the rest to their helmet feeds." Jerr ignored the sweat rolling down his face. Now, more than ever, he had to trust what the Shroud showed him.

She nodded. Within seconds, the soldiers cursed, whispered, or stiffened in denial.

"What you're seeing is evidence of Dominion crimes," Jerr said. "The reason they keep growing us. We rape and murder for them. We are their slaves. Skilled just enough so they will never let us die."

The soldiers aimed at him. Their expressions of awe and fury pained Jerr's heart. Tunva tensed, blade in each hand. Xade simply watched, her eyes scanning them with computational intensity.

"What the fuck is this shit?" one soldier called.

"This isn't what I was trained for," another said.

"It's a lie!" one yelled.

Tunva gave him a warning look. Even Xade indicated the Dominion ships with a glance. He knew they'd be surrounded, but he had to make the reborn understand.

"There's thousands more like us, growing in vats across this planet," Jerr said. "They've all been woken up, shown the same thing. Some will still fight for the empire, but others will make the right decision. Which will you be?"

"I say we destroy them!" a reborn shouted.

"You're full of shit," another one said.

"I know how you feel," Jerr said. "We're not special. Our DNA has been abused to kill innocents on who knows how many worlds. Then we die and do it all over again."

Another reborn spoke up. "You're wrong. I like being this way. Knowing I'll rise again, defending our people. Living eternally as a guardian of humanity."

Some of the reborn nodded. Xade shot Jerr a doubtful look.

"Sure, you'll live eternally." Jerr slowly walked up to the man. "You might even be celebrated as some great hero for centuries to come. But you'll only know how to kill. Your only skills will be in the trade of death. You'll never have a real family of your own. And you will only be useful, only be reborn, as long as you kill for them."

Their collective anger woke something within him. So many lives had been stolen by the Dominion this way. So many families wrecked, like his, or Wanrys's. Dreams shattered simply to patrol star systems and fight small wars for a system afraid of itself.

"Look at me!" Jerr yelled. The soldiers stopped short. Xade and Tunva flanked him, eying the troops carefully. "I have your face! Your voice! You think I like dying over and over again, just so I can be regrown in a place like this? We mean nothing to the empire. Is that who you want to be?"

Anger drained from their faces, replaced with fear or resentment.

"I want to be a man again. One that can die, one that can have a family, a life outside of Dominion control. Follow me and I know we can find it."

"Follow you where?" One soldier stepped forward. "If you're like us…a reborn…how do we know we can trust you? How do we know you're right?"

Jerr pointed at the next soldier. "Because this one here will ask what goddamn right I have to tell you where to go."

The other man stomped forward. "How the hell did you know that?"

Jerr gestured skyward. "You see that? They're coming for us. They want to destroy every last one of us, to ensure our DNA doesn't survive."

"Why?" the first soldier asked.

"Because they can't control us anymore," Jerr said.

Security troops were moving across the causeway toward the facility. Somewhere within, Holte screamed for Jerr's arrest. Tiny flares in the sky indicated the approach of marines in Starjumpers, their thrusters mimicking a meteor shower. Small arms fire echoed in the canyon-like streets below. Explosions and smoke came from an adjacent rebirth facility until missiles darted from the atmosphere, leveling it.

"What if I shoot your ass?" One soldier aimed his gauss cannon at Jerr.

"Then I'll be dead," Jerr said. "But you'll still be their tool."

"So?"

"So look around," Jerr said. "The empire is killing all the reborn on this planet. Some are trying to fight back. Will you resist, or let them exterminate you?"

The man didn't back down. The other reborn traded doubtful glances.

"Jerr is not brave," Tunva whispered. "Jerr is mad."

"You should see me when I'm drunk. And naked."

"Scandalous." Xade smirked. Tunva's smile was razor-sharp.

"See that other facility?" Jerr pointed eastward. "Three rockets will hit it, killing everyone inside. All because they look like you and me."

"Bullshit," the soldier said.

No sooner had the man spoke, than a trio of objects slammed into the building. It blew apart in a massive fireball. The screams of civilians reached Jerr's ears.

"You could've called in that airstrike," the soldier said.

"Really?" Jerr indicated other Dominion fighters bombing the city.

The soldier slowly lowered the cannon.

"We must escape," Jerr said. "But not on the ship we arrived in."

A reborn frowned. "Huh? What else have you seen?"

He jetted his thrusters, queued his gauss cannon. "More than I ever wanted to."

⚜ ⚜ ⚜

Still armored, Balyra stood beside the Matriarch in the Sanctum. Hundreds of Sisters lined the causeway in full uniform. It had been a long time since she'd seen so many arrayed at once, like the parades of old. She'd never realized how artificial they looked. Faces sculpted via surgery. Bodies augmented beyond the human threshold for pain, strength and fortitude. There was an underlying homogeneity despite the variety of flesh tones, ethnicities, or names. They were mirror images of an ancient ideal long outdated. The Matriarch hoped to convince their visitor that it mattered.

Balyra knew he wouldn't care.

A procession came down the causeway, a ritual she'd not seen in two millennia. Several Kieta formed the vanguard, their thin bodies like strands of liquid silver, without torsos, heads, or anything denoting them as sapient in human terms. The Kieta twirled forward in tandem with each other. The effect was disturbing on a primal level despite all Balyra's years of travel and experience. Though defeated in the Armada Era, they were one of the few species spared the genocidal purges following humanity's victory.

Revor should have let her kill all of them.

Next came four Theux, all of them assuming a genderless humanoid appearance, their exoskeletons and dermaflesh mere facsimiles of humanity. After them came a cadre of Class III Repta, frightfully human-looking, yet powerful enough to crush a soldier in a Starjumper. Each carried a rifle topped with a glowing blue shard.

These living trophies preceded Revor, greatest of the Curators. Despite the distance between them, Balyra felt his eyes on her.

He wore white muscled armor draped in blue silks with a benevolent-looking silver mask. Drones flanked him, bearing realizer recreations of the galaxy's spiral arms. As if Revor was the center of their island universe with all revolving about him.

The procession neared the dais. The Matriarch made a visible effort not to tremble as she bowed. Her metalloid body embarrassed Balyra, who knew what Revor truly thought of Vestal House and its rituals. Much to her surprise, he ignored the Matriarch and continued staring at her.

"Curator, you do us great honor." The Matriarch spoke with a hint of seduction, a touch of subservience. But Revor merely lifted the Matriarch to her feet. Sisters along the causeway held their torches at attention, looking like primitive hags in the presence of one who created the future. Balyra hated him all the more for it, but she smiled back. She knew one who could pierce that future.

"The honor is mine." Revor's voice filled the Sanctum. "It is a pleasure to see Vestal House still obeying tradition. Especially while facing such a threat to the empire."

"Yes, Curator," the Matriarch said. "We do our—"

"Confessor Balyra, you came into direct contact with this threat." Revor walked over to her. "Your skills never cease to amaze. You will be commended, of course."

"Thank you, Curator." Balyra curtsied in the archaic Elder States fashion, when women had worn the great gowns of their houses, passed down generation to generation.

Revor took her hand. "Your respect for convention always leaves me nostalgic. But I am not here for reminisces. I am here to ensure that it is the Dominion's traditions which are kept. Getting me here in time strained *Liberator*'s resources."

"Vestal House's resources are yours, Curator," the Matriarch said.

Turning in a circle, Revor stared at the Sanctum's far reaches. "Was there ever a time when that was different? I never realized, that when I gave Vestal House this ship, you would fill it with such petty reminders of imagined glories."

The Matriarch bowed, though terror filled her eyes. "Yes, Curator."

"I never realized one reborn could destroy it all." Balyra did not curtsy again.

A nodus terminal showed the unfolding battle on—and above—Third Echelon. A Veja Qor fleet had appeared. Thousands of reborn were in open revolt, planetside.

Revor stared at her for several moments. "He will be eliminated."

"When has a Curator seen to such a trifling task personally?" Balyra asked.

The Matriarch gave Balyra a dangerous glare. Below the dais, thousands of attendants and Sisters remained still, far out of earshot.

"Nothing is trifling that can challenge the gods." Revor beckoned. One of his Repta guards came forward. There was an etherspace box fitted to its rifle barrel. The size of a child's fist, the box's semi-transparent, metallic surface gleamed blue beneath the Vestal lamps. Shaped like an octahedron, each of is eight faces bore a Kieta inscription. Balyra wondered how many that box had sent to a timeless hell.

That hourglass would be broken. Soon.

"Jerr Manivo stole one of these, meaning he knows what it can do," Revor said.

While the Matriarch backed away, Balyra held her ground. "Are the gods afraid?"

"They should be." Revor waved the soldier away. "The Rebirth Initiative has allowed humanity to thrive in the cosmos. Without it, who would rule our many worlds? Who would protect us from our enemies? It is the foundation the Dominion was built upon. It cannot be endangered or compromised."

"Your servants cannot rein him in?" She nodded at the Kieta on the causeway.

"I asked them." Frustration entered Revor's voice. "They cannot locate him."

The Matriarch frowned in disbelief. "They showed us how to destroy the Weavers. The Shroud is their domain. They taught us its variances, its dangers!"

"It is time for the student to become the teacher," Revor said.

"How?" Balyra asked.

"Vestal House has a chance to prove its worth." Revor said. "Kill him and his Theux. Bring the etherspace box back to me. Do not deviate from this."

Balyra met his stare. Revor didn't look away.

So he suspected her. His appearance on *Prophetess* was simply a veiled threat.

"Of course." Balyra had not felt so alive in a very long time. It was almost over.

"And the rest of Manivo's reborn, Curator?" The Matriarch, trying to be relevant.

Revor kept staring at Balyra. "On every world they are grown, every ship they serve, every theater of operations they occupy—destroy them."

For the last time, Revor's words decided what Balyra's next action would be.

Chapter 20

Upon their inception, the reborn were the pariahs of modern galactic civilization. Despised by the poor, the politically progressive, and countless xenophobes alike. It wasn't until the common citizen realized the reborn contributed to the state, and not the individual, that these quasi-immortals became nameless, faceless, disposable products.

Elder States Archives, Volume LXXX

Upon Xade's preset command, *Bhaellator*'s engine reversed its flow of energy.

The resulting explosion was like a third sun over the planet, flaring painful white with a fiery blue corona roiling from the edges. The shockwave struck the atmosphere and generated a thunderclap so powerful it threw people to the ground. Things closer to *Bhaellator*—orbiting stations, fleets, and other aeronautical strata—were drawn into the blast by the reversed gravity and atomized. Though further out in the system, *Prophetess* and *Liberator* still received superficial damage.

Jerr hoped it would be enough for Veja Qor to make a difference.

"Avenge us."

The familiar voice echoed in Jerr's psyche. A ghost whispering across time.

"It unravels. Before you, behind you."

The sky morphs into a thousand different horizons. Each another world he's visited—or will visit. The situation never changes. Leviathans in orbit. Death below.

As he'd feared, Third Echelon was simply the beginning of Revor's policy.

"It unravels."

Every sensation in Jerr's body dulled. Sounds muted, nerve endings went numb. Everything was blurry. He thought about whiskey. Decided he didn't want any.

"You cannot stop it. But you can weave the future anew."

He floats above it all. A god without wings. A catalyst without boundaries.

"Chivalrous…"

That voice…it made him grin.

"Chivalrous…"

"Xade?"

Shuts off his boot thrusters. Allows himself to freefall.

Jerr sucked in a breath as reality reclaimed ascendancy of his consciousness.

In the minutes after the explosion, Jerr and the freed reborn took flight over the city. Their Starjumpers were fully armed and fueled. Tunva acted as Jerr's lieutenant while Xade waited on a causeway below, connected to the planetary network. She provided intel on enemy deployments and helped them target isolated units.

Dominion forces attacked them in wave after merciless wave. Another building toppled in the distance. Debris clouds bowled down the canyon thoroughfares. The gunships and fighters now struggled to contain the other freed reborn, loosed all across Third Echelon. It provided no respite for Jerr and his Immortals.

"Xade, you still okay down there?" Jerr banked away from a missile salvo and strafed the gunship. The cockpit exploded and the craft spiraled to the street.

"Chivalrous!" The anger in her voice made him grin.

"I'm coming back for you, just hold tight!" He glanced at his HUD. "Shit."

Jerr shut off his boot thrusters and allowed himself to freefall. The three marines in pursuit darted after him, flying right into

Tunva's sights. Her diffusion blaster melted them to bones and slag. Jerr fired the thrusters and joined the rest of his reborn.

The causeway was covered in dead imperial troops and not a few reborn. Glowing hot gauss rounds and missiles zipped back and forth over the erstwhile battlefield, terminating in red clouds as bodies were disintegrated by the onslaught.

"Second Platoon, cover our flank or we'll be digging scattershot from our asses!" Jerr flew back over the causeway and blasted two more marines. The armored men blew apart only to be replaced by ten more. Tunva, leading First Platoon, intercepted them.

"Expeditious." Xade remote-loaded a real-time map of the area on his HUD. He'd lost over eighty reborn so far, but Dominion casualties numbered in the hundreds on the causeway alone. Like Jerr, his reborn could react before their enemies. Imperial marines died before they even knew where they should shoot. But two brigades were converging on their position, augmented by an entire fighter wing. It looked hopeless.

"Veja Qor is engaging the Leviathans," Tunva said.

"They're not brave, they're mad," Jerr said.

"Tunva is not drunk or naked." She shot a marine off his tail. "At least, not yet."

Jerr couldn't hold back a laugh. "Well, let's hope your friends aren't either."

He'd hold until the vision came true. Without *Bhaellator*, it was their only chance.

As he flew down to the causeway arch where Xade took cover, Jerr barrel-rolled away from piercer fire. Each shot, every explosion, flashed in his thoughts before actually happening. Likewise, some of his reborn died horribly. He could have saved them. Choosing which future to make real was like murdering a piece of himself each time.

"Second Platoon, tell me what's happening over there," Jerr said.

There was no response.

"Second Platoon, copy that?"

"They are gone, Jerr Manivo," Tunva finally said.

Jerr glowered at his HUD. "Immortals, regroup near the arch. My thrusters are nearly exhausted, but we must hold this causeway."

Explosions popped over the clouds ahead.

"They are gone!" Tunva yelled over the radio.

"What?" Jerr studied his HUD mapping as he landed near the arch. First and Second Platoon had broken all unit cohesion. The remnants were fighting their own individual, personal wars with the Dominion. Committing berserk attacks.

Some were even strafing civilians.

"Goddamn it." Jerr tried hailing them even as more missiles struck the other end of the causeway. The rogue reborn ignored him. The rest—less than a hundred now—rallied around the arch. He sensed they followed him not out of loyalty, but out of self-preservation. Darei had been right. Jerr did expect these men to behave like him.

Xade broke cover and hurried to him. "Tumultuous!"

He grabbed her and knelt behind a fallen railing. "I know, but we have to wait!"

The security forces now hemmed them in near the rebirth facility, but Jerr knew his vison would become reality. He'd seen the vehicle arrive, seen the figures step out. Seen these people die. It was a burden, a curse. He hated himself for needing it.

"What now, Jerr Manivo?" Tunva landed with a handful of Third Platoon, her armor charred from combat. "Tunva's ammunition runs low."

"We hold this position." Jerr scavenged a gauss magazine from the dead.

"Tenuous!" Xade ducked as a piercer round melted through the wall behind her.

"Stay behind me," he said in her ear.

Xade shook her head, messaging all the other reborn on Third Echelon. Asking for their help. Even while facing such destruction and death, she wasn't giving up.

A shot zipped past his shoulder and struck a reborn. The round plowed through the man's armor and out his back. He fell, dead.

"They betrayed us. They will come for you, too."

Jerr rolled aside and shot the marine on the arch above. The body plummeted hundreds of feet below. "Tunva, Xade, hold! The rest of you, form up and cover me!"

But his reborn were already in action. One duo ambushed and slaughtered a security squad down the platform. Another reborn ducked and rolled, drawing fire while his comrades gunned down two dozen troopers—but the man was wounded and unreachable now. Jerr felt a perverse pride, glad some remembered their training.

Wind scattered over the platform. He checked his oxygen supply. Less than half an hour left. He knew it wasn't normal weather, bringing such a breeze. He had to be patient. The future came in its own good time.

"Now!" Jerr rushed from cover as his reborn enfiladed the ledge above the platform with diffusion fire. The bright rounds slipped through armor and flesh in unstoppable light beams. The dead slumped over in heaps. Jerr kept running. He saw in his mind the man about to shoot him, then Jerr ducked and shot him first. The Shroud's visions warned him of the squad flanking the power generators at the end of the causeway, and of the heavy gunner team setting up in the facility's entrance.

Jerr signaled his reborn and they acted in quick, deadly concert. They surprised the squad, spraying piercer rounds into helmets and chests. Bodies toppled into the urban vastness. Fireballs gushed into the air as the heavy gun was destroyed by Tunva and Third Platoon, acting more on instinct than thought. The reborn cheered.

All around, the metropolis burned. Wails of the wounded, of the terrified, filled his aural sensors. Stronger winds stirred the ashes of the dead. He glanced up at the sky.

The craft was finally descending.

Jerr's breath caught as Xade embraced him. They shared a brief smile. Maybe it could still work, all these sacrifices could be justified—

A blast tore three nearby reborn apart. Debris struck and busted his faceplate. Slivers of Starjumper armor clattered over the platform. Tunva held her side where a small piece of shrapnel protruded.

Xade lay beside him. Missing her left hand and part of her forearm.

Jerr hugged her against him as he returned fire, killing four marines. He wondered if he were shooting other reborn. It didn't matter. The craft was getting closer.

"Xade? Hang on, it's almost here." He ripped off his helmet. Shot another marine.

The causeway shook.

"Betrayed us."

"No," he murmured, as Tunva shouted something.

"They will come for you …"

Chunks of the causeway tore free and crushed many buildings underneath.

A Kieta appears several feet away. Swirling, morphing. Coming for him.

"No!" he cried, as if the wind could bear his denial to the heavens.

The causeway shattered as the craft settled on the platform. A cascade of pure energy darted from the sky. It struck a rebirth facility to the north. The energy obliterated it, leaving little more than a crater of smoldering masonry.

"Jerr, Veja Qor is waiting!" Blood flowed from Tunva's side as she shot two more marines coming their way. Three more of his reborn fell dead.

"Xade?" He cradled her close as a piercer round melted the decking near his right boot. "Xade, we're going to make it. I saw them coming. They're here. I saw them …"

She touched his face. "Chivalrous."

He started to say more when the craft lowered its hatch. The marines ceased fire and strengthened their positions. Tunva gasped, sword at the ready. The reborn waited.

"You cannot weave our strands back together. But you can weave your own."

The vision came true.

Holding Xade under one arm, he leapt up and raced toward the Vestal shuttle. Behind him, dozens more reborn followed, screaming their rage, their freedom.

Across the planet, thousands more fought on, slaves no more.

Just like he'd seen it.

On the shuttle's ramp, Balyra stepped aside. Allowing them entrance.

In the premonition, Jerr had led the reborn in taking over the shuttle. Balyra hadn't been present, much less inviting him in. He loaded his final gauss round.

The marines down the causeway waited in tense silence. Balyra waved Jerr in.

"Sinistrous," Xade said.

"On the honor of Vestal House, I grant sanctuary," Balyra said. "Please. Hurry."

"Tunva knows what honor is," Tunva said between labored breaths. "Tunva will restore the honor of her people. Tunva swore an oath."

"Let me help you keep it," Balyra said. Two morga helped Tunva aboard.

Jerr walked up the ramp, leading Xade by her good arm.

"The frayed ends cannot be repaired."

"Why?" he asked.

Balyra's cold beauty softened. "Because I think you are the key."

Moments later, the ramp closed. The marines on the causeway stared in confusion. Onboard, several morga tended the reborn, who had fallen silent.

Jerr nodded, having seen it. "Tell your Sisters we have an injured Theux."

"Ridiculous." Though her arm didn't bleed, Xade's grimace hinted at her pain.

The shuttle lifted off the causeway while Balyra messaged the authorities that she had Jerr and his accomplices in custody. Battles still raged over the planet. Once they cleared the stratosphere, Balyra took Jerr outside the cockpit.

"There is a greater Leviathan in orbit," Balyra said. "With a Curator onboard."

"I know." Jerr met her eyes. The mixture of fear and hope in them unnerved him.

"Good." Balyra hesitated. "They were closer to the shockwave than my ship. We might still have the advantage. I've gambled on you knowing what happens next."

Jerr stared at the dried blood on his armor. "That makes two of us."

Chapter 21

It wasn't easy convincing the old guard in Vestal House to surrender their human biology for circoids and cyborg bodies. The ranks of Sisters had shrunk over the centuries and the House wished to preserve its best minds to help the organization survive. In the end, most acceded to the new rules, but a few had to be coerced. Thus, we gained immortality with a price. Only, Vestal House forced others to pay that price.

Psychopomp Errata, Sector 698, The Matriarch, Vestal House

The shuttle hatch opened. Through the exhaust, Jerr made out dozens of perfect feminine visages. Goddesses from a prehistoric religion here to save him.

Jerr exited after Balyra, his banged-up Starjumper clanking and echoing through *Prophetess*'s hangar. He kept his diffusion blaster charged in the event the Vestals betrayed them. He still clasped Xade's remaining hand, afraid to let go of her again. Despite her wound, she was a firm pillar of support. Her eyes were confident. Strange how she could be calm, when he was the one who saw the future.

Vestals glared at him and his reborn as they packed the hangar. Morga nurses waded among his bloodied yet defiant soldiers, their guileless, blank faces offering little welcome. Tunva was laid on a stretcher, but she refused to give up her blades.

Jerr extended a hand to Balyra. "Give me your sword."

The Vestals whispered in disbelief. Balyra gave him an unreadable expression. As a Confessor, her word was law to these women and morga. For all their intrigues, Vestals wouldn't dishonor themselves by attacking him if their leader surrendered. And though he'd foreseen this initial situation, he had no idea how she'd answer.

"Is this what you saw?" Balyra asked in a low voice.

"You say you gambled on me," Jerr said. "Don't question the stakes."

With obvious resignation, Balyra unsheathed her sword and handed it over. The other Vestals stiffened, their jaws firmed into stoic acceptance. Jerr's reborn cheered.

"Taking a Leviathan is unheard of," Balyra said. "Now you have captured two."

"That won't make Revor stop," Jerr said.

"Do you need more proof of the danger you represent to the empire?" Balyra asked. "That it's timeless, endless 'peace' is a fallacy that could be brought down by a single individual? One being in a galaxy of trillions upon trillions, and it's you."

"I'm just a soldier." He glanced at his reborn.

Balyra indicated the hangar with a sweeping gesture. "Then welcome aboard, Captain Jerr Manivo. Or have you chosen a different epithet to designate yourself from every other traitor and common criminal?"

He scowled until she leaned in close.

"If you raise the stakes, you must play the role," Balyra whispered.

"Then let me see the stakes." Jerr walked over to the nearest viewport.

The sheer power of the spectacle took his breath.

Three other Leviathans had arrived in the system from neighboring sectors. *Bhaellator*'s destruction would register to all of them, the blast's gravitational shockwaves sped across the galaxy via the Shroud. A silent, powerful message that all was not right with their precious empire.

"Jerr was right," Tunva breathed, holding her side. "Now they will see."

"What?" Balyra scowled out the viewport.

Liberator fired white-hot beams down upon the planet. Swiping through the remaining rebirth facilities, laying waste to any adjoining structures.

"Is it as beautiful as the version you foresaw?" The scorn in Balyra's voice was thick. "Thousands dying, because of you?"

"The empire is desperate," Jerr said. "I'm not the one giving those orders."

"They are orders to destroy you," Balyra said.

"You act like I wanted this to happen," Jerr said. "That mass murder down there isn't all I've seen. It isn't all that you hope I've seen."

Balyra's cool exterior cracked for a second, then she regained her composure. "My anger is not directed at you. Revor's madness must come to an end."

"We should leave," Jerr said. "Xade has the coordinates."

"Where?" Balyra asked.

"The Faqar Belt. More of my reborn are grown there. I want to release them."

"And start this insanity all over again?" Balyra asked. "You cannot be serious."

"At least I'm giving them a chance," Jerr said. "The empire will kill them now."

"Revor will follow us." Balyra's tone was more reflective than threatening. "But you will pass through the Shroud. Giving you more prescient advantages. I have no—"

"Idea what I'm capable of," Jerr said.

Balyra stared back, then spun on her heels and activated her earbud. "Bridge, travel to the coordinates this Theux uploads. Priority Yellow."

While Xade sent the data from her nodus, Jerr faced the reborn who'd made it onboard. Perhaps seventy had survived, some escaping from adjacent facilities.

"You've seen what the Dominion does," Jerr said. "They want us dead, just for being who we are. I say we fight back."

"Why?' one reborn asked. "Hell, we can go anywhere in a Leviathan. Let's start over somewhere else." Several nodded in agreement.

"I'll fight," another one said. "They made us for one purpose. What else am I going to do with my life now?"

"We deserve a choice!" a third reborn called. "Not all of us want to follow you on some dumbass suicide mission. I want off this ship the next system we come to."

"I'll not ask you to do anything I wouldn't do myself," Jerr said. "But if you want out, I won't stop you. Remember: we're all outlaws. Targets. Alone, we'll die."

"Jerr Manivo is right," Tunva said, now swathed in bandages. "Tunva saw her own people massacred by Dominion soldiers, by Dominion reborn. Tunva could have found a clutch mate and bred a new family. But Tunva came here and bled for you."

The reborn looked at each other. Dozens of people with his face, his voice. He knew what they felt, he still felt lost himself. Finally, they agreed to accept his leadership. He had no illusions about how long their obedience would last.

"Thanks," he whispered to Tunva.

"The other Jerr Manivo never thanked Tunva."

"Guess I'm the softer one." He clasped her hand and grinned.

She flicked her tongue and lay back in the stretcher. Trying not to grin back.

"Ambiguous?"

Xade's question made Jerr turn. She stared at Balyra, holding her nodus up for all to see. The coordinates still hadn't been approved by the bridge crew.

Eyes darting here and there, Balyra tapped her earbud. "Bridge?"

The other Leviathans were surrounded by Veja Qor ships, but it was like flies attacking a house. Unless they left soon, *Bhaellator* would've been destroyed for nothing.

"Bridge?" Balyra's jaw stiffened.

She wasn't certain her order would be carried out. If Balyra failed to help them escape, he'd have to hijack the damn ship anyway. He'd no idea what weapons Vestal House carried aboard *Prophetess*, but he hoped it was more than religious scrolls and icons. Otherwise he'd have no more chance than ice on a lava world.

"Treacherous," Xade whispered.

He rubbed the tip of his finger along her hand. "Trust me. This will work."

Her look said she'd always trusted him.

Prophetess shook slightly. Balyra's stiff demeanor assumed its typical haughtiness. The Vestals straightened, looking even more arrogant, if that were possible.

The battle outside the viewport morphed into a blurred starfield.

"We are in the Shroud," Balyra said.

"The Kieta refused to listen. They too untangled the strands to see."

Jerr caught Balyra looking at him. "We need to talk."

"Come." Balyra gave Xade a grudging look, then led them both to an elevator.

Morga nurses and med drones gave Tunva and the reborn the best care, living up to Vestal House's healing reputation. It provided a lull Jerr doubted would last.

"We wish to use one another," Balyra said as the elevator whooshed them up. "The question is, how far can we trust each other?"

"Spare me the Vestal mind games," Jerr said. "And take us up another deck. I'm not interested in talking to your security morga."

"Perhaps I was simply testing you." Balyra sent the elevator to the next deck.

"Perhaps." Jerr kept the diffusion blaster on standby.

The doors opened. Balyra led them into a great arching chamber, its walls fashioned with ancient stone. Paper-like murals and icons decorated the space, along with candelabras from a thousand different worlds, lit by candles from ten thousand others. Vestal saints, now cast into obscurity, were shown in idealized statues and paintings. Many other sculptures stood on pedestals. Real flowers surrounded these treasures.

"You need my ship." Balyra walked here and there, examining some of the statues as if she'd known them in real life. "You'll need support once Revor is deposed."

"You want my abilities," Jerr said.

"You have a way of finding out things that has nothing to do with the Shroud."

Balyra said something else, but Jerr's mind filled with new images. A desert planet. Old memories. A Leviathan, torn in half. Balyra screaming as light swallows her.

Xade nudged him and he realized Balyra had asked a question.

"You saw something just now." Balyra's eyes narrowed. "How did it feel?"

"How the hell is it supposed to feel?" Jerr rubbed his temples. "Or have you already forgotten your interrogation data? You know, when you tortured me."

Balyra fumed. "I had to. It was—"

"Wrong?" Jerr asked.

"Do you think yourself a god, seeing our futures, our mistakes? You know what I say before I say it. You know who will die before they feel it. Like those on that planet."

Jerr paced the chamber. "I'm no god."

"Then what do you want?" Balyra asked. "You commanded your own Leviathan. You could have went anywhere in the galaxy. Perhaps even the universe. Yet you have traveled to two different Hub Worlds to find your other reborn, even though they distrust you. You have risked the end of an existence that most citizens in the Dominion would kill for. Do you know the percentage of people that actually get reborn?"

"It's pretty small." Jerr avoided her eyes as images continued entering his mind: *craters in the desert, a glowing blue shard. A bay filled with non-human creatures.* A lensing effect covered it all, as if he viewed it from a porthole inside the Shroud.

"Presumptuous." Xade's nodus showed an incredibly small number.

"It is a fraction of a percent," Balyra said. "Of all the trillions of people who have families, who create art, who inspire others—who love others—they are allowed to die. Die forever, Jerr Manivo. Yet tools like you are rebirthed by the thousands, until you have amassed far more human experience than an entire city of people."

"Is that how you see me?" Jerr asked. "How long have you lived in that body? How many times have they regrown the flesh on your face?"

Balyra's eyes flared red. "I have sacrificed a hundred lifetimes of emotional and physical experiences to have this body. I am one of the few people who can further the path humanity has taken."

"Bullshit," Jerr said. "Vestals have aided every tyrant and butcher since before the Armada started scorching every planet it disagreed with. You're a fucking hypocrite."

Balyra moved to slap him, but Xade caught the Vestal's hand. An unbending will dominated Xade's gaze, though not a trace of anger. Something wilted inside Balyra as she stared back, some internal revelation that made her shudder and turn away.

"What is it you want? You're hiding it from your superiors, whatever it is." He ran a hand through violet and yellow wildflowers, wondering if the rest of their home world had been just as beautiful. Wondering how many more worlds might be destroyed.

"Tell me what you saw." Balyra yanked her hand back from Xade.

"Some craters on a desert world," Jerr said. "A blue shard. Then a starship bay crammed with bodies."

"Did you see me?" The eagerness in Balyra's voice pierced her austere demeanor.

"So Vestals do possess vanity."

"Wrong—I must know if what I have undertaken has any hope of success," Balyra said. "Such as aiding the galaxy's most-wanted criminal."

"And I need to know why you're helping me." Jerr crossed his arms.

"It is time for Vestal House to depose the Dominion's autocracy and assume control of humanity's future," Balyra said. "That means Revor must be removed. It is his policies that spawn continual unrest in the galaxy."

"What're your policies?" Jerr kept his voice neutral.

"A more benign control." Balyra ran a finger down a statue's cheek as if tracing a tear. "Humanity's history is one of suffering, then occasional evolution due to that suffering. Such is the way of Vestal House. We understand pain and the growth required afterward better than anyone. That growth is now stunted due to Revor's greed."

"You're not greedy?" Jerr snorted. "You've done whatever it takes to remain alive all these centuries, you keep armed morga—"

"Only because I've had to. Vestal House didn't require endless armies to keep the Elder States in line. The Dominion under our rule would be no different."

Xade shook her head. "Pendulous."

Balyra scowled at her. "The Dominion's structure sags because of Revor's callous management. The reborn never truly grow as individuals. That system must be eliminated. No more reborn. Under me, the empire could—"

"Under you?" Jerr's brows raised.

"Why not?" There was an edge in Balyra's voice. "Should it be you? A reborn that common people already loathe? A man who destroys a Leviathan on a whim?"

"I had to so we could escape," Jerr said.

"So you knew those other Leviathans would appear?" Balyra asked. "How?"

"Think about what drives these ships," Jerr said.

Balyra watched as Xade drew up a Leviathan schematic on her nodus. "I do not require a physics lesson."

"A gravity engine," Jerr said. "It creates an artificial neutron star every time a Leviathan travels. That gravity is pushed outward, creating a rift in space-time."

"Go on." Balyra stood very still.

He almost didn't continue, having already heard the same conversation.

"What if we could reverse that gravity? What if the Leviathan draws things to it, instead of pushing them away?"

Xade's nodus displayed the results.

Balyra's eyes widened. "No. That would mean—"

Jerr nodded. "I know what it means."

"That sounds like how the Weavers were trapped." Balyra rubbed her shoulders. "Revor's ships crippled one of their vessels. One that contained a peace delegation, after his Armada had nearly annihilated their race. The disturbance in space-time prevented them from escaping. You did the same so Revor could not easily follow us."

A faraway look entered Balyra's eyes as she touched the statue of a young woman in ancient robes. The sculpt was so lifelike Jerr expected it to open its eyes and speak.

"Then he sent in the Kieta to finish the job?" Jerr asked.

Balyra blinked and left the statue alone. "Yes."

"So, how does Revor control them? Their alliance can't be a willing one."

"Your voices haven't told you?" Balyra sniffed.

"You don't know, either," Jerr said. "Because, if you did, you would've—."

"The Kieta must be kept under control," Balyra said. "They would destroy us otherwise. They do not want anyone else traveling through the Shroud."

Xade's brows lowered. "Contentious."

"Then maybe humanity doesn't need the Shroud anymore," Jerr said.

"Without it, humanity cannot grow. If it cannot grow, then it will wither and die. I cannot allow that!" Balyra ambled among the statues, then knocked one over. It smashed on the floor, little marble pebbles spreading like stars flung from a dying cluster.

"Then…what do you want from me?"

Balyra knelt in the rubble and gingerly picked up a few pieces. "Let Revor reduce the Dominion, and the reborn, to ashes. Let his foolish, costly edifice collapse. Vestal House can lead humanity into a future where no one is enslaved lifetime after lifetime, where we can move on to other galaxies—but only after it has been purged."

"Hideous," Xade said.

"Growth does not come without sacrifice," Balyra said. "Humanity has festered into a boil that must be lanced. You can help me do it, Jerr."

He shook his head. "Why should you be trusted with this?"

"Because Vestal House has purged itself for millennia." A terminal bitterness underlined her tone. "We have merely waited for the rest of humanity to catch up."

"And it will start on a little desert planet? One you swore never to return to?"

Balyra looked away and nodded. "Yes. Kadah IV. Where Revor met the Kieta."

Xade's eyes widened at the planet's mention.

"What about your superior? The Matriarch?"

"She will remain ignorant until the time is right. Now…excuse me." Balyra walked back through the chamber until Jerr lost sight of her among the statues and icons. A ghost returning to its resting place.

The statue she'd knocked over had Balyra's face.

At the door, a morga sentry appeared. "Your accommodations are ready."

"Okay, then. Show us to our cabin."

The morga said nothing as she led Jerr and Xade through *Prophetess* on a tram. As they sped through dim tunnels, he spotted apartments that might have been villas from humanity's past. After exiting the tram at the next dock, the morga directed them through a world straight from a primeval fairy tale.

Vines and flowers wound around columns, porticos, and atriums, all crafted from stone. The facsimile streets smelled of fresh flowers and citrus. The lighting resembled daylight on a world with a middle-aged, main sequence sun. Even the gravity adjusted to suit Jerr. He walked comfortably on real, living grass.

"Luminous." Xade took his hand in hers.

"Yes. It certainly is." The effect was such that Jerr almost forgot about reality outside the picturesque realm they now traveled. People dressed in elegant robes tended gardens, prayed at Flame shrines, or engaged in religious discourse in amphitheaters. Disguised as caryatid columns or statues, a few Sisters kept a cautious eye on the trio.

"Balyra's planning a coup," Jerr whispered. "She'll use us to take over Vestal House. Then, to topple Revor. But I don't trust her."

He stopped talking until after a monk walked by.

"Vestals are obsessed with the past. They live in it. That's why they're afraid that I see the future. They're afraid of the voices, because they tell me the Vestal's crimes."

Xade said nothing, examining her damaged arm.

"Guess you know more about the past than any of us," he said. "But you're not afraid of anything. Not me, not the Dominion. Not the truth. Wish I could be like that."

She smiled sadly, squeezed his hand.

The morga stopped before a small cottage, complete with fountain and flower garden. Fresh food and a change of clothes for Jerr waited within. A cube of biomech substrate to replace Xade's hand lay on a table. She regarded it with sadness. Maybe the cube reminded her of her own homeworld, wherever that was.

After removing the Starjumper, Jerr sat in a wicker chair. He gripped the carved wooden armrests. He'd not seen wooden artwork in several lifetimes.

How many lifetimes had Xade waited for someone like him? And now, the Vestals had invested themselves in his plight for a reason. He needed to find out why.

Chapter 22

The Weavers were never slaves,
Yet shackled themselves with doubt,
Bowing to that callous master, time.
The Weavers were never heroes,
Yet fought and loved as martyrs,
Failing and dying as villains.

Epiphanies of the Shroud

After Jerr and Xade left, Balyra turned to a statue sculpted like a fellow Sister. It wasn't one from her collection. Balyra kept her arms loose at her sides. Ready to strike.

The statue moved, being a sentry in disguise. Never before had Balyra been spied on. Only one person knew she frequented the art chamber.

"Your actions conflict with the Matriarch's orders." The Sister frowned.

"Jerr is our prisoner," Balyra said. "We cannot simply kill him."

"You are making arrangements with him that Vestal House cannot comply with," the Sister said. "I must report this."

"We each have our duties." Balyra walked around her. Not breaking eye contact.

The Sister scowled. "May the Flame guide my—"

Balyra's left hand whipped out. The Sister blocked it. Ready for such a move, Balyra struck with her right, crushing the woman's neck. The Sister still struggled, though, and Balyra kicked her in the chest. Flesh and ribcage caved in.

The Sister backhanded Balyra to the floor. Balyra rolled aside as her former comrade slammed statues over in an effort to crush her. The sculptures snapped apart in dust clouds filled with marble shrapnel. Balyra leapt up and punched her to her knees.

The other woman reached for a pistol inside her robes.

She overturned a statue onto the Sister's head. With a wet crunch and a pop, the woman stopped moving. Blood and servo fluid pooled from under the statue.

For the first time in ages, Balyra was breathing hard after killing another person. If Vestals were still people. Was it murder, slaying one that had lived, stolen, and lied for so many centuries, just like herself? She summoned a drone to clean up the mess.

Balyra squeezed the dead Sister's hand. "Forgive me. I do this for the good of all ..." She gazed at the one statue that mattered to her. It remained intact.

Her betrayal was complete. It was blasphemy to spill blood on a ship that was Vestal House in all but name. Gods and voids, how long she had avoided it. No more.

She'd contemplated this course of action. Unlike Jerr, though, she had no idea where it might lead. The Matriarch would find out Balyra needed to have everything prepared by then. But Revor would follow *Prophetess* once Third Echelon was ashes. Perhaps the fool was fulfilling the very thing he feared—imperial collapse.

Sands were plummeting through the hourglass. There was no turning back now.

As the drone cleaned up the corpse, Balyra stared at the icons, the priceless artworks celebrating the order she'd helped survive. There was a time she'd held crying children in her arms, comforting them. Aiding the diseased, or the wounded, in one of the galaxy's countless calamities. But that person died long ago.

She studied herself in an ancient mirror, its border featuring saints accepting the solar power packs in place of their hearts, and the holy vat flesh grown from the original Vestal, in place of their own. Very few knew that. Wearing the cloned flesh of a woman long dead, even sharing some of her facial features. On some Elder

States worlds, the faithful called her kind angels. They worshipped as all disciples do: without question.

That was how she'd served. In the end, the differences were mere semantics.

One alcove in the chamber held an energy field. Within the field hovered the remains of Vestal armor. The winged cuirass was scorched, the red unisuit shriveled and blackened. The person who wore it was long gone. Killed by the Kieta.

Balyra stormed past the alcove. The promises she'd made that day, to see her safe, still gnawed at her conscience. Balyra remembered that scream. Remembered picking up those scraps since nothing else remained. And Revor had proclaimed it a victory.

This time she would finish the job. All the Kieta would die for what they did.

She had suffered all of her existence for the sake of others. Now they would suffer in turn. The apocalypse ushered in by Revor and Jerr would create victims by the multitudes. Begging for Vestal House—for her—to save them.

And with Jerr under her control, spotting future traitors or rivals, she would know who deserved saving. Who deserved to die.

Controlling Jerr would be no problem; he was a grunt and could be placated with wealth, power. Sex. Simple pleasures that Balyra had long mastered. But Xade would be an obstacle to Balyra's thrall over him. She would have to be eliminated.

The easiest way would be to undermine Jerr's trust in his pretty robot.

She left the chamber and headed for the Sanctum. The Matriarch might be afraid, but she was no fool. There would be many guards. Many she had known for centuries.

Balyra would have to be quick.

Xade paced the atrium with nervous energy. She avoided eye contact.

Jerr rose and embraced her. Though Xade didn't shy away, she remained tense.

"I'm worried too, but we need to know what Balyra wants from us," he said. "That's how we'll stop the Dominion. That's how…"

Everything in his sight blurred at the edges. He gripped Xade tight, afraid he might lose her as the chamber rippled. It was as if he viewed reality underwater. His sight became distorted, bloated. There was a tug at his being, stronger than gravity.

"We did not wish this upon you. But we cannot wait any longer."

Jerr grunted as a flurry of images invaded his mind. By now, he'd grown accustomed to the unbidden missives. The more he traveled the Shroud, however, the more he saw. The easier it became, forgetting where present ended, and future began.

Standing with Balyra on a desert world, overlooking two craters. Fighters strafe a dropship. Meteors tumble over the landscape. The resulting smoke and dust plume, making him cough and squint as Balyra vanishes in silvery swirls.

He couldn't see who attacked them. Or, rather, who would attack them.

"Carry it into the Shroud. Do not let it out. It must die there."

"What must die?" He crushed Xade against him.

His vision changes from the desert world to a massive bay, extending for miles. All gray and chrome bulkheads. Near-infinite tiers of vats and growth tubes rise in an edifice mind-numbing in its implications.

"It must die."

The hull splits open.

Jerr fell to his knees and cried out as the visions departed. While he blinked away their remnants, all reality was altered. He visualized a slight lensing affect around everything. The chair, the grass outside the atrium, even the light waves emanating from the globe far above. Even Xade in his arms, who cradled his head with her single hand.

"Horrendous," she said.

"What?"

Xade's palm nodus activated. It showed the image of a man. Silver mask. Black uniform. Eyes obscured by tinted glass.

"Revor." It wasn't a question.

The image switched to a video feed. It showed Revor commanding a large battle fleet. Leading human forces against Idreuns, Repta, Squidrans, and finally, the Weavers. His orders were genocidal. His manner, cold and calculating. World after world, incinerated to the crust.

"The Armada," Jerr said.

He'd fantasized about those battles as a child, playing with model ships or fighting hordes of Class I Repta with a stick in his high gravity yard. Jerr smiled; he'd not remembered that for a long time. But the smile waned.

"How'd you find this data?"

The feed showed Xade herself on the bridge of Revor's command ship. The same blue dermaflesh, dark blue exoskeleton … but her pale blue eyes lacked their current emotional depth. Her face had been just as lovely then, but without expression, like one of the statues in Balyra's art chamber.

Jaw tight, he started to speak, but she shook her head.

The feed changed again. This time, Xade knelt beside Revor on the bridge. Outside the viewports, his fleet laid waste to a world completely covered by machines: 78 Vaaqa D. A dizzying array of orbital platforms, solar arrays, starports—connected to facilities all the way down to the planet's surface.

It was Xade's homeworld.

"Shit," Jerr breathed.

As the destruction rained down, pieces of the planet morphed and convulsed as if trying to shrug off the great assault. But in the end, the planet became a darkened ball of cooled slag. Revor forced Xade to fire the final destabilizing blast, sending the world out of its original orbit. In time, it would leave its parent system entirely, becoming a rogue world drifting between the stars. An orphan abandoned after the murder of its parents.

The feed showed one final image. Xade experiencing her first emotions: despair, shock, anger. Fused into a perpetual guilt.

"I can't…" Jerr leaned on the chair for support. His head swam with the images. The Shroud's lensing made them all too real, like he'd been there.

As the feed continued, Revor told her the same would happen to a thousand other worlds if she didn't serve him. He scattered her species across the galaxy and hoarded the surviving biomech substrate cubes—the substance used to heal themselves, even create new Theux. After the Armada's final victory, Revor stationed her on *Bhaellator*. Knowing she'd always keep her oath, so no other worlds would be destroyed.

"Enough." His voice was tight. "I don't want to see any more."

She reached for him, but Jerr stepped back. Her lower lip trembled.

"You killed your own people," he whispered.

Face scrunched with grief, she slowly nodded.

"To save the rest of us? How can I believe that?"

Not until she shrank back did he know he was shouting.

The nodus switched to another feed: Xade studying the Shroud. It couldn't be inhabited unless one was a Kieta or aboard a starship. For centuries Xade had computed the likelihood of that changing. Jerr watched as the feed showed her efforts over time. The equations and variables were near infinite to his untrained eye.

The feed continued. Xade had calculated that of all the species to access the Shroud, humans would be the first changed by it at the cellular level. Thus, her race had selected humanity as its role model afterward. Copying them, learning their emotions.

Jerr scowled. "You served Revor. You aided him in destroying worlds, whole solar systems. The genocide of intelligent species. All so you could be like us?"

Ancient videos played one after the other on the nodus. Showing Vestals killing those same species, firsthand. Balyra was in some of them, leading thousands of troops.

A rebirth vat appeared in the feed. Xade stood over it, studying her nodus. Tweaking a mutation she'd discovered, then ensuring it appeared in every future rebirth.

Jerr's rebirths and no others. Not even his DNA twins on *Bhaellator.* Only him.

He kept glaring back and forth from her, to the video feed.

Tampering with a reborn's DNA template was illegal. But Xade had done it over and over, each successive clone a new experiment, a new test subject. Risking her life.

She was responsible for his precognition.

The videos revealed that the Shroud contained the echoes of all events, past and future, in a never-ending reverberation through space-time. His sensitivity to the Shroud allowed him to see some of those echoes. Hear the voices of the dead and the unborn.

"Why?" he whispered.

Xade avoided Jerr's eyes.

The illusionary vat became a nodus library. Xade stood surrounded by holographic displays of countless alien species. Many of them were extinct. Slain during the Armada Era. Xade learned all she could about each one, over many thousands of human hours. Over time, the coldness in her stance gradually gave way to slumped shoulders, pinched expressions. Shuddering on her knees, face held in both hands.

Some of Jerr's anger waned. Xade had learned emotions the harshest way. Maybe she'd hated herself for millennia. Punished in ways far worse than physical pain or death.

Xade faced him while the feed continued. Her species had waited until a race developed a sensitivity to the Shroud. A species that was capable of prescience might prevent their own destruction and, statistically, prefer peace with others. With such clairvoyance it could hear the cries of the dead, forever echoing in space-time.

Hear those cries and thus reveal the Dominion's crimes.

The feed completed. Neither spoke for a time.

"How long have you known me, then?"

Her nodus displayed him boarding *Bhaellator*: the log indicated it was the first time. In a series of classified feeds he outperformed all the other soldiers, even sacrificing himself to save Xade during an Idreun raid on *Bhaellator*.

His first death.

"What? Play…play that part again." His skin flooded with heat.

The feed rewound and played. Idreun rebels had managed to sneak aboard *Bhaellator* in a captured Dominion shuttle. Jerr and Xade waited in the hangar, thinking it a routine security check. But the hatch flew open. Weapons fired, bodies fell. One warrior shot a piercer rifle at Xade. Jerr leapt before her in time, taking the hit in the chest.

He'd perished instantly. Even after the battle was won, Xade knelt over his body. Clasping his lifeless hand tight.

"I died…saving you?" Jerr's knees weakened until he finally sat down.

She nodded.

"And all the other rebirths since then? You watched over me?"

Eyes closed, she nodded again. The realizer showed each of his combat deaths. Mouth open, Jerr witnessed all his glories, in battles now legendary in their respective systems. Dossiers of his deeds, filed away for the good of the empire.

"You think that makes up for what you did?"

She regarded him with sorrow.

"Don't look at me that way. You can't erase the past by helping me."

"Piteous," Xade said.

"I don't need pity!" He stormed over to her. "When I die this time, will you watch over the next Jerr Manivo? Will you tell him all of these things? That you care about him only so you can make yourself forget about serving Revor?"

She hung her head.

The Dominion had used him all his many lives, but this was different. He felt like the tool of someone he truly cared about. He wanted her feelings to be real in ways his old wife and son weren't any longer. They might as well have been dreams now.

And the way Xade always touched his chest … it was how his wife liked to touch him. A hand over his heart. A barrier against the horrors of the world outside the one they'd created together. No doubt she'd copied it from his mind. Emulated it to perfection. The worst part was not knowing whether she'd done it to gain his confidence, or because she meant what that touch implied.

"Continuous," she whispered, eyes filled with apology.

He stalked into the galley and found a bottle of red Luorn wine. Such a vintage would've cost him a month's pay on *Bhaellator*. Thinking about his former home—hell, prison—made him smash the neck on the counter's edge, bypassing the need of a corkscrew. Maroon liquid sloshed over his hand, splattering on the floor.

"I don't give a damn if you can't talk." Jerr embraces Xade. "All I care about…"

His grip on the bottle shook. Its vanilla and dark berry bouquet made him salivate.

One taste. Everything would be okay. Just one taste.

"All I care about…"

Jerr exhaled slowly. Walked over to the galley drain. Poured out the wine.

He walked back to her. "Will you love the next version of me?"

Xade deactivated her nodus and straightened. Not backing down from him.

"Answer me."

Xade nodded, blinking as if she were crying. Which a Theux was incapable of doing, lacking tear ducts.

"Will you?" He grabbed her by the shoulders and shook her.

Trembling, she punched his chest. "Continuous. Continuous!"

"What does that mean to me?" he shouted. "Did you tell that to all the others? Everyone you watched die, every fucking reborn that you—"

Xade knocked him down and straddled him. Slapping, punching. "Continuous!"

Jerr grabbed her fist in both hands, barely stopping her despite his own strength.

She yanked free, started to punch again, then flung her arms into the air and mouthed a wordless scream. The agonized shame in it broke Jerr's heart.

Lying still, arms splayed out, Jerr tried to catch his breath. He knew she'd not meant to do those things. That she was trying to bring Revor down so it could never happen again. What had really angered him was the fear that her affection might be false.

She lay overtop him, caressing all the places she'd struck. Shuddering all the while, like someone who'd wept to the point of exhaustion.

"Reveal us."

He wrapped his arms around her. She sagged onto his chest, breathing heavily against his neck.

Jerr stares out at a dark, lifeless void, floating between star systems. Something glows blue in his hand. Balyra stands nearby, tattered red cloak fluttering.

Xade whispered over and over in his ear. "Continuous… continuous…"

"Yeah," he said. "Me too."

There was an extra contingent of armored morga outside the Sanctum. Though alarmed, Balyra nodded and continued as if she'd been summoned.

"Confessor, the Matriarch has forbidden any audience until she has discovered why *Prophetess* departed Third Echelon," the morga captain said.

"I am here to update her on that information," Balyra said.

They stared each other down. She'd come too far to be turned away now.

"Very well, Confessor." The captain stood aside and the morga cleared a path. As she walked between them, Balyra stung with the thought they could simply stab her all at once, like something from the grand assassination legends of the Elder States. But they let her pass unharmed. The great door disappeared behind her as she entered.

The Matriarch paced the causeway in a translucent red robe, metalloid nudity gleaming underneath. She was breaking protocol, being mobile—and they weren't alone. Balyra regretted not bringing another null dagger. One wouldn't be enough.

One of Jerr's reborn knelt before the Matriarch, consternation and fear on his dusky features. The Matriarch smiled.

Gods and voids, there would be death before that door opened again.

"Confessor Balyra," the Matriarch called in a light feminine voice, lending her the air of a younger woman. "I am glad you have come. And at so opportune a moment."

Carefully walking forward, Balyra's skin prickled upon seeing no guards. "It is my pleasure, Matriarch. What, in all your wisdom, have you discovered?"

The Matriarch ran her fingers down the reborn's cheek. "You did well, bringing me such a prize. Revor will be even more pleased."

"He is quite a specimen," Balyra said. "Trained to fight in multiple arts—"

The Matriarch waved a hand. "I do not care about his martial abilities. I am interested in what he knows. What he has told me."

Balyra let her hand dangle near the null dagger hidden at her thigh. "Indeed?"

"He says Jerr Manivo implored them to rebel." The Matriarch sauntered around Balyra, the hem of her robe teasing Balyra's figure like the caress of a lover. "Not just himself, but tens of thousands of other reborn. Perhaps in other systems."

"That is extraordinary," Balyra said. "Has he told anyone else of this?"

"Oh, no," the Matriarch said. "The Sisters brought him here at his request, but unlike the soldier you interrogated on Ghela Beta, this one surrendered information."

"I live to serve the Dominion, Matriarch," the reborn said.

"He must be studied," Balyra said. "Might I take him for a psychopomp session?"

"Unnecessary," the Matriarch said. "It is amazing what the human mind can manage, isn't it? Why, Jerr Manivo saw the future as much as any telepath in a fable. But his brain is young. It has not endured the centuries like ours. It has not been replaced at the cellular level with stem injections or circoid dumps. It has not aged to the point that he cannot recognize himself as a human, thus losing his empathy."

Balyra kept her hand near the dagger. The Matriarch had never spoken like this.

"Empathy is what keeps us human," the Matriarch said. "Generating concern for our fellows, our comrades. Our allies."

The null dagger was an older design, but one swipe would destroy a target's circoids, disable all network connections, and force adrenaline reserves into the subject's heart, killing them. She had not used it for three millennia.

"It makes them warn us of those who would betray us." The Matriarch scowled.

Balyra went for the dagger but four reborn in Starjumpers rocketed up from under the causeway. She smashed one's helmet, then kicked another aside, but they came again. Armored fists crunched into her abdomen. A diffusion blaster leveled at her head.

Ramming a knee through a faceplate, Balyra freed the dagger. A diffusion beam zipped past her temples, burning off the end of her braid. She thrust and swiped. Two reborn collapsed, clutching their chests. A third fired at her again, but she kicked one of his dying twins into the line of fire. Superheated light blew through armor and flesh, flinging the dead man off the causeway. The blast threw her off balance. Balyra rolled to shield her fall and caught sight of the Matriarch. She threw the dagger.

A morga leapt into the weapon's path. The blade sunk into its chest, killing it.

The other two reborn and a squad of morga tackled Balyra to the floor. Soon she was forced to her knees before the Matriarch. Dozens of Sisters entered the Sanctum.

"He told me you took Manivo prisoner instead of killing him," the Matriarch said in a deeper voice. "I gave you that null dagger long ago. Now you would use it against me? Against Vestal House, and the Dominion itself?"

Balyra didn't struggle. "Not against what is in my heart."

Emotions played across the Matriarch's features, but Balyra knew her lover would never voice them publicly. Not even to save her. This betrayal was personal.

"Revor ensured humanity's survival," the Matriarch said. "Jerr's death will guarantee it. Can you not see? There is peace in slavery and corruption. Jerr's rebellion will only beget death, disruption. Vestal House cannot allow it."

"You'll always be a servant," Balyra said. "To the Flame, to Revor. To lies."

The Matriarch pried the dagger from the morga and slit Balyra's unisuit. "There will indeed be a psychopomp session, Confessor. But it will not be to your liking."

Chapter 23

The only way to maintain a military in peacetime is to invent threats or antagonize weaker states into a state of aggression. Thus large arms budgets, zealous patriotism, and combat deaths become acceptable to a society that only hears about, yet never sees, these threats. Making these acceptable to the rank and file requires far less.

Narrative of the Armada, Chapter 2

"Reveal us, Weaver. The thread is in your hands. Don't let them unravel it."

Jerr awoke at the voices whispering in his ear. A collective plea from the Shroud.

Xade sat beside him on the cot, replacing her lost hand with the biomech substrate. She attached it to her forearm. One moment it was a cube; the next, it was as if it'd simply been her balled fist all along. She studied the new appendage, then clasped it to her chest. Only now, knowing the fate of her people, did Jerr realize why the cube healed her body while piercing her heart.

A stifling silence hung over the area outside.

"Has anyone checked on us?" Jerr rose, scanning the room.

"Erroneous," she said.

"It must die, before it devours you all."

He eased up to the atrium doorway and peered around. No one tended their garden. The shrines were empty. He glanced at the ruined Starjumper's weaponry.

Balyra appears in his mind: beaten, hands sliced off, bowels opened—yet she stares up at someone with defiance. The background is decorated in icons, shadowed by the vastness of a great drop. The Sanctum.

Jerr hurried to the Starjumper. "We need to find Balyra."

Xade clicked her new hand into place and flexed its fingers. "Dangerous."

Six reborn fly over the gardens, firing at him as soon as he leaves the atrium. White-hot rounds sear through his skin, incinerating organs as he shoots back.

"Shit." Jerr detached the diffusion blaster from the suit and secured the heat sink unit to his belt. Using Rezal state, he calculated the paths the reborn would take once they flew through the deck entrance. "Stay close. There's going to be trouble."

They were turning on him. Whether out of loyalty to the Dominion, coercion from Vestal House, or revenge for bringing this upon them, he didn't care. He'd kill them.

"Before it devours you all."

The whine of boot thrusters reached his ears.

They shared a look. He squeezed Xade's hand, then flung the Starjumper outside.

A barrage of diffusion beams turned the armor into glowing orange debris. Jerr fell into Rezal, judged the location of the shooter based on the firing trajectory, and shot through the atrium's wall at an angle. Someone screamed. A burning airborne figure flew over the atrium and crashed into a nearby crop field.

"Move!" Jerr ran outside as gauss rounds flattened the atrium walls. Masonry and dust blew over the area. Xade appeared beside him as they fled through an orchard. Scatter shot and gauss salvos shredded tree trunks, branches. Jerr grabbed Xade and ducked past a tree, knowing it would fall. Dodged a piercer shot, having already seen it rip through his shoulder. Fell prone and blasted the reborn waiting outside the fence.

His adversaries were fast, smart. Tenacious and merciless. But he saw their next move by a fraction of a second.

"Go!" Jerr shoved Xade toward a shrine. Gambling with her life. He hated himself for doing it. Yet, as he'd already envisioned, a reborn jetted for her, autoloading a gauss shot. Rezal allowed Jerr to pinpoint the exact area to hit, the exact second to fire.

Eyes closed, he squeezed the trigger.

His diffusion shot struck the reborn's gauss magazine. The blast disintegrated the man, as well as blinding two other reborn flying toward the shrine. Jerr opened his eyes and enfiladed the pair. The shots liquefied armor, dissolved bones.

"Xade, only one—"

A boot slammed into his back, flinging Jerr into the shrine wall. His cheekbone, left elbow, and ribs shattered. Air was knocked from his lungs.

"More?" The final reborn hovered over him, boot thrusters flaring like twin suns.

Jerr held down the trigger, but the reborn kicked away both weapon and heat sink before they charged to dangerous levels. Gasping, Jerr scratched fingers through the dirt, trying to rise. A piercer barrel touched his neck.

"You stupid bastard," the reborn said. "I had a career ahead of me. Shoot some dumbass rebels, put down a few riots. And if I die? I get to come back. Like you."

"They're … using us …" Jerr grunted as pain stabbed through his body.

"I don't care." The barrel pressed into Jerr's back. "Who the fuck are you to decide my future? You had your chance. Now it's my turn."

"Don't …"

His kick flipped Jerr over. Jerr sucked through his teeth, trembling with agony.

"Look at me, asshole." The reborn flung off his helmet. It was a younger version of himself. "Look at the future."

"Fatuous."

The reborn spun around as Xade slammed a large rock through his skull. The body fell, convulsed, then lay still. She stood over it, eyes haunted with despair.

Using the shrine wall to brace himself, Jerr got to his feet. "Thanks."

His voice made her blink. She hurried over and steadied him. "Atrocious."

"We need to keep moving. More will come, once these don't answer back."

She examined his wounds. "Contentious."

"Not now." He grimaced at the raw aches. "We need to find Tunva—"

Xade placed her fingers against his lips. She was trembling. Looking back and forth from him, to the reborn she'd just killed.

"That wasn't me," he said. "You had to do it."

Her face pinched with anguish. "Villainous."

"Help me into his Starjumper," Jerr said. "It's the only way I'll walk out of here."

Thanks to Xade's quick hands, she had him in the dead reborn's suit within minutes. Though blood still stained the collar and chest, he didn't care. Wearing a Build 7.0 at least secured his broken ribs and cushioned his footsteps against the pain.

He made sure to secure the etherspace box in an empty ammo magazine.

They left the deck and walked down a great hall. Xade accessed *Prophetess*'s network despite its powerful encryption. Her nodus showed all decks on alert.

"Then where the hell is everybody?" He glanced up and down the hall, checked his sensors. Nobody.

"Suspicious."

"Yes, I…" The hall rippled in Jerr's sight.

The floor shakes. An alarm echoes down the ancient corridors. Xade stares at her nodus, shaking her head in disbelief. The entire hall quakes, then all is still.

Her nodus shows their deck has detached from Prophetess. Marooning them forever in the Shroud.

"Grab onto me!"

As soon as Xade wrapped her arms around him, Jerr fired his thrusters. They rocketed down the hall, past lacquered icons, vine-draped balustrades. Flying for the exit.

Xade patched his HUD into *Prophetess*'s network. Five seconds until release.

They wouldn't make it.

Jerr fired three gauss rounds at the access hatch as the deck separated from *Prophetess*. The explosion punched through the hatch and bulkheads. Holding Xade tight, Jerr flew straight through the explosion into space. Finding himself in the vacuum between the ship and the detached deck. He'd never been in the Shroud like this before. Always onboard a Leviathan—never outside it. He fought back nausea.

The Shroud had a drifting, weightless quality, akin to typical vacuum. The similarity ended there as stars lensed around them— like they were close one moment, then light years away the next. Blips of light popped across his vision. The ghostly afterimages of worlds, ships, and galaxies appeared and vanished.

"Do not let go of the thread."

All of his senses surged with a fluidity he couldn't control. Unable to shut off the thrusters, they jetted for the adjoining deck's hatch. It was slowly receding as *Prophetess* journeyed on.

Trying to use Rezal, Jerr focused on the hatch. Focused on his firing controls. They were close enough that he and Xade were still part of *Prophetess*'s gravity well. Still a chance of reaching the vessel before the ship left them behind in the Shroud.

Xade stiffened as the exoskeleton covered her entire body, sheathing her in a navy blue shell. Her eyes glowed azure through a full-face mask. But it was too late.

Prophetess drifted farther away, and with it, the influence of its gravity well. The spiral arms of the galaxy distorted around him like the tendrils of a great beast, refusing to release him. Time slowed. The Shroud would claim them after all.

"Reveal us, Weaver."

Jerr fired the cannon. The rounds streaked lazily through the expanse. Independent actors free of his control. Much like his reborn. Darei had been so right.

"The thread is in your hands."

The rounds blew through the other hatch. Seconds crawled by as Jerr witnessed the shattering of metal, the release of atmosphere, in terminal slow motion. Vestals and reborn spilled into the darkness, their mouths open in silent screams.

Sound scraped his eardrums as Jerr flew through the ruined hatch. His thrusters barely kept the decompression effect from tossing them back out, but seconds later, a Vestal secured the blast shielding. A wall of solid metal slammed over the breach.

Outside the nearest viewport, the detached deck—where he and Xade had just been—drifted away, only to be destroyed by *Prophetess*'s starboard batteries.

Not just marooned, then. They wanted him dead.

Now, inside the safety of *Prophetess*'s gravity, the passage of time normalized.

Still in Rezal state, Jerr identified, targeted, and shot eight opponents before the rest recognized his threat. By then, only two Vestals remained standing, hands up.

"You must be desperate trying something like that." Jerr released Xade, whose exoskeleton receded to normal. "Where is Confessor Balyra?"

"May the Flame burn you!" one Vestal said, setting off a new alarm. "May it—"

Jerr bisected her head with a piercer shot and aimed at her comrade. "Where?"

The other Vestal swallowed.

"Odious." Xade shut off the alarm on her nodus, but shot Jerr a look.

Jerr switched to the diffusion blaster. "Last chance."

"She has been taken to the Sanctum," the Vestal blurted.

"Xade, find the closest tram dock. Then we'll go get Tunva from Med Deck." He wrenched the Vestal's hands behind her back. "You're coming, too."

"Harmonious," Xade said in a sarcastic tone.

"One big happy family," Jerr said. "But it's them or us at this point. I choose us."

⚜ ⚜ ⚜

Kneeling before the Matriarch, Balyra was reminded of her initiation ceremony nearly twenty thousand years ago. Wearing nothing but her underveil, a flimsy garment intended to remind Sisters of their chastity, their purity. Their oath. Supposedly the Vestals of old had worn these and nothing else, even on new colonies filled with lonely, abusive men. Vestal House had never feared confrontation.

Neither did she. She'd played her hand.

Balyra mentally counted red grains slipping through an hourglass. On her desert homeworld, the ancient, sand-filled chronometer represented one's life. Many were the times she'd flipped that hourglass, via technology and cybernetic transplants. No more.

Two Martial Brides held her down, dressed in black robes. They were the Matriarch's personal guard. Vultures trying to be angels.

The Matriarch brandished the null dagger like a prize. "This is something not seen by Vestal House in nearly a millennium. The Rite of Chastisement. Bear close witness and remember it well, my Sisters. This is the penalty for betrayal. This is the fate of a traitor, who is worse than a heretic—for this Sister knew better and still transgressed."

The reborn that first spoke to the Matriarch stood nearby, watching without emotion. His martial mind offered no mercy to traitors. To him, her punishment was just.

The Matriarch sliced off a lock of Balyra's hair. She loosed the strands over the side of the causeway, where they floated into the blackness. "Thus we cleave you from us, like an infection, so you will not taint the whole. For Vestal House is incorruptible."

"Incorruptible!" hundreds of gathered Sisters cried. They lined the causeway on either side, attired in full armor and robes. Thousands of morga knelt, holding lamps.

Balyra stiffened as the dagger neared her face.

"You were given the beauty of the original Vestal," the Matriarch said. "You were charged with representing her to the best of your ability. You have failed."

The edge sliced into Balyra's left cheek. Blood flowed from the cut, running over her jaw, down her neck, and staining her underveil. The unspoken statement being her spiritual hymen was broken for all to see. She was a Flame virgin no more.

Oh, how she'd bled for them over the millennia. In wars, raids, in the beds of men or women. She'd bled for them by the gallon. This was nothing.

"I know why you did it," the Matriarch whispered. "I should have suspected you sooner. She would be ashamed of you."

"Not of me," Balyra said. "Of you."

The Matriarch ripped away the underveil and ran the dagger's edge between Balyra's breasts. "Now must the sacred heart come free, to find solace in a worthier Sister. One who will not hang from the Shame Pillar, nor turn the heart black with evil."

The blade paused over her heart. It wasn't her original one, but it still beat to keep her alive. It was an animal trait, requiring a heart. Pumping the blood of life and warmth. The Matriarch had no such heart. That removed any compunction to take it from others.

"And now..." The Matriarch paused and glanced around.

A commotion built up in the Sanctum's vastness. The Matriarch turned all way round. The other Sisters stared down the causeway. The reborn armed their weapons.

Balyra smiled.

"You did as I ordered?" the Matriarch said. "You released Agri Deck 15?"

"Released and destroyed, Matriarch," a Sister said.

"I told you," Balyra said in calm voice. "He sees the future."

"Blasphemy," the Matriarch said. "No one could have—"

The doors to the Sanctum opened. Jerr entered in a Starjumper, limping. Xade and Tunva followed with a Vestal in tow. The Matriarch took a step backward.

The gathered Sisters and morga drew their weapons.

"Are you so afraid of me that you'd detach an entire deck, just to assassinate me?" Jerr's question echoed down the causeway. "Is this how Vestal House honors an oath?"

"You dare lecture me on my own ship?" the Matriarch cried.

"I was promised protection by Confessor Balyra Peran." Jerr paid the armed host along the causeway no mind. "A sacred Vestal oath. And now you're about to kill her."

"Silence the liar!" The Matriarch jabbed a metalloid finger in his direction.

Tunva pushed the captured Sister forward, who raised her voice. "It is true. We were directed to eliminate Jerr Manivo by separating his deck from *Prophetess*. His reborn were promised rewards if they helped."

Vestals were trained not to lie, at least to their own, from the first day of indoctrination. If one Sister's word was doubted, then the entire order would be open to question. No one had broken that taboo and lived.

The Brides holding Balyra loosened their grip. She hid her smile.

Arguing voices resonated through the chamber. All the while, the Matriarch screamed for someone to defend her honor and the sanctity of Vestal House. Combat robos flew in by the dozens and hovered over the causeway. Skiffs flew from the Sanctum's dark confines, filled with heavily armed morga.

Aiming at the Matriarch, not Jerr and his friends.

"You could not help yourself, could you?" the Matriarch murmured. "You will do anything, even destroy us, to get what you want."

"How many times did you help yourself to me?" Balyra stood as the Martial Brides stepped away. "Yet I am the one who has given everything. It is mine, by right."

"It is forbidden to shed blood in Vestal House," one Sister said.

The Matriarch tried to appear stern. "Sisters, believe me, I..."

"It is forbidden to break an oath," another called.

Balyra's own hypocrisy was for the greater good. Though she too had besmirched Vestal House, killing that Sister in the art chamber, no one would remember it.

"It is forbidden," a Martial Bride said. Scores of voices repeated the mantra.

"You pervert what we are, who we are!" the Matriarch shouted.

Balyra yanked the null dagger from her superior's grasp. "What you were."

The traitor reborn raised their weapons at Balyra, but the Martial Brides moved aside, allowing Jerr to come forward. He scowled at the faraway icons, the goddess-like colossi that offered nothing but cold dominance.

"Lies!" the Matriarch cried. "Jerr threatens all we have protected and fought for! Do you truly believe a man who sees the future will help us? He has done nothing but destroy and disrupt—"

"The Chastisement will take place," Balyra said. "But upon you, Matriarch. Vestal House is supposed to protect humanity. You would destroy it at Revor's bidding."

"Protect humanity?" the Matriarch asked. "You lying—"

"At Revor's order, you have kept the knowledge and gifts of Vestal House to yourself," Balyra said. "You have crammed it all aboard this ship, hiding behind the Shroud, but I see through you. We see what you have hoarded while millions suffer."

"No!" the Matriarch cried, but Balyra continued.

"We have let Revor tell us what to do. We have upheld a lie—his lie. We have killed in his name, strengthening his rule while we grow weaker. I say Vestal House should continue its true purpose. I say Vestal House should be the entire galaxy, not confined to one single Leviathan, where we dwell in darkness rather than light!"

Shouts of agreement resounded through the Sanctum. The Brides aimed at the dozen traitor reborn who refused to stand down.

Jerr walked right up to his irascible twins. "Which one of you betrayed me?"

"You'll kill us all anyway." The leader maintained his aim.

"Jerr's reborn is wrong." Tunva, though bandaged, still appeared menacing.

"Inglorious." Xade summoned her nodus and displayed images of Tunva fighting alongside one of Jerr's previous rebirths. Their camaraderie, their victories. His death.

"Bullshit," the leader said.

The other reborn shut off their weapons. Sweat trailing down his face, the leader grimaced in angry refusal.

"It doesn't have to be this way," Jerr said.

The leader aimed the piercer at his temple and fired. The headless body fell.

"You knew he would do that," Balyra said. Jerr said nothing, staring at the corpse.

"A new era begins now." Balyra faced the crowds gathered on the causeway. "No one can deny the future from those who can see it."

She clasped Jerr's hand and raised it. The Sisters saluted with upraised swords. After a few moments, Jerr pried free and shot her a look. Though bloody and naked, she returned his stare with a dignified nod. Appearances were more important now.

"Take her." Balyra contained her joy while two Brides led the Matriarch away. The metalloid bitch screamed and shouted orders, but none obeyed her. Two other Sisters draped a sheer red robe over Balyra's shoulders. Jerr looked on and blinked.

"You saw this, too." Balyra casually stepped around the dead reborn leader. "The future is but an extension of your senses. But can you control your reborn? Veja Qor?"

"They don't need control," Jerr said. "They need a plan. They need hope."

"You have provided the latter," Balyra said. "Allow me to provide the former."

Jerr watched a morga platoon escort his other reborn away. "Like you did with your superior? You knew she would try to have me killed. You're using me already."

Balyra made herself not bristle at his criticism. "As you will soon use me. First, we must talk. Privately." She wondered how much sand the hourglass retained.

As the morga led him into Balyra's quarters, *Prophetess* resonated with Vestal hymns, sung by the faithful in minarets on each deck.

The pleasant, ethereal voices clashed with the silence he'd grown accustomed to on *Bhaellator*. But the songs didn't calm him. Balyra didn't want Xade or Tunva in their discussion, and since a new Matriarch hadn't officially been chosen, Balyra refused an audience in the Sanctum.

Jerr didn't mind the last part. He needed no further reminders of Vestal crimes.

The cabin's simplicity startled him. Every inch of *Prophetess*'s interior, even storage areas, was decorated with ancient stylings or Flame artwork. Not so the quarters of the would-be Matriarch. Sparse furniture, no realizers or nodi. No bed, for Vestals rested in upright charging alcoves. No memorabilia, despite Balyra's long existence.

The only denial of the white-walled austerity was an hourglass, filled with red-tinted sand. Though resting on a corner table, it dominated the room.

Dressed in a scarlet unisuit, Balyra stared out a wide viewport, her back to him. A med drone hovered nearby, repairing the cut on her cheek. She didn't flinch.

Jerr waited until the morga left. "So, here we are."

"This was once the Jhoa system," Balyra said. "Seven populated worlds, sixty-three inhabited moons. Eighteen billion beings altogether. All gone."

Slowly approaching her, Jerr's heart chilled at the scene. Mangled derelicts orbited a brown planet bearing massive dark scars. Violent fires still burned in the depressions, flickering through the smoky atmosphere. The Shroud gave it all an interspatial quality, making the collection of dead worlds shimmer in the void.

"Revor?" He stood beside her.

"Yes. This will be repeated if his reign continues." She faced him. "Only now, with my manufactured beauty compromised, do you hide your revulsion of me."

"Old habits die hard."

"Humanity must develop new habits," she said. "Will you help me teach them?"

"Thought I just did."

"With control of Vestal House, I can return the favor."

Jerr turned away from the viewport. "There is an endgame available to us. It might cost us everything—but all of this would stop."

"One cannot gamble while worrying about the cost," Balyra said. "Tell me."

Standing with Balyra on a desert world. Two huge, empty craters. Fighters strafing a dropship. Meteors tumbling over a dead reborn.

"What's so special about Kadah IV?"

Balyra hesitated several moments, lips pursed. "Revor forged his alliance with the Kieta there. No one is allowed to enter the system."

"So if we threaten it, he'll come?" Jerr asked.

"Perhaps." She glanced at the hourglass.

"He's a Curator, one of the so-called 'Ageless'. You're a Vestal. Other than nostalgia, what could possibly be on Kadah that would—?"

"Revor gifted me that hourglass after the defeat of the Weavers," Balyra said. "The sand was taken from Kadah IV…my homeworld."

"Why would he use your homeworld to forge an alliance?" Jerr asked.

"Kadah IV was a Vestal stronghold," she said. "Our very best resided there. Their fighting skills were required to secure that so-called alliance."

"What happened?"

"You see it in the sands of that hourglass." Balyra swallowed. "Stained red with the blood of my people."

Jerr neared her. "Why would that bother you now? You've done much worse."

"And you haven't?" The hurt in her eyes stung him. "How many have died at the hands of your past rebirths? All your hundreds of thousands of reborn?"

"Then tell me how you'd change all that," Jerr said.

"With your precognition, Vestal House could stop wars before they began. Learn about diseases and plagues before they could spread. The greatest dangers—supernovas, asteroid impacts, solar flares—could be avoided, or at least, their damage lessened. Knowing the future is the same as guaranteeing galactic peace."

Studying the hourglass, Jerr rubbed his chin. "Who enforces this peace?"

"Vestal House," Balyra said. "If placed under my command, the Leviathans could respond to anything."

He kept looking at the hourglass so he wouldn't glare at her. "You want to rule."

"Why shouldn't I?" Her voice sounded so innocent he turned and stared.

"You're no better than Revor, then."

Balyra glowered. "Look at me, Jerr Manivo. Do you know why Vestals must undergo so much surgery, so much augmentation? Why we willingly endure all suffering across human experience? Do you even comprehend our purpose?"

"Power, immortality—"

She circled him, fists clenched. "We do it so that the rest of you won't have to. So that we may learn ways to control such agony and move the human race forward. Who else can lead you after Revor falls? Who else can show the galaxy a better way?"

"People deserve a choice," Jerr said.

"Remember the choices your fellow reborn made," she said. "They turned on you. Let me provide the guidance to avoid such mishaps."

"Why doesn't Revor try the same, instead of killing my kind now?" Jerr asked.

Balyra smirked. "He fears what he cannot control."

"And you think to control me?" he asked.

"I won't have to." The med drone sealed Balyra's cheek injury with a slight pop.

"Why?"

"Because we want the same things." Her smile was too full, too beautiful. "Revor defeated and the Reborn Initiative brought to an end."

"Then tell me about Kadah IV. What's Revor hidden there?"

"There are rumors." Balyra's smile waned into a frown.

"I'm not risking everything on rumors," Jerr said.

Balyra shooed the med drone away. "Some say he imprisoned the last Weaver there. Others think the secret to his identity is hidden in those deserts. Revor hasn't shown his face in many millennia. Even I have never seen it. Then there is the story that the world is precious to the Kieta, so he guards it to protect their alliance."

"So?" Jerr crossed his arms. "Stories won't save us."

"*Liberator* always appears and destroys whoever intrudes upon the system."

A desert planet. Old memories. A quick Rezal calculation gave Jerr an idea.

"Then Kadah IV is where we'll lure him."

"And what then?" Balyra asked. "*Prophetess* cannot engage his ship. He will have hundreds of thousands of reborn soldiers at his command."

"I'm not going there to fight," Jerr said. "I'm going to reveal his secret."

"And that alone will give us the galaxy?" Balyra laid a hand on his shoulder.

"I don't want the galaxy." He moved away from her. "I need to discuss this with Xade. We need her for this to work."

"She was Revor's servant, once." Her lip curled. "You trust her with this?"

"Yes." He knelt over the hourglass. "You should, too."

"That Theux has obeyed him for thousands of years—"

"So have you," he said.

Balyra glared out the viewport. "Then what role does she play? Have you ever wondered why she conspired with Veja Qor to free you?"

"There's a lot about her that is still a mystery to me." Jerr gently touched the hourglass's surface, then faced her. "Her loyalty and friendship aren't."

Her lips formed an uncompromising line. "I hope the Shroud hasn't misled you."

"I don't need voices to tell me what I already know." He walked out.

Chapter 24

After the Armada Era a new social stratification arose. One where those who traveled the Shroud, living onboard Leviathans, considered themselves superior to those who lived their entire existence on a single world. This sentiment grew as Shroud voyagers enhanced their bodies. Miming the old gods, racing between the stars, while ignorant peasants remained in thrall, barefoot in the dirt of their terrestrial prisons.

Elder States Archives, Volume LXXX

Prophetess remained on alert after the reborn mutiny and the Matriarch's imprisonment. The surviving reborn had been consigned to the onboard penitentiary, which was little more than a prison deck without cells. Jerr had no sympathy for them.

They'd betrayed him. Loyalty to the Dominion, to the glories of a martial existence, was bred into his erstwhile progeny. Even he found it difficult, solving their current dilemma without resorting to violence. It was all he knew. He hated it.

Outside the Sanctum, two morga tried assisting Tunva back to Med Deck, but she rebuffed all further aid from their robotic hosts. "Tunva will stand on her own now."

Jerr leaned close and lowered his voice. "Sorry. I didn't see this happening."

"Tunva is not angry with Jerr." She hesitated, then gripped his arm. "Did Jerr lie to Darei, about what Jerr saw? Before Darei died?"

"You mean, about Darei's future?" Jerr sighed and looked at the floor.

"Exiguous," Xade said.

"A lie is still a lie, Xade," Tunva said.

Jerr faced Tunva. "I wanted him to have some comfort before he died."

Tunva's grip tightened on his arm. "Tunva does not need comfort."

"I haven't been shown your future," Jerr said. "But if I ever see it, I won't lie to you. You have my word. Besides, you've always trusted what I saw before."

"Tunva still does. But so does Balyra Peran."

"I don't trust her," Jerr whispered. "But we need her right now. *Prophetess* will get us to the Faqar Belt, then Kadah IV. Plus, Balyra won't give me up to Revor as long as she thinks I can benefit her."

"Then Jerr is living a lie," Tunva said. "Balyra is still Dominion."

As Tunva left with the morga—limping, rather than accepting their help—Jerr caught Xade's sad look. He took her hand and walked to a tram in silence.

Balyra delayed further talk to allow him rest and recuperation. Provided with a comfortable cabin, he'd not refused. A med drone set his ribs and reconstructed his cheekbone. Xade insisted on completing the rest herself. Though they spoke less than usual, they made love anyway, despite his aches. But she made little eye contact.

Hours later, Jerr sat up on the bunk and yawned. Xade reclined in a chair opposite him, most of her flesh exposed, toying with her nodus. It was a strange comfort, how she'd lie beside him after they finished, not leaving the bunk until after he fell asleep.

Hell, when he could sleep. As long as they remained in the Shroud the visions came at all times. The scale of it left him in a fatigued awe. He wondered how well Xade would process it, if she were having the same experiences. But then again, the Theux brain mystified him. Capable of running the affairs of a large city or starship… incapable of understanding that he saw through her façade.

Xade might love him, but he knew she indulged him, his lifespan as ephemeral as a breeze on a tropical planet. He'd be long dead, while she lived far into the future.

He studied her sitting there, legs splayed, back straight, little blue toes digging furrows into the moss carpet. He could get used to that. Jerr's skin chilled.

Reborn again and again, he'd relive such moments with her, every lifetime. She would care for and love every future version of him. After a time, more out of duty than emotional connection. He couldn't know for sure, but he suspected. The idea saddened rather than angered him. Burdening her for centuries to come. She deserved better.

Xade caught him looking at her.

He tried to smile, but her gaze bored into him with a focused intensity. He cleared his throat and started to rise, but she came over, placing a hand on his chest.

"You're going to wear me out."

"Pretentious." She kissed him, clasping his head in both hands.

"What's wrong?" He traced her jaw with his thumb.

Her mouth opened to answer, then two Sisters entered the cabin. Xade spun around and placed herself between him and them.

"Vestal manners are lax these days." Jerr tensed, ready to spring.

"The Confessor wants to see your Theux," a Sister said.

Jerr slowly stood. "She's not 'mine'… and she has a name."

Xade clasped his hands and gave a feeble smile. They escorted her from the cabin.

Several moments passed before Jerr realized he was shaking. Balyra said she needed him and his visions—but Vestal House was infamous for its intrigues. He was a soldier. Point and shoot. Unraveling schemes wasn't his style. Tunva was right, he was living a lie. Yet the visions in his head had never lied.

"Where are you now?" he whispered, glaring at the bulkheads. "Where are you when I need you?"

The voices didn't answer. No precognition of what would happen. No hints or glimpse of what Balyra had in mind for him, or the woman he'd come to love.

In the art chamber, wearing the Matriarch's robe, Balyra clutched the null dagger. Two dozen soldier morga remained hidden but she doubted they would be needed.

Xade entered, her exoskeleton receding, copying the underveil Balyra had worn just hours ago in the Sanctum. Her blue dermaflesh was like a cool body of water in the bone-dry, antediluvian chamber.

"You think I brought you here for Chastisement?" Balyra asked. "That implies you have crimes to answer for. You do … don't you?"

Xade paused before the statue of a Vestal saint, her armor torn, sword held high against heretics. The white stone took on an azure tint. Like she was implanting herself on it. Balyra knew all too well how a Theux could mimic nearly anything.

"You may have charmed Jerr with your silence. Do not insult me by assuming—"

Xade walked around Balyra until she stood before a mirror where they both were visible. The surgeons had healed her cheek and the stylist had rooted new hair.

"You seem a greater version of myself. One that can self-repair, take different shapes. A doppelganger of anything Jerr thinks he cares about. Even loves."

"Continuous," Xade whispered.

"So you claim. I also know what else you harbor that is never-ending."

"Ridiculous."

The null dagger would have little effect on a Theux, save to disrupt Xade's internal network for a few seconds. Unlike other species, every Theux cell constituted a copy of the whole. Each one was a version of Xade. The dagger might shut off the brain, but the other cells, with their own neural centers, would assume control.

It wasn't Balyra's only weapon. A Vestal never hunted without an extra snare.

"Even you have an agenda," Balyra said. "Or do you still obey Revor's bidding?"

"Contemptuous!" Xade's fists clenched. Was it an act, or had this Theux really assimilated human emotions so strongly? She'd watched the security feeds from the cabin assigned to Jerr and Xade. Their lovemaking passed scrutiny, even the way she laid with him until he fell asleep. It could still be a ruse. Either way, if Balyra hoped to control Jerr, Xade could not interfere. His affection for the comely android would cloud his judgement. Balyra was the only counsel he needed. Until she no longer needed him.

"Did the Weavers tell Jerr how to use the etherspace box he took on Gnebus?" Balyra kept her hand near the sheathed dagger. She hoped Xade saw it, distracting her.

"Abstentious," Xade said.

Balyra laughed. "That is not a denial. What did you learn? That he will destroy your former master? That he's the one all Theux hoped for, to avenge their dead worlds?"

Xade touched an angel statue, fingers sinking into the marble. The sculpture came alive, possessing a blue tint. Its head turned and spoke in Xade's voice. "Spurious."

It took all Balyra's will not to back away. She'd never seen, nor heard, of a Theux animating and controlling objects. "I've visited the spherical cinders that used to be your homeworlds. If not vengeance, then what is it you want?"

Xade withdrew from the statue. It resumed its shape.

"Revor delivered you," Balyra said. "He gave your species a purpose."

Xade shook her head.

"Then what?" Balyra leaned in close. She tried masking the desperation in her voice. "Why are you doing this? You know Revor and

Jerr will destroy each other. You know it is up to me to ensure that the galaxy has leadership afterward. So why?"

Images of worlds popped up on Xade's palm nodus. Planets ravaged by war. By Revor and Vestal House. The hologram displayed ships filled with reborn, landing on those worlds. Repopulating them. Humans, Repta, and many others.

"What an infantile enterprise." Balyra smirked. "You really expect clones, trained only for one role, one purpose, to live together on those worlds in harmony?"

"Auspicious." Xade indicated herself, then pointed at Balyra. "Preposterous."

"So you believe you can achieve this, where I cannot?" Balyra scowled, gripping the dagger. "Unlike you, I am human. You only think you know passion. That you feel emotions like a creature born of the womb, not the forge. You are nothing but—"

"Piteous," Xade said.

Balyra yanked out the dagger. "I've lived twenty millennia, and you, a biomechanical doppelganger, think I deserve your pity?"

Xade approached a certain statue. She touched its outstretched hand.

"Don't you dare." Balyra brandished the dagger.

Even as the dagger neared her throat, however, Xade didn't move away from the sculpture. There was no fear in her eyes. Cool as ice on an asteroid.

The statue assumed a blue glow and came alive for one precious moment. The eyes blinked and focused on Balyra. Marble lips parted into a warm smile.

Balyra stumbled backward. It was as if she were alive again, standing before her and Xade. There was so much she wanted to say. So much she had done in her name.

"Piteous." With a sad smile, Xade offered Balyra her hand.

"Stop it!" Balyra cried. "You don't understand...how can you understand..."

Xade withdrew from the statue. The beloved form was once again inanimate.

Balyra breathed deep, containing her anger. "If Jerr succeeds, you will have to face Revor again. We will see who is piteous, then."

As the morga led her out, Xade gave Balyra a depthless, unreadable stare. Very little blue skin showed now. Her exoskeleton covered all but her face and hands. She was on the defensive. But it brought Balyra less comfort than she thought it would.

CHAPTER 25

Once a human reborn's sensitivity to the Shroud was discovered, the mutation was accelerated. A process that should have taken millions of years was accomplished in thirty thousand. It was time to turn humanity's focused aggression, misplaced entitlement, and serial overachievement to a better purpose.

Theux Codex, 78 Vaaqa D (reconstructed), banned excerpt

The blackened worlds of the Matrisse system no longer reflected light from their parent, blue dwarf star. Now they only reflected the truth of Jerr's words. He'd been right, that Revor would attack Hub Worlds in the Faqar Belt next.

They had arrived too late.

Standing before the wide viewports on Bridge Deck's observation lounge, Balyra wore nothing but a thin robe. She knelt and started to say an old Vestal prayer for the dead, but a terrible anger rose within her. Suffocating the pompous, empty words.

Two sectors from Third Echelon, and the repercussions from Jerr's actions were already in play. Veja Qor-sponsored uprisings had spread to eighty systems so far. It was a hopeless revolution, and like the destruction of *Bhaellator*, would be hot but short.

Revor's brutal responses to the rebellion were paving the way for Balyra to swoop in with Vestal House, once Jerr destroyed him. The people would beg for her help.

Yet the interim was vexing. She rubbed her temples with both hands. For the last few days, tensions had grown between her and her new 'allies'. Jerr claimed the visions and voices were silent, and

Xade loitered around restricted areas such as the Records Deck. Balyra had to play the host, allowing them freedom on *Prophetess*. It galled her.

"Confessor?" a voice asked from her earbud. "This is Bridge."

"Yes?"

"The Theux isn't in Manivo's quarters. Again. She cannot be found on the Med Deck with her Repta ally, either. Security feeds have revealed nothing. Some are offline."

"Double the patrols," Balyra said. "That Theux has hacked us. I want no harm done to Manivo, but prevent them from entering Clearance III areas and above."

As the crewwoman acknowledged the order, the Matriarch wheezed a laugh.

Balyra rose and turned. Crucified to the Shame Pillar, the former Matriarch now lacked legs. Both arms were affixed, with spikes through the palms, into the Pillar's outspread metal wings. Naked, she writhed under the heat of the wings' constant flames. Slowly licking at metalloid flesh. Neither killing, nor relenting.

"You think Manivo will do your work for you?" the Matriarch asked.

"You could have helped me set them against each other, but you refused." Balyra walked up to the Pillar. "Why?"

The Matriarch grimaced as flames lapped at her thighs, her wrists.

"Why, Kerase?" Balyra whispered. Using her former superior's real name.

Arrogance melted from the Matriarch's face. "Never call me that. That woman—"

"Is still in there somewhere." Balyra swiped a hand, dowsing the flames. "Isn't she? The same weak-willed sycophant that claimed credit for all of my glories."

"Because I envied you. Then I loved and hated you for it."

"Again, why?" Balyra swiped her hand, activating the Pillar's motion controls. The former Matriarch squealed as her legless stumps crackled with fire.

"Because I knew you would be our salvation. Our future. You are the brightest star Vestal House ever produced, with more fortitude than even I thought."

Balyra poked a finger into the woman's melting thighs. "Then why did you accuse me in the Sanctum? Revor isn't the real demon you fear. Neither is Jerr."

"You know why." The Matriarch twitched and groaned. "At least, you should."

"Tell me!" Balyra hadn't suffered such a loss in self-control for centuries.

"I was jealous," the Matriarch said. "That you chose ambition over me."

"You grow desperate on your funeral pyre," Balyra said. "Sentiment will not save you. How many thralls did you watch rape me on my initiation before you said 'enough'? How many plagues did I spread for you, while you took credit for ending them?"

"We once found identity in each other," she said. "We found passion!"

"I loved you once," Balyra said. "But you chose ambition over me long ago."

"I hear the truth in your voice." The Matriarch sobbed. "Please, have mercy."

"You lie to yourself." Balyra's lips tightened. "We surrendered truth to Vestal House long ago. We scorched away identity and passion in the Eternal Flame, so that we could remain eternal ourselves. And I saw your mercy. You would have killed me just to please Revor and keep your position. That isn't love."

"I … I am sorry."

Balyra stood on the Pillar's base, putting their faces at the same level. "You are?"

Pity entered the Matriarch's red eyes. "I am sorry that you never learned. That you fight so hard to be something you've long lost. I am sorry I helped you lose it."

"Tell me." She tried to caress the Matriarch's face, but gripped the neck instead.

"Your humanity."

Lips parted, Balyra searched for words while the Matriarch watched with scorn. Once again she was being judged. Once again, all she had endured still wasn't enough.

"You lost yours centuries before I met you," Balyra said.

"That is why yours mattered all the more to me. Why couldn't you see that?"

Balyra sobbed and caressed her burnt face. "I tried!"

"Revenge blinded you," the Matriarch said. "None of this will bring her back!"

"Then you are a fool." Balyra swiped.

Flames gushed from the wings. The Matriarch screamed, but Balyra held on until her robes were ashes on the floor. Held on until the Matriarch's eyes darkened, until her own nails melted off her fingers.

Held on until she was sure her own tears were real.

Stepping back, smoke trailing off her charred limbs, Balyra wiped her cheeks.

"Goodbye, Kerase. May your Flame burn…may it burn forever…"

The squirming form's moan dropped into mechanical octaves as Balyra ran out.

It could've been worse. At least, that's what Jerr kept telling himself.

Xade had left their quarters while he'd slept. It wasn't the first time. Ever since Balyra had assumed power over Vestal House, Xade always sneaked out after Jerr fell asleep. He'd not questioned her, knowing she would tell him when she was ready.

This time, though, she'd taken the etherspace box.

While he hurriedly dressed, the Vestal proverbs and icons on the walls insulted him. Demanding he seek salvation, as if he were less than dirt. Even the silverware provided by the Sisters was inscribed with some trite prayer.

But he knew what Balyra truly held sacred: her right to power.

Standing with Balyra on a desert world. Two empty craters. Fighters strafe a dropship. Meteors tumble over the landscape. The resulting smoke and dust plume make him cough and squint as Balyra vanishes in silvery swirls.

Jerr paced in circles. The vision was of Kadah IV, where Balyra said Revor had met the Kieta. There had to be a connection, something Revor didn't want uncovered.

The door opened. Tunva entered. Her limp was less pronounced. Though most of her bandages were gone due to Vestal medical care, her eyes sought violence.

"What's wrong?" Jerr asked. "Have you see Xade?"

"Morga patrols prevent Tunva from mounting a proper search. Jerr must come."

"You think I'll have any better luck?"

Tunva yanked him toward the door. "Balyra needs Jerr, so her metal guards will not hurt Jerr. But Xade cannot see the future. Xade is in danger."

"Balyra wouldn't do anything to piss me off," Jerr said. "At least not yet. But I agree. I don't like Xade running off by herself in this nest of vipers."

They left the room and traveled the halls at a brisk pace. Every time they spotted a morga patrol, Jerr and Tunva backtracked and took an alternate route. With Xade missing, the extra sentries meant Balyra wanted to restrict their movements. Vestal House was filled with so many secrets, Jerr wasn't sure where to start.

What could Xade be looking for?

"Where would Xade go, Jerr Manivo?" Tunva whispered in his ear while morga passed them in an adjacent corridor.

"Was hoping you'd know."

"Tunva doesn't see the future."

"Neither does Xade…so she would examine the past." Jerr's brows raised as an idea materialized. "How far away are we from the nearest Records Deck?"

"Two berths up," she said. The morga's footsteps faded down the hall.

He spotted a tram dock down the next hall but morga already guarded it. They'd have to be quick, though Tunva would slow them down. "I'm going to carry you."

"Tunva is not that wounded." The pride in her voice made him grin.

"They won't shoot you for fear of hitting me."

Before she could reply, Jerr hauled her over his shoulder and raced to the dock. The morga shouted warnings. Others fired 'lectropulsers, which would end Jerr's little investigation. Two morga tried physically stopping them, until Jerr plowed right over them. The next instant, he flung Tunva into the tram and followed. They sped away.

"Jerr touched the back of Tunva's pelvic area."

"It was an accident. Hell, they were shooting at us!"

"Tunva is not complaining."

Records Deck 5 was chilly but dry. Icons, statues, even lamps were absent, thus granting all space to data storage in every known form. So Vestal House did hold something in higher regard than itself. For all his anxiety, Jerr slowed down, appreciating the ambiance. Tunva followed, flicking her tongue in aggravation.

"Tunva warns Jerr to never speak about carrying her from battle."

"I promise I won't tell anyone how much you weigh." He peeked around a corner.

"Tunva is sufficiently athletic!"

"Fine," he whispered. "Now be sufficiently quiet."

Her tongue playfully slapped his ear.

The Vestals' preoccupation for documentation bordered on mania, putting *Bhaellator*'s archives to shame. Vacuum-sealed shelves held books many millenniums old. Several antiquated machines used for feed playback were maintained in pristine condition: two-dimensional screens, headset projectors, and other devices he'd never seen. There was even a rusted typster, each key bearing the letter of a long-dead alphabet.

It was a testament to Vestal obsession with the past, as he guessed everything on the devices had already been digitized onto their network. He hoped so, anyway.

But for all its combined knowledge, Deck 5 felt like a tomb.

No alarms blared. Not even a security robo appeared. Jerr knew Balyra wouldn't dare risk harming the archives. So the guards would continue using nonlethal methods.

He continued through an aisle filled with handwritten manuscripts and tomes, shielded by energy barriers. Light levels remained low, preventing further damage to the arrayed treasures. Jerr wondered who possessed the patience to write so much.

Something moved a few aisles over. He tensed.

A deep, warbling noise thrummed in the archive. He and Tunva fell still.

"The Kieta will cut your thread as they did ours. Beware of their weapons."

Exiting the aisle, he caught sight of an exhibit isolated from the rest of the grimoires, magnetic tapes, and psyche uploads. It consisted of half-melted polyhedral artifacts, each isolated on separate pedestals. Kieta boxes.

Standing in the exhibit's center was Xade. She waited before a pedestal that held the etherspace box they'd taken from Gnebus. Her nodus was downloading data.

"Hey," Jerr whispered.

Xade turned and nodded at them, then continued downloading.

"Balyra has patrols out looking for you." Jerr hurried to Xade's side. "Even if you hack into *Prophetess*'s security systems, they'll eventually find you here."

"Xade has found something important?" Tunva asked.

"Outrageous." Xade's nodus pulsed with new data streams.

"We better go. You can show us later."

Focused on the etherspace box, Xade slowly shook her head. "Dissentious."

"Huh? Why?"

Tunva looked around as if expecting an ambush. "Xade and Jerr can argue later."

Xade's nodus displayed records of the Vestals helping Revor defeat the Kieta. Jerr and Tunva both leaned forward, unable to look away.

The ancient video feeds showed Revor allying with the Kieta, pledging to help them drive the Weavers from the Shroud—the Kieta's home. Their meeting took place on Kadah IV, an old human colony just inside the Settled Zone. The swirling forms produced an etherspace box. A Vestal held it up for Revor's examination.

The Vestal resembled the statue Balyra kept in her art chamber.

"So Balyra does know what's there," Jerr said.

Static filled the feed, then it displayed the Kieta attacking the same delegation. Revor fled in a shuttle while the Vestal with the etherspace box led hundreds of her Sisters against the silvery beings. After the shuttle had reached a certain distance, a beam darted from it and struck the box. The Vestal, her comrades, and the Kieta hordes were disintegrated. The explosion flattened the surrounding cities and crystalized sand dunes.

"So Revor pretended to offer peace—before he betrayed them," Jerr said.

"Why would Revor do that?" Tunva asked.

The feed shifted. Now Dominion soldiers wielded etherspace shards like swords. Carried guns with the boxes attached to the barrels. Imperial engineers installed the blue octahedrons into starship batteries. Ensuring every shot, every strike, would not only slay, but exile one to the Shroud forever. The Vestals also waged war with zeal. Slicing down Weaver drones. Incinerating entire vessels with the new weaponry.

Other boxes were detonated like bombs. The effect not only ripped the Weavers' Leviathans apart, but forced them from this universe into the Shroud. Being a hive mind A.I., the Weavers could have spread their collective consciousness to another ship, another host body. But this way, Revor ensured their total elimination from this reality.

It didn't end there. Any species that resisted Revor and his Armada were disposed of in the same manner. The Shroud was filled with his victims. Their voices.

None could call it genocide without the evidence.

Tunva's back scales bristled. "And they call Tunva's people monsters."

"They burned our thread away. We are all but forgotten."

Jerr, despite his combat experience, wanted to look away. But a blue hand gently touched his chin. Keeping him focused on the images.

The sadness in Xade's eyes was now his own.

A third set of feeds revealed the Vestals using the boxes on the Kieta. Though Vestal House lost thousands of morga and Sisters, they fought the Kieta to a standstill.

They were led by Balyra.

Jerr shared a look with Xade and Tunva. "I'll be damned."

While the Kieta battled the Vestals, Revor entered the Shroud and stole the Kieta children. Since they always brought their young along in the Shroud concurrent to the Kieta's location in this universe, Revor accomplished this easily. The tiny, gleaming forms could only gestate in the Shroud. Revor hid them on Kadah IV, guaranteeing the Kieta's servitude. Their losses had been so great, the Kieta couldn't create a new generation. Held outside the Shroud, their progeny couldn't mature.

"That explains what happened on Kadah," Jerr said. "But who was that Vestal?"

Xade pulled up the information: Aylea Peran. Balyra's older, biological sister.

"Holy shit," Jerr said.

"Balyra fights for a vendetta," Tunva said.

"And she'll kill us all to see it through." Jerr exhaled and rubbed his face.

Revor had deceived and betrayed so many. And with Vestal House, Balyra had participated in the Weavers' genocide, and the Kieta's servitude, at every level.

"Weave a new thread for our old enemies. The Kieta must not share our fate."

Prophetess shuddered.

"Damn, we've left the Shroud," Jerr said.

Xade's nodus blinked and showed their location: the Kadah system.

"Let's get out of here," Jerr said. "We have what we need, I'm not playing this stupid game with Balyra anymore. Bring that box. If I touch it, I might go nuts."

"This no time for Jerr to eat hard-shelled fruit," Tunva said.

"Huh?"

"Facetious." Xade nudged them onward.

They hurried to the nearest exit from Deck 5 using Xade's nodus as a guide. Jerr kept looking from its deck plan schematic to their surroundings. Finally, he let Xade lead, which tore at him. She was unarmed and he wasn't sure if the morga would kill her.

Now that they'd uncovered the truth, Jerr wasn't about to test Balyra's hospitality.

Though it took them a little longer, they went to a different tram dock. The corridors were silent now, with no hymns being sung. Not a patrol in sight. Jerr regarded Xade and Tunva with a warning look.

"Nervous," Xade whispered.

Jerr studied every corner, each alcove. "Me too."

Tunva passed him one of her Onashi blades. He nodded in thanks.

No one stopped them from entering the tram car. Jerr's skin prickled at the total lack of activity. Tunva cycled her pistol. She only had eight shots left.

Xade piloted them through *Prophetess* to the hangar containing *Lux Aeterna,* Balyra's cruiser. Again, they faced no resistance. No vision of what was to come.

The cruiser awaited them without challenge, an older vessel commonly used in the Affiliate. It was half a mile long, with cylindrical berths protruding from the lower deck. The Vestal emblem, a red flame bisected with wings, was backlit on the hull.

Xade flew the tram right up to the main airlock. They ran to the hatch.

"Can you hack the lock code?" Jerr asked.

"Contentious." Xade's brows lowered in concentration, swiping her nodus.

Jerr watched every doorway and corridor, the tram dock, the service lifts.

No one was stopping them.

The code was bypassed and Xade helped them into the airlock.

"Tunva doesn't understand." She leaned on him as Xade entered the cockpit.

"I think I do," Jerr murmured.

Standing on *Prophetess*'s bridge, Balyra watched *Lux Aeterna* depart. She'd followed Jerr's progress on the security feeds. Loaded his Starjumper onboard. Ordered the guards to stand down. Even weathered the scolding looks of her fellow Vestals when she allowed them to escape after Xade's data theft.

After discovering who Revor had taken from her.

But there was still a chance Jerr would destroy Revor—she need only follow.

Chapter 26

It wasn't enough to simply conquer all non-humans in the galaxy. Their physiology had to be reshaped to suit human standards. Our geneticists and eugenicists pooled their skills into a bioengineering feat worthy of legend. Evolution's gifts to us—opposable thumbs, a bipedal configuration, large brains—was awarded to those who embraced progress. Those who refused were discarded to the Shroud.

Narrative of the Armada, Chapter 42

The Faqar Belt gleamed with a billion young suns, the blue-white orbs like sapphires melting on velvet. A spiral arm jutting away from the Settled Zone, the Belt had been the next destination Jerr's visions showed him. He gazed at it through *Lux Aeterna*'s cockpit viewport. Cursing his failure.

They were still minutes from Kadah IV. Jerr knew *Prophetess*—and Balyra—would be right behind them.

"Malicious." Xade swiped the cockpit nodus. It detailed Leviathan attacks on Prioa 49C and Matrisse, Hub Worlds within the Belt. The same worlds he'd told Balyra about, where more of his reborn were grown. Judging from the military transmission Xade had just intercepted, the planet's reborn facilities were now destroyed.

Tunva slumped in the navigator seat. "Revor moves too quickly. We are lost."

The broadcast showed news from other Leviathans but Xade swiped them off.

He kept staring out the viewport. "Play it."

"Impetuous." She touched his arm.

"No, I'm not about to do anything crazy." He faced her. "Play it."

She swiped and resumed the feed. The Dominion had put down eighty-two uprisings across the Elium Rim and Affiliate Worlds. The pattern was spreading to the Settled Zone, the heart of the empire. Each revolt was a large scale affair involving fleets, planet-side engagements—but Veja Qor had yet to achieve a single victory.

"Balyra let us go," he said. "*Prophetess* should've overtaken us already."

Xade deactivated the nodus and watched him.

"She expects me to lead her to … what? The end of the empire?"

"Balyra wants Jerr to kill Revor for her," Tunva said. "Then Balyra will kill Jerr. The galaxy will see Balyra as their savior."

"Yes, but he has to be stopped," Jerr said.

"What do the Weavers tell Jerr?"

"I don't know."

Tunva stood. "Jerr must know. Tunva has come so far—"

"Damn it, I said I don't know!"

Jerr left the cockpit and strode around *Lux Aeterna*'s command deck. Though he assumed the vessel had carried Balyra across the galaxy for centuries, it featured no personalization. Not a single image of a loved one, no mementos. Like her quarters on *Prophetess*, the ship contained no trace of her. It was similar to the way she'd used him. Surrender no information that could be used against her.

And unless he did something, there'd be no trace of the resistance once Revor was finished. Yet for each vision he'd seen, a hundred other things transpired that he had no warning of. Though he needed the voices more than ever, they remained silent.

"I didn't see what would happen back there. The Weavers haven't spoken to me."

Watching him from the cockpit, Xade swallowed. "Valorous."

"Lot of good that's done us. I'm not blameless. Goddamnit, I should have learned how to use this ability, this power, whatever it is. I should have …"

"You have done more than anyone dreamed, Jerr Manivo," Tunva said.

Xade came up behind him, rested her head against his back.

"We'll never win," he said. "Revor and his Leviathans are too powerful."

"Callous," Xade said.

"I can't help it. They made me this way."

Xade yanked him around so they faced each other. The hurt, the anger creasing her brow was nothing compared to how her mouth struggled to enunciate it.

"You can't do anything to change that."

Shaking her head, Xade continued trying to form words. Refusing to give up.

"I don't give a damn if you can't talk." He embraces her. "All I care about—"

Lux Aeterna gave a slight shudder.

They stared around as the stars outside the viewports lensed over.

"We're back in the Shroud," Jerr said. "But how? This ship can't—"

Pearly shapes morphed into existence around them. Sleek, silver tendrils spun inside each. Streaks of color dragged across Jerr's eyesight as the Kieta encircled them.

Pistol in one hand, blade in the other, Tunva waited.

Xade brandished the etherspace box, keeping Jerr behind her. "Preposterous!"

So the Kieta really could appear anywhere they wanted. Without a Leviathan.

Yet they remained still. Swirling in place.

"Wait." Jerr raised a hand. "I don't think they want to hurt us."

Four Kieta shimmered and spun like miniature, argent galaxies. Viewing them inside the Shroud, Jerr could discern more detail on their forms. Halos of dust-like material clung to each being, never straying far from the host body. Each gleamed like tiny stars. He wondered if the Kieta weren't individual universes unto themselves.

"They know you are not their enemy. They must still serve Revor, or their progeny will be destroyed. Their race would perish."

Jerr shared a look with Xade. She lowered the etherspace box.

"Why are you here?" he asked. "How did you take us into the Shroud?"

One of the Kieta spun faster. A yellow dodecahedron appeared among its tendrils. One of the metallic sides slid open. Jerr sucked in a breath.

It was a narrative box, like Jhe 97 had described on Gnebus. Staring into it made everything around them bleed into a focal point of light and color. Its epicenter was utter darkness. But the longer he stared, the more Jerr discerned shapes moving therein. Images, sensations. A flipbook of captured moments, everlasting within the Shroud.

Moments became scenes, and scenes transformed into impressions that could only be called memories. Jerr's own recollections blurred, collating into distorted retentions.

He sensed, rather than saw, the Kieta dwelling in the Shroud. Entering and leaving it at will. A handful of them could transport a vessel from his reality to the Shroud, as had just been done with *Lux Aeterna*. It was their home—until the Weavers discovered it. Exploitation followed. Then war. Both races refused to share.

Revor tried to wrangle the secrets of such travel from the Weavers. They rebuffed him, so Revor befriended the Kieta. Though promising to help them drive the Weavers from the Shroud, he played them against each other. Afterward, he stole Weaver technology and traveled the Shroud anyway—the very thing the Kieta had fought against.

"Unscrupulous," Xade said.

"We were all such fools. Strangling ourselves with the strands we had woven."

Another side opened on the box. Light and shade refocused on the sandy dunes of Kadah IV. Jerr's Urian eyes glimpsed a corona of gravitational radiation pulsing over the landscape. Shining buildings appeared on the horizon, then were crumbling ruins. Clouds swept over the sky, only to vanish the next moment, like time had lapsed in fast-forward.

As if space-time on the planet was in flux.

"Our final tomb served as a crib for their captive young."

Jerr gasped as the box refocused on one more scene. Reality seemed to peel away on Kadah IV: skies melted, structures blew away like dust in a storm. A huge shape coalesced on the planet's surface. An ancient vessel, broken in half.

"Reveal us."

A Weaver starship.

Deep within its gutted confines lay its gravitational reactor. Still active, its power kept the vessel in the Shroud—along with thousands of Kieta young. The reactor's strength was too much for their underdeveloped forms to escape, trapping them inside. Revor's forces moved them there while Balyra faced the Kieta in her anguished conflict.

"Reveal us avenge us weave a new thread reveal us avenge us weave a new—"

Jerr fell to one knee, clasping his temples against the mental onslaught.

Trapped in the Shroud, wrecked on Kadah IV, the Weavers had made their final stand. Now the Kieta's children were held inside in the ultimate reminder of arrogant power: obey Revor or suffer their rival's fate. Guarded by marines armed with etherspace box shards. If threatened or ordered, they could destroy the Kieta's future.

"You want our help," Jerr breathed. "That's why you haven't killed us."

The Kieta swirled faster, each becoming a distortion of motion and light. Reality unwrapped itself in waves of color until Jerr worried the very hull around them would shred apart. But the next moment all was normal. The Kieta were gone.

The cockpit console beeped. The Kieta had pulled them back out of the Shroud—and into orbit above Kadah IV. Granting them a slight head start on Balyra.

Jerr had to sit down, the experience leaving him shaken. He'd felt those memories. Shared the glories, the tragedies.

She reverses the energy flow in the vessel's reactor. Instead of exploding, like Bhaellator, the ship's connection to space-time stabilizes. Echoes build in the Shroud.

"Slumberous?" Xade wiped his brow as her nodus showed his fatigue at 82%.

"I'm not sleeping yet," Jerr said. "Not until you get a shuttle ready and send out a message to all Veja Qor cells."

"Fabulous." Smiling, Xade nodded in approval.

"Ask as many ships that can to gather in the Kadah system." Jerr took her hand and gazed out the viewport again. "Tell all the rest in the other systems to stand down."

"Is Jerr turning into a hard-shelled fruit after all?" Tunva smirked.

"I'm not nuts. Stand down until they hear from the Shroud. From the Weavers."

Confusion became concern as Xade cocked her head.

"Finding that ship and freeing the Kieta's young—it's our only chance." He thought of the vision he'd just received. Echoes…

Xade's hand shook in his grasp.

"You'll have to trust—"

Xade touched his lips and slowly smiled.

"I know that you do." He held her close. "I just hope we can trust what I saw."

Standing alone in the Sanctum, Balyra studied the icons and proverbs on the distant hull. Really examined them, something she'd not done for centuries. Too long she had sacrificed herself—and others—to uphold the virtues the imagery and words espoused. Too long she'd played goddess's advocate, when there were no deities, save those invented out here in the void, to attribute one's guilt and remorse.

Those, too, were ephemeral, emotional crutches. She wanted free of them.

Jerr could offer that. There would no blame, no censure, if one saw the future.

"How many?" The skin on the small boy's lips puckered with sores.

Balyra didn't flinch from his fetid breath. Like he was already dead inside. "You should focus on the joys and comforts awaiting you in the arms of Vestal House."

Her retinal HUD displayed his temperature as eight degrees above normal and his blood pressure far too high. Plague had hit the colony before her ship arrived. Three thousand had died before her first evening on the planet. Two weeks later, she'd had to increase that total to seventy-two thousand. The old vaccines weren't working.

"Please … how many do I have left?" The boy clasped her hand.

She smiled sadly. If not for her augmented body, his touch would be a death sentence. But common people didn't know that. Whenever she shook a hand, or touched a cheek, the smiles it provoked filled her heart. Though dying, these people were delighted to see her. They saw her as an angel, a goddess.

They were wrong.

She had targeted their world for a test of the plague to see if their genes could resist it this time. If she was an angel, then she was a killing angel. The gain in knowledge was worth it, meted out for the good of humanity. But she was still guilty. Whatever would make their passing an easier one, she was willing to entertain.

"A day. Perhaps two." Balyra pushed damp hair from his face. Some of his flesh peeled off. She flung it off her fingers where he couldn't see, still smiling at him.

"Will you stay with me?" the boy asked.

"Of course."

But she never returned. Since the mission was complete, and her task done, she'd left the boy to his fate. Vestal House used the data to create better vaccines and epidemic response systems for the empire. Though tragic, the boy's death had served a purpose.

That was how she could justify what Jerr was about to enact on Kadah IV. She was willing to risk him reactivating the Weavers' last starship if that meant Revor would hurry to stop him. If Jerr succeeded in killing Revor, then the soldier-turned-prophet would have inadvertently given her the galaxy.

If Revor killed Jerr, though, she could simply regrow Jerr from his DNA sample. Pretend fealty to the Dominion. Wait until she was ready to strike again.

It wasn't what Aylea would have done. She had been the paragon. The one who originally pulled Balyra from that garbage trough and showed her an existence filled with virtue and light. The real flame that had illuminated Balyra's life.

All reservations had died in Balyra the day Aylea died. All mercy.

A sudden chill overcame her despite her bionically controlled body temperature. She slowly sat on the causeway, crimson robes receding over the surface like blood. A long time she stared off into space, struggling with how much she missed Aylea.

"The armor suits you." Smiling, Aylea cinched the cuirass's straps as Balyra stood with her arms straight out. "Even if you are taller than me now."

Balyra laughed. "Not where it counts." She whirled around and struck a pose.

They stood on a mesa overlooking the chapterhouse grounds on Kadah IV. Vestal banners flapped in the breeze along with Aylea's blonde locks. Balyra ran a finger through them. Hoping she'd be just as beautiful one day.

"So where is my first post?" Balyra asked. "Will you be there?"

Aylea smiled sadly. "You will be in the Affiliate helping plague victims. I have to stay. The Dominion is meeting an alien delegation here soon."

"Then I'll make it quick." Balyra twirled her new red cape.

"Hey." Aylea gently took her hand. "Being a Vestal will test you to your very core. Promise me you will never let the horrors out there change you. Promise me you'll remember your training, and resist our baser instincts."

Balyra hugged her so Aylea wouldn't see the tears in her eyes. "I had the best trainer in the order: you. I can handle anything this universe throws at me."

"Promise me, Balyra," Aylea whispered.

Hugging her tighter, Balyra whispered in her ear. "I'll never fail you. Promise."

She intended to honor that promise the best she could.

A morga approached with an activated nodus: *Prophetess*'s scanners had detected the exit of *Lux Aeterna* in the Shroud. The Kieta must be aiding Jerr. She still knew how to fight those creatures. Once Revor was gone, and Jerr under her control, Balyra would destroy the Kieta for battling Aylea. Had they not attacked, Revor might not have fired.

"Very well," Balyra said. "Prepare the shuttle. Bring my hourglass."

If the galaxy were to have peace, there could be no rivals for use of the Shroud.

Though the Xade had doctored the wounds he'd suffered, Jerr took his time getting into the Starjumper. She waited nearby in the hangar, ready to help, but he did it all himself. Every time he tightened a joint, or brought a servo online, he recalled Darei's skills in doing so. Remembered those insults. That chuckle.

Only half-equipped, Jerr slumped in the Starjumper, reminiscing. Laughing with Darei in the mess hall. Getting drunk in that spaceport on 51 Mahd B, then puking on the showgirls afterward. Rescuing a platoon from a crippled dropship in the Affiliate.

Shivering, Jerr hurried with the rest of the suit. Secured an extra gauss magazine, double-checked his oxygen supply. Reconfigured propellant ratios in his thrusters.

"The threads are frayed. You cannot save them."

"Damn it." He dropped a wrench. Xade offered to help but he waved her off.

"Conscientious." Her sarcasm made him sigh, then smile.

"You know me. Stubborn to the end."

Xade grabbed the wrench. Two seconds later, his armor was ready.

"Thanks." He checked the suit's glycogen boosters, ready to inject for Rezal state. Without it, he'd not stand a chance against the marines on the Weaver derelict that guarded the Kieta young. Revor would have only the very best serving in that capacity.

Jerr cradled his helmet. "What will you do if you see Revor?"

She lowered her eyes, quivering with pent-up emotions.

"Yeah … me too."

Once again she tried to speak different words. Lips pursed, then flattening in frustration. Veins bulged in her neck. Her eyes narrowed to furious slits. She finally stamped a foot and looked away.

"I don't need words, or voices in my head, to tell me what I already know."

Xade lifted the etherspace box, then stared up at him. Her nodus indicated the damaged artifact had only a 12% probability of functioning. That his chances of using it successfully against the Kieta were 7%.

"What are you really trying to say?"

"Anxious."

She feared for him. Despite all their shared hardships, Xade had never expressed doubts about his safety. Her predictions were scientific, rooted in numbers and data. His precognitions came from the echoes of space-time, from voices long-dead. But now they came from his instincts, which ignored the integers of possibility, the odds of mortality.

Though he towered over her in the Starjumper, Jerr reached down and gently lifted her face up by the chin. "Continuous."

"Continuous." Her slender blue fingers clasped his armored ones.

Tunva's holographic image appeared on his faceplate HUD. "Jerr, we are ready."

Lux Aeterna's hangar lights flashed red. He entered the shuttle with Xade, where Tunva stood in her own Starjumper. Kadah IV awaited them below.

True to a vision he'd already seen, *Prophetess* exited the Shroud seven hundred thousand miles away. Xade's nodus confirmed it. Like a scavenger, Balyra wouldn't attack until her prey was mortally wounded. But he was the Dominion's finest predator.

"Reveal us, Weaver."

Jerr stilled himself as the hangar door opened.

Chapter 27

The light bleeds through our eyes,
But we are not blind.
The darkness pulls us under,
But we are not dead.
Our screams travel between the stars,
But we are not heard.

Epiphanies of the Shroud

The surface of Kadah IV was a golden red, covered in ever-shifting sands. Mountainous dunes towered over deep canyons and valleys where tattered spires of ruined cities poked through the powdery regolith. Xade piloted *Lux Aeterna*'s shuttle over the arid expanse while Jerr adjusted his Starjumper's equilibrium. The planet's gravity was slightly higher than his native tolerance. The last thing he needed was nature dragging him down while dealing with elite commandos, Kieta, and whatever the hell else guarded Revor's greatest secret.

"Inconspicuous." Xade kept refreshing the scanners, but a heavy band of gravitational radiation surrounded the planet, preventing her from discovering the Weaver derelict. Her sidelong glance at Jerr made him sigh.

"Tunva agrees," Tunva said. "There is nothing here but dust and memory."

"Just keep flying northeast," he said. "I know it's there."

He didn't mean to sound uptight, but ever since entering the atmosphere, he'd received no more visions. Heard no voices. It bolstered the impression that he was sneaking into a graveyard.

Worse, they had little time. Revor would be aware of ships entering the system, like Balyra had told him. The gravitational signature of *Prophetess* alone would alert the Dominion. Unless his plan worked, Kadah IV would indeed be a tomb—his own.

As the shuttle flew past another mesa, Jerr glimpsed two large craters ahead. Tunva leaned forward, having spotted them as well. There were no doubt plenty of craters on the planet—but years of sandstorms had filled them in.

These two were empty, clean. As if something invisible still rested therein.

"There," he murmured.

Xade flew in closer. "Mysterious—"

The shuttle's instruments went dead, came back online, then displayed a complete different set of readings. Reality outside the viewport became total void. Before Jerr could move or speak, the void peeled away in wisps of light and color, revealing two huge objects. Each was surrounded by a debris field more static than a still image.

Two halves of an ancient vessel. The predecessor of the Leviathans.

Bands of multi-colored light swept all around the derelict, coming and going. Distant systems and galaxies lensed and stretched, then zipped past like cosmic will o' wisps. Jerr lifted his arm, but there was no transitory, visual clue it had moved. One moment it was at his side; the next, it was raised before him.

Other objects and beings repositioned themselves the same way. Xade was sitting—then, she stood beside him, the shuttle's airlock now open. Tunva reached for her weapons. An eye blink later, she held pistol and sword ready.

Everything was stationary, inertial. But still traveling from one point to another.

"We're physically in the Shroud." He waved, testing the displacement effect.

"Obvious." Xade clasped the etherspace box.

"Don't get smart, Miss Blue Theux."

She gave a shy, wide grin.

"Let's go make our friends proud, Jerr Manivo," Tunva said.

Jerr led the way out of the airlock. Xade followed, exoskeleton covering her entire body like it had when they'd been jettisoned from *Prophetess*. After taking her hand, he jetted his boot thrusters. They darted toward the wrecked ship's larger half. Tunva flew after them, bringing up the rear.

Outside the shuttle, Kadah IV was no longer visible around them. All was jet black void, occasionally pierced by whorls of light and motion. Some of these Jerr felt rather than saw. The lights on his Starjumper illuminated nothing beyond a few yards.

The derelict's halves floated before them, wreathed in a flickering afterglow with no visible source. Like nothing else existed in the universe. Jerr held Xade tighter.

Once they avoided the jagged edges around the breach in the hull, Jerr flew deeper into a yawning interior. Much like modern Leviathans, the bulk of the Weaver vessel was a giant, empty space meant to contain the energies released by its engine. Though no engineer, Jerr was surprised at how little the design had changed. Tens of thousands of years later, and Revor had done nothing to perfect the Weavers' genius.

Initially, Jerr, Xade, and Tunva stared in wonder at the gargantuan craft. Their amazement turned to melancholy as they encountered the first Weaver drone corpses. Triangular forms in black, obsidian-like armor floated in the vastness. Their limp tentacles gave the impression of marine creatures drifting in watery depths.

Human soldiers gunning down alien troops, of a species he can't identify. They resemble floating, inverted triangles, with tentacles grasping weapons.

The vision was made real, its actors in perpetual, ghastly repose. Though the drones were mere shells the collective Weaver mind had inhabited, he'd no doubt they had felt the pain of these 'deaths'. Each a piece of the larger atrocity.

The bodies grew in number—hundreds, then thousands—until Jerr had to push them aside to reach the engine far ahead. Xade tapped his faceplate, pointed at his HUD. He'd not have enough fuel to fly back to the shuttle.

"Tunva's suit was fully charged," Tunva said. "Tunva will save you."

"No, I need you to activate the engine cores," Jerr said. "Judging from our scans, they should be far to our left. There's four of them, split into two groups."

Lights appeared in the darkness. Swirling, shimmering. The Kieta.

"They'll try to stop us until we can free their children," Jerr said. "Xade, I'll hold them off while you help Tunva turn on the engine. Each of you get two cores."

Xade looked at him as if he were mad.

"It's our only chance." He snapped his wrist thrusters onto her arms.

Her nodus feed appeared on his HUD, saying he'd lost 15% maneuverability.

"Let's hope I'm a better dancer than these things. Go."

With a forlorn glance, she swept her arms back and jetted into the alien abyss.

"The stars be with Jerr Manivo." Tunva rocketed off toward the cores.

Jerr clutched the etherspace box as a dozen Kieta approached. They stopped a few feet away, barring his path. Spinning. Waiting.

"You know why I'm here," he said.

The Kieta slowed their rotation and moved away.

Jerr fired his boot thrusters once and coasted past them. They followed on either side of him, gliding through the murk. Moments later he passed the first bulbous engine core, spying a tiny blue shape flying around it. Xade.

She reverses the energy flow in the vessel's reactor. Instead of exploding, like Bhaellator, the ship's connection to space-time stabilizes. Echoes build in the Shroud.

Ahead, the glowing energy cores lighted several exposed berths. Miles of decks, hangars. Most were scorched through, with melted bulkheads and twisted framing. More Weaver carcasses rested there, along with thousands of dead, floating Vestals. Their red cloaks and braided hair jutted at strange angles, not influenced by any gravity. All were as beautiful as icicles in Urian winter, and just as cold.

Jerr was speechless. The battle, the slaughter, the butchery—it defied human comprehension. For outside the craft, tens of thousands more bodies floated. Dominion marines, Weaver drones, Vestals and morga. All caught in the blast of an etherspace box.

For the first time Jerr felt some sympathy for Balyra. Her sister was likely here.

"First core activated." Tunva's voice was filled with static.

His HUD showed that Xade had also turned one on.

"Good job, we almost got this." Expending the last of his fuel, he flew over the final energy core. He dared not stay long. The radiation would kill him despite his Starjumper's shielding. The Kieta children had to be here. He had seen it.

Dozens of marines in Starjumpers appeared from behind the cores. As the light from the cores shone on them, Jerr realized the luminance didn't come from the cores themselves. Rather, the oval machines were coated in thousands—perhaps millions—of tiny, swirling shapes. The engine's power held them in place like a magnet.

The Kieta young.

"Shit the escape pod." Jerr's HUD targeted and tracked the marines, but there was too many. Even with Rezal he couldn't win.

"Xade has the third one online," Tunva said. "Tunva is flying toward the fourth."

The Kieta gathered around him, swirling. They had no choice but to obey.

"Tunva, turn this heap on, then reverse the power. Like we did *Bhaellator.*"

Static came over his radio.

He lifted the etherspace box as the Kieta closed in. 'Xade, you hear me?"

The marines fired at a shape zipping along the last core. It was Tunva.

"Well, fuck." He picked off one of the marines, who plummeted into darkness. The others focused on him—showing Tunva their backs. She shot four down.

"Tunva is fine." He could hear the smirk in her voice.

"Show off." Jerr jetted backward as a shot flew past his helmet. "Xade, we got their attention, make this count!"

"Jerr pressures Xade too much." Tunva sniped three more marines. The bodies, sizzling with sparks and leaving a trail of red globules, slowly drifted away.

"Huh?" Jerr traded fire with another marine while trying to monitor the Kieta.

The marines came around again, but Tunva blasted another two, covering Xade. Working the manual releases, Xade nearly had the fourth core online.

"In Tunva's culture, Jerr would be Xade's caretaker. And less demanding."

Jerr snorted. "Well, I guess I don't know everything about—"

A platoon of marines appeared from behind the Weaver corpses. Behind Tunva.

He didn't have time to shout a warning.

The marines fired.

A barrage of piercer rounds burned across the darkness. One blew off Tunva's right hand. Two melted through her chest. Another seared away part of her helmet.

Without thinking, Jerr waded among them, discharging all weapons. He went into Rezal, calculating when a marine would turn, when one would fire. How long it would take to burn through armor, and how long he'd have to recover and shoot again.

Seconds later a dozen corpses drifted around him. Xade spoke over the radio, but her words seemed muted. All he heard was the silence of empty victory.

Tunva floated near the final core, her one remaining eye staring at him.

Daring him to turn back.

"You must weave a new thread for those who were our enemies…"

The vessel tore away around him in splashes of color and radiance. The dead marines, the engine cores, Tunva's body—all drained from his eyesight as if he were pulled into a vortex of shadows and lightning. He was leaving the Shroud.

"Xade!" he shouted.

The Kieta weren't attacking. They were forcing him out of the Shroud.

"No, I'm…here to…"

The words slurred in his ears. Jerr swung the box at the Kieta, but it snapped apart into glowing azure shards. Jhe 97 had been right. It was broken, useless. He clasped one last shard as he passed into a maelstrom of blinding light.

Desert winds tossed Balyra's diaphanous robe, spreading behind her like vermilion wings. Kadah IV smelled the same: of dust, salt. Terminal decay. Something, like the world beneath her feet, she'd thought to have abandoned long ago.

Her knee-high boots sunk into sand up to her ankles. In the distance, the remnants of the mesa and Vestal chapterhouse poked above the dunes. City ruins glittered here and there for miles around. After the battle where Aylea perished, Revor had ordered the planet vacated. Now it languished in devastation, the desert reclaiming its kingdom.

She scanned the twin craters just beyond the desolate horizon. Waiting. Though armed with his visions, Jerr lacked Revor's cunning. The Kieta young would be too heavily guarded. He'd not have enough time to reverse the engine's power.

But Revor had grown vain, arrogant. He would want to see the man who had almost ended the Dominion, face to face. Meaning

Jerr and Xade would be captured and taken aboard *Liberator*. Balyra needed to ensure that Jerr would be angry enough to kill Revor, regardless of the consequences. Xade's death would be that catalyst.

Sunlight gleamed off the hourglass at her feet. Each grain a crime she'd paid for. Her fist crashed through the glass. Fingers dug through the bloodied sands of her homeworld, then clasped around a polyhedral object.

An etherspace box.

She'd kept it hidden within Revor's 'gift' to her. Though he had ordered all of the devices confiscated from Vestal House after the Kieta's defeat, she'd managed to hide one. The best glassmakers of Vestal House had refashioned the hourglass afterward.

It was a final gamble Balyra had taken. She could still win.

"*Liberator* has entered the system, Confessor," one of her morga said.

A gale thrashed at her robe. Lights stirred in the canyons below. They could've been torches carried by herself and Aylea from the chapterhouse twenty millennia ago.

A flash came from the craters. For a split second, Balyra saw the halves of the derelict—then it was invisible once more. Not here or there.

Jerr fell from midair and plowed into a nearby dune. Sand puffed up in a cloud. The morga and marines—Jerr's traitorous reborn from *Prophetess*, now under her command—raised their weapons.

"Hold." Balyra had seen the Kieta thrust people from the Shroud before. They had done so to her fellow Sisters after Vestal House obeyed Revor's order to bring the silvery creatures to heel. She slid the etherspace box under her robe.

Xade zipped into existence several feet away. Morga surrounded her.

In a blast of sand, Jerr erupted from the dune, boot thrusters flaring. He looked all around, though his disorientation lasted but a second. His teal gazed leveled on her.

"You could have warned us," he said. "You could've helped us!"

"You would not have believed me." Balyra glanced at the craters. "Revor cannot be fooled. This was a mistake."

"It's what I've already seen," Jerr said. "That was your mistake."

"Will you allow Revor to benefit from it?" she asked. "We share a common goal."

"And one of my friends died to reach it," he said. "Go to hell."

Her lips parted to answer when thunder rumbled across the sky.

"Confessor, sixty other vessels have entered the system," Bridge Deck radioed.

They looked skyward. Two larger shapes traded fire with many smaller ones.

Veja Qor was engaging *Liberator* and *Prophetess*. Already, meteors scorched a path across the sky as ships exploded. Debris from the space battle.

"You could fight him with us," Jerr said. "But you're too afraid."

"We are all afraid, Jerr. You, me. Xade. We stand on the cusp of a paradigm shift, with you at its apex. I need you to clear your mind. Revor is not the same man you saw on the realizer, commanding the Armada. He is worse."

"No worse than you." He powered up his diffusion blaster. "I know about Aylea."

"Then you know I will not stop," Balyra said.

A flash stole the sky. Shockwaves roiled the clouds. A deluge of meteors fell.

"Confessor, we have been—" *Prophetess*'s audio feed went dead.

Balyra braced herself as tendril-like forms appeared from out of nowhere. Kieta.

They didn't speak, gesture, or attack. They merely surrounded her. An invisible force pressed against her as the horizon melted into the earth. Colors exploded, blurred, twisted into shapes that might be glimpses of the past, or from countless futures.

It had been so long since she'd traversed space-time in such a manner. Part of her wished it could last forever. But once she fired the pistol hidden within her thigh compartment…forever would be an ephemeral term.

The next moment she stood in a great starship bay. Far overhead, she barely made out distant bulkheads hundreds of miles away. Tiers of vats and tubes lined the walls.

Xade stood nearby, flanked by two Kieta. *Lux Aeterna* waited in a nearby hangar.

The Kieta had brought them aboard *Liberator*.

Balyra hid her smile.

The Kieta surrounded Balyra as Jerr attempted Rezal state. Dominion fighters dove from the sky and streaked over the canyon. The reborn flew in different directions. Balyra vanished, transported by Kieta to the stars knew where.

His Rezal concentration faltered. The Kieta had taken Xade, too.

It was an ambush. Revor had been waiting for them.

A fighter shot down two reborn. Repta warriors opened fire from a nearby dune, peppering the Vestal dropship and morga guards. Two seconds later the morga were all destroyed. Another fighter strafed the area. The dropship exploded. Sand became glass.

The blast threw Jerr across two dunes. The impact knocked out a knee servo in his suit. His concentration broken, Jerr could only watch as three more reborn were disintegrated. Lights flickered across his HUD. He tried injecting the glycogen dumps.

More flashes in the sky. More meteors. Revor was leaving nothing to chance.

Everything happened with brutal speed. Jerr shook, realizing he still hadn't seen what came next. He couldn't predict where they'd shoot, where he could dodge.

Another reborn was blown to pieces in the sky, his scream a cruel coda.

A Kieta appeared several feet away. Swirling, morphing. Coming for him.

"Their children are still in danger, so they fight. You must reveal us!"

Grunting, Jerr slammed the glycogen release button and jetted into the air. The syringes stabbed his abdomen. Within seconds, he trembled with unspent energy. He reentered Rezal just as two fighters zeroed in on his position.

He regained control of himself. As dozens of Kieta appeared and disappeared all across the landscape, Jerr calculated his next move. His skull numbed from the work.

The Kieta must have taken Balyra and Xade to Revor's flagship, *Liberator*. That meant it was already orbiting the planet.

The remaining reborn darted and weaved between meteors, but multiple Kieta tore them apart. Jerr fought to maintain Rezal as he banked and rolled away from the fighters. Below, the Repta added their small arms fire to his challenges.

He had to get on *Liberator*. Xade was there. He had to hurry.

Actions came before thought. Without the Shroud's help. It was all he could manage, dodging the meteors or avoiding the Kieta. They swirled faster as they pursued him, vanishing with greater regularity. Taunting, confusing. Jerr gritted his teeth and—

A meteor slammed into the ground several hundred feet away. The blast flung him through the air. G-forces crushed him in a vise of agony. Fiery debris raced past from the meteor's impact. One piece burned through his left forearm, armor and all. A second melted his gauss cannon's control coupling. His HUD flared red.

The pain and shock tore his mind from Rezal state. Jerr spiraled to the ground along with all the other meteors. A fighter flew over him, then was vaporized by the relentless, fiery downpour. Yelling, Jerr hit the sand. Pieces of armor flew off him. The diffusion blaster malfunctioned, firing upward, disabling another fighter.

A cinder liquefied his faceplate. Jerr ripped it off before his face caught flame.

A Kieta appeared before him, then teleported out of the hellish rain.

"Xade …" Jerr coughed, the mic smoldering from the faceplate damage.

A thud sounded and Jerr was lifted a few inches off the ground. A second thud. A third. Closer, stronger. The fourth threw Jerr into the air several feet. Super-heated sand grains and fire clouds blazed over the dunes. Breath held, he managed to roll over.

Meteors decimated the area. Another would do more than toss him into the air. There were no time for screams, no way to tell what debris had been bedrock, fighter craft, or Repta limbs. Jerr tried to rise.

His glove crunched on something.

It was the etherspace box shard, still in his grasp. It gleamed white-hot.

Jerr stares out at a dark, lifeless void, floating between star systems. Something glows blue in his hand. Balyra stands nearby, tattered red cloak fluttering.

Four Kieta closed in on him. Jerr brandished the shard.

"The Weavers are dead."

He crawled to his feet, lungs burning from holding his breath.

"But you can create new strands."

Tried to fire the diffusion blaster, switched to the piercer.

"You can end all of this."

One Kieta swirled faster, then zipped out of existence. The energies it released snapped the piercer apart. Jerr's arm numbed from the jolt. The same Kieta reappeared.

"Reveal us!"

The other Kieta loomed over him. The etherspace shard shook in his hand.

His mind swirled with possibilities: the Kieta ripping him apart with gravity as they depart. Another future, where he shoots the box and it explodes, killing them all, melting sand within a quarter-mile. But a third option presents itself.

One of the Kieta swiped at him but Jerr struck it with the shard. The jagged, glass-like edge glowed blue. The creature disintegrated in a fading whirlpool of light.

The others swirled like miniature hurricanes of silver fury.

"I'm pissed off, too." Jerr's voice was hoarse. "Take me to her. To Xade."

Their tendrils slashed around him. A great chill spread through his body. Blue energy arced over the shard. He screamed in pain.

Colors roiled and exploded in his eyesight. The dune flung itself up into the meteoric barrage, then morphed into utter black void. A flurry of stars blew past Jerr. The shard grew hot but he dared not let go. They kept falling as galaxies blurred around them, then lensed into a tunnel where space bent and curved like it was painted on a cylinder.

They were traveling through the Shroud. Realities melted from one to another.

Jerr and the Kieta shot through the tunnel. They sped to a massive shape, a declaration of life within the Shroud's inertia: a Leviathan. The next moment they stood in a large hangar bay. The Shroud melted away, revealing a starship's interior: *Liberator.*

"Reveal us."

Jerr sucked in air as if he'd been underwater. Only after a few glorious, refreshing breaths did he think about alien atmospheres, noxious gases. But he still lived.

Two Kieta slinked away from Balyra and two more from Xade. The bay extended for miles, all gray and chrome bulkheads. Near-infinite tiers of vats and growth tubes rose in an edifice mind-numbing in its implications. Humans, Squidrans, Avae, Repta, and dozens of species he'd never seen. Thousands upon thousands of reborn.

Enough soldiers to fight a thousand wars, for a thousand years.

The Starjumper whirred and popped as Jerr stood. He swallowed, looked around.

"What a magnificent recreation. It must have taken you millenniums, Xade."

The voice was familiar. Jerr's skin chilled.

A figure in a black and white uniform approached, wearing a featureless mask. Two dozen Class III Repta provided escort. They all had Tunva's face.

Revor. The ghost haunting his Shroud dreams, made real.

"Revolution?" Tunva laughs with a slight hissing sound. "Tunva doesn't want revolution or revenge. Tunva wants release." So Tunva had known the fate of her reborn.

Jerr reached for her Onashi blade on his belt. Nothing remained but a charred, jagged hilt. The Repta aimed piercers at him.

"What have you done to *Prophetess?*" Balyra's tone was demanding.

"She remains unscathed at the moment." Revor walked around her. "Like you."

Balyra displayed no concern. "I see time has not dimmed your arrogance."

"Space and time are infinite," Revor said. "My patience isn't. I have given you leeway to correct your errors of judgement. I even allowed you to take *Prophetess* from your own Matriarch. The game is up, Confessor. I know everything."

"No one can know everything," Balyra said. "Especially—"

"The secrets of Vestal House?" Revor shook his head. "Spare me those trite Vestal platitudes. The Matriarch's memory circoids told much. I have you at my mercy."

A nodus drone hovered nearby, showing *Liberator* engaging the Veja Qor fleet. Twenty ships had already been destroyed. It was a hopeless battle.

"Mercy?" Jerr scowled. "I saw what you did to Third Echelon. To Prioa."

"You tried to take what was mine." Revor's voice was cold iron.

Jerr shook with fury. "They were never yours. I was never yours!"

"And yet, you are." Revor indicated the vats. "Like all these others."

"Monstrous," Xade said.

"Ah, my dear Xade." Revor smiled. "You enabled all of this. Aiding Veja Qor, giving the rebels hope that your vat-grown messiah would save them. Think of the millions who have died believing in your cause. And you call me monster?"

"Only a monster would make her destroy her own world." Jerr glowered at him.

"I made her do it?" Revor removed the mask. "Are you certain of that?"

The man had Jerr's face.

Chapter 28

The Kieta evolved with the ability to physically traverse space-time. When we captured a specimen, its genome could not be sequenced due to constant shifting in and out of our dimension. We turned our attention to the Weavers, an artificial intelligence navigating the Shroud in large vessels. They refused to share this knowledge, so we attacked them. In denying humanity its destiny, the Weavers had woven their own noose.

Only later would we know why.

Elder States Archives, Volume XLV

"Reveal us."

"No," Jerr said. "You're not me. You can't..."

It took Jerr a moment to realize he'd fallen to his knees.

"The old legends are made true." Revor smirked. "You kneel before your god, crafted in his own likeness. My DNA is the original template. You are simply a clone."

"I am my own man!" Jerr's voice cracked with anguish.

"Man?" Revor asked. "What do you know about being a man, a human? You are what I wanted you to be. Nothing more."

"Murderous!" Xade cried. Four Repta restrained her.

"You can end all of this."

"How?" Jerr's voice came out in a rasp.

Four Kieta appeared. They slinked and twirled into a perimeter around him. The silvery smooth bodies caught the light like comets streaming in slow motion.

They would only help him so much while Revor had their children.

He stepped toward Revor. One Kieta twirled around a captured morga and the thing exploded in a red cloud. The action blurred at the edges of Jerr's vision.

"I would take care," Revor said. "Kieta aren't known for taking prisoners. Their command of gravity is deadly. Despite your efforts, they still serve me."

On the drone's display, *Liberator* destroyed another rebel ship.

Revor smiled. "Your tactic was sound, thinking to cut my hold over the Kieta. But that Weaver cruiser is ancient and wrecked. Its engine is only powerful enough to hold the children of my allies captive."

"Doesn't matter." Jerr shared a glance with Xade, who looked even more worried. "Even now, Veja Qor is giving the Dominion back to the people."

Revor gestured. The Kieta closed the perimeter around Jerr, less than four feet away. "Give it back? I made it. Without me, you would not even exist. Humanity would not exist unless my Armada had guaranteed its survival. Safety and progress have a cost."

"Bullshit!" Jerr cried.

"I recognize your anger," Revor said. "Your 'righteous' cause. Yet you made the assumption of all conquerors and martyrs: you think everyone wants what you want. That, if you but topple the figurehead, all will change. You really think citizens want a reborn telling them that their lives are slavery, that humanity must abandon the Shroud?"

"We deserve the choice," Jerr said.

"You, and all your so-called clones, are extensions of my choices." Revor's voice softened. "I trusted no one else to rule and defend this empire. Do you know how many traitors and sycophants I had to eliminate, before realizing that the only person I could rely on was myself? I made clones I could trust. I made you immortal."

Liberator shook. The realizer showed an energy source spreading from the planet below. The Kieta shrunk back. Intercoms buzzed with static.

He caught Xade's eye, not daring to hope.

She winked.

The realizer displayed the Weaver starship engine starting up after millennia. It had taken the cores several minutes to build up the requisite energy.

Against all odds, Tunva had reversed the energy flow in the vessel's reactor. Instead of exploding, like *Bhaellator*, the ship's connection to space-time had stabilized.

Echoes built in the Shroud. In his mind. Jerr wanted to cover his ears.

"Reveal us avenge us weave a new thread reveal us avenge us weave a new…"

The voice, now a chorus, was no longer in Jerr's head. It came from every intercom, each helmet speaker, every nodus and realizer on *Liberator*. The nodus drone behind Revor showed that the signal had a galactic reach. Every device in the empire would play it. The voices of the Dominion's victims would be denied no longer.

"Gods and voids." Balyra reached inside her robe.

"Glorious," Xade said.

Jerr smiled at her; Xade returned it. No matter what happened now, he was glad to have helped her give voice to the voiceless.

Revor shook his head at Xade. "That is the same word you used to describe my orders for the Weavers' destruction. You have learned a great deal since then. You act totally human now. If I did not know better, I would believe the earnestness of your smile, those expressive eyes. Yet you will always be a Theux. I knew what you were. What you wanted. That is why I conquered your race before you did the same to us."

"That is true," Balyra said. "Vestal House—"

"Knows nothing." Revor tore off her cape. Balyra didn't flinch. "Do you have any idea what would have happened if your power play had succeeded? Had I not destroyed the Weavers and enslaved the Kieta, they would have wiped out humanity. Only we can be trusted with such power. Not a common grunt, as you've come to believe!"

"Erroneous," Xade said.

"This is not the mission I gave you," Revor said. "You were to eradicate any mutations. You were to guarantee my reborns' docility. Instead, you have betrayed—"

"Erroneous!" Xade yelled.

"Only a machine could display such a lack of imagination," Revor said. "You carried out my orders then because you were a machine. You might imitate us, but you will never be our equals. Still just machines. I proved that when I subjugated you."

Xade's glare could have burned through steel.

"Then punish her and be done with it," Balyra said. "Or have you grown soft, languishing on this ship while—"

"Aylea was loyal until the end," Revor said. "She knew I would destroy the box in her hand. A Vestal who knew her duty. She would have put you down. For me."

Balyra glowered. "You lie."

"It is true," Revor said. "All of this has been for your vanity, not her memory. But like Jerr, you cannot harm me. That is the conditioning placed on all clones. All Vestals."

Jerr went numb. He'd not been able to harm Garrand, either. He looked at Balyra.

"You are different, Jerr," Balyra said. "You can end this!"

Revor laughed. "One servant trying to convince the other."

Clasping the shard, Jerr risked moving forward a few more steps. "The Kieta only serve you because you threaten their children. That won't last."

Revor regarded Jerr with lowered brows. "My pact with the Kieta has worked for millennia. Yet you have endangered that partnership. Endangered the galaxy."

Jerr swiped the shard around. The Kieta backed away, swirling faster.

"Then prove you aren't an emasculated despot," Balyra said. "Punish Xade."

"It is not your decision," Revor said. "Be silent."

Liberator shook again. Alarms sounded. Revor shouted orders at the Repta, but they waited. The other soldiers tapped their earbuds or swiped their nodi. The nodus drones displayed images of the Weavers being slaughtered by the Armada. By Vestals. Again, the message was sent across the galaxy. The soldiers lowered their guns.

"Stop playing these lies!" Revor shouted.

The drones continued showing video feeds, though, revealing Dominion reborn committing atrocity after atrocity. The original Repta, Squidrans, Avae—all massacred. The survivors were pressed into imperial service. The dissenters ... trapped in the Shroud.

Revor's troops stirred with confusion, guilt. Anger.

"I order you to stand at attention!" Revor called.

Balyra stepped behind Revor. "You would look weak before your troops? Perhaps Jerr really has what it takes. Xade did betray you for him, after all. She even loves him."

The beam burns through Xade's chest ...

"I said silence!" Revor yanked a pistol from a nearby soldier.

A hole smokes through her chest, out her back.

"No!" Wielding the etherspace shard, Jerr plowed through the Kieta around him. Two disintegrated. The others whirled away from him. Augmenting his leap with a blast from his boot thrusters, Jerr hovered and landed beside Xade.

Two pistols fired.

Balyra's shot hit Jerr instead of Xade. The beam struck him between the collarbone and right shoulder. But Revor's shot ...

Xade crumbled to the deck. A hole smoked through her chest, out her back.

Jerr's hands shook. His throat went dry.

"I knew you would see that," Balyra said. "But you couldn't block both."

"Goddamn you," Jerr breathed.

"Avenge her," Balyra said. "You can break your conditioning. Avenge her, Jerr, as I would my sister. Do it for the galaxy. For yourself."

"You traitorous slut!" Revor turned, then backed away as Balyra held her own etherspace box. "You will never escape this ship. I swear it."

"Vestal House will soon control it. Not you." Balyra destroyed two Kieta with deft strikes of the etherspace box. The rest hovered out of her reach.

Jerr shoved the shard into the remains of Tunva's sword hilt.

"Kill them all, now!" Revor shouted.

The Kieta didn't move.

Revor scowled at the silvery creatures. "Have you forgotten your oaths to protect the empire? Tell those marines to destroy the Kieta children!"

None of his soldiers obeyed.

Balyra aimed at Revor, but the gun shook in her grasp. The conditioning was real.

"Your sister would be embarrassed." Revor shot Balyra in both legs, then in the stomach. She fell to her knees and tried to fire. Revor shot her in the chest. Sparks flew.

"Do it, Jerr!" Balyra screamed. "End it!"

Jerr entered Rezal state again. Aimed his makeshift dagger. Calculated the throw's trajectory, how fast the soldiers' reactions would be.

"End it," Balyra whispered, her eyes moist.

Revor aimed again. Xade rose and charged forward.

Jerr raised the shard as the Shroud warped around him. Space-time went into flux due to the energies from the Weaver derelict. Memories from previous rebirths flashed through his mind. One moment he was aboard *Liberator*; the next, reliving another life.

He raises his rifle, but not in time. The Mu cultist shoots him with a solid phosphorous round. Jerr screams as the chemicals blaze a deadly trail through his flesh and bones. Falling to his knees, Jerr still manages to fire. The cultist drops dead, but the phosphorous keeps scorching through Jerr. He writhes in agony as it burns out his back.

"No!" Revor fired.

Jerr cries out as the private fails to grab his hand. She careens off the hull into vacuum as more diffusion shots zip past. She'd completed her training only a week ago. Across the terminal expanse, they stare at each other. He finally mutes his radio as her sobs become choked, running out of air. He almost lets go of the edge himself, ending this horrible life, fighting war after war…

Revor's shot grazed Xade's side.

His hand rests on the side of a burning tank. It was overturned near the Idreun bunker, where dozens of their soldiers lay in charred heaps. Outside in the mud, scores of his own troops lay dead, piercer rounds still smoldering in their armor. The shit stink of sludge and burnt metal aromas make him gag. But looking at all the dead faces, mangled limbs… it hasn't made him sick in a long time.

"Captain, your team is to be commended," Garrand says as reinforcements arrive. The bastards trudge right over the dead in their clean combat suits. "You secured this zone and eliminated all the Idreun scum."

Jerr barely returns the salute. "My team is dead."

Garrand doesn't miss a beat. "Then you shall have a new one. Yes, we really need you for that mop up on the eighth moon. You know, that little bright turd in the sky right there? They think they can declare independence. After all we do for them."

Jerr looks over the mangled bodies, the sergeant he had a drink with the night before, the corporal who did hilarious imitations of the top brass. He's done all he could for them and they are still dead.

"What are you waiting for?" Revor cried. "Kill them all!"

The stench of amino solution makes Jerr gasp as he rises from the growth vat. A med drone helps him from the yellow muck. It slides down his naked form in fat, greasy drops. His muscles quiver. Each breath hurts as if he's never used his lungs before.

He hacks up a great gob of the solution, then gazes around. So he's really died. Reborn again, like the contract said. But how many times does this make?

Screams and gunfire competed with the alarms on *Liberator.*

The last gunship explodes, a brief yellow spark fading to black cloud on the horizon. A hush steals over the burning facility, as if breath has been sucked from all the corpses surrounding Jerr. Some of them have his face.

"Tunva is sorry." She closes the eyes on a dead reborn and stands.

"You say…there's another rebirth facility on Stavia X?" His words come out calm, despite having lost his right arm. His cracked HUD blinks red.

She catches him before he topples over the hillside, nearly joining his ill-fated twins on the slope. "Yes. Tunva and the other Repta are also rebirthed there."

They stare at each other as his breaths become more labored. Her scaly hand is tight around his armored one. Finally, he smiles.

"At least you got a drink of Yuggan whiskey this time."

"Tunva enjoyed that. Very much." She grins, eyes full of emotion. Jerr embraces her as Dominion troops flee Boschalan. Even as he bleeds to death.

"Stop her." Revor's voice sounded haggard. "Stop her!"

Jerr went numb as the Shroud lashed his consciousness. There was no up or down. No life or death. It was everything and nothing. He heard the battle around him, but colors shredded and light dissolved in his eyesight. He tried to move, tried to …

Iliea slams the door in Jerr's face.

"I can't stop being a soldier, goddamn it! You think this is what I want? It's what the Dominion wants. It's in my contract. I told you it would be like this!" Jerr grabs the door handle and shakes it. His strength rattles its hinges. "Iliea, let me …"

Jerr gazed around. "…in."

Balyra offered him her hand. Xade ran on, her body afire.

Liberator's walls had morphed and folded in on themselves, revealing stars.

Iliea?"

He stands in a crowded apartment with a metal grid floor, pipes visible underfoot. The walls are thin bulkheads scavenged from scrapped vessels. Paper scribblings in various colors cover them.

One has a smiley face with a word scrawled under it. His own face scrunches up as he reads it aloud.

"Daddy," he whispers.

Two more shots pierced Xade's body. She didn't stop.

Knees weakening, he stumbles into the wall where other drawings show three stick figures: at a floating arcology, or visiting a realizer zoo. One shows the trio in a rocket headed for a moon bounded in red rings. He touches one image after another.

"Iliea … Ghalas …"

His wife and son.

"The strands cannot be rewoven. The Weavers are dead."

The voice was distant now, as if he'd been moved from its source. Swells of gravity became visible through the ship's hull, even beyond the starfield outside. Strands waving, converging. Like threads of fabric, woven by cause and effect.

"Daddy?" Ghalas enters the room, clutching his stuffed Urian bear. Jerr had spent a month's pay just to get one this far from the Affiliate, where his homeworld is.

Jerr smiles and sobs at the same time. "How's my little man?"

He reaches for Ghalas, but the room blurs around them. Ghalas's form stands there, holding that bear … lensing out of existence before Jerr's eyes.

Space-time corrected. The Shroud released him.

"No … no!" Jerr grabbed at the air. His wife, his son … mere transients in his existence now. Apartment faded back into starfield, back into *Liberator*. Jerr glimpsed Weaver forms around him, then Kieta ones. Numbering in the thousands, the former enemies now manipulated the Shroud around both Leviathans orbiting Kadah IV.

"We have showed you who you were. Now become who you want to be."

The voice came from everywhere as *Liberator* fluxed back and forth in space-time. Jerr shrugged off the soldiers barring him. Two marines tried to fire their weapons but the Kieta tore them into wet chunks. The other troops retreated in confusion.

"Curator, *Prophetess* is changing course!" a voice called.

Xade kept running. Revor fired.

Jerr tried to throw the shard at Revor. Tried again. It was no use.

"Jerr!" Balyra met his eyes, then rolled the etherspace box toward Xade.

Since she was defenseless without the box, the Kieta mobbed Balyra.

Jerr threw the shard.

Before the Kieta reached her, the shard struck Balyra in the heart. She gasped, closed her eyes, and died. Her body flickered out of Jerr's universe and into the Shroud.

A group of diehard reborn still protected Revor, trading fire with the horde now surrounding them. One after another they fell, with Xade heading straight for Revor. She'd been hit several times. Another shot passed through her stomach.

"Xade!" Jerr screamed.

Liberator rumbled and shuddered. A distant explosion rocked the deck.

"Curator, the Kieta have taken control of *Prophetess*!" a voice cried over the intercom. "It's ramming us!"

"Xade?" Jerr coughed, reaching through the haze. Blood slid from his wound.

The smoke cleared as Xade, staggering and smoldering, finally reached Revor. He fired the pistol into her chest, thrust a null dagger into her stomach. Still she came.

The last marines loyal to Revor collapsed in shattered heaps. Soldiers and reborn from ten thousand worlds, along with the Kieta, watched and waited.

Gasping, Xade fell to one knee. Her blue flesh was darkened in melted splotches.

Energized by fear, Jerr leapt up and ran for her.

Xade grabbed Balyra's etherspace box from the deck.

Revor fired again. And again. The left side of Xade's face was scorched away.

Jerr's scream echoed through the Shroud. Joining the voices of Revor's victims.

With one final lurch, Xade smashed the etherspace box down into Revor's skull. Azure splinters flew as the object shattered. He cried out, flickered in and out of reality, then collapsed. A bloody halo pooled around the body before the Shroud claimed it.

Xade gave Jerr a sad smile. As she started to speak, she tumbled to the deck.

Liberator's hull split open as the bow of *Prophetess* sheared through the vessel in a great spray of debris, bodies, and explosions. Cracks dozens of miles long snaked across the bulkheads. Berths blew apart in brilliant infernos, only to darken in decompression and vacuum. A shockwave rippled along the hull, the deck. Most of the soldiers, already in Starjumpers, survived by flying out the breach. *Prophetess* was already jettisoning its remaining berths, saving what Vestals and history it could.

Jerr reached Xade as the hangar berth detached from *Liberator*. He grabbed her with one hand, held onto a deck plate with the other. Wreckage and corpses flowed out the breach in a river of misplaced intentions and tyrant's dreams.

"Continuous." He attempted a smile even as he felt his breath leaving.

Xade's lips trembled, trying to speak. He blinked back tears.

Outside, *Prophetess* and *Liberator* released their remaining berths. The ship cores drifted into orbit around Kadah IV, their engines silenced forever. Millions of small forms—debris, bodies, shuttles—glittered like crushed jewels above the desert world.

Dozens of Kieta appeared around Jerr and Xade. Twirling faster than before.

CHAPTER 29

To star's end, we call
To life's end, we fall
Until, in starry death, we are reborn.
To futures past, we lie
To futures lost, we die
Until, in the Shroud, we are one.

Epiphanies of the Shroud

The starfield outside blurred and rippled. Jerr struggled for air.

"Continuous?" He ignored the Kieta. Her face was the last thing he wanted to see.

Her mouth tried to form words. Despite the growing vacuum chill, he snapped off a glove. Touched her face, his skin to hers.

"I don't give a damn if you can't talk." Jerr said. "All I care about…"

The door finally opens. Iliea's cheeks glisten.

"See?" Jerr says, holding Ghalas. "Mommy's okay."

He stops, because if he says more, he will cry. Iliea looks from him to Ghalas, then sobs and hugs them. Jerr squeezes them both against him.

"Daddy, can we play when you come back?"

"Sure thing," Jerr murmurs into his son's ear. "I promise."

"Jerr?" a voice said in his ear.

Light flared around them as Jerr put aside the memory and looked to the future.

The next moment, he lay inside *Lux Aeterna*, outside the cockpit, still holding onto Xade. The cruiser remained in one of *Liberator*'s hangars but the berths around it were missing. Kadah IV gleamed below, filling the cockpit with golden-red shades.

The Kieta hovered around them for a moment then disappeared. Revor's former slaves had saved them, placing them aboard Balyra's personal ship.

"Jerr." Tender fingers wiped his damp cheek.

He froze, realizing it was Xade who had spoken, not a voice from the Shroud.

Of all the words she could have said, over countless millennia, she had selected his name. Coming from her, it represented far more than an appellation. It was a denial of apathy, a thing of beauty. A cypher for her love.

"I love you too." Jerr bent over and kissed her.

"Jerr." Her wide grin rivaled the glorious view below, her cerulean presence a hot young star, ready to light a new world.

Jerr tried rising, but sharp pains stabbed through his torso. Xade cradled him.

"Feverous." She caressed his hair.

"Well, I have had a rough day." He tried to smile but coughed up blood.

"Analogous." Her palm nodus showed a rebirth vat in *Lux Aeterna*'s med deck. So Balyra had really intended to regrow him if he hadn't agreed to join her.

"No." Jerr cupped her face with shaking hands. "No more rebirths."

"Contentious." She clasped him tight, breathing hard. "Delirious."

"Promise me."

Eyes closed, she shook her head.

"Xade? Promise me."

Messages beeped on the cockpit console.

Xade connected the feed to her nodus. It displayed queries from the berths that had survived the battle; *Liberator*'s, Vestal House, and the remaining Veja Qor ships. All were asking what should be done. Who was in control. If the rebellion had won.

What he intended to do.

He stared out the viewport. Wondering if his visions would lead them to prosperity or disaster. If he really was worthy of Weavers' help and the Kieta's trust.

"Jerr?"

"Tell them…" Jerr's mouth went dry. Knowing his next words might be remembered, studied, even repeated for generations. Knowing he couldn't do it alone.

Xade squeezed his hand and nodded. A med drone started treating his wound.

Ideas came to him. All the reborn, all those damaged worlds. The former could repopulate and rebuild the latter. It would take time. Perhaps more battles, if the other Curators tried to maintain control. But their genocidal secret was out.

"Tell them that Curator Revor and the Dominion are dead. Tell them each world can elect its own leaders. Say that Balyra Peran died bravely, fighting Revor."

Xade frowned, but he shook his head. "We need Vestal House to help rebuild, so they need to hear that. I think Balyra found some peace in the end. I'll not take it away."

She closed her eyes and nodded.

"Also… tell everyone that the reborn are finally coming home."

He wheezed as Xade keyed in his reply. Balyra's shot had been true. The med drone could seal the injury, but the internal damage was too much. He was dying.

"Congruous!" Xade searched through the biotics Balyra had kept on *Lux Aeterna*.

"I told you," Jerr managed through the pain. "No more… rebirths."

She found a biomech substrate cube and ran to his side.

"Wait, it's too late—"

Jerr cried out as she planted the cube into his shoulder wound. Sleek black tendrils spread from the cube and inserted themselves into his flesh. He sucked in a breath. The cube pulsed blue. His pain vanished. Xade straddled him, smiling.

The hole in his torso was now filled with light blue material. Symmetrical veins spread from it and connected with his own biological ones. He felt new nerve endings across the synthetic skin, as if it were the same he'd been born with.

"How...?" He remembered a Theux could assume any shape. And Xade had used something rare, a remnant of her past that could never be regained, to save him.

Her own body morphed and repaired itself from the remainder of the cube.

"Congruous." She raised her brows.

Jerr laughed and squeezed her close.

The cockpit console beeped again. They studied the ecstatic reactions sent back from Veja Qor, the remnants of Vestal House, and nearby worlds. All agreed with his suggestions. Jerr smiled, yet Xade regarded him with anxious curiosity.

"What is it, Miss Blue Theux?"

She brought up Uria on her nodus and cocked her head. His homeworld. The white-blue sphere was still beautiful. But he no longer yearned for the past.

"No." He laid a hand over her heart. "This is where I want to live now."

About the Author

"*Only when facing the extremes of environment, physics, and reality, do my characters realize who they are. Then I realize who I am.*"

Tony Peak is an Active Member of SFWA and an Affiliate Member of HWA. He is represented by Ethan Ellenberg of the Ethan Ellenberg Literary Agency. His debut novel Inherit the Stars was published by Penguin Random House in November 2015. His interests include progressive thinking, transhumanism, and planetary exploration. Residing in southwest Virginia, he has a wonderful view of New River. Find out more at: www.tonypeak.net

About the Publisher

This book is published on behalf of the author by the Ethan Ellenberg Literary Agency.
https://ethanellenberg.com
Email: agent@ethanellenberg.com